T0363392

MEDICAL

Life and love in the world
of modern medicine.

**Falling For The Single
Mum Next Door**
Fiona McArthur

A Kiss Under The Northern Lights
Susan Carlisle

MILLS & BOON

FALLING FOR THE SINGLE MUM NEXT DOOR
© 2025 by Fiona McArthur
Philippine Copyright 2025
Australian Copyright 2025
New Zealand Copyright 2025

First Published 2025
First Australian Paperback Edition 2025
ISBN 978 1 038 94050 6

A KISS UNDER THE NORTHERN LIGHTS
© 2025 by Susan Carlisle
Philippine Copyright 2025
Australian Copyright 2025
New Zealand Copyright 2025

First Published 2025
First Australian Paperback Edition 2025
ISBN 978 1 038 94050 6

MIX
Paper | Supporting
responsible forestry
FSC® C001695
www.fsc.org

Published by
Harlequin Mills & Boon
An imprint of Harlequin Enterprises (Australia) Pty Limited
(ABN 47 001 180 918), a subsidiary of HarperCollins
Publishers Australia Pty Limited
(ABN 36 009 913 517)
Level 19, 201 Elizabeth Street
SYDNEY NSW 2000 AUSTRALIA

Printed and bound in Australia by McPherson's Printing Group

Falling For The Single Mum Next Door

Fiona McArthur

MILLS & BOON

Also by Fiona McArthur

Second Chance in Barcelona
Taking a Chance on the Best Man
Father for the Midwife's Twins
Healing the Baby Doc's Heart

Discover more at
millsandboon.com.au.

Fiona McArthur is an Australian midwife who lives in the country and loves to dream. Writing Medical Romance gives Fiona the scope to write about all the wonderful aspects of romance, adventure and medicine, and the midwifery she feels so passionate about. When she's not catching babies, Fiona and her husband Ian are off to meet new people, see new places and have wonderful adventures. Drop in and say hi at Fiona's website: fionamcarthurauthor.com.

Dedicated to my dear friend, Tracy Brenton,
who helped me understand Nadia.

PROLOGUE

Almost five years previously
Henry

DR HENRY OLIVER, paediatric registrar, hadn't thought he would fall for someone at first sight.

Heck, Henry loved the company of women, enjoyed the rapport between colleagues in the hospital and supposed, after careful consideration, he'd one day settle down and have a family with a like-minded partner most probably in the medical profession.

But on this day, at work, his romantic soul felt captured by the mother of a patient—a woman in a wheelchair, as pale as death—so not in his plans. He'd been standing beside a wall, writing notes on his tablet about a tiny prem, unaware that his life was about to change direction.

Henry's boss, Simon Purdy, consultant paediatrician and neonatologist, was the one who pushed the wheelchair towards the open crib and Henry looked up to see the woman's golden hair wisping around her fine-boned cheeks like pale sunrays. The young mother held one delicate hand under her chin as if her head felt too heavy for her slender neck to carry the burden as she gazed upon her child who had been fighting for survival but refused to succumb.

Henry felt as if he'd been blinded by fog his entire life.

The fog instantly dissipated and even from across the room Henry could see the enormous sapphire eyes fill with maternal angst and the sparkle of unshed tears as she lifted her chin to Simon. Henry needed to be there for her.

She was a patient's mother, yet without even noticing his presence he felt her call to him. An unexpected wave of protectiveness tightened his chest and Henry reached out to touch the wall to steady himself. His body went cold and then heated. He had never had such feelings before, except perhaps as a young boy when his single mother had worked too hard. He'd wanted to nurture and protect her like this, and had failed. But this woman was not his responsibility.

At least he was older. Wiser. Not a child. He knew from Simon that this woman was a recent widow and was surrounded by family and grieving—nowhere near being emotionally available.

No room for him to be more to her—possibly for years.

This feeling of recognition was crazy, unexpected, but it seemed to hold such significance he couldn't brush it away.

Thank goodness he was leaving soon for London, but still his eyes fixed on the angel in the blue dressing gown, confirming who she was, her premature baby and her scarily efficient sister, intensivist Isabella Hargraves. And Simon, his senior consultant, who was his boss and her baby's doctor. But he'd never actually seen *Nadia* until now and that must be why his world had tilted.

Over the next four weeks, before Henry left for the new appointment in London, he made himself available to Nadia when she needed extra support, not pushing, answering her hundreds of questions as her baby grew, staying quietly in the background, and acknowledged ruefully that he wasn't visible to her even though she felt seared into his heart.

Strangely, the crazy concept didn't rattle him. He had nothing to offer her at this time and she was grieving. Immersed in the needs of her tiny daughter. Lost in being a widow and single parent. Surrounded by her family. He was invisible.

Lucky he was going, it really was, because here there was only heartache for him.

Almost five years later

Dr Henry Oliver signed on the dotted line and the pretty red-headed Realtor sat back and fluttered her extra-long eyelashes in an I-could-give-you-more-than-legal-papers-if-you-want look.

In London, Marco, his ex-flatmate, certainly would have been eager to secure a phone number.

Not Henry. Not now. Not on the Gold Coast back in Australia.

This was the real world and he'd be too busy at work for romance in the next year or two.

Henry felt delighted about the signing but not tempted by the pretty girl. He'd just bought his favourite apartment, ocean view overlooking Rainbow Bay, Queensland, top floor, in a small block of units that each took up the whole floor. He'd always loved this apartment.

Though he believed it was good business sense, even if it had cost a packet, he couldn't help but wonder how much of this decision was tied to the woman who, he'd just discovered, still lived downstairs.

No. He'd bought the place because he'd always fancied it when he came to visit his boss, Simon, when he'd worked for him as a registrar. The hospital where he'd be spending a lot of time working was one street away and Simon's partnership in his thriving Gold Coast paediatric practice was not much further to walk.

It just felt so good to be back in Australia after years at London's GOSH, the Great Ormond Street Hospital for Children, though he had thrived working in paediatrics under leaders in the field. His work and living away from Oz had been exhausting, though Marco had made it fun.

Henry had flat shared with an Italian colleague, Marco, who pushed weights in his off time and dragged Henry with him to the gym until Henry had never been so fit or confident in himself.

Henry enjoyed the company of women but, apart from forced double dates with his flatmate's latest girlfriend's girlfriend, he rarely thought of anything but work.

Now, back in Australia, he'd achieved the professional goal of paediatric consultant he'd always dreamed of becoming while still being one of the younger specialists at thirty-four.

And then his boss—no, his colleague—Simon had oh-so-casually mentioned that his sister-in-law Nadia was still single.

Henry's heart quickened, but that was because of his purchase—heck, he'd always loved Simon's home. Nothing to do with Nadia.

Yes. He'd bought the place because he loved the apartment.

None of that decision had been tied to the single mother who lived downstairs.

Nothing to do with Nadia.

CHAPTER ONE

Nadia

NADIA HARGRAVES PUSHED the base of the child's swing harder and Katie, a very mature almost five-year-old, giggled in the strapped swing seat.

'Push me higher, Mummy.'

Nadia watched the mane of her daughter's blonde hair streaming in the wind as they both faced out over the waves and across the bay to Surfers Paradise with each push.

On their side of the water, the white sand of Rainbow Bay, so aptly named as a place of hope and new beginnings, stretched to the break wall where the waves crashed and creamed up the side of the jagged rocks. Every now and then a larger set of waves would shoot droplets into the sky with a snap and a fan of crystal water. Ahead, surfers swooped forwards or slid backwards off waves, while seagulls cawed above.

Here was so much better than Sydney's snarling traffic or Brisbane's constant roadworks. This tucked-away southern corner of the Gold Coast had become Nadia's favourite place in the world.

Here she had her daughter Katie, her only sister Bella, plus, of course, Bella's caring husband Simon and their son Kai and her grandmother Catherine, all close in one apartment block—and they were the most important people in her world.

Occasionally her professor father visited briefly from Sydney if he had a business appointment in the Gold Coast, but years of work-related neglect from him meant none of the women in his life had expectations of a lasting connection. Even for his favourite, Isabella, Dad could easily visit the hospital next door and not even consider calling in to see his grandchildren before he flew way again.

Nadia had learnt in childhood that she could survive without her father, any man really, in her life. Until she'd fallen for Alex. But he was gone. Wrapping his expensive new car around a telegraph pole and leaving her just enough of her own savings to buy the apartment outright and barely any savings to survive on. She'd managed to navigate pregnancy, widowhood, moving, a difficult birth and motherhood without Alex.

Maybe because as a young girl her famous father had always loved his work more than his two motherless daughters, she'd understood that for Alex she'd taken second place as well.

The number of times she'd watched fruitlessly for Dad to arrive at childhood occasions and been disappointed. Birthdays, awards, graduations, he hadn't come to any. Piers Hargraves had taught Nadia well that complete immersion in work was a bad thing, so marrying a doctor had been out. Her dear old dad might be an expert neurologist in Sydney, but he knew little of the caring side of his brain and Nadia had finally given up trying for his approval. Even when she'd voiced her dream of being a nurse like Bella, more for him than herself she suspected now, hadn't made him see her.

But she'd fallen for her handsome husband, had thought easy-going Alex was the answer, but that hadn't worked out either. He'd been too busy socialising to be there for her, despite taking her surname when they'd married. Nadia had secretly questioned whether he'd hoped to become the favoured son-in-law and benefit financially from her dad.

Poor Alex had turned out to be less than perfect, uninvested in anyone apart from himself, and had left her an impoverished widow when he'd wrapped one of his fast cars around a pole a few months before their daughter had been born.

But she had loved him, although she'd been disappointed by who she thought he was when he'd died, until the reality of the financial disasters he'd wrought in so short a time had become apparent and she'd had to climb out of a financial hole.

The drone of a plane rose above the din of the surf for a moment, interrupting her thoughts, and as its wings came in low to disappear behind the hill of apartments to her left to land at the hidden airport, Nadia remembered her broken arrival that fateful year.

Refuge in Gran's apartment had saved her, and then using her savings to make her own home in Gran's block.

She'd been pregnant and shell-shocked at the loss, but Gran and her sister had steered her safely to finding her feet in the spacious ground floor unit near family.

Best move ever.

'Ahoy, you two,' a familiar voice called out. And here came the dearest member of her family now.

Her sister Isabella, tall, blonde and very pregnant, strode, only slightly ungainly despite her huge baby bump, across the grass towards them. Nadia shook her head in admiration. Nothing slowed Bella down. Not even a watermelon-sized belly.

Nadia let go of the swing and reached out to hug her sibling, the big bulge in the way making her smile widen. 'How on earth can you still move so fast? It defies mechanical physics.'

Bella shrugged. 'Women are designed to be adjustable when pregnant.' She waved at her niece. 'Hello, darling Katie.'

'Hello, Auntie Bella.' Katie blew a kiss, then set her chin and began to lean forward and backward, trying to get the swing to increase momentum on her own, while her mother stood distracted.

Bella rubbed her hands. 'Guess what!'

Nadia steeled herself for what she suspected might be coming. 'What?'

'We sold the unit.'

Nadia's heart sank and she tried not to let disappointment show. Bella was moving out. 'That's great news for you all. Yay. Simon will be happy.'

She could see that, uncharacteristically, Bella was oblivious of her sense of impending loss. She must be very excited because her sister rarely missed anything.

Bella burbled on, 'Kai will be so happy. He can learn to ride a pushbike in his own backyard. I'll have space for baby and spare rooms as well.' She laughed. 'Several rooms. It's a big house.'

'And you'll have areas for entertaining.' She knew Bella and her friends were multiplying children and the unit was proving too small for social events. 'The buyer must have snapped it up as this is the first I've heard.'

'He did. But then he'd seen the place years ago. Do you remember Henry Oliver, Simon's registrar from when Katie was born?'

Henry Oliver? On hearing his name, Nadia found it surprisingly easy to conjure kind brown eyes and very short brown hair. Henry Oliver. Good grief. She'd liked Henry. A tall but slim man with a diffident manner and the nicest smile. 'Yes. I do remember Henry.'

He'd been so attentive, caring and thoughtful of her feelings. Unlike Alex. Where had that thought come from?

She steered her thoughts away. 'Didn't you take him under your wing and teach him some tricks for difficult cannulas?'

'Good grief, I'd forgotten that.' Bella laughed. 'I was feeling protective of Katie, and you weren't there.'

No. She hadn't been there when her precious daughter had been admitted to the NICU at thirty-two weeks. And her husband had been dead. She'd been in Intensive Care with severe hypertension of pregnancy, fighting for her life, while her prem daughter had been watched over by her fierce neonatal nurse aunt Bella.

Nadia whispered, 'I'm fairly sure you told Henry he wasn't allowed to attempt to cannulate my baby again until you gave him some lessons.' She was teasing but even the memory made her want to hug her sister.

Bella nodded, a little pink in the cheeks. 'It was four a.m. I wasn't allowed to treat a relative, so I made him ring Simon to come in.'

'That's when you fell in love with Simon.'

'Not that night,' Bella said with a laugh. 'But soon after.'

Her sister and brother-in-law were a besotted couple and their love gave her hope for some distant time in the future.

'I remember Henry told me you terrified him.' Nadia laughed at her sister's expression. 'You do get scary when you're in NICU.'

Bella couldn't help being an extremely skilled nurse when she wasn't on maternity leave. As their father still said, she should have been a doctor. But Bella loved hands-on paediatric intensive care and had no desire to work in medical rooms half the time seeing patients.

Bella laughed. 'Oh, piffle. But you'd better not remind him I was pushy because he's joined Simon's practice as a consulting partner and coming to work at our hospital.'

For some reason Nadia doubted the Henry she had memories of would hold a grudge. He hadn't seemed that type of person.

She felt a flash of delight at the news. Probably because she now knew there wouldn't be strangers in the top unit. He'd been good to her when he'd been the neonatal registrar, when Simon or her sister had been busy elsewhere, and Henry had always eased her worries when she had something on her mind.

Yes, Henry had helped her understand about prematurity and the temporary heart murmur they'd found in Katie, and all the other things a newly widowed mother would worry about with her prem baby. Yes. He'd been very kind.

She wondered if she'd ever thanked him.

CHAPTER TWO

Henry

HENRY HAD ALWAYS been methodical, perhaps stemming from when he'd hunkered down and tried everything he could to not be a burden on his hardworking mother. If he wanted something he worked steadily towards his goal, using his own tenacious resolve to achieve said objective. A year or two of knuckled-down hard work and he'd achieve all he wanted here too.

In the last three days Henry had accomplished a lot. He had furniture ready to go into the apartment when he took possession. He'd settled into the specialist practice he'd bought into. And he'd acquired his own residents, Tom and Sam, and Amelia, a brilliant and careful registrar, to share the workload and create his team.

He'd taken on the hospital consultant paediatric position for both the Emergency Department and Children's Ward, quite a workload, when he started at the hospital next week.

Rainbow Bay Hospital had proved not as large or imposing as London experience had taught him to expect, but he preferred the modern and more patient-centric model, with hopefully more time to get to know patients and parents.

His new office with its large windows looking over Coolangatta Beach showcased everything he'd missed about living in Australia. Blue skies, sparkling ocean, a laid-back but surprisingly efficient secretary of his own, and a stellar senior partner to forge ahead with in his professional life. Hard to believe it was the Friday of his first week because he felt as if he was finally home.

Right now, after work, Henry carried a bottle of Tasmanian Coal River Pinot Noir, a red wine he'd missed and aspired to open. He straightened his tie with his other hand as he stepped out of the lift, casting slightly proprietorial eyes around the foyer outside his soon-to-be front door.

He'd been looking forward to Simon and Isabella's farewell party in the flat and been invited to come early. In fact, he'd spent far too much time today anticipating the moment he arrived.

Because tonight he would see Nadia Hargraves. He hadn't caught a glimpse of her for almost five years. There was no doubt that she had been on his mind but he'd probably blown the whole attraction-at-first-sight thing out of proportion. Most likely, it had just been a protective instinct since he'd known her circumstances.

Anyway, he'd also see Nadia's daughter, Katie. He couldn't imagine that tiny, thirty-two-week baby as almost five years old. Of course, for a paediatrician there was nothing more satisfying to see than a struggling baby become a healthy and happy child. Nadia's child.

He knocked, and after some delay the door opened slowly to reveal a waist-high, woebegone blonde-haired little girl with two big tears sliding down her pink cheeks. She looked healthy but not a happy child. Despite the mermaid suit.

The tiny mermaid sniffed and rubbed the back of her hand under her nose. He glanced behind her but there were no adults that he could see. Odd? But kids didn't faze Henry. He enjoyed and admired children. Spent his days with them.

He tilted his head, crouched down and said, 'Hello. I'm Dr Henry. What's wrong, sweetheart?' He pulled out the large white handkerchief he always carried and dabbed her cheeks, then handed it to her. 'Blow.'

She took it and with a surprisingly vigorous trumpet she blew, and he couldn't help but smile.

'Better,' he said, taking the screwed ball of his handkerchief back carefully to keep his hands clean and tucking it into his trouser pocket to sanitise later. 'Now, tell me what's made you feel sad.'

'Mummy and Auntie Bella are dressing Kai, and I was feeding Ernestine...' She stopped. Held up a much-loved rag doll.

'Something happened?' Henry glanced around the room until he saw. Under one of the low tables a tipped plate of biscuits and several rounds of cheese had ended up in a scatter of food and crackers on the pristine tiled floor. 'Did your doll bump the plate?'

Another sniff. A nod. And big beautiful green eyes swam with tears again.

Henry stood up. Held out his hand. 'Oh, no, you don't. We'll just fix the plate, and you and your doll will say sorry to Auntie Bella and Mummy, and everyone will be happy. Okay?'

'You sure?'

'It's not a big thing. And we can fix it. Lickety-split.'

The little girl blinked and lifted her chin. 'I'm Katie.'

'I thought you might be. I met you when you were a tiny baby. You're a big girl now.'

'I am.'

They crossed to the scene of the accident and Henry used a biscuit to push the cheeses back onto the plate and into some semblance of attractive arrangement while Katie picked up the biscuits. 'Are there more biscuits in the kitchen?'

Katie nodded.

'Let's put these ones in the bin and put out new ones when you wash your hands.'

When Katie frowned at him he added, 'I don't think Auntie Bella would mind.'

'Hello, Henry.' His new partner's wife gave him one of her warm smiles as she walked in. She was wearing a tent. It was a very pretty tent, but my goodness she was pregnant, Henry thought in some awe.

She raised her brows at her niece. 'What wouldn't Auntie Bella mind?'

Isabella glanced at the biscuits in Katie's hands and the one in Simon's and smiled. 'Ah, I see. The cheese fell. And we need new biscuits. I don't mind at all.' She stepped forward with her hand out. 'Let me take that plate.'

'I have to wash my hands.' Katie waved them in the air. 'Dr Henry said.'

Another movement from the bedrooms. 'Hello there, Dr Henry.'

And there she was. The woman he'd tried not to think about for far too long. Dressed in a floating white beach dress with a low neckline, a peppermint beaded necklace nestled against her brown skin between the curve of her breasts. Her blonde hair, like spun gold in some fairy tale, hung loose to her shoulders and caught the light from the big windows.

She'd grown even more beautiful and there was an air of confidence and serenity that she hadn't had when he'd first seen her.

His heart went boom and his breath caught. *Nadia Hargraves... be still my heart.*

The seconds seemed to stretch as his gaze snagged on the woman he suddenly realised he'd measured every other female in London against, finding they fell short. He'd been an idiot.

He stepped forward. An idiot with great taste. The rest of the room was forgotten.

His hands stretched out to take hers. 'Nadia.'

The word was a breath as he captured her slim fingers, her skin as warm and soft and exquisite as he'd imagined it would feel beneath his. If he'd thought before that he'd come home... For one crazy moment he believed he really breathed *home*— which was ridiculous. They were practically strangers.

To his delight, she leaned forward and kissed his cheek. Not quite beyond his wildest dreams but pretty darn near it. 'That's to say thank you for all the times you reassured me about Katie in the NICU. I don't think I did say thanks.'

'You are very welcome.' He forced himself to release her hands. Remembered where he was. Who he was. Though he didn't really know who she was now.

He turned back to the others, who were watching. 'And Katie has grown up to be a beauty like her mother.' He smiled. 'And her aunt.' He needed some sanity. 'Where's Simon?'

He noted that Isabella watched them both with a definite twinkle in her eyes so like her sister's, though she glanced at the door. 'He was called back to the unit but shouldn't be long. He's been gone an hour already.'

At that moment a key turned in the lock and the door swung open. 'Perfect timing,' his wife said as Dr Simon Purdy, tall, debonair, greying a little at the temples and Henry's senior partner, entered the room.

'Uncle Simon—' Katie grabbed Henry's hand and pulled him towards the door '—this is Dr Henry.'

Everyone laughed and poor Katie frowned as Henry gently squeezed her tiny hand and crouched down. 'You didn't know but Uncle Simon and I have known each other for a long time. But thank you, it was very kind of you to introduce me. Did

Mummy tell you that I'll be moving into this flat when your auntie Bella and uncle Simon move to their new house?'

She turned to her mother. 'Is that true?'

'It is,' Nadia confirmed.

'That's nice,' said Katie, shrugging off her confusion. 'We'll be able to come up and visit, just like we do with Auntie Bella.'

Henry stifled a laugh and looked innocently up at Nadia. 'You and Mummy are welcome at any time.'

Nadia murmured, 'Oh, please, don't tell her that,' but the awkward moment passed as the doorbell rang.

Simon opened it to a dark-haired man and his blonde wife, their tow-headed twins and one dark-haired baby.

Henry knew Malachi Madden and his wife Lisandra and their two little boys. His eyes widened. 'My goodness, look at your boys, Malachi.'

He smiled at Lisandra, a woman he admired very much, and shook hands with Malachi. Lisandra leaned in and kissed his cheek. He hadn't met the baby in Lisandra's arms. 'And who is this little pearl?'

'This is Angelica. She's eight weeks old today.'

Katie's little voice said, 'You really do know almost everybody.'

'I know these people,' Henry said as he smiled down at her. 'And these boys, though they were only slightly bigger than you were when I left.'

'We're at school now,' Bastian said. 'But Bennett's not in my class.' He sounded miffed.

The boys weren't shy then.

Henry said sagely, 'I heard they do that with twins.'

CHAPTER THREE

Nadia

NADIA WATCHED HENRY assimilate into the close group with ridiculous ease—not the quiet, diffident man she remembered but a man who stood out even in this crowd of men who shone. This version of Henry Oliver seemed larger than life.

Way larger than life. Good grief, no diffidence here, just confidence, and those shoulders and arms—he could lift her up and toss her over his shoulder without breathing hard. Now why on earth had she thought of that? But she couldn't help the smile at the ridiculous picture.

As if echoing her thoughts, the latest man to arrive, and her own obstetrician, Malachi Madden, spoke up bluntly as usual. 'What happened to you, Henry—take up bodybuilding in London? You're twice the size you were!'

'A bit of exaggeration there, Malachi.' Henry laughed and the deep, rumbling sound rolled over her, tingling her skin. 'Flat-shared with a paed from Italy and we stayed fit at the gym. Had to because it felt like we spent twenty hours a day at the hospital.'

Nadia frowned as she heard that and thought to herself, *Twenty hours a day at the hospital? Good grief. Men. Just like her father.* She mentally nudged away any thoughts of being attracted to Henry. *Shame, that.*

'Maybe I could go run with you here?' Henry said to Malachi. 'I'm a social animal. I like company when I exercise.'

Malachi grinned. 'You can try to catch me.'

'Or not.' The men sized each other up with amusement. 'A race never bothered me.'

Nadia decided that Henry didn't look worried or hang back from being competitive. He really was not the Henry she remembered. And that was enough thinking about Henry. She wasn't the woman he remembered either, she imagined.

'No running on Saturdays,' Isabella stated. 'Lisandra comes surfing with us. We go every week while the men mind the children.'

Simon touched his niece's blonde head. 'And Katie's a big help when I mind Kai, aren't you, sweetheart?'

Katie nodded importantly.

'I might have to take up surfing myself.' Henry's gaze shifted from Katie to her, a brush of teasing, and Nadia felt it as if he'd lifted his finger to her cheek. Why was he looking at her when he said that? She wasn't surfing with him.

She did not want a man in her life, or if she ever did... It wouldn't be a career consultant like her father.

Oh, boy, no.

Henry Oliver had just admitted that he lived and breathed the hospital and buried himself in work. Even worse, she didn't need another man who would draw the eye of every woman he passed like her departed husband had. And there was no doubt that this new Henry would do that too.

Henry tilted his head when she didn't answer. There was a smile on his face, darn it, a really too handsome face, waiting for her to smile back. 'You surf too, Nadia?'

The doorbell rang again.

She lifted her chin. 'Bella and I surfed for years. Our gran was one of the original Bondi Girls and she taught us both. Gran was a champion.'

Simon ushered in Catherine, speak of the dear devil, just as she uttered that. Nadia saw that Elsa Green, the lady from two floors down, was with her, along with her visiting granddaughter, Lisa, whose eyes jumped straight to Henry with speculation. Really? Lisa was just going to stare at him with big eyes?

She heard Gran say sedately, 'Did I hear my name?'

'We were talking about surfing,' Bella said. 'So of course your name came up.'

There was a general surge of people hugging and kissing and suddenly it was crowded with nine adults, three children, a baby and an enormous pregnant belly in the unit.

Nadia stepped back and away and Henry moved with her, saying from her other side, 'I think, yes, your sister needs a bigger house.'

Nadia had to laugh. 'Despite my loss. I fear so.' She looked at him then while the others exchanged pleasantries. 'Are you excited about moving in?'

He took in the layout of the apartment and she studied him while his attention was focused on the room around them. Sexy, confident, muscular, gorgeous—not descriptions she would have thought of for the old Henry, which was strange—but certainly fitting now. And in this setting, with people she knew so well, it was surprising that he looked so very much at home.

'It's great to be back,' he murmured. His eyes sparkled as he looked over his shoulder at her. 'And yes, I've always loved the view from this unit.' He gestured with his arm to the small balcony, inviting her to step out there with him.

She didn't know why but she followed him, leaning her elbows on the rail and turning her face to watch his expression as he leaned his strong arms on the warm metal.

'I love the ocean. The colours. All of it. When Simon said he was selling I decided to go for this.'

She thought about that. About what she knew of him, which wasn't much except he'd been good to her and Katie in the past. And now he'd come back a very well-built paediatric consultant working with her brother-in-law—no doubt after long hours of intense medicine and loads of experience.

She thought again of his care of Katie. 'I'm glad. You work hard and deserve a place you can relax in.' That was true. He'd been incredibly knowledgeable five years ago. He'd be more so now. The hospital was lucky to have him back. And now he was Simon's partner, she guessed, she'd see a lot of him.

She thought about that and a strange, agitated feeling grew inside her, but her expression must have stayed the same because he only said, 'Thank you. I appreciate that.'

'Anyone special in your life to share your view?' Now why had she asked that? Good grief. Her eye caught on Lisa, watching them through the glass. You'd think she'd pretend she wasn't watching Henry. Nadia looked away. And why did she care?

His teeth flashed in a quick white grin. 'Not yet. Currently, I'm footloose and fancy-free.'

At the wattage of his smile her attention zeroed in on him. 'Hardly footloose, buying into Simon's practice and working at the hospital all hours. What about your parents? Siblings?'

'No family.' The smile died and there was something quiet in his tone that didn't match the man, the view or the conversation. He directed the topic away from himself. 'Do you still enjoy living here?'

No family? Curiosity stirred and she tamped it down. Then frowned at herself. She shouldn't even have started asking questions. Let it go.

She remembered he'd asked a question. 'Here? Good grief, I love the place.' Glad to change the subject with him.

She gestured with her hand at the park below and the expanse of water around them. 'This is my world. I'm in charge. I'm in control.' She heard the words, the assertion—she'd said that almost defiantly. It was true but... Good grief. Talk about putting it out there and waving it like a flag.

His eyes twinkled. 'Sounds like a castle with a moat.'

Her cheeks felt warm. 'It does.' And maybe that was too stark for this conversation too.

She relaxed her shoulders and glanced back inside. 'I'll miss having Bella upstairs, but Gran is still here, and we'll all visit her. And Katie loves the park. And the beach.'

'When does Katie start school?'

'It's Queensland, so she'll start prep school this year because she turns five before the thirtieth of June. She's in childcare now. They don't call it kindergarten up here and it's not compulsory but I work two days a week. I think she should get used to school rules.'

'So proper school next year?'

'She says she wants to stay home with me for another year.'

'Tricky.' He smiled. 'I bet you've worked something out.'

'I have.' She smiled back. 'I bought her a surfboard for Christmas and promised to start teaching her on the weekends once she's big enough for Prep.'

He looked mischievous for a few beats, as if not sure how she'd take his next words. 'Maybe you could teach me to surf at the same time? I'm serious about learning.'

Oh, yeah. She could just see that. This big, well-muscled guy, wobbling on a board, all bare skin and sex appeal. While she was supposed to be watching her daughter. Not on your nelly.

'It's the Gold Coast. You have the means. You can pay a surf instructor.'

'You wound me.'

She huffed out a laugh. She enjoyed this sparring too much. 'I doubt that. After years in London staying warm, I imagine your skin is thicker than it looks.'

'It is. But... Wowser. Where's the fun in that?'

'Tough luck.' She glanced back inside. Away from those laughing liquid eyes. Found Lisa's still on Henry. Frowned. 'Food's on. Better go help in the kitchen.'

CHAPTER FOUR

Henry

HENRY WATCHED HER walk away. Blonde, beautiful and swaying like a gorgeous golden sunflower in the light sea breeze. He'd done that before—watched her walk away, just before he'd left for London, but this time maybe they could be on an equal footing. Nadia was not his patient's mother. 'You've been away nearly five years. No rush, Henry,' he murmured to himself.

He'd taken himself to London and Great Ormond Street Hospital without making plans for the future.

Now he was back, a consultant in his own right, and he found himself far too delighted that Nadia was still single, and even more dazzling in his eyes. Not only that, she and her daughter lived just downstairs from his new penthouse, so there would be chance encounters apart from socialising with the Purdys and the Maddens.

He had some serious thinking to do and this time she wasn't a grieving widow he had to walk away from. Now, Nadia was an independent woman, in charge and in control of her world. Her words.

He smiled. He liked that in a woman, in Nadia, but hopefully there was room for him somewhere in her world too.

Simon appeared beside him. 'You're not checking out my sister-in-law, are you, Henry?'

Henry dragged his gaze away from Nadia's back to his new partner, who'd appeared at the door. 'Maybe.'

'I did wonder if that was always the plan,' Simon said, a gleam in his eyes. 'But you were away for a long time... I thought I had it wrong.'

Henry shrugged. He'd been determined to come back a success.

'I enjoyed London, enjoyed the experience gained with great mentors. Stepping more into paediatrics than neonatal suits me.'

Simon nodded. 'It's a good move. Works well for our practice to have both covered.' Simon's eyes twinkled. 'Did you know that Nadia works as admin in our children's ward?'

Henry stared in delight. 'You're kidding me.'

'Nope. Wouldn't kid about that. She works Mondays and Tuesdays. With the possibility of an increase when Katie goes to Prep full-time.'

'Now, that is interesting news.' He wouldn't have to keep thinking of ways to run into Nadia.

'I thought it might be.' Simon glanced back inside. 'My wife is waving us back to the party.'

Henry grinned and preceded Simon into the warm and noisy room.

Suddenly he was surrounded by family and friends—an unexpected feeling and something he hadn't felt since his alcoholic father had deserted his mother when he was seven.

Henry pulled his thoughts away from the dark times, the times he'd hidden behind his quiet façade and pushed himself to learn everything he could to help, the times he'd watched his proud mother work too hard to keep them fed and housed because she refused any help.

It was too late to save Sara Oliver now, his mother's heart had given out at fifty, but Henry's future wife and children would never be reduced to that penury, and he'd set himself to make a solid foundation that would never leave anyone needy.

But he'd been away a long time and it was nice to feel included here. He'd enjoyed London, although he'd missed Australia, but Marco had been distracting and a good friend. He'd also seemed to have no extended family—which was strange for an Italian—but Marco had never talked about his family either.

Heck, there'd never been anything that wasn't testosterone driven with his Italian flatmate. Transitory girls, gym competitions and long hours at work. The years had flown as he'd raced towards his goal.

And now he was back, he owned an apartment, and was more than ready to take on the world saving sick children.

He might not be ready just yet to settle down with a woman and spend the rest of his life with her, but some down time with Nadia did feel more promising than he'd expected. Now he had to find out if Nadia thought that a good plan.

CHAPTER FIVE

Nadia

MONDAYS WERE ALWAYS a struggle. Katie didn't like Mondays, which put a bit of a dampener on them for Nadia as well.

She understood that while her daughter enjoyed being with the other children at childcare, she would very much prefer to be home with her mother every day. Well, she was home with her four out of seven days.

Nadia had wanted to spend as much time as she could with her workaholic dad after their mother died, but she had received even less attention than Bella—though Bella had always been like a surrogate mother for Nadia to make up for it.

The real *world* meant Nadia needed to work at least part-time, and Katie needed to understand that, because she wanted her daughter to grow up independent and self-sufficient.

But, unlike when her dad had been tasked to pick the girls up from school or events, Nadia made sure she *always* arrived. Usually before the rest of the parents at preschool.

On Mondays and Tuesdays Katie went to childcare, and Nadia jammed in two days of children's ward admin, which she loved despite the busyness. It paid the bills while her photography business paid the extras and built up her savings, which had taken such a beating by her husband. She'd never rely on a man or be left in debt like she had been when Alex had died.

Her friend Carmen, another widow, worked the other three days and was flexible with extra work, so if either of their children were sick, the other had cover.

Carmen's little boy went to preschool with Katie, so both were at ease in the other mother's care. Other days, Gran or Bella could care for Katie if needed. But it was rarely needed.

Yes. Her world worked well. And nobody let her down.

The children's ward had recently been upgraded, with everything made modern, and the caring staff, including Nadia, were delighted with the new furnishings.

This morning when Nadia walked in there was a subdued hint of excitement in the air because today they had a new paediatrician starting and everyone wanted to meet him.

Henry Oliver. In her ward. Nadia couldn't get her brain to sit right with that concept. Simon had told her after the party, and she wondered why Henry hadn't mentioned he'd be the new children's ward consultant.

She supposed he hadn't known she worked here.

Their last boss, Dr Steel, had been a gruff, intelligent and caring man, but with little sense of humour. He'd suddenly retired with an unknown illness. Dr Steel had liked children well enough but had always talked down to them.

Somehow, Nadia knew that wouldn't be Henry's style. The idea made her smile. He'd been marvellous with Katie at the party on Friday afternoon and their children's ward just might get a lift it didn't expect.

She'd almost had to run to get here on time this morning, so unusual for her, until finally Katie had called, 'Come on, Mummy, we'll be late.' Dithering with her hair wasn't her usual style, but this morning...

Digital clocks had a lot to answer for, Nadia thought, stowing her bag in the drawer. When she'd been four, she hadn't been able to read a clock face and tell an adult they were late.

But her hair had been a mission. Normally, she just brushed it out but, for some silly reason, today she'd decided to straighten the ends. And it just hadn't hung right. Now, she feared, it looked like a toilet brush.

A shadow fell across her desk. A tall, well-built shadow.

'Good morning, Nadia.' The deep voice and blinding smile hit her. 'Wow. Your hair looks amazing this morning.'

Fighting the blush and borderline annoyed with herself for such a girlie action, she gathered her wits before she looked up. Suddenly, she realised why she'd been so fiddly. Good grief, she'd done it for Henry. No!

Henry stood just a little back from her desk, as though he wanted to take in the whole picture, ridiculous thought, and it looked like he'd taken pains with his appearance too.

Her brows rose in amusement, and appreciation at the panda bear tie covering the buttons of his well-pressed shirt. A shirt that moulded his shoulders and chest as if it had been made for him. Maybe it had—what did she know? This was a new Henry. A pretty darned fabulous Henry. So much so she needed barriers against all that charm because she was an independent woman, not a fool to drool.

She realised he was waiting for her to answer. 'Oh. Good morning, Dr Oliver.' She stood. 'I'll just take you over to Sister Taylor. She's been waiting for you.'

'Formal,' he murmured for her ears only and smiled. 'It's great to see you here. And I look forward to meeting everyone.'

Tara Taylor was in her office, already rising from the chair behind her desk. Nadia gestured with her hand. 'There she is. I'll leave you in her capable hands.'

'Thank you, Nadia.'

Tara, a tall brunette with red highlights and a big smile, tilted her glossy head at Nadia as if to say, *Do you know him?*

Nadia felt her cheeks warm. 'Dr Oliver was a registrar when Katie was in NICU as a baby.' She smiled at Henry. And yes, he'd been great. Just the thought of those days had her softening her awkwardly stilted attitude towards him. 'He's very patient with explaining things.'

Tara smiled at Henry with approval. 'That's lovely. The parents will appreciate that. Welcome to our ward, Dr Oliver. We're very excited to have our own consultant again. We've been struggling with locums.'

Nadia stepped back and away and returned to her desk, where she had a clear view of Henry charming Tara into a laugh. Tara charmed right back. Oh, goodie. She'd get to watch flirting. Not. And where was all this dog in a manger stuff coming from?

Tara and Henry disappeared into a room where Nadia knew a child had not been recovering as fast as everyone had hoped.

Henry stayed in the room for a long time while Tara came and went with trolleys and IV poles and several trips to the medication room, until finally the door opened and Henry emerged with the child's mother.

'I think Joseph will improve more rapidly now, Dawn. But I'll come back at lunchtime and check on his progress.' From her vantage point near the exit to the ward, Nadia watched the worry recede from the mother's drawn face with his promise.

'Thank you, Doctor.'

Henry the doctor. He was invested. She remembered that from when Katie was born. At least that hadn't changed.

Then Henry was off again to walk around the ward properly, making sure each child knew he had time for them and their parents before he left. There were a lot of laughs and smiles from the staff and even the children seemed brighter by the time Henry had finished his ward round.

She heard him say, 'When I come back after lunch, I'll look for those results coming for Anna, Tara. Let's see if we can get her home.'

'Thank you, Henry, that would be great.'

Seemed everyone was on a first name basis after one visit. Dr Steel wouldn't have been happy, and Nadia smiled down at her keyboard.

'See you later, Nadia.' Henry lifted one hand as he passed her desk, and she lifted her face and met his smile.

'Bye-bye.' Oh, good grief. *Bye-bye?* Too late to suck the words back in. Was she four? She'd been a toddler's mother too long and now she spoke like one.

Henry grinned and kept his hand still while he waved his fingers up and down—just like Katie did. She shook her head and went back to work. The guy was a flirt with everyone, not just her, and just because of their previous friendship she wasn't going to be one of his conquests.

Though maybe she needed instructions for building that Henry barrier. Because that was a spectacular smile he'd just sent her, and like everyone else in the ward she'd felt special too.

Apparently, Henry came and went while she was at lunch, but while she was packing up to go home he returned and appeared beside her desk, where she'd been preparing the next week's theatre list patient files.

'Have a good day, Nadia?'

She tilted her head sideways and met his warm brown gaze. He was flirting again. Her newly constructed forcefield went up with only a little delay.

'Hello, Henry. Yes, thanks. And how was your first day?'

He looked across at the nurses' station. 'Great. It's a well-run ward and the staff are very friendly.'

With your winning ways, I bet they are. Now that had been a snarky thought, and she suspected he didn't deserve it. Protection, Nadia, not snarky, she chastised herself.

'I'm glad.' It was the truth.

'Are you going to get Katie now?'

She wondered why he'd asked. 'Yes. Monday is shopping day, and she likes that. I needed something to help get her over the Monday blues.'

His head bobbed once. 'She has Mummy-going-to-work blues, does she?'

He understood, then.

'Yes. Tough love to leave her two days a week.'

'Two seems very reasonable in this day and age. Kids adjust. It's amazing what they'll adapt to.'

'Actually, three. I have Thursdays on my own at home.'

She was thinking there was something there, a shadow of the past in his eyes, something she hoped he'd share...but he didn't.

'Enjoy shopping,' he said instead and walked past her into the ward.

She might have barriers up against Dr Henry Oliver, but just maybe the intriguing man had a few brick walls of his own to keep out the world.

On Tuesday Henry's spectacular smile seemed a little dimmer as he went past her desk. 'Good morning, Nadia,' he said as he paused.

'Good morning, Henry. Nice bags under your eyes.'

'Yes.' A rueful grin that made her want to reach up and touch him in sympathy. 'A late one in Emergency last night, but we won. It's a wonder you can't hear my stomach rumbling.'

'No breakfast?'

'No dinner. I really need to stock my fridge with snacks for Mondays when the fast food shops all close early.'

'I guess I could be neighbourly tonight and invite you to dinner, until you get stocked.' Feeling awkward but somehow driven to say it, Nadia added, 'Home-cooked spaghetti bolognese on Tuesday nights. There's always enough left over for an extra person.'

'Can I say yes before you change your mind?'

She smiled at that. 'We eat around six.' Waved him off. 'Katie will probably talk your ear off.'

'Katie has wonderful conversations,' he said and went on his way.

She watched him go straight to the room with the closed door and she knew he'd be pleased at how much little Joseph had improved. Everyone was talking about it this morning.

The day passed swiftly without her seeing Henry again and she cleared her desk and went to pick up Katie.

Afterwards, she and Katie went up to watch the furniture removal people empty the upstairs apartment to take to the new house. Katie had been tasked to help keep Kai amused and out of the way.

'Is Dr Henry moving in soon?' Katie asked as she and Kai built blocks on the kitchen floor. Nadia sighed. Third time she'd heard that question.

Bella cocked her ear at the words and her lips lifted but she spoke to Katie. 'As soon as the cleaners Uncle Simon organised have made it all shiny.'

Nadia heard her sister's wry tone. She knew Bella hadn't been happy with that.

'You should have heard him,' Bella said. Her sister needed a rant, Nadia thought fondly. Hormones and pregnancy—gotta love them all.

Bella lowered her tone to a deep voice that came out very similar to her husband's baritone. 'You can't go cleaning around a pregnant belly.'

Nadia laughed.

Bella went on, 'Which is just ridiculous because I'm as strong as a horse. And pregnancy and birth is a normal thing for women.' She threw up a hand. 'Some women work in the fields until they deliver and then they go on working in the fields with the baby in a sling.'

'Not around here,' said Nadia, laughing. 'In fact, not anywhere in Australia, I think.'

But she did feel secretly glad, after her own eventful pregnancy, that her usually easy-going brother-in-law had put his foot down. Nadia needed everything to go perfectly for her sister after her own disaster. 'You don't want to go into labour exhausted from *silly*—' she used her sister's word '—cleaning that you didn't need to do.'

'Hmm,' said Bella, because there really was no argument to that, and they both watched the last armchair being lifted out of the door. Suddenly, it was all gone. The apartment was empty.

They looked around. Bella said slowly, 'I had so many lovely times here and I will miss the view.'

'But you're more excited about the new house,' said Nadia.

Bella flashed her a big smile. 'Absolutely. I cannot wait to have all the furniture in and sorted.'

Nadia raised her brows but didn't comment that apparently her sister would miss the view but not the relatives she was moving away from.

Bella was quick. 'Oh. That was tactless of me.' She hugged Nadia. 'I will miss you, sis.' She looked down at her niece. 'And of course I'll miss you, Miss Katie. It's been so wonderful being so close and watching you grow up every day.'

Yes, that had been a blessing she should count whenever she missed her sister, Nadia thought.

'We'll come and visit often.'

'And Dr Henry will be here,' said Katie.

Bella laughed. 'He's really made a conquest there, hasn't he?'

'Yes,' said Nadia dryly and Bella tilted her head.

'He hasn't made a conquest of you?'

'Henry is lovely, of course. But he's way too much like Dad. No way I'm going to fall for a man who puts his work first. And the man is a flirt. All the women in the children's ward hang on his every utterance and are offering to follow him home.'

'A flirt? I don't think that's true,' Bella said mildly. 'The flirt thing. Do you think he wants women to follow him home?'

Suddenly, Nadia felt just a little cross with her sister for poking her nose in.

'I don't have any idea what Henry Oliver wants.' And for some reason she didn't mention she'd invited him for pot luck.

'And, sadly, you speak the truth,' said her sister cryptically. 'But I'm off home to make sure these fellows put all the things in the right place. The cleaners will be in tonight.'

'Tonight? Is Henry in that much of a hurry to move in?'

'I imagine so. He's living in a hotel and goodness knows what he's eating. Wouldn't you be?'

And now would be a good time to mention that he was coming for a meal at her apartment tonight. But she didn't. 'Hmm. I suppose so.'

Henry arrived promptly at six p.m. Katie opened the door and gave that little jump up and down she did when she was excited. 'Mummy, it's Dr Henry!'

Nadia, stirring the mince, lifted one hand from the kitchen

nook. Seemed he had another fan girl. 'Hello again, Henry. Ask him in, Katie. He's coming for dinner tonight.'

Katie gave another bunny hop. 'Because he's living in a lotel?'

'Hotel,' Nadia corrected with resignation. Big ears.

Henry's amused gaze met hers from the door with a quirk of his brow and she said, 'We watched Bella's removalists upstairs this afternoon and she mentioned you would be moving into the top floor as quickly as possible.' She tilted her head at her daughter. 'Some people don't miss anything.'

Henry laughed, stepped in and closed the door behind him. 'Mummy invited me to have spaghetti bolognese with you tonight, Katie. I don't have a kitchen. Yet.'

'You'll get Auntie Bella's kitchen soon.'

He smiled. 'I will.' Nadia watched him glance around. 'You have a lovely unit, Nadia.'

She warmed at his praise. Yes, she'd tried hard to make it a happy and comfortable home for Katie.

'I always feel like the garden's coming into the house, with the windows and the courtyard. We catch lovely sun in the mornings.'

It was a little awkward. But what did she expect? It had been years since they'd known each other. And there hadn't been that much private conversation during Bella's party.

He was in her home.

'Sit down. Would you like a drink? I have a can of beer left over from when Simon was here a few months ago. I don't know if they go out of date?'

He shook his head, amused. 'No, thanks. I had coffee with a worried dad not long ago.' He smiled and lowered his big body into her couch. He looked good there and she turned towards the kitchen, blocking the picture, in case he read something on her face.

'Then I'll dish up.'

As they ate, Katie carried much of the conversation and, to her surprise, Nadia found Henry's presence unexpectedly restful.

They talked about her photography business a little. He conversed easily with Katie and complimented Nadia's cooking. His obvious enjoyment felt somehow satisfying and she realised she'd missed that feeling of appreciation from a man when she cooked a meal.

A sudden bitter memory of a special meal she and Bella had slaved over for their father's birthday came back to her. He hadn't turned up and later he'd brushed it off, saying he'd already eaten.

Bella had been philosophical but Nadia had cried in her room afterwards. Henry wasn't her father but she wouldn't be getting used to another consultant at her table.

Henry's phone rang not long after they finished and he excused himself, apologised for not helping with the washing-up and left. Nadia felt vindicated by her earlier reservations.

Wednesday she and Katie spent with Bella, helping her open boxes and stack cupboards. With Bella on maternity leave, the move had been good timing to have it done and dusted before the baby arrived.

Thursday had become Nadia's favourite day. Thursday, she enjoyed a full day of photography, shooting scenery, promoting her website and taking or editing portraits for families, and she had a portfolio order to drop off this afternoon.

Katie went to childcare, which she didn't mind on Thursdays as her special friend, Lily, went that day as well.

This morning had been particularly productive, though she hadn't got around to breakfast and suddenly her tummy rumbled at the same time as the phone rang.

She didn't recognise the number. That was the problem with the business number being the same as her private one. She had to answer phone calls even if she didn't know who was on the other end of the line.

'Nadia Hargraves, Hargraves Photography.'

'Nadia, it's Henry.' Deep voice, instant picture—her heart-rate did not just leap.

Her hand lifted to her chest and then fear shoved everything else aside. Her throat was suddenly tight. 'Is Katie okay?'

'I thought she went to childcare on Thursdays?' Henry questioned.

'Yes.' Of course. Childcare would have rung her. 'She is. Yes.' She felt like slapping her head. 'Sorry. I just had a little panic attack that the doctor was ringing me.'

'No. Sorry.' A pause, then Henry said almost gently, 'Last thing I want to do is cause you worry. Not ringing you as a doctor. Is that okay?'

'Of course.' Now she felt super silly.

But Henry hadn't sounded as if he thought she was silly.

'You said you have Thursdays at home. I wondered if you felt like taking a break and coming down to the beach café for a quick bite.'

'Did my brother-in-law give you my number?' And of course he'd tell Bella that Henry had asked for it. Nadia frowned.

'No.' There was a pause as if he was thinking through her question. 'I looked up Hargraves Photography.' She suspected he was smiling because he did sound amused.

'Okay.' She'd pay that. She forgave Simon for a deed he didn't do. And she was hungry. And it was only Henry. Only Henry? Nothing 'only' about Henry, no matter how she pretended.

'I'm a couple of minutes away from our foyer. You could come down the lift as soon as you're ready. I'll wait.'

She thought about busy Henry waiting. 'No. You go ahead and get a table. It's always busy at lunchtime.'

'I've already booked a table.'

More amusement in his voice. What was so funny? Had he expected her to leap at the offer? She frowned again. Did he think her predictable?

'Not sure of yourself at all?'

'Not at all. I booked for one and said possibly two.'

And that silenced the internal witch. Enough guessing at Henry's motives since she'd got most of it wrong.

'Thank you, Henry, I'm starving, so that would be nice. A walk outside will do me good.'

CHAPTER SIX

Henry

AND SEEING YOU *will do me good*, thought Henry, delighted she'd agreed. Though she had been slightly combative, which was a little disquieting. Had he annoyed her?

She hadn't sounded overjoyed. Oh, no. It wasn't him she was coming for. It was because she was starving. She needed to get out for a walk.

Lucky he didn't have an ego when it came to women.

That was okay. He'd asked her today to return the hospitality of Tuesday's dinner and he knew she was home on Thursdays and Katie was at childcare.

His thoughts rambled on, creating a scenario he enjoyed. Maybe a casual lunch here and there, depending on their work commitments. She had to eat and so did he.

He liked the idea that she was hungry and he could meet that need for her. Of course, him paying the bill might be a problem but he wouldn't fight about it today if there was a struggle.

Maybe a future dinner date with Simon and Bella, with Nadia and Katie travelling in his car. Simon had mentioned that he and Bella had bought a new child restraint seat for Kai with the new baby coming and hadn't got around to throwing the old one out yet. He could ask for it to keep in his garage if needed for Katie.

Henry was feeling pretty happy today, for some reason.

Nadia swept out of the door of the units just as he reached their steps. Dressed in a knee-length skirt and blue sandals, the cream blouse glued itself to her svelte figure and made her tan glorious. In fact, all of her looked glorious. And then she smiled at him.

There, that was it. That was what he needed in his life.

'Hello, Henry—this is a nice idea.' She smiled sunnily at him. 'But don't think you're going to make a habit of it.'

He blinked, still slightly dazzled. 'Why's that?'

She raised her brows. 'Thursdays are mine.'

Henry thought about that. 'I'm pleased you could come, then. I understand work commitments.' That he did.

'Yes, you would.' Her tone was dry.

No idea what that was about, but he let it go.

'It's a beautiful day,' he said as they began to walk towards the café. 'I'll be finishing late this evening, so I thought I'd better have a decent lunch in case I don't get dinner.'

She turned her head his way and for a moment he thought he'd said something wrong.

But then she smiled brightly at him. 'Seems to happen often. Working late. Not getting dinner.'

He shrugged. 'Often enough. It's easy to do in a hospital.'

'Lots of after hours, then?' Something in her voice made him cautious.

'I've only been on the ward four days. It's a lot quieter than London.'

She stopped and turned to him, still smiling brightly. 'So, just clarifying, you're one of those doctors who is always there for his patients. Whenever they need him.'

He frowned. 'I hope so. Not much use being someone's doctor if you're not there when needed.' He'd worked darned hard to get where he was and yes, he was a dedicated doctor.

She nodded as if something had been confirmed but they'd arrived at the café and he wondered where that conversation had been going.

He considered his answers. Nothing he would change. But the thoughtful expression on her face said he'd confirmed something for her she'd had a preconceived idea about. It was curious...disquieting. But they'd arrived.

The coffee shop sat perched above Rainbow Bay, with high stools and tall benches under red umbrellas all facing the waves. Jars of pretty purple-blue knives and forks sat in the middle of the tables. Henry loved the beachy feel to it after London.

The proprietor, a young woman with a dozen piercings, her hair shaved so close to her head it would prickle, grinned at him. 'Henry, your table's over here.' She smiled at Nadia. 'Hello, Nadia. How's Katie?'

'Happy and healthy, thanks, Lulu. And the twins?'

'Full of mischief.' She patted her pocket and pulled out a pen and notebook. 'Want to look at the menu or do you both know what you want and ready to order?' Lulu was used to medical staff in a hurry.

Nadia said, 'I'm ready, thanks, Lulu. I think Henry needs to get back to work and I do too.' She turned her face towards him. 'Is that okay?'

Henry nodded. 'Sure.' Maybe Thursday lunch wasn't going to be the thing.

Nadia said, 'I'll get the smashed avocados and eggs, thanks, Lulu, and a rainbow juice, please.'

'You know your sister orders the same thing when she comes?'

Nadia smiled. 'You do it so well we can't resist.'

Lulu smiled and then lifted her brows at him. Henry allowed his slight tension to slip away. 'And you, Henry?'

Order. Right. Stop thinking disappointed thoughts about his lunch companion's lack of enthusiasm.

'The full all-day breakfast, thanks, Lulu, and a large cappuccino, please.'

'On the way,' she said and winked so of course he winked back.

Nadia sat back in her chair. 'You've only been back in the area a week and already you're Lulu's new fave person?'

He smiled after the waitress slash proprietor. 'She's a gem. Remembered me from when I was here before and welcomed me back like a long-lost friend.'

That bright smile again. 'I can see the ladies do like you.'

He sat back in his own chair and sifted through the messages that were mixed and perturbing. Resisted the urge to say, *I'm sure the men like you too.* Because Nadia was hot.

Instead, he turned his head and allowed his eyes to roam over the bay, before tilting her way and saying calmly, 'I love sitting here. I thought of this exact spot in London when it was sleeting outside. I could see the waves in my mind and the red umbrellas.' He blew out a breath, more settled in himself just remembering that.

Then he shrugged and said very quietly, 'A couple of times I thought of you sitting with me here, when I was in London.'

CHAPTER SEVEN

Nadia

OH. HE DIDN'T just say that. Nadia felt her cheeks heat, mortified. She had no idea why she was in such a foul mood. And taking it out on poor Henry, who didn't do anything wrong except ask her for a friendly lunch.

Still, that tiny picture he'd just painted, so unexpectedly, had derailed her determined hunt to find reasons she shouldn't want to be out for lunch with him. Which was her problem, not Henry's.

This nice man had invited her in the middle of his busy day because he might not have a meal tonight and had asked her to join him.

Here she was whining about a waitress smiling at him when they all knew and loved Lulu, who smiled at everyone. What was wrong with her?

Yes, he spent a lot of time at the hospital, but that wasn't her problem. The fact that he was a caring doctor was a good thing. It didn't mean he was like her father, and while she had to admit it would be a problem for whoever he spent his life with, that too was not her problem.

Because she wouldn't be looking for a part-time husband and a part-time father for Katie. Still, she was jumping way out of line and that thought, and the consequences, were not for today. Or ever.

His last words, though, had whipped the wind from her black sails and stopped her destructive path. She brushed his fingers across the table in apology before drawing back.

'I'm sorry, Henry. Seems I'm a little belligerent today. My bad. I'm out of practice lunching with a man. Haven't done it for years. And you copped my nervousness.'

'Really. That's not a bad thing to hear.' He smiled at her. 'I'm very pleased about that for the past. But allow me.' He waggled his brows. 'I'd be very happy to help you get back into training. Get rid of those nerves for you. Maybe on Thursdays?'

He was teasing. She knew because his brown eyes were twinkling at her and she could see the cute crinkles. Despite herself, she smiled back.

'I'm very protective of my world.'

He nodded solemnly. 'Yes, you told me.'

'And I'm very protective of Katie.' Her voice dropped. 'She's already asked me why she doesn't have a daddy like the other kids at school.' Another huge worry.

'Tricky,' he said, and she could see she had his full attention.

She nodded. 'So I've avoided the idea of her attaching herself to someone who's not around. Or someone who will leave.' She shrugged. 'Hence, I avoid the complications that going out with a man could cause.' But maybe that didn't count with Henry since he was a part of the family and social crowd they circulated with.

She felt her eyes widen as sudden insight penetrated. 'Good grief. It's not just for Katie. I'm scared for me.'

She heard the words. Hadn't meant it to come out. But knew it to be true. She put her hand on her throat.

'That's not so surprising,' he said gently. 'As a widow, your world would have been upended, adrift while grieving. Now you have your world stable. You told me. You want to keep control.'

He did understand, but if she was honest with herself that wasn't the whole problem. She just wondered if he needed to hear the rest of the reasons. And since she didn't want to encourage him—really, she didn't—she guessed he did deserve it.

'Losing someone I loved is a part of it—the death of a spouse does change everything. But there's more to it than that.'

Henry's gaze held hers and he leaned forward, full attention on her. Softly, he said, 'Can you tell me the *more*?'

How did she explain? She sighed. Henry had been open and honest with her. Could she be the same?

She sat up and straightened her shoulders. 'My husband was a very handsome man. I loved him.' She looked down at the pretty knife and fork she'd put in front of her as she waited for the meal. 'But all women loved him.' She added dryly, 'And... he loved women.'

'Okay,' said Henry, letting her know again she had his full attention.

She went on, 'I don't believe he was unfaithful, but I felt I faded into the background when other women surrounded him. Maybe I was just young and insecure.'

There was silence, not uncomfortable, more of a moment for her to catch her breath after saying things she hadn't said before. Had never allowed herself to think. She appreciated the minute to let it settle.

He touched her hand briefly. Just a quick connection like she'd made and then gone.

'I'm sorry. That must have been hard. But I think he was a fool.' He shook his head, still with that warmth making his brown eyes look very dark and a little too mesmeric. 'He had you. You're amazing. What more could he want?'

She felt her cheeks heat. 'Good grief, Henry. Extravagant compliments today.'

He spread his hands and slid them on the table as if feeling the grain of the wood, a crooked smile on his face. The silence lasted a little while again, not awkward, just both of them...thinking.

She broke it, saying, 'And my husband loved fast cars. He spent almost all of my savings on a stupid car that killed him.' She looked up at him. Narrowed her eyes. 'What type of car do you drive, Henry?'

He laughed. A deep rumbling roll of delight that made her skin prickle and her belly warm. Good grief, that was a sexy laugh. Half the women in the restaurant looked up and smiled.

She watched him force his face into serious lines. 'My car? Oh... It's a Volvo.'

She felt her face pull into a smile, her shoulders sagged as tension left and amusement replaced it. Her turn to laugh.

'You do *not* own a Volvo.'

He smiled at her. 'No. But if it's a deal-breaker for lunches I could buy one.' He was teasing.

'Noted. So you're rich enough to afford a penthouse and a Volvo. And you're a funny man.'

His face looked suddenly serious. 'I'm more than that. Way more. But that's for another day.'

She raised her brows. 'There's another day?'

'Of course.' He rubbed his hands together. 'You've got lots of lunch practice to get in.'

'Spare me,' she said.

'I will. But how about today we just have lunch? Enjoy this

beautiful place. With excellent company. Without worrying about the fears and the future.'

She felt her shoulders drop, her facial muscles ease. Even her fingers relaxed.

'Thank you, Henry. I can do that.'

So they did. Until the child at the next table began to choke.

Henry was up and out of his seat, lifting the wheezing, purple-faced toddler out of his highchair and into his lap while he slipped into a chair at the mother's table. 'Do you mind? I'm a doctor,' she heard him say, and he leant the toddler forward and tapped his open hand firmly between the child's shoulder blades.

Nadia followed—she'd done her emergency first aid certificate, she wouldn't be as useful as her sister Bella or a doctor, but Henry nodded approval. 'Nadia. Great. Can you check his mouth after every tap, and clear it if something dislodges?'

She nodded and crouched down in front of the child as Henry firmly tapped his back. Once. Twice. Three times. The horrible purple of the child's face had deepened, and the mother clutched her throat in panicked terror.

Suddenly, a piece of fruit flew into Nadia's hand and she whipped it away as the little boy sucked in a gasping breath and wailed.

Henry sat him up and rubbed his back as his breathing settled, despite the cries of distress and fright.

Once Henry was sure the boy would recover he smiled reassuringly at the mother and handed the little boy back.

Lulu appeared beside them and offered a packet of baby wipes to Nadia as she stood up, and one to the mother.

'Oh, good grief, that was frightening. Thank you, Dr Oliver,' Lulu said, making sure everyone heard that Henry was a doctor.

Nadia felt her heart thumping in her chest as her own fear settled. The other patrons sighed in relief and clapped.

They were the centre of attention of smiling fans and she wanted to hide.

They finished their lunch more quickly than they'd previously intended and Henry left her to return to work.

Nadia found herself looking out through the garden window of her unit and staring at the frangipanis more than she should.

He'd thought about her in London.

At least that was what he'd said. A couple of times. Her?

Then it was most likely true, the sensible part of her brain said. Henry had always been honest. Even when there'd been tough news to share in the NICU he hadn't tried to avoid it.

People trusted him with their unwell kids. Huge trust. The woman today had trusted him to save her child. And the children's ward already adored him.

She thought about his sincerity as he'd held her gaze and said those startling words. He'd thought of her. Thought of her in London. But only a couple of times.

Henry had moral fibre. She struggled with the thought because she didn't want to label Alex, her husband, a dead man, as lacking, but yes, really, she'd loved a man who hadn't existed. Her husband had lacked maturity, responsibility and principle and she'd grown a strong wall around her heart after he'd died. She wasn't likely to fall into that silliness again.

Henry was different, but she still wasn't willing to let him in. Henry was reliable and honourable and honest, which for her was one of the most important qualities in a man. And apparently Henry liked her.

She thought of the drama of the café and the fact that Henry would always be the doctor who rushed in to save. Like her dad. That was a good thing, a great thing. Did that make her a bad person because she didn't want any of it?

At two p.m. she packed the new portfolio into a protective folder and took her car out of the underground garage to drive to her client's house. She didn't drive all the time, except for her photography business and picking up Katie from the pre-school and shopping days—otherwise, everything else, including work, was within a short stroll. Though now they'd have to drive to Bella's new house.

The road seemed busy, and she decided she'd ask Gran if she wanted to come with her out to Bella's when she picked Katie up from daycare. Gran didn't like driving on busy days.

Most of all, both Gran and her sister were sensible women who would listen to her ridiculous anxiety over going to lunch with the first man since becoming a widow.

Nadia's grandmother, Catherine Goodwin Hargraves, had been an adventurer in her youth. She'd slowed down now, especially after a nasty hit-and-run accident five years ago that had left her unconscious for weeks, but now her green eyes, so like her great-granddaughter's, although faded slightly, were clear and shrewd.

If it hadn't been for Gran, Nadia and Bella wouldn't have had anything like a normal childhood. They would have spent their holidays locked in the house with part-time nannies, waiting for a crumb of attention from their workaholic father, but instead they had Gran, always smiling and suggesting adventures perfect for children.

When they were teenagers, Gran had moved to Rainbow Bay to look after an ailing sister who had since passed away, and the girls had started flying up from Sydney for occasional weekends when they were older.

For Nadia, living in the same block of units with Gran and Bella had been an incredible support after she'd brought Katie home from hospital. And the inclusive family she and Katie had been surrounded with still felt priceless.

'Have you been out with anyone yet?' said Gran, forthright as usual as soon as she was settled.

Bella thought how typical that statement was as a conversation starter. She'd been hearing it a lot for the last few months. To give her grandmother some leeway, Nadia knew the accident had shaken Catherine's world view of being here for many years to come. She wanted Nadia settled before she died. Hopefully married with more children.

Nadia concentrated on navigating the busy streets to Bella's new house. Katie was in her booster seat in the back, immersed in a singalong on her tablet which was connected to the rear of the passenger seat, and hopefully would miss the opportunity to hear this and repeat it at the most awkward moment.

'Well, I went to an impromptu lunch with Henry Oliver today. Does that count?' She didn't mention the neighbourly dinner.

'Did you?' Her grandmother straightened in her seat. 'I like Henry. A caring man, I feel.' Nadia could sense the searching look coming her way, but she refused to intercept it. 'And how was lunch?'

Nadia kept her expression serene. She badly wanted to say, *Sometimes awkward, sometimes wonderful*, but didn't.

'Fine, until a child choked and Henry saved the day.'

'Good grief, how horrible. What happened?'

'A piece of apple happened. Then Henry was up, boy on his lap bent forward and striking the little chap on the back. The apple dislodged.' She thought of that happening to Katie and shuddered. At least she'd been reminded to know instantly what to do. 'I'm glad he was there.'

'I'm sure the mother of the child was as well. How horrid for everyone.'

'Yes. All very dramatic and it sort of ruined the lunch.'

'I imagine so.' She felt her grandmother's gaze on her. 'And before the drama? How was lunch before that?'

'Pleasant.' Nadia flicked a quick glance to see the response.

'Pleasant.' Catherine moved her mouth as if the word was distasteful.

Nadia turned back to the road and grinned.

'I'm so pleased,' Catherine said dryly. 'I would have preferred delightful, exciting, great fun. But I'll take pleasant. At least he asked you.'

'What makes you think I didn't ask him?'

'My own lamentable lack of imagination,' her grandmother said dryly.

True, but not very complimentary.

'Are you saying I wouldn't have asked Henry out myself?'

'Yes.'

Well, she had asked him to dinner. So there. But Nadia only laughed.

'Okay, he rang me on his way walking past and said he was going for lunch. He had a big afternoon at work coming up and needed a decent meal.'

'Poor man.' Catherine tsked. 'He needs a wife.'

Not this little black duck, Nadia thought, so she ignored that.

'I was hungry, so I said yes.'

'Good, because he's a very *pleasant* young man.' Copying Nadia's description. Silence built between them. The faint strains of a child's song drifted from the back.

Nadia remembered Henry's words and almost blurted, *He says he's more than that*, but she didn't.

Finally, she said very quietly, 'We went to the beach café.

Glorious weather. All done within an hour, including the excitement. And I may have behaved badly at the start.'

Catherine drew in a surprised breath. 'Did you? Strange. You never behave badly.'

'Well, only initially. And thank you for that vote of confidence. But I was extremely snarky with Henry.'

'Really?' She could feel her gran's scrutiny. 'What about? And why?'

'Stupid things. Women fawning over him. His workload. My world I was protecting.'

'Good grief.' Gran snorted. 'Did he enjoy the fireworks?'

'He seemed fine. I said I was out of practice with men.'

Gran turned in her seat to look at her. 'You are. Very.' She smiled. 'And what did he say?'

'Henry said he'd help me get back into training.'

Gran laughed. 'I do like this boy. Though I'm not sure a bare hour for lunch constitutes going out, but it's a start.'

'Thank you. But I'm not looking for a man. Yet.'

'I see. So when? It's more five years, dear.'

'Gently, gently, Gran.'

'Yes, dear,' murmured Catherine.

CHAPTER EIGHT

Henry

HENRY'S AFTERNOON PROVED too busy, working with the excellent team at the children's ward, to be able to dwell on his lunch with Nadia. He smiled and made decisions and concentrated on each diagnosis.

Yet every time he had a free moment Nadia's face seemed always there at the back of his mind, and he thought of that word she'd used. Scared.

Well, yes, shocking, but it made sense if she was feeling threatened by the concept of forming a relationship. And it had worked in his favour while he'd been away because she wasn't settled with someone else. But still, he felt sad that such a beautiful woman had those limitations in her life.

As long as she didn't feel threatened by him—or the concept of him intruding into the safety of her world—he could see how a shift in her world view as a single parent would be a valid concern for her.

So, what were her other fears? And why was he so intrigued when Nadia's signals today had been mixed at best?

Judging by the veiled accusations of him being a ladies' man—which was just not true—and something about spending excessive time at the hospital—which couldn't be helped—

it was probably linked with her past. He just had to find out what it was.

Her deceased husband was the easy answer. She'd intimated the man had a roving eye at the very least.

He'd actually spent the plane trip home from the UK alternating between wondering if she was still single since the last time he'd asked her brother-in-law, an irregular occurrence, and fantasising about how he would find her if she was.

And the answer to that, after today's revelations, was cautious. He needed to talk to Simon.

When Henry had finished his tasks, he took himself through the hospital to the NICU—Neonatal Intensive Care Unit—which was Simon's domain.

His friend stood conversing with Carla, the unit's nurse manager and a friendly face from the past.

Carla looked up and greeted him with a smile. 'Hello, Henry. Lovely to see you. I heard you were back.'

'Greetings, Carla. Love your new hairstyle.'

'Goodness, London has polished you.' But she patted her hair.

'Ah, I've been trained by a master. My Italian flatmate encouraged me to actually appreciate little things like that.' He remembered Nadia's accusations, grinned at her and held up his hands. 'Not flirting.'

Carla laughed. 'Good to know.'

'The unit looks great.'

She smiled with delight. 'Happy to take the compliment. We have great staff. How are you enjoying the children's ward?'

'Ditto on the great staff.'

'Yes, clever bunch over there,' said Carla. 'And the new refurbishment is great. I'm guessing you've come to talk to Simon, so I'll leave you to your discussion.'

Simon studied him with a slight smile on his face.

Henry put his hands out. 'What?'

'Something for later. And you did come back smooth.'

'Maybe, and maybe it's a problem,' he said. 'I think I need a buddy pep talk.'

Simon smiled. 'Walk me to my car.' He glanced at his watch. 'I'm late for dinner and I try not to be.'

Henry's head went up. 'Is that a big deal?'

'Yes. Because Bella and Nadia's father... You've met the professor?'

'No, I don't think I have.'

'A joy waiting for you, then.' Simon beeped his car open but didn't get in.

Henry stilled as all denominations of coins fell and pushed the right recognition buttons. 'Oh...'

'Right. Solved one of your problems already, have I?'

'Maybe. Thanks.' He patted Simon's arm. 'You should go.'

Simon smiled, went to climb in and then stopped. 'You said maybe coming back "smooth" would be a problem. Why?'

Henry sighed. 'I went to lunch with Nadia today.'

'Fast work.' Simon grinned. 'Not surprised, but I'm impressed.'

'Impromptu. Anyway, do you know anything about her ex-husband?'

Simon's grin faded. 'A bit. But that's Nadia's business. Ask her.'

'I will. But not soon. I'm going slow.' In fact, he wasn't even sure he had the qualities Nadia wanted in a man—apparently, he was like her father.

Looking thoughtful, Simon considered that. 'Very wise. Come around on the weekend. See the new house. Borrow the car seat.' He grinned. 'If you think it's safe to pull it out this early.'

'Might not be a good idea just yet.' Henry thought about the belligerent Nadia he'd first met outside the units, not presuming anything, and he expected to be busy at work this weekend as his registrar was away on a course. 'But thanks.'

CHAPTER NINE

Nadia

NADIA AND CATHERINE arrived at Bella's new house at Bilinga and were greeted by the new housekeeper, Mrs Tierney, a plump, perpetually smiling woman with pepper and salt hair who ushered them in with undisguised delight.

The two-storey house sat barely four kilometres from the hospital and across the road from the grassy Bilinga Beach, one of the quietest beaches on the Gold Coast, with sand and sea beyond. The yard had a tall surrounding fence with electronic gates and was set on a double block with a gorgeous outdoor entertainment area.

The well-fenced pool came with a children's slide and spa for the adults. The house itself held six bedrooms and four bathrooms. Nadia agreed with Bella's husband that her sister needed a housekeeper and possibly a gardener.

If Bella hadn't been pregnant and on maternity leave she might have complained more strenuously about the idea of needing help twice a week, but for the moment she'd adapted to the idea. And struck gold.

Nadia knew Mrs Tierney came in on Tuesdays and Thursdays and Mr T accompanied his wife and managed the gardens. Already, Kai had taken a shine to Mr T and the gruff Irishman, who only slightly resembled a garden gnome because of his rounded low stature and beard, allowed the little boy to watch him as he pruned and tended the flowerbeds.

Not long after Nadia and her grandmother followed Mrs T through the house, Katie took herself off after Mr T as well and pelted him with questions.

'Let's have a cup of tea in the sitting room before Mr and Mrs T go home,' said Bella. 'Before the children come back in.'

Gran said, 'Where did you find that delightful couple?'

'So fortunate.' Bella smiled at the memory. 'Simon looked after their daughter's premature baby last year, and we ran into them one day at the shops, both looking very woebegone.

'Mr T asked if we had any gardening he could do as they'd sold their house and moved into a unit.'

'Ah. Yes, I understand that,' said Catherine, who'd always had a green thumb.

Nadia smiled and didn't comment. She kept fake plants in the house to save the death and destruction she caused to anything with real leaves but the garden on the other side of the low wall that gave her such pleasure was maintained by the units and flourished gloriously.

Bella went on. 'While we were talking, we discovered their daughter and husband had had to move away for work, and the couple missed their grandchild dreadfully. Said their lives felt empty except for the times they performed their duties as traffic wardens for the school near their home. Mornings, they patrol the zebra crossing for the children who cross to school between seven and nine a.m.'

Nadia glanced at Gran, who raised her brows.

Bella waved her hand. 'They're great. She manages me, just by smiling sweetly. Simon's delighted. So yes, I think I work for them rather than the other way round.'

'Well, your house looks like you've lived here for years.' Nadia gazed around in wonder.

'Good,' said Gran. 'I'm pleased. It always amazes me how many women move house when heavily pregnant. Such a lot of work when you've got a busy time coming up.'

Bella smiled. 'Yes, you made your view very clear when we first mentioned we were moving. I thought you'd be happy that I have some help.'

She turned to Nadia. 'But enough about me. Tell me about your world. How's life in the units since I've gone? How's business? Have you seen much of Henry?'

Nadia didn't look at her grandmother. 'Life's good. Photography's doing well. And, ah, yes, I went to lunch with Henry today, as a matter of fact.' Again, no mention of the dinner because then she'd be interrogated by Gran for not mentioning it. She wished she'd never invited him. A small voice inside whispered, *Liar.*

'Did you?' Bella didn't quite clap her hands, but she looked very pleased.

Nadia tried to play it down. 'It was just an impromptu friendly lunch.'

'Sure. Of course it was.' Her sister leaned towards her. 'You know he fancies you, don't you?'

Nadia remembered his comment that he'd thought of her in London, but she wasn't sharing that. Again, not sure why.

'I'm not looking for a man.'

'Keep telling yourself that. One day you will.' Bella sat back as Mrs T put a tray with a teapot and cups in front of them. 'Thank you, dear Mrs T.'

The older woman smiled serenely and left.

Gran murmured, 'No reason two pleasant people can't get together.'

'It was one lunch.' *Spare me, Gran,* thought Nadia. 'It wouldn't work with Henry. You know as well as I do that he works long hours. And probably will for the rest of his working life. He belongs to the hospital.'

Bella raised her brows at that. 'He works with Simon too.'

'Yes. A full load. I don't want to live with someone like Dad again. And I certainly don't want my daughter to have a fragment of a part-time father either.'

Gran interjected, 'Your sister's managed to make it work.'

Nadia sighed. 'Yes, but Simon's an established consultant. He can make his own rules. Henry is just starting out and I understand that he wants to be there for everyone.'

Gran harrumphed but Bella nodded. 'I understand that. And I have to admit it was a sticking point for Simon and me.'

Despite Bella's agreement, there was something determined and older-sisterish in her eyes that portended advice that might prove unpalatable.

Silence, except for the muted sound of tea pouring into cups, hung heavy over the table.

Gran groaned loudly. 'Your father has a lot to answer for. Problems in Bella's relationship. Difficulties with Simon's workload. And now you. I'm sorry for you girls. I'm sorry I didn't do enough to see that Piers' obsession with work didn't damage you.'

They both leaned forward. 'You did so much, Gran. You were amazing,' said Bella.

'Every holiday, most weekends. And always at the end of the phone,' added Nadia.

Catherine didn't look happy. 'Yes, I tried. But you're still scarred by it, aren't you?'

This conversation had turned out way more depressing than Nadia had thought it would. 'No, Gran. It's not just that.'

She looked at her sister. 'I've been married. I know what it's like to fall madly in love with someone and then to come second to something else in their life.' She shrugged. 'After the freedom I've had for the last few years I'm not sure I want to do that again.'

Gran huffed. 'Apples and oranges. Henry is twice the person that man was.'

'You never liked Alex?' Nadia blinked. 'You never said.'

'Not my place. But I'm sorry, dear, no. Didn't trust him as far as I could throw him.' Seeing that Gran was about twenty centimetres shorter than Nadia's husband had been, that wouldn't have been far, and Nadia decided to redirect this uncomfortable conversation.

Besides, she had another good reason.

'Katie's got all of me now.' Nadia held Bella's gaze. 'Think of all the disappointments when Dad didn't come to school events. The awards. Graduations.'

'Simon will be there for our children,' said Bella firmly.

Nadia opened her mouth to dispute that, but her sister held her hand up. 'Katie sharing you is a good thing. Plus, one day Katie will go away and have a life of her own, so you have to make yours. You'll be the person who gave her everything and was left behind.'

Gran huffed again. 'And I have to mention that you have no male friends, so any male role model would be an extra.'

So much for *support*, Nadia thought gloomily as her grandmother sat back, having made her point. All this because of one lunch. And they didn't even know about the dinner. That would teach her to break her own rules.

CHAPTER TEN

Henry

HENRY DIDN'T HAVE time to run into Nadia over the weekend. He'd spent most of Saturday and Sunday in and out of the hospital at all hours, arriving home after midnight.

Devlin, the four-year-old boy he'd spent most of the time with, had remained in Intensive Care but was improving after Henry had treated the correct diagnosis.

His resident had admitted the child with scarlet fever, but the little boy's red, cracked lips and his swollen tongue had raised Henry's suspicions. Even the palms of Devlin's hands and feet had been swollen and red. And peeling.

Henry had seen Kawasaki disease in London and had been quick to instigate the treatment of gamma globulin. Crucially, they needed to prevent heart damage for Devlin, something that could happen if treatment didn't commence promptly.

This morning, Henry felt a quiet satisfaction with Devlin's recovery and lack of new symptoms, and the young boy looked on track to be transferred back to the children's ward today.

On his way to discuss the good news and the boy's admission with Tara Taylor, the idea of seeing Nadia at her desk at the front of the children's ward quickened his step. He hadn't managed to pass either Nadia or her grandmother in their mutual foyer for days.

And there she was. Henry blew out a breath he hadn't re-alised he'd been holding. His very own daffodil on a busy day, easing the tension in his neck just by seeing her.

Except she wasn't his.

A small red warning light came on in his brain. *Be careful*, it blinked. *Slow down. If Nadia can't feel the way you do, then what are you doing? You don't have time to pursue someone who has reservations.*

She looked up and saw him and that smile she sent him ex-tinguished his little red warning light with a pop of disdain. Ha! She wasn't immune to him.

His mouth curved with pleasure. 'Good morning, Nadia. You are just what I need to see on a Monday morning. You look wonderful.'

'Thank you.' Her smile faded as she studied him. 'Can't say the same for you, Henry. Looks like you've had no sleep. Again.' She lifted her gaze higher. 'Have you been pulling your hair?'

At least she saw him, then. She even noticed his tiredness. Excellent, he thought, if a bit flattening that she thought he looked rough.

'If I bend so you can reach, will you pat my spikes down?'

'No.' The answer was short, but the smile had returned to her sapphire eyes and she shook her head. 'No PDAs here.'

'Happy to go somewhere else?'

She had him. Yep. Something about this woman…

She raised her brows in *This is work* disapproval. But he just knew she was holding back amusement.

To redeem himself he semi-explained. 'One of my patients. A little boy who's been very sick is on the mend. I haven't had the relaxing weekend I expected, but he's recovering now so it's all worth it.'

He watched her brows draw together and remembered her accusation that he lived at the hospital.

'Of course.' She looked away and that movement caught his attention. She nodded, not looking at him, staring at something else. 'It always is.'

'We'll bring him downstairs today.' He didn't know why their mood had flattened, but he wouldn't talk about little Devlin here. He was tired. She was acting oddly. Best strategy might be to exit until his brain started working better. 'Is Tara in?'

'Just back from a department heads meeting. She could be in the staffroom if she's not in her office.'

'Right, thanks.' He nodded and forced himself to leave her and get on with his work.

He didn't get to talk to Nadia again that day, though he dropped by a couple of times because he still felt uneasy but, not finding her at her desk, he shrugged his unease away.

When a surgical consult about a child with a ruptured appendix kept him busy until she'd disappeared home, he didn't have time to think of her again.

On Thursday Henry warned his secretary that he really needed to have a lunch break today. Often, he just worked through if there were appointments that needed urgent consults.

Today, his plan included mooting the idea to Nadia about him driving her and Katie to Simon and Bella's proposed house-warming barbecue on Saturday.

Most of all, he just wanted to sit down with Nadia in a pretty place and spend time with her. And maybe make up for the last drama filled lunch. But he still hadn't called her. She'd been difficult to pin down on Monday and Tuesday, except for that first sighting of her at the beginning of his workday, and he'd thought he'd catch sight of her or Katie before now, out and about.

Nope. That hadn't happened. He found himself hoping it was bad luck and not machinations on her part to avoid him.

He shrugged and pressed her number.

'Hargraves Photography.'

'It's Henry. How are you?'

'Good, thanks, Henry.' A brief pause. 'You?'

'Fine. I'm passing for lunch in a little while and wondered if I could entice you out again. Try for a non-drama-filled lunch. Surely lightning can't strike twice in the same place?' He found himself a little too invested in the answer.

'Well, I haven't eaten.' A pause. Reluctance? 'Thank you. What time are you thinking of going?'

Relief sagged his shoulders. This was ridiculous and he needed to work through her reluctance or drop the whole idea of pursuing Nadia.

'My last patient is at twelve so, all going well, say twelve thirty-five.'

'Same place? You've booked a table?'

'I have. For one, maybe two.' It amused him to remind her about her comment of him being sure of her last time.

'Then that sounds fine. Are you planning on phoning me every Thursday, Henry?' There was wryness in her tone and he felt himself smile though she couldn't see him.

'I'd like to do more than that, but yes, I'll settle for Thursdays at the moment.'

Maybe he shouldn't have said that.

There was a pause and she murmured, 'I see. Then, in that case, I'll choose where we go next Thursday.'

Relief washed through him again. 'Absolutely. Sounds great—we could alternate with choices.'

'There's going to be that many Thursdays?'

'That's the plan. I'll see you outside the units. At twelve thirty-five.'

Ridiculously, his heart felt as light as one of those seagulls flying outside his window. *Careful.*

CHAPTER ELEVEN

Nadia

So THERE WAS a plan? Nadia thought as she put her phone down, and she couldn't help admitting she might just have missed him the last few days.

As long as she was careful. If Henry was looking for a relationship, she needed to make up her mind if she was interested or too...scared? Scarred? Sensible? She wanted to... But something dark and frightened inside her still wasn't sure what she wanted.

It seemed dishonest not to tell him he might be better spending his time with someone else, unless he wasn't looking long-term. Ooh, a fling? No.

Asking for that wouldn't be awkward much. No!

She shook her head at her idiocy and glanced at the clock. She had an hour before lunch and thirty minutes of work to do before then. Maybe she'd think of something to say.

She really tried to work. But it was hard to concentrate. Thoughts of when she'd seen him on Monday morning and how tired he looked. How she'd avoided him on Tuesday, catching glimpses and forcing herself to go the other way.

Henry had moved in upstairs and there was a little ridiculous pique at not being invited to see what he'd done with the big space. He had her number.

Then there were the thoughts of him going upstairs and grabbing whatever he could from the cupboard to eat after a long day. Going to bed and getting up again to answer calls.

She liked Henry. She really did. Liked him a lot.

But all the markings of someone who just wouldn't be there for her and Katie were bright and clear for anyone with her past experience.

She'd seen how consultants could be sucked into immersion at the hospital…have no other lives…desert their families. Thoughts of all those disappointing moments in her childhood when her dad had not been there resurfaced. But this was Henry, she had to remind herself.

She didn't want that to happen to Henry's family. Or have Henry make it happen to her family. Because no, she didn't want it to happen to her and Katie.

But right now, she needed to get this portfolio of baby photos completed and get herself to the front door by twelve thirty-five.

She was early. She saw him walking up the street at a brisk pace, on his phone, probably crisis managing long-distance. She'd seen her father with his phone in his hand all her life.

But this tall, handsome man wasn't her father, she reminded herself. Instead, she forgot to think and just watched. She drew in the sight of him, striding, confident, smiling at the world as he talked the whole time. The glints of gold in his brown hair that hung a little bit too long for fashion over his brow. His strong shoulders stretching the button-up shirt, sleeves rolled up, showing powerful arms. Long, confident strides towards her, strides that quickened when he saw her waiting.

Nadia couldn't deny the flutter of excitement and warmth that leapt inside her. Oh, dear. That flutter was a worry.

'Hello, Nadia.' The words were deep and soft, like the smile on his face, and the warmth turned into a hot glow curling like melting toffee spiralling inside her.

Henry leaned forward and kissed her cheek, his mouth warm and firm against her skin.

She hadn't expected that. Her surprise must have shown on her face because he stepped back and said, 'It's always so good to see you.'

'Nice to see you too, Henry.' She resisted the impulse to touch her face where his lips had been. She was seriously out of practice with a man.

Had she always been this awkward?

Had men always been this smooth?

What did other women do? No, she couldn't go there. Henry would have to deal with what Nadia did. 'No dinner for you tonight, again?'

They started walking, their steps easily falling into a rhythm that matched.

His brows went up in mock surprise. 'Are you offering to feed me again?'

She spluttered. 'No!'

'Shame.' He quirked a grin, then turned his expression to mournful and sighed. 'My cupboards are bare and it's take-away Thursday.'

She refused to feel sorry for him. He'd made his choices.

'Poor you. What you need is a housekeeper now you have a home. To leave you a meal and shop.'

The grin came back. 'Are you looking for a job?'

She spluttered again. 'No!'

He patted her shoulder, his fingers warm and strong against her bare skin. 'I'm joking. I'm fine. I just want lunch.' A brief pause. 'With you.'

There he was again, flirting.

'I'll get Simon onto you. He believes in outsourcing to make time. He'll get you a housekeeper.'

They arrived at the beach café and Lulu waved to a well-positioned table for two. Menus lay on the table beside a bottle of water.

Henry pulled out her chair and, when she was seated, sat down himself and poured two glasses of the water.

'Cheers,' he said as he held his glass up.

'Cheers,' she repeated, and they clinked glasses. She couldn't help smiling. 'I believe this is a wonderful vintage.'

'Oh, I agree,' mused Henry, his expression pulled serious. 'I think it's the tangy quality of the chlorine that makes it particularly palatable.'

She nodded sagely. Took another sip. 'Young. Fresh. A bold little white.'

They laughed. It was so silly, but sitting here with Henry, shaded from the sun by their red umbrella, the ocean in front of them, it was even more delightful than last time.

'You have no idea how much I enjoy hearing you laugh,' Henry said.

'Why, thank you, kind sir.' Despite the flippant reply, Nadia remembered that moment last week when he'd thrown back his head and done the same. 'I enjoy your laugh too.' And all the women in the restaurant had smiled, drawn to him. There was that. Her mood flattened a little.

He leaned forward. 'Do you know I've fancied you from the first moment I saw you in that wheelchair, coming to visit Katie in the NICU?'

He said the most astonishing things. She thought back to that hazy time. 'You mean sick, wild-haired, in a hospital gown?'

His expression softened and he shook his head minutely. 'Your hair like gold, you were pale, beautiful, and you had a blue dressing gown,' he corrected her. 'But I found out you were newly widowed and had a prem baby demanding all of your attention. And you were my patient's mother.'

She didn't know what to answer to that. Where to look. This was unexpectedly frank of him.

She managed, 'I must admit it's all a blur back there.'

His gaze held hers, gentle but sincere. 'The time wasn't right for me to intrude. I knew you needed your family around you, I needed to advance my career and, like the song, London was calling.'

'I'm sure you had a wow of a time in London,' Nadia replied, trying to lighten the mood.

His warm gaze didn't leave hers. 'Nobody in London matched up to you.'

She sucked in a breath. 'Stop flattering me.'

Heavy praise she didn't quite believe. And she'd had no idea he fancied her back then. Though the thought did strange things to her squirmy stomach. Things she told herself she didn't want to think about.

He tutted. 'Truth, not flattery. I told you I only went out with the girlfriends of my flatmate's girlfriend.' He shook his head sadly. 'Poor Marco was always devastated I wouldn't go on a second date with any of them.'

Striving for composure, she said, hopefully in a disbelieving tone, 'I'm sure your work took up most of your time.' But she was thinking, *No second dates at all?*

He shrugged. 'Work. Of course. That's why I was there. But no women I remember like I remembered you.' The words were soft but sincere and slid past her guard like a silver arrow.

Oh, my. Her sister's words came back to her. *'One day Katie will go away and make a life of her own, so you have to make yours.'* Was she being stupid to push a man like Henry

away before seeing what they could have together, too scared
to even try?

Thankfully, Lulu arrived with her notebook and pencil,
and Nadia looked up, so relieved she offered a huge smile.
Lulu looked tired.

'Hey, Lulu, how are the boys?'

'Jake is home from school with a sore throat and terrible
aches and pains. Haven't had much sleep. My mother's mind-
ing him.'

'I'm sorry.' She hated when Katie was sick, though it didn't
happen often. 'Kids get sick fast, don't they. Hope they get
better even faster. Fingers crossed that's soon.'

Henry nodded. 'Most recover quickly. But if the boys are
not any better tomorrow, bring them into Emergency, Lulu.
I'll get my resident to phone me when they come in and I'll
check them out for you.'

'Thank you.' A wan smile for Henry. 'I will.'

Henry frowned at the worry clear on Lulu's face. 'If you're
concerned you can bring them earlier. You know that, right?'

'I will. Thanks, Henry.' She lifted the notebook. 'What can
I get you two?'

Henry looked at Nadia to order first and she stared at her
menu. Her brain still swirled from his comments and her stomach still twirled in a dance she didn't seem to be able to stop.
Menu. Right. She needed something heavy to sit on her belly
and make it stay still.

'I'll go for a chicken burger, please, Lulu. And a skim latte.
Thanks.'

'Got it. Henry?'

'That sounds good. Same, except I have a full cappuccino
in a mug, thanks.'

She hurried off when someone waved at her.

'Poor Lulu. She looks stressed.'

'She does.' Henry watched her walk away. 'I hope the boys feel better soon. She seems very concerned. I'll talk to her again before we leave.'

Above and beyond.

'That's very nice of you, Henry.'

'Not really. But I promised you lunch.' He smiled at her. 'Back to our conversation. The one I started when we arrived here, and when we spoke on the phone.'

She picked up her water and sipped because suddenly her mouth felt dry. 'Oh?' was all she could manage, still hiding behind her glass.

He reached across and gently pulled her hand down so he could see her face. 'I want to see you more than just lunch on Thursdays, Nadia. I'd like to take you to dinner. Maybe a trip with you and Katie in my car. Even if we just go to see Bella and Simon to start.' He was watching her with too much focus.

He'd included Katie and her sister in his plans. He really did have plans. 'Um... What do you want me to say?'

He gave a short laugh but there wasn't much humour in it, which seemed out of character. 'I'd like you to say what you think and feel about that.'

Well, that dropped the conversation on her side of the table. All the things she should say warred with wanting to say, *Yes, I'd like that, Henry*. Because who wouldn't enjoy his company? But in fact she didn't want to fall for Henry, which she knew could be very, very easy to do. She had promised herself Katie would not have the life her dad had given her and Bella.

Instead, she said, 'Well, of course that's very pleasant...' She had a sudden thought of her grandmother grimacing at the word. 'Really lovely,' she amended. Though that wasn't much better. 'Thank you,' she hastily added on. 'But...' Nadia drew a breath and squared her shoulders '...I'm worried about you, Henry. I'm very happy to become friends. But I'm not planning on a relationship. And from some of the things you've said, I'm guessing you're coming from a different place. I've told you I'm happy with my own status quo.'

He watched her thoughtfully, the silence a little more strained this time. Finally, he said, 'And that leaves me where?'

Fair enough.

'So as long as you're aware of my reluctance to commit, I'm sure I'd enjoy going out with you.'

He sat back. 'Do you find me attractive at all?'

She raised her brows. Almost snorted. 'You're joking, right?' Had to laugh. Pointed her finger at the centre of his awesome chest. 'Look at you. You're a hunk, Henry. Gorgeous. It's not that.'

He smiled, his cheeks a little pink at her comments, which made her smile again.

'More information than I expected,' he said. 'Thank you. So do you mean by not being in a relationship that you'd be free to date other men?'

Her eyes went wide. 'Good grief, no, I wouldn't do that.' She laughed. 'Haven't dated in the last five years, so not that.' *Apart from lunch with you*, but she didn't say that. 'Except for social events with Bella and Simon, I don't get to dress up, go out at all. You know? Have fun. With adults. You're offering me that and I'd be crazy not to say that sounds like fabulous fun.'

'Better. Fabulous fun is good.' He tilted his head. 'So, you're saying if I'm willing to risk my heart you're happy to spend time with me? With Katie, on jaunts around town.'

She thought about that.

'Yes.' But there was some reluctance and she suspected he didn't miss it.

He didn't comment on that. 'Good. How about I take you

and Katie to Simon and Bella's barbecue on Saturday, instead of us taking two cars?'

She blinked. That had come out of left field. He'd had that ready. 'I was going to take Gran.'

'We can include your grandmother as well. Lots of room in my Volvo.'

She laughed. 'Bought one this week, did you?'

'No, but there's room in my other car.'

Still smiling, she nodded. That actually sounded good, she decided.

'Lovely. Thank you. I might even be able to enjoy a glass of wine, which I can't if I'm driving.'

'Excellent. I'll pick you and your little family up at your door on Saturday at eleven.'

The word manoeuvre came to mind. Had Henry just manoeuvred her? With perfect timing, their meal and drinks arrived in a rushed slither at that moment.

'Sorry,' Lulu said and turned away.

'Lulu.' He caught her sleeve and she spun towards him. Her normally mobile face looked strained and frightened.

'What's happening?'

'Oh, Henry... Jake went to lie down after lunch. I thought he was just tired. But he woke up with a stiff neck and now he has a raging temperature and my mum said he's taken a turn for the worse. I have to go upstairs.' Lulu lived above the shop.

Henry stood without hesitation, though he did glance at Nadia briefly in apology. 'I'll come with you, Lulu.' He touched Lulu's arm.

Nadia blinked. But another look at Lulu's stricken face and she was up too. 'I'll come as well. Maybe I can help.'

'What about your lunch?' Lulu looked torn.

Nadia brushed that away. 'I'll ask them to make it takeaway and then follow you both upstairs.'

* * *

In the surprisingly spacious flat above the café Henry took one look at Jake and said to Nadia, 'Please call an ambulance.'

She could do that. At least she could be useful.

To Lulu he said, 'Jake needs to be in the hospital. I'll stay until the ambulance arrives and then I'll meet you in Emergency.' Lulu sank onto a chair and covered her face but she was nodding.

When the paramedics came more quickly than expected, Nadia shooed Lulu away with Jake. 'I'll bring your overnight bag.' Henry sent her a grateful look and left at a brisk walk when they did.

She stayed with Lulu's mother and his frightened twin brother, Jackson, until the necessities were packed, phone chargers and a change of clothes and toiletries for Jake and Lulu. This was Henry's medical world, not hers.

But ten minutes later, after picking up their boxed lunches, Nadia carried the small overnight backpack past her own unit and on to the hospital for Lulu. As she walked, she mused on the fact that, yes, here was another interruption to spending time with Henry. But what was happening to Lulu as another single mum, and a friend of sorts, made Nadia's heart thump in fear.

The fact that Henry proved a hopeless lunch companion was a moot point. Thank God for him being there for Jake.

CHAPTER TWELVE

Henry

ONCE HE ARRIVED in Emergency, Henry saw his registrar had already found Lulu and the paramedics. Jake was being pushed into a cubicle.

When the ambulance personnel left, the petite registrar lifted her head and spoke concisely. 'I've taken bloods, sir, and because of his stiff neck asked the nurses to set up for a lumbar puncture.'

It was so good to see Amelia more confident as each week passed. He'd kept telling her she was brilliant and to use her instincts.

Henry nodded. 'I will be doing that. And your examination?'

'Jake's drowsy, slightly confused to which day it is, and sensitivity to light is noted as well as the stiff neck.'

'No vomiting?'

'No.'

'What about a rash?'

'Not that I saw, but they're changing him now into a gown so visibility will be better.'

'Okay, let's go see him.' He touched the distraught mum's arm. 'Come on, Lulu, you're with us.'

Henry's second impression confirmed that Jake looked very

unwell. The nine-year-old was usually robust and noisy. The fast-breathing, pale and limp child in front of Henry made his own heartrate spike.

'What are his observations?'

Amelia repeated them instantly. 'Temperature's thirty-nine. Pulse one-forty. Blood pressure eighty on fifty.'

All signs of galloping infection.

'How long ago did you send the bloods?'

'Five minutes.'

Henry nodded. 'Get on to Pathology. Ask how long before we get some results.'

Amelia sped off.

The nurse in charge of Emergency appeared at his elbow. 'Anything I can do for you, Henry?'

'Afternoon, Jolene. Yes, please. Open up that LP set you have ready. I'll do it in this small suture theatre if it's free. And grab a consent form for Lulu, thanks.'

Jolene sped off. He turned to Lulu. Her eyes were wide and scared.

'What's wrong with Jake?'

Henry hated this part. 'My first thought is infection. I'd like to do a lumbar puncture. That's placing a needle into the fluid around his spine. He has to curl up for the procedure so the vertebrae open and I can draw off some spinal fluid from the space. It would help if you cuddle his neck and shoulders while we do it. You up for that?'

Lily nodded emphatically. 'I'm up for that.'

Henry smiled at her. 'I never doubted it.'

She brushed that aside. 'So? What are you thinking, Henry?'

'Could be just a nasty virus, but also a bacterial or viral illness which could possibly have progressed to create swelling in the brain. We won't know that until we get the results back from the spinal fluid.'

'How long does that take?'

'A while. But we can start treatment after we do the procedure, not before, or we might mask the organism before we can isolate it.'

'Will he be all right?'

'Results say how we can treat it. But I think Jake has all the symptoms of meningitis. Except maybe a sore throat.'

'He had that this morning, but I thought it was left over from last week.' Lulu pulled on the stud in her lip. 'But you can treat this?'

'Yes. As soon as we get that lumbar puncture done. In case it's bacterial we'll give him antibiotics directly into his vein. He already has the cannula, so he doesn't have to have another drip. We'll add IV fluids to prevent some dehydration through that. And if he gets breathless we'll be giving him some oxygen through a face mask, so he doesn't have to breathe too hard and fast to get what he needs.'

'Will he be in the children's ward?'

'In a day or so. For now, I'll send him to Intensive Care so I can monitor his heart and blood pressure more closely. He'll be in hospital for a few days to a week if all goes well.'

Lulu nodded. 'Is it contagious? Should I bring Jackson in to get checked?'

Henry touched her shoulder again. 'If he's well, he's fine. If he's not well, bring him in.'

Lulu nodded. She was doing a lot of that, pale and shocked by Jake's rapid decline. But her sensible questions had Henry amazed at her composure.

'I thought they'd got over what they had the other day.'

'This is probably something different.'

The charge nurse pulled back the curtain and asked Lulu to sign the consent while another nurse and an orderly unlocked

Jake's bed and began to move it out through the curtains. They had a plan and everything would happen fast.

Henry explained the risks and reasons for the lumbar puncture and when Lulu had signed the form they followed Jake's bed down into another, walled room with a door, not just curtains. Once they were inside, the nurse shut the door.

Nadia was waiting when they left the treatment room, and Henry felt that little skip his heart made every time he saw her unexpectedly. He smiled and she smiled back, but there was something he didn't have time to interpret in her eyes.

She made up for that when she handed Lulu the overnight backpack and Henry the packed lunches.

'You haven't eaten,' she said to him. 'Put them in a fridge somewhere.'

His stomach rumbled in agreement.

'Thank you.'

She nodded, hugged a grateful Lulu and left them.

Lulu followed Henry to Intensive Care, where Jake had been moved, lying flat after the lumbar puncture. Henry sat Lulu down in a small tearoom, put the food from Nadia in the fridge for later and made the stressed Lulu a cup of tea.

'The fluid that I took from the space in Jake's spinal looked cloudy, Lulu, which suggests an infection we need to treat. His blood tests confirmed that.'

Lulu paled even further, if that was possible. 'So, meningitis?'

'Yes. Likely. We've started the antibiotics and if Jake shows more symptoms of swelling around his brain we may add steroids to his medications to reduce symptoms.'

Lulu sobbed once. 'Swelling around the brain is bad, isn't it.'

'Not good.' He pushed her cup closer. 'There are risks, Lulu.'

Her eyes were wide and terrified. 'Like what?

He didn't look away, saying softly, 'Worst case scenario, it could cause damage.'

Lulu's eyes widened even further in horror. 'You mean brain damage?'

'It's a risk, but not yet. I have to add there's also a chance of hearing loss, but we're not there yet either. We brought him in early, within a few hours of the first symptoms, so Jake's got every chance of being back home with you in a few days to a week with no problems.'

Lulu closed her eyes. 'Okay.' She gulped. 'Not to worry about that today. Got it.'

But Henry could see the swallowing of horror as she breathed.

He stepped in and hugged her to his chest. Her body shook with distress. Single parents did it even harder, which made him think of Nadia and Katie and the fact that they didn't have arms to hold them.

He stepped back, letting his arms fall. 'We're on this, Lulu. He'll have the best care. It's what we do here.' He gestured to the ward. 'You can't have a bed here, but you can sit in a chair a lot of the time. And when he goes to the children's ward you can stay with him overnight there, in a bed. Okay?'

She clutched his sleeve. 'You'll watch him when I'm not here, won't you, Henry?'

'He'll be watched. Either me or my residents or registrar will be coming a lot and the nurses here are experts at critical care nursing. He'll sleep for a few hours now. If you need to go home and see your mother, now's a good time. Give me your mobile number and I'll text you right now, so you have my number.'

Quickly, he entered her details and texted *Henry* to her phone. It pinged straight away.

Lulu blew out a big breath, looking at the text. 'Thank you. I really appreciate this.'

'You're welcome. You go home now and reassure them. Update your mother and Jackson, and I'll sit here for a bit while I write up my notes.'

Henry watched her go, aching for her distress, but he would do everything in his power to get Jake home to her, undamaged.

Then his eyes were drawn back to the boy lying so pale against the white sheets. Jake lay deeply asleep, moaning softly every now and then, and Henry suspected his headache caused him distress. The boy's chest rose and fell with the rapid breathing and Henry glanced at the monitor to see the telltale sign of desaturation in the pulse oximeter numbers that had come down just a little.

He looked up at the nurses' station and instantly the nurse who was caring for Jake appeared. On the ball, he thought approvingly. The staff everywhere in this hospital were top-notch.

'Thanks, Helen. I'll order a dose of IV Panadol for pain, and see if you can put some nasal prongs on if Jake will tolerate them. If not, then a mask at two litres a minute.'

The nurse nodded. 'To bring his respirations down a bit and his O2 saturation up.'

Henry smiled. 'Yes, and can you make sure his mother, Lulu, is looked after and can come in any time?'

'Of course.' She turned and left to collect the medication and pass on the orders.

Before she could get out of earshot he added, 'Phone my registrar Amelia immediately if there are any concerns and me if there's any delay getting onto her.'

'Will pass that on.'

Henry would document all those orders in the patient notes,

but it never hurt to back up the orders with verbal ones as well. Sometimes staff became so busy they didn't get a chance to read the latest notes until it was too late.

He wasn't having that happen to Jake or any of his patients.

Henry stayed with Jake for an hour, not seeing any improvement despite all his positive vibes, and when Lulu came back he left her there. He ate the delayed lunch in the fridge that Nadia had brought, ate hers too as he hoped she'd expected and then took himself to the children's ward for a round.

Everything was fine. He could go. Had to.

He started to walk home, worrying about Jake and the stricken Lulu and wishing he could talk to someone.

Friday had proved too busy for the spot of consolidating Henry had hoped to achieve after work. He'd been thinking about an impromptu invitation to Friday night pizza, relaxing in his place or hers, but in the end he made it home and fell into bed at ten that night.

He took himself to the gym on Saturday morning because his morning runs with Malachi Madden were weekdays only and he needed to burn off nervous energy. For some reason, he felt that today's family visit could be a pivotal moment in his budding relationship with Nadia.

On the blokey side, he enjoyed the dawn outings with Malachi's amusingly blunt pronouncements as they ran along the foreshore paths. Malachi and his family were coming this afternoon for the barbecue, he thought as he pumped iron at the gym, and he enjoyed the clatter of lots of children. He'd been looking forward to Simon's barbecue for days.

And chauffeuring Nadia. His first tenuous inclusion in Nadia and Katie's world. Musing on the progress of his pursuit of Nadia Hargraves, because that was what it was becoming—a pursuit. She certainly wasn't doing any of the chasing.

At least he'd discovered she found him attractive. Relief there. He laughed at himself. Marco would be rolling his eyes. Henry didn't believe he was gorgeous but still, it was better than Nadia saying he left her cold.

He still believed the main stumbling block was rooted in the past. Maybe her dad, who Henry really wanted to meet now, to suss what all that was about. And maybe try to ask her about the dead husband with the roving eye. But he needed time to draw it out of her.

All in all, perhaps they had progressed, though not in the easy manner Henry had hoped for.

He had a date on the weekend, which was what he'd been aiming for. And she had said dinner would be fun. And perhaps when they had Catherine in the car, not the planned inclusion on his little family day out, she could prove a bonus. He liked Catherine, and knew she often minded Katie when Nadia had to work out of usual times. Maybe she would offer to babysit for them to go to dinner. Yes. All in all, lunch had worked out well, if not very well.

Fifteen minutes before the departure for Simon's house his phone rang, and his stomach sank. Amelia's strained voice, requesting assistance. One of his small patients had relapsed and his registrar felt concerned enough to want an onsite consult.

Of course he would go. Now. As soon as he explained to Nadia.

When he knocked at the ground floor, Katie opened the door. She stared up at him, her little face alight with expectation.

'Dr Henry! We're going to Auntie Bella's in your car!'

Oh, dear heaven.

'Darling Katie, how are you? Is Mummy there?'

Nadia stepped from the bathroom with a hairbrush in one

hand and a curve to her lips that made him want to kiss her lovely mouth. Her hair gleamed and face looked serene as she smiled. 'Hello, Henry, you're early.'

'Sadly, I'll be late.'

'Oh.' A cooler voice.

'I'm sorry. I've just been called back to the hospital. I'll have to meet you at Simon's later. They've just phoned from the children's ward.'

'Of course.' He saw something he didn't want to see cross her face. But she smiled carefully and nodded. 'Sure, we'll see you there.'

He looked down at Katie's frowning face. 'I'm sorry, sweetheart.'

'Aren't we going in your car now?'

'Next time. A little boy is sick and I need to go to the hospital to see him. That means I can't come with you yet.'

'Like Uncle Simon does sometimes?'

He nodded. 'Yes. But I have to go now.'

Nadia said, 'Of course. We hope the child gets better soon.'

When he still stood there, she waved him away. 'Go. I know you're in a hurry.'

He blinked. 'Thanks. Sorry about that. See you.'

'Sure,' she said. 'Shut the door, Katie.'

By the time Henry made it to Simon's barbecue he had no doubt that if any of the food was left, his would be plated and covered with foil.

The first person he saw was little Katie. Her bright green eyes narrowed on him. 'You missed the barbecue.'

As the words left the child's mouth, Nadia appeared behind her with her tote in her hand. She said calmly, 'How is your patient, Henry?'

'Improving, thank you.'

'I'm glad for them.' She said to Katie, 'Doctors have to be there for their patients, Katie. When people are sick, that's more important than everything else.'

Henry frowned. The words were basically correct, but something was off, and Henry felt the sinking in his gut deepen.

'More important than us?' In surprise, Katie swung her face between Henry and Nadia. Henry knew exactly what Nadia was going to say, and he jumped in.

'Nobody is more important than you and your mummy, Katie. But sometimes I have to miss out on fun times even when I don't want to.'

'Yes,' said Nadia neutrally. She gave him one of those unconvincing smiles he was beginning to dislike intensely. 'We're just about to leave. Malachi and Lisandra have gone. Gran's tired and my sister has finally noticed she's heavily pregnant. She needs a nap.'

'Of course,' he said, cursing under his breath. 'Do you have plans for tomorrow?'

'Let's just see how it pans out,' she said vaguely as her family drifted out behind her, congregating towards the door, where they all hugged and kissed.

Bella came up to Henry. 'Welcome! I'll just see this lot out.'

Everyone greeted him, but in this instance he felt like an outsider. It was something he didn't like to feel. In fact, it made him feel like the ostracised kid in the mended clothes with no dad, the one he'd been at school. Especially when weighed against the sense of inclusion he'd savoured the last time this group of people had gathered.

Simon turned to Henry. 'Sorry you missed out on lunch.'

Everyone left and Bella returned. 'There's a full plate in the fridge for you. You should eat before the salad goes limp.'

Simon touched his wife's shoulder. 'I'll sort Henry and you'll go and rest.' Henry felt his friend's sympathetic gaze on him. 'I'll make sure he gets his lunch. Henry and I will have a very comfortable afternoon doing blokey stuff.'

Bella said, 'But...'

'And we'll empty the dishwasher now it's finished and listen for Kai if he wakes.'

As this domestic jostle progressed, it dawned on Henry that he was so late that even the dishwasher had finished its cycle after the event. He'd missed it all. Completely.

Five minutes later, when they were both sitting at the table, Simon with a coffee and Henry carving into a reheated tender wagyu with lashings of potato bake, Simon said, 'Bad luck on that timing, mate.'

Henry put his fork down and stared glumly at his plate. 'I think I may have gone back four steps.'

Simon sipped his coffee thoughtfully. 'At least four.'

He didn't get it. 'What am I supposed to do? This is my job. That's why I studied and trained. I'm a doctor who is called into work. It's what I am.'

'Finished wallowing?'

Simon's soft voice had Henry's chin up in no time. He wasn't wallowing.

The aggravating man opposite had his hand up in amusement. 'I get that. It's what you do. What we do.' He paused. 'Listen to me. We love our jobs, but if we want to keep the women we love you need to understand that our work is not who we are.'

And how did that pan out?

'I'm pretty sure Nadia wouldn't want me to not care about my patients.'

And that hadn't sounded sulky like a child, Henry thought, wishing the words back. He really had worked himself up and he didn't like it.

'I'm sure Nadia admires your dedication,' Simon said dryly,

'but she won't be admiring from up close. As for missing lunch, today wasn't a big event, just a little family barbecue. There was no tragedy or disruption to anybody because you weren't here.'

Ouch. Henry didn't like the sound of that, but had to accept it was true. He put down his knife and fork, his appetite satisfied and his heart heavy.

Simon wasn't finished with the tough love. 'But if it had been, say…a formal event with Nadia all dressed to go, and your resident called you with exactly the same phone conversation, would you go?'

'Yes. Of course.' He heard the words before he thought it through.

Simon nodded. 'I applaud you for it. But if there is something budding between you and Nadia, that lack of forethought might just cost you a family.'

Henry shook his head. 'People marry doctors. They're happy. This can't be right.'

'Your dilemmas were mine four years ago,' Simon said.

'What am I supposed to do?'

Simon rubbed his chin. 'Talk to Nadia. Find out what she thinks. I can't help you there.'

Henry shook his head. 'I thought there was a good thing happening here, Simon.'

'I'm seeing that. And I can share that Nadia cast more than a few glances towards the door today. She looked disappointed when you weren't there.'

That was something.

'Do you think it's too late?'

Simon held up his hands. 'Over my pay grade as your mentor-slash-buddy. Depends how hard you want to try.' He stood and walked to the fridge. Came back with two beers, handed one to

Henry. The silence lengthened between them. Simon patiently sipped.

Henry said slowly, 'When I thought I might have to fight for Nadia, I thought it would be against another man, not against my work.'

'Hmm. Does it change how you feel about her?'

Henry's whole being rebelled. 'No, of course not. Just makes me depressed.'

'Oh, spare me that too,' Simon murmured, and Henry had to smile.

He had sounded pathetic. Maybe he could explain. 'Not something I talk about, but my dad left when I was seven. My mum worked really, really hard to keep a roof over our heads. She died young.'

Simon said quietly, 'I'm sorry.'

'Other people have it worse.' Henry took a sip of his beer and put it down again. 'A big part of my work is making sure that I have a solid base. When I do find a partner for life, no way will she ever have to work like my mother did. She'd never be left destitute.' He looked up at Simon. 'If it was Nadia…I would keep her and Katie safe.'

Simon put his beer down and sat back in his chair, a perplexed frown on his face. 'Admirable sentiments and sympathy for the young Henry. But saying that out loud to Nadia could get you thrown out. Which century are you living in?'

Henry blinked.

Simon laughed and waved an apologetic hand. 'Nadia is an independent woman. Self-sufficient. Doesn't need you to provide, because she can meet every material need she and Katie have.'

The words were colder on his skin than the beer he rested his hand against. It took a few moments for them to sink in past the gooseflesh.

Oh, damn. He sat back. He'd been so stupid.

In London, sixteen thousand kilometres away, he'd been so focused on achieving his career goals so he could nurture and care for his future partner, like he'd wanted to nurture and care for his mother, he'd dropped reality.

While he'd been in London, his memory of Nadia had been based on the beautiful but fragile young widow in a wheelchair with a premature baby, the mysterious woman he'd been attracted to at first sight. He hadn't been able to care for her five years ago because she had her family. But he had built a fantasy world around the whimsical possibility that he might in the future.

In fact, she still had her family. She had herself. She didn't need him.

A lot of that self-loathing must have crossed his face because Simon said, 'Before you take yourself off to drown your sorrows, listen to me.'

He dragged himself out of despair and looked up.

'Women have other needs than a roof over their heads, though that is essential too. If you want to be a part of Nadia's and Katie's lives, be an equal partner and parent. They need your presence more than they need you to provide anything.'

And how did he do that?

'Not much of me to go around. I work ten to fifteen hours a day. I've been stupid. Patriarchal. Maybe I don't have anything they need.'

Simon looked at his empty stubby as if it had let him down. Sighing, he said, 'Yes, you do. You have you.'

Henry grunted. Pushed away the small bottle in front of him. This was bad.

'I should just back off. This isn't going to work.'

'And you heard me say she cast more than a few glances towards the door today.'

'Sure.'

'She did. You're in a tough place, Henry. First dates and starting out as a new consultant. Finding your feet and making connections with colleagues. Moving up. If you want Nadia, you're going to have to figure out the balance. We can't put our wives and families on hold whenever it suits us.'

Simon finished his beer. 'And that's enough about you.' He shook himself as if it was all too much. 'I want football. The Broncos are playing South Sydney at Suncorp Stadium in five minutes.'

Henry held up his hands. 'I'm done.'

Simon had given him some advice. If he wanted to pursue Nadia, he needed to figure this out for himself. There were very capable doctors a few suburbs away, working at other hospitals. Maybe he needed a bigger team.

He sat back. Thought that through. He knew of several good paeds. He could cultivate some backup.

CHAPTER THIRTEEN

Nadia

DRIVING HOME FROM BELLA'S, Nadia glanced in the rear-view mirror. 'Katie's gone to sleep already,' she said to her grandmother.

'Lucky Katie,' said Catherine and put her hand up to cover her yawn.

Nadia smiled. 'You'll be having your own little nana nap in fifteen minutes. The traffic's heavy, so it will take us a bit to get home.'

They drove for a few more minutes until they stopped at a traffic light behind a long line of cars. Catherine shifted in her seat and faced her. *Here it comes*, thought Nadia, heroically not sighing out loud.

'So? Are you going to forgive the man?'

And that would be Gran, not beating around the bush.

'I'm still too annoyed to think about it.'

'He looked like someone popped a paper bag in front of his face when you left.'

'He probably didn't even notice the time while at work,' said Nadia. 'Just like Dad. Too busy being that consultant.' When Catherine didn't say anything, she went on. 'I'm more angry with myself. I knew this was going to happen. And yet I opened myself up to disappointment. Katie was disappointed.'

Yes. Definitely more annoyed with herself. And, sadly, definitely disappointed with her idea of Henry.

'But still annoyed with Henry,' said Catherine.

'Oh, yes.'

'The man has a dilemma, you know.'

His problem, thought Nadia, feeling snarky.

'Well, I don't. I'm not having that life. Lovely man, lovely fairy tale. But, in reality, I want a man who's there for me.'

Catherine huffed. 'Oh, for goodness' sake, Nadia, stop. What man is there for you now? What perfect paragon is going to meet all your needs in exactly the way you want?'

Oh, dear, Gran was on a roll, thought Nadia with an inner wince. Thankfully, the lights turned green to go and she could watch the road and avoid those all-seeing eyes.

'If you don't start accepting people aren't perfect, then you will always be alone. It will become harder and harder to connect with someone who could be your life partner.'

Ouch. Gloves off, Gran. It would even be painful if she hadn't heard it before.

'Take second best, you mean?'

Gran growled.

'Okay.' Carefully, she said, 'You're saying I just forget that this was the first time we actually looked ahead? A proper planned outing. That he had advance notice for.' She really didn't want to say *date*. 'And just forget he didn't turn up until it was all over?'

'Yes,' said Catherine simply. 'He's a new consultant. His patient was sick. He's never held this position before. He has to find a way to arrange his life balance.'

'All perfectly reasonable, even admirable, for a doctor. But not my dream person, and not someone I plan to pin my life on.'

Catherine pushed on. 'Give him a bit of leeway to make mistakes.'

'You think today was a mistake? He didn't realise?' She

could hear the incredulity in her voice and toned it down. Said quietly, firmly. 'I think it's the beginning of a pattern.'

'Of course you do. You've been hyperalert for traits of your father since you started dating.'

There was a silence then. Nadia feeling cross with her grandmother now and no doubt Gran struggling not to say what Nadia knew she wanted to say. *And you married the wrong man because of that.*

More calmly, Gran said, 'If I know Simon, he'll have given him sensible advice already.'

Nadia thought about her big brother-in-law—a mentor Henry looked up to, the man married to her sister. A little of her ire seeped away. Yes, Simon would have advice. Could it help? Would Henry listen?

Catherine said, 'Give him another chance.'

Nadia blew out a big breath. She enjoyed Henry's company and his attention. Found herself thinking of Henry when she shouldn't. The man was intruding and if he wasn't going to be there it had to stop. Stubbornly, she asserted, 'An over-committed consultant is not what I want for Katie and me.'

Gran snorted. 'Well, pull up your big girl panties and tell him. If that's the big problem, don't whistle down the wind until you've had a chance to tell him why.'

Thankfully, they were just pulling into the underground car park of the units. Katie woke with the sound of the rumbling roller door. 'Home,' she said sleepily.

'Home, darling,' Nadia said. And that was the thing. More than anything, she didn't want Katie to have a part-time father.

When she'd gone to bed last night Nadia had listened to her relaxation track to calm down and in response she'd had a good night's sleep.

So when Henry phoned the next morning, she knew it was him because she'd swapped in his new number for his old.

Funny that. His old number had been in her phone all the time since Katie had been born. Because, yes, he'd been so very good when Katie had been in the NICU, so she smiled and answered.

Thought about her grandmother's words. Maybe she would give Henry somewhere between one and four chances.

Before he could say anything, she said, 'Good morning, Henry. Happy Sunday.'

There was a moment's silence at the other end of the phone as if she'd interrupted his prepared speech. She smiled. Good—got him off-balance instead of her.

After just a beat he said, 'Happy Sunday, Nadia. Would you and Katie like to go for breakfast at Greenmount Surf Club this morning? And the markets are on at Coolangatta. I thought you might like to walk through there after?'

That did sound lovely.

'Thank you, Henry. I've been meaning to get to the markets for ages. Hadn't realised it was the second Sunday today. What time were you thinking of leaving?'

'Whenever you're both ready.'

She glanced at the clock. Seven-thirty.

'Half an hour?'

'I'll be at your front door at eight.'

Henry arrived promptly at eight. Possibly a few minutes before. This time Nadia opened the door for him.

Before she could say hello, he said, 'I'm sorry about yesterday, Nadia. I'll try to do better in the future.'

And that just took the wind right out of her sails.

'Okay, Henry. And I'll try to give you some leeway. But understand that my childhood meant being stood up by my father at important times. Every time. I'm not planning on doing that for the rest of my life.'

'Noted,' he said, and cautiously both smiled at the other.

'Right,' she said, 'I'll just grab my backpack.'

Katie ignored him as she played with her doll in the corner—scolded the painted face, probably for being late. Nadia thought with a smile that she was mimicking her mother, like she normally was.

'Come on, Katie, Dr Henry's here.'

Katie bounced up with her doll under her arm. She crossed the room to Henry. Tilted her head up at him. 'Mummy said we're going in your car this morning. Is that true?' She didn't look convinced.

Nadia had to suppress the smile. Poor Henry had two women on his back.

He crouched down to Katie's height. 'Yes, Katie. I'm sorry for yesterday. I borrowed a booster seat off Uncle Simon. So I've got a car seat in the back of my car already.'

Katie skipped up and down. 'You have?' Which was just what Nadia was thinking. She'd planned to grab Katie's from the back of her own car on the way through the garage.

Henry glanced over his shoulder at her. 'I did.'

Nadia raised her brows in ironic approval while Katie tilted her head in enquiry. 'Do you have an iPad behind the seat?'

Nadia grinned at Henry's sudden freeze. 'Um…no. No, I don't.'

'Mummy does. And I sing songs while the grown-ups talk in the front.'

Nadia bit her lip to stop the laugh.

Unfazed, Henry agreed, 'I'll have to get one.'

Katie picked up her doll. 'Then I'm ready.'

Breakfast was easy and fun. Greenmount Surf Club overlooked the waves and the sun beat down on the sand in front of them while gulls squabbled over morsels found at the edge of the water.

Katie had been given a pack of crayons and paper by the staff and was happily drawing stick figures on a sunny day.

She and Henry had fallen into a desultory ramble of comments and observations and Nadia realised that, despite all her protestations of being happily single, she had desperately missed adult male conversation. And Henry's company was pretty darn special.

And maybe the admiring looks whenever Henry glanced her way were very nice too. Which was often. And very warming.

'Looking for anything special at the markets?' Henry asked.

'Little things for a Miss...' She spelled out Katie's age. 'Next month.'

Henry's smile made her catch her breath. White teeth, sexy lips curved and his dark brown eyes crinkled with delight. 'Are you having a...P-A-R-T-Y?' He spelled out the word. 'May I come?'

'Yes. At Bella's with three extra visitors coming.'

'What time?' he asked.

She tilted her head and narrowed her eyes at him. 'Eleven. I'll see you there.'

She actually thought he gulped, and she softened. 'Or not. It's entirely up to you, Henry.'

'I will do everything in my power,' he said. And, strangely, she believed him.

The markets proved fun, but by the time they'd finished, Katie's head drooped and she fell asleep even before Henry drove them back to the units.

'I'm going to put Katie to bed for a little nap with her doll. Ernestine's tired,' she said.

'You could carry Ernestine, and I could carry Katie up for you?'

And didn't that just make her smile. *Oh, Henry, you are a charmer.*

'If you do that, I could offer you a cup of tea.' Because she wasn't ready to say goodbye to him yet either.

CHAPTER FOURTEEN

Henry

HENRY CONSIDERED HIMSELF very fortunate to be sitting one down from Nadia on her three-seater couch with the teacups and pretty teapot on the table in front of them.

Katie hadn't woken when Henry put her into bed. Feeling Katie's cheek against his shoulder and her small hands around his neck had been the most amazing sensation. He'd been surprised how fortunate he'd felt to be trusted by the child and her mother.

He'd lifted kids before, many times, but not one he'd known since birth. A little girl he found himself growing more fond of every second, and little Katie's freely given trust and snuggle-ability made a strange protective urge surge unexpectedly inside him.

He'd watched as Nadia slipped her daughter's shoes off, tucked her doll—Ernestine, Henry reminded himself—beside her and covered her up. It was almost as if he was a part of her family. Nadia's family.

Dear heaven, was this where he wanted to be?

Now, Katie's bedroom door stood ajar, which kept their voices low, and in the background, country music played softly as the open veranda door allowed the sea breeze to flutter the curtains.

'You can pull up the tab at your end of the lounge, you know, to give you a footrest,' Nadia said.

Lazily, Henry raised his brows at her. She demonstrated and once she'd kicked off her blue sandals her feet were bare and suspended above the tiles.

His gut twisted at the sight of her bare toes. So exposed. Fragile. Womanly toes. He moistened suddenly dry lips.

'You have beautiful feet.'

'Thank you,' she said.

He so dearly wanted to cup them in his hands.

'I give a great foot rub.' He had a sudden, very graphic fantasy of lifting one slender leg and kissing those feet. His body stirred.

She turned her head and quirked an eyebrow at him. 'Do you?'

'So I've been told.' It had been his mum, but he wouldn't share that.

Or maybe he could. Maybe he should. He forced himself.

'My mum said that. Dad left when I was seven. She worked really hard.' He wanted to push those memories of his exhausted mother away, but perhaps Nadia needed to know. 'Sometimes I'd rub her feet for her after work.'

Nadia stared at him. The glorious blue of her eyes went so soft his breath caught. But he wanted understanding, not sympathy, so he changed the subject.

'Anyway, dear Nadia, one day I'd like to rub your feet.' He watched as her sympathy turned to something else as he imagined again holding Nadia's slim feet in his hands and let it show on his face.

Her cheeks pinked and her mouth curved. With her response, instantly his body stirred until he had to force cooling thoughts—icy showers, polar bears, Nadia being scared. That worked to cool him. Not tonight. But soon.

'But…' back under control '…I won't say no to the footrest.'

She murmured, 'And I won't say no to some future foot rub.'

Henry glanced back at her toes, mesmerised. She had small slender feet with perfect nails painted pink at the tips. There was something private about those toes that he'd been allowed to see. He couldn't remember feeling this at home with a woman. Ever.

He tried his own footrest and took the weight off his legs like a…husband? Leaned back and closed his eyes.

'All we need now is a movie and some popcorn for the perfect Sunday afternoon,' he murmured, to lighten the unexpectedly heavy impact of that thought.

Nadia laughed. Her voice was a whisper of dancing notes in the quiet room. 'That does sound relaxing. Do you watch many movies, Henry?'

He opened his eyes. 'None in the day. At night, when I can't sleep, sometimes.'

She leaned with her cheek on her knuckles, elbow resting on the side arm of the sofa as she watched him. 'What sort of movies do you watch?'

'Prefer old ones.' His drowsiness receded. 'But anything that's on, really.'

'Yes, but what's your favourite?'

He closed his eyes to think because he couldn't while he watched her. Thought about what he enjoyed. 'Old Westerns. Clint Eastwood. Saloon girls and rough, tough ranchers.'

He heard her laugh softly and his lips curved. He loved that sound. Could easily love her, he realised. That hadn't taken long. Damn. He was already in too deep for his precarious position.

'You like romance and bromance. I love it.' She was on another page. As usual.

He blinked. Bromance? Where had that come from? he

thought, and then remembered the conversation before his own internal revelation.

'Um…yes. What about you?'

'Rom-coms.' Her eyes sparkled and he sat straighter in the chair, reducing the angle.

She had a faraway look in her eyes and a reminiscent smile on her lovely face that he wanted to see when she thought about him. 'Ones that make me laugh and then make me sad and then smile again. And yes, the old ones are fab, just like your Westerns.'

Pulling the chair out of its recliner mode, he put his feet back on the floor. *Ground yourself, mate.* Because he just wanted to reach sideways and pull her to him.

'Name one.'

She shrugged. '*French Kiss* with Meg Ryan. *Sleepless in Seattle. The Princess Bride. Notting Hill.*'

'Nope. Don't know any of them. But the kiss one sounds promising.' He fancied a bit of French kissing.

'Seriously? Never watched any of them?' Her eyes widened and he smiled. She'd missed his innuendo.

'Cross my heart.' He mimed the action.

'Well.' She put her own footrest down with a click and stood. 'Stay there. You need educating. I'll just put the popcorn maker on.'

'Please do.' Suddenly, he wasn't sleepy. At all. He stood too. 'But let me help.'

She waved him back. 'No. It's a small kitchen and I'll get flustered with your big body in there with me.'

Hell, yeah.

He grinned. 'I'd like that.' He loomed as much as he could without crowding her.

'I'm sure you would.' Primly, she pointed to a wall but with laughter in her eyes as she moved towards the kitchen.

He didn't sit. Instead, he shifted so he could lean on the wall near the kitchen with his arms crossed across his chest and watched her economical movements as she pulled a small red contraption out of the cupboard and put it on the granite bench. Plugged it in.

Watched her lithe yet luscious body stretch up to a top cupboard, her breasts outlined as she stretched the bodice of the lacy shirt and lifted out a container of rattling beads. His mouth turning dry. Hungry. Not for the popcorn.

She must have felt him watching.

'Haven't you ever seen someone make popcorn?'

'Not like this.' And he wasn't talking about the roasting. Nothing like this. His mouth a desert, he searched for an answer. 'Maybe in the movie theatre.'

'Only in the movie theatre? Didn't your mum make you popcorn?'

He didn't answer. Didn't want to go there again this afternoon and kill the magic.

Finally, he said, 'No. Do you put oil in there?'

'Not with the machine. You do if you put it in a pot on the stove, though I did read they turn out better if you don't.'

She concentrated on the task at hand and he could see she was only half listening to him. Good. Easier to watch and savour. He knew nothing about the intricacies of popping corn. But maybe it was his new favourite pastime. Absolute fave. That would be watching Nadia make popcorn. She took about a quarter of a cup of bright yellow corn kernels from the cannister and poured them in the top of the machine and turned it on. She looked quite satisfied with herself and he smiled.

'What movie are we going to watch?'

'I think *French Kiss*. Kevin Kline does it for me.'

Now that she was just waiting, he decided it should be safe to crowd her a little.

'Yeah? Well... You do it for me.' He moved in and stood close behind her as she faced the popcorn maker. Slid his arms around her waist. 'I'd like to do it for you, but I don't think we're quite at that stage,' he murmured, his voice amused. More softly and seriously, he whispered, 'But I would like to kiss you.'

She spun slowly, her body turning within his arms, thankfully not pushing him away, until she faced him and looked up. Still in his circle. So close. A teasing womanly smile tilting that gorgeous mouth.

Very softly, very near to his mouth, she whispered back, 'If I was honest, Henry, I'd have to say I'd like to kiss you too.'

His heartrate spiked. 'Fortunate.' His voice coming out deep and low. Breathing in her scent. He leaned across the tiny distance between them to brush her mouth oh-so-gently with his.

Heaven help him, her lips were so soft. His arms tightened, pulling her close against his body. So warm. So soft.

Behind them, the first corn kernel popped and he felt her lips smile against his.

The kiss deepened and he was lost in the heat. The taste of her mouth. His tongue nudged against softness and she opened to him, offering her breath, herself.

Henry groaned and kissed Nadia until his head swam, not demanding but savouring, learning, losing himself in her, with her, entwining and tangled and tormented. A whole world of sensation which was new and wonderful, even for their first time.

By the time he stepped back, the last pops from the machine were sporadic and Nadia's eyes were shut. Her breasts rose and fell, rose and fell with her rapid breathing and he savoured the feel of her soft body squashed against his.

Henry leaned past her and switched the machine off at the

wall, with no idea how to turn it off at the control panel and not really interested enough to ask.

He came back to her and smoothed her velvet cheek with a reverential finger, watching her face, the roses in her cheeks, the thoroughly kissed blush of her mouth.

Nadia blew out a slow breath and opened her eyes. Her lips curved, slightly swollen, pink and delicious.

'Well, Henry Oliver,' she whispered, 'it seems that's another thing you do very, very well.'

He felt his smile stretch. 'Ditto, dear Nadia. I could kiss you until the whole world was full of popcorn.'

CHAPTER FIFTEEN

Nadia

OH, MY. NADIA felt like fanning her face. Henry was just too dangerous. In fact, she was feeling a tad daring herself right at this moment.

The silence stretched and she realised the popping had stopped.

'Oh, popcorn's ready. Don't want it to burn.' Inane but better than the silence.

She spun to see the popcorn maker. It lay full and silent.

'I turned it off,' was his laconic response.

How had she missed that? She knew how.

'Did you? Oh. When?'

'Just a second ago. Before you opened your eyes.' His brown eyes were watching hers with a decidedly masculine appreciation. 'Can we do that again?'

'We don't need more popcorn,' she said, pretending to misunderstand him, and spun to lift the lid. 'We've probably got thirty minutes of movie watching time before Katie wakes and wants to sit between us.'

He stepped back to give her room, but didn't leave the kitchen. Leant back against the doorway in that pose he seemed to like. Tall, arms folded, watching.

'Does that mean we get to snuggle on the couch until she does?'

That didn't sound too bad.

'Maybe.'

'And *French Kiss*,' he said. 'Definitely *French Kiss*.'

She laughed. 'Of course you're talking about the movie. I'll get right on that.'

She had no doubt that her cheeks had flamed red. And she wanted to lift her fingers to her lips because oh, my, she could still feel his oh-so-sexy mouth on hers. Her belly still jumped and writhed too, and her hands felt empty without the hold she'd had on Henry's muscular back. It was very lucky that Katie was in the other room, keeping her mother just a little bit sane.

'Do you want something to drink?'

'Cold water would be good,' he said. 'I'm feeling a little warm...' He waved his palm back and forth as if creating a breeze, like she'd wanted to do moments ago. His eyes twinkled. 'Really no idea why.'

'Right,' she said as she lined up two glasses from the cupboard and took down two bowls for the popcorn. Though she didn't need to keep their bowls separate as they'd already plastered their mouths against each other. Dipping in and eating the same popcorn wasn't going to make a difference. Thoughtfully, she put one dish back.

'You put the popcorn in the bowl. I'll fill the water and find the movie.'

Five minutes later, they were settled, no 'Mind the gap' between them. Hips touching, arms brushing, shoulders heated. No gap at all.

As the movie intro began to roll, Henry reached down and took her fingers in his and cupped her hand. Yep, she couldn't help the smile on her face. She looked down at his fingers and the popcorn on the small table and decided maybe they should lift the bowl into her lap. For safety. For the popcorn. And for her.

She reached and juggled until she had it settled. 'Holding hands does make it awkward.'

He shrugged. Dug into the popcorn. 'Bringing that popcorn closer is a great idea.'

By the time Katie pulled open her door, rubbing her eyes with her fists, they were engrossed in the movie. Henry had laughed more than a few times at the witty repartee, and she loved the sound of his deep laugh as much as she had the first time she'd heard it. Maybe more.

'Hello, darling. Come sit up here.' She patted her lap. The bowl had been moved for safety a long time ago. 'Henry's watching a movie with me.'

Katie shuffled across and instead of sitting on her mother's lap or at her side, as she had wryly expected, she stood between them and wriggled her body until there was space for three on the lounge like sardines.

Henry met Nadia's eyes over the top of Katie's blonde head as her daughter settled in between the adults. 'This is nice,' he mouthed.

Nadia agreed. Fabulous, but also terrifying. Still, she consoled herself, they were only watching a movie.

And they'd only kissed.

Yeah. Only, huh?

Quite a few times, actually, while the movie ran. But everything would be back to normal and slow down now their chaperone was here.

When the movie was finished and they started *Saving Nemo* for Katie, it proved more fun as the adults chuckled while Katie sat immersed in the movie, occasionally glancing at them as if wondering why they were laughing.

A perfect afternoon.

* * *

When it was over Henry stood to help her clear up dropped popcorn from the floor and empty glasses, and slowly her sanity returned.

He tilted his head and suggested, 'Would I be pushing my luck if I offered takeaway pizza at my house?'

'I think so,' said Nadia quietly. 'It's been a lovely day, Henry. Thank you for taking us out for breakfast and the markets.'

'Watching movies with you and Katie has been the nicest Sunday I've had for a long time,' he said.

Nice. For some reason, she thought of her grandmother and her dislike of *pleasant*. Nadia decided she didn't like *nice* either.

'I hope we do it again,' he said.

His words stole her amusement away. She sucked in a breath.

Shifting her hip back his way until they were touching again, she whispered, 'Henry, you're just the dream man, aren't you?'

'It's what I've been telling you.' He went on, 'Sometimes you are so slow.'

She laughed.

'Now. Come out on a date with me. A real evening date, dressing up, with a proper restaurant. Can you find somebody to mind Katie just for one evening?'

Suddenly, she felt unsure of herself. Her friends-with-benefits thought might be a double-edged sword.

'Gran already offered.'

'Good. How about we go out on Wednesday night? My worrisome patient should be well on the mend by then and I'll arrange call cover with another paediatrician.'

Strangely, she approved of his concern for his patient, even when it meant making her wait a few days, and yes, she could do that. A couple of days to think about it would be a good thing.

He stood. Reached and pulled her up and into his arms. Leaned his face down and kissed her thoroughly until she forgot where she was, any objections and concerns about the future, in those moments of bliss, the world as distant as the weather or the waves outside the window.

Henry eased away, stared into her face and seemed satisfied with what he saw there—probably a gaping fish, the way she felt—and strode to the door.

'Wednesday. I'll pick you up at six. We're going to have drinks and a posh dinner and maybe go dancing.'

'I haven't danced for years.'

He looked smug. 'I'm very good.'

She laughed. Who was this new Henry?

'And you have tickets on yourself.'

'I'm pinning them up there so you can see them and feel reassured I will stop you treading on my toes. My only reason for bragging.'

'Ah, thoughtful of you.'

'I'm nice like that. Then we'll come back to my place and watch the moon rise over the ocean.'

'That does sound amazing.' Getting dressed up and going out with a man for the first time in years...with Henry. That idea was terrifying and exhilarating. She wasn't sure which emotion was winning. But no strings was good, though Henry hadn't been as eager as she'd expected.

She'd never wanted to risk her heart, and this wasn't a stranger she would see once and never again. This was Henry and she had taken steps to not get in deeper than she wanted.

'Then another day we'll take Katie out.' He grinned at her. 'There are all sorts of fun places we can go to on the Gold Coast. I'd love to spend Sundays with the two of you.'

Before he could say more his phone buzzed quietly, but he didn't answer it. Just texted quickly. Then smiled at Nadia. 'Lucky you were throwing me out. Bye-bye, Katie,' he called, and her daughter looked up from where she was talking to Ernestine about the fishy movie.

He leaned in and kissed Nadia's still sensitive lips very softly before she realised his intention.

Then he was gone before she could kiss him back, his voice trailing behind him. '...I'll see you tomorrow at work.'

As she closed the door, Nadia turned and rested against the hard wood, cool against her back.

Thinking about the day. Thinking about the kiss. And thinking about the trouble she was in if she didn't want to fall for Henry.

CHAPTER SIXTEEN

Henry

HENRY WALKED AWAY from Nadia's door with his phone to his ear. 'I'm on my way. Five minutes.'

The small change he'd made to his callback protocol had worked well. After Simon's insight he'd considered his options. For normal weekends with no concrete plans he'd cover himself, but he'd told his registrar to text first and then ring if he didn't answer within a couple of minutes. Which gave him a chance to extricate himself without blatantly stepping away from Nadia to answer his phone. He still had to attend, that was the job he loved, but his leaving would not be so in her face.

The whole time he walked towards the hospital he ran over the last eight hours of absolute bliss in his head. It really had been the best Sunday afternoon he'd experienced for years. As for his revelation of moving from desiring Nadia to imagining a possible future with her—that was something he couldn't think about now. But it could stay at the back of his mind, along with those delightful memories of kissing Nadia and holding her in his arms.

But all that needed to be put away as he walked through the front entrance to the hospital.

CHAPTER SEVENTEEN

Nadia

WHEN HENRY LEFT, the room felt suddenly empty and colour-less.

She persuaded Katie into the bath, where her daughter always made lots of noise, which helped dispel the hollow quiet of the flat. Still unsettled, she wandered aimlessly until she had a shower herself.

It had been a big day and she felt strangely agitated and unable to settle to any of the tasks she usually performed on Sunday evenings for the week ahead.

Eventually sorted for the week, she glanced at the clock and decided she could make dinner and maybe they'd just go to bed early and read.

It was only when Katie, looking adorable in her unicorn pyjamas, was deep in conversation with Ernestine again that Nadia began to feel more like herself. She listened to her daughter, couldn't help smiling, and waited for a pause in the conversation, shaking her head at the chatter.

Finally, Katie drew breath and Nadia asked, 'What would you like for dinner, darling?'

'Pizza.' Her daughter's instant reply made Nadia frown.

Little minx, she must have heard Henry when he'd mentioned pizza earlier. At the time she'd looked so immersed in playing with her doll, Nadia thought wryly.

A good reminder that Katie missed little.

'I could make pizza. On those flatbreads—you like them, don't you? What sort would you like?'

'I like all your pizzas, Mummy.'

Not helpful.

'Well, choose. Pineapple and ham? Pepperoni? Or just cheese and tomato?'

'What sort does Dr Henry like?'

Nadia blinked. Yes, if she'd needed proof that her daughter was aware of everything going on, that was it there. And she'd just got the pesky man out of the forefront of her brain.

'I have no idea what sort of pizza Dr Henry likes, but he's not coming to dinner tonight, so it's about you and me.'

'Ernestine wants to know why he can't come to dinner tonight.'

Oh, spare me.

'Because he's not here.'

Her daughter looked at her as if she were such a silly thing. 'He's just in the flat upstairs.'

As if.

'He had to go to the hospital.' She assumed that was what the text message was all about. And she'd seen enough of Henry Oliver to stop her sleeping tonight, already. She did not need to think about him any more than she had already.

Her belly squirmed. But it had felt good, snuggled up next to Henry and with Katie between them and, judging by his tentative suggestion they do pizza tonight, he'd enjoyed it too.

She could ask him? No doubt about her daughter's feelings on the matter.

Nadia sighed. He probably wasn't back from the hospital anyway.

She watched, as if she were a being taken over by an alien, and her fingers typed a text to Henry.

I'm making small pizzas on flatbread. If you're not busy and you'd like to join us you're welcome. N

The answer came back swiftly.

Have a patient I'm worried about but would love company if you don't mind me dashing away as needed.

And didn't that just epitomise Henry's openness? His disclosure, general though it was, even put a different slant on her aversion to doctors being on call.

Her dad had never made it personal, so she guessed she'd never thought of the reasons he'd left as real dramas for real people. Most likely because of the privacy door that had always been slammed in their faces.

And Henry said he was worried. He wanted company and she had a sudden insight into the loneliness of his life if he didn't have anyone to talk to about those worries. He had put it out there, just like him, despite knowing she could be annoyed if he was called back to the hospital, and even risking her rescinding the dinner invitation.

Strange, she mused, not understanding her own acceptance. Thoughtfully, she texted back.

You have to eat. If you leave, they're small enough to take with you and gobble on the way. N

Sounds amazing. I'm on my way. H

Which was how Henry ended up back on the couch in Nadia's lounge room and she had to admit he looked good there.

Katie had been very satisfied when Henry turned up at the door and couldn't wait to ask, 'What's your favourite pizza, Dr Henry?'

'Whatever your mummy makes, Katie.'

'Me too.'

The pizza was gone—all types, all variations—and the conversation had been desultory until Katie went to bed.

Henry made no move to go and, strangely, she didn't push him to, and it wasn't even because they'd ended up back on the sofa, hip to hip, drinking tea.

'You said you were worried about a patient?' And that was opening herself up to a snub. Any time she'd tried to ask her father he'd slammed the privacy and Hippocratic oath at her. She could remember being crushed enough to let the subject drop.

Henry said, 'I am worried.'

'I know you can't tell me who, but I'm happy to listen to why you're worried. Maybe it will help to talk.'

The look he gave her was something she'd never seen on a man's face before. Certainly not on Alex's. Her husband had always looked like a reckless teenager bent on some new adventure, and their relationship hadn't been this...equal? Giving? Trusting?

Her heart did a little gallop inside her and her hand lifted of its own accord and lay warmly on his thigh for comfort. She'd seen something like that expression when Katie was sick and Nadia stroked her brow.

Just for a moment, she could see the young Henry, not much older than Malachi's twins, needing comfort after his dad walked out. And later, when his mother worked hard. The expression disappeared. But she'd seen the worried child from the past. The boy who cared too much.

A rush of tenderness she hadn't expected made her hand slip from his leg to take his hand in hers to listen.

'This morning this little boy, who is going through chemotherapy, was reasonably well. This afternoon he's critical, confused and in distress. I had to tell his mother he has no immunity at all and at risk of any infection attacking him. I'm afraid he won't survive if he catches something. If that happens, I don't know how I can comfort her. How I can forgive myself for not being able to make him well.'

'Oh, Henry. You comfort her by keeping him alive and giving her hope,' she said quietly, wanting to ease him. 'I'm sure she knows you care. Knows you'll be there when needed. You're a wonderful, compassionate paediatrician, Henry. I saw that myself when Katie was a baby.'

And that was her problem right there. He'd always give to others when needed, even if she needed him, but at this moment it wasn't important.

'You give—be careful you don't give too much. Because you and your skills need to be there for the next little kid and the next.'

'But how? How can I be there and still have what I want for myself in my other life away from work? How do I meld the two worlds?'

Yep. Problem there. And she didn't have the answer.

'I don't know, Henry. I suppose it depends on what you want.'

He turned his head and his gaze held hers. His chocolate-brown eyes suddenly filled with despair. Uncertainty wasn't something she was used to seeing in Henry. And then it was gone. She'd have missed it if their gazes hadn't locked.

He lifted his free hand. 'What we had today. I want this.'

'Except when you get called away.'

'Yes. Except for then.'

'So where do you see this going?'

'I think we could have something good together...if you can take a chance on me.'

She'd wanted to explain. This was her opportunity, but she felt as if she were on a precipice and what they said here could make or break whatever fragile thing there was between them.

'There's a big part of this I want too, Henry.'

'But not all of it?'

'No. I told you about my dad letting us down. We lived with him, loved him, but he wasn't there at all for us. He lived for his work. I will not have that for Katie. I can't fall for a guy who can only give half of himself.'

'And are you, Nadia? Falling for me?' His eyes burned into hers. 'Is that so bad?'

Yes. Yes, it was.

'You make me feel things I haven't felt for a very long time.' Maybe never, she thought. 'It's taken me all this time to rebuild my life. I'm happy with that status quo. Secure in what I have and what I am.'

He put up his hand. 'You're your own woman. I know that. See that.'

'And Katie and I are happy.'

He leaned forward. 'What if I could make you happier? Both of you. A bigger world.'

She heard the words. Wonderful words. But...did she really want that?

'I tried that. I wasn't happier with Alex. And Katie is my first priority now.'

He shook his head. 'For goodness' sake, just because your husband was less than you expected doesn't mean Katie shouldn't have a dad.'

'You don't know anything about Alex.' She glared at him, not wanting this conversation to go there. But she'd been the one who had brought up her marriage.

'No, I don't know anything.' For the first time she detected a glimmer of bitterness in Henry's quiet voice. 'And I really, really would like to. But you're as prickly as a pear.'

She had caused this trap herself. She tried to divert him. 'Pears aren't prickly.'

'Prickly pears are. You're one of those.'

She shifted until their hips weren't touching. 'Nobody asked you to come and pick the fruit with spikes.'

'I know.' He touched her cheek very, very gently and, despite the bitter little spat they'd almost had, she really, really wanted to cover his fingers and hold him there. Feel his warmth and tenderness against her face.

This whole disaster was so stupid and she'd promised herself she would not confuse lust and love again. If she could just keep it to lust.

He went on softly, as if to himself, almost rhyming, 'I have a thing for this particular prickly pear. And no matter what, I cannot change it there.'

'And I don't want to fall for a doctor.' The words fell like stones between them. Silence followed.

When he didn't say anything, she said, 'Can't we just be friends?' Whispered, 'Maybe even friends with benefits, when Katie's not here. Let's not talk about this future stuff. Just enjoy each other's company?'

She watched him as he stopped what he'd been going to say, saw a strange...could it have been hurt, cross his face?

Decisively, he shook his head. 'No. I don't think so.'

'Why not?' And that hadn't sounded like a petulant child. Much.

'Because,' he said simply, with just a little bite, 'a fling is not what I have in mind.' He got up and, to her chagrin, he left.

She wondered if she still had a date.

CHAPTER EIGHTEEN

Henry

HENRY SHUT THE door behind him quietly, careful not to wake Katie, when in fact he wanted to slam it. Friends with benefits. No strings. No commitment.

That way disaster lay—for him, anyway. He didn't want to give up on Nadia—he was falling deeply for her, but equally he couldn't give up being the sort of doctor who was there for his patients. Maybe this wasn't going to work.

He hadn't made it to the lift before his phone vibrated in his pocket. It was a message from his registrar, Amelia. Little Gregory—his heartrate had spiked. He probably should have spent the last couple of hours getting in a power nap because he suspected he'd be up all night.

He chose the down button instead of up and sped out of the door and towards the hospital, lifting his phone as he walked. He stabbed the number for his registrar. 'What's happening, Amelia?'

'Henry, Gregory's temperature just hit forty,' she said, concern clear in her voice. 'I thought you'd want to know.'

'Yes. Always. I'll be there in three minutes.'

'That's good.'

'Is his mother there?'

'Yes.'

'Okay, I'm coming.'

Henry was right. He was up most of the night, but in the early hours of Monday morning Gregory's condition turned the corner and the child settled into a more peaceful sleep.

Henry went home to catch a few hours' rest. When he checked in when he woke, his patient had continued to improve.

Henry felt like a deflated punching bag and decided a run with Malachi might just get him through the day.

Malachi was jogging on the spot when Henry arrived. *Oops.*

'Sorry. Took me a little longer to get here than I thought it would.'

'I'm not that far ahead of you.' Malachi cast him a glance. 'Rough night?'

'You could say that.'

They jogged along, slowly increasing speed. 'I get tricky mums and babies. You get tricky kids.'

It had been a big week with his sick patients, Jake and Gregory. Silence.

Malachi concluded, 'We love what we do.'

Shame everyone didn't, Henry mused silently, thinking of Nadia.

'Does Lisandra love what you do?'

Malachi's expression didn't change. 'She's a midwife. She gets it.'

'And Bella's a nurse, so she gets Simon's work.'

'Which would be Simon's business.' They jogged across a road to a park and began to circle it. Finally, Malachi said, 'You're wondering because Nadia isn't a nurse?'

'I guess.'

His friend grunted. 'She works in the kids' ward. She'll

get it.' They ran a few more metres before he added, 'If she loves you enough.'

Henry winced as he ran. And that was the kicker. How did he make that happen? Could he? Of course not. She had to do that.

But Malachi wasn't finished. 'The job isn't worth losing them. The job has to give too. Not just them giving. Learned that.' He didn't speak again while Henry ruminated over the wisdom.

Afterwards, when the burn and aches were showered away, Henry felt the exercise had brought him some calm because, strangely, the slap of their feet on the concrete, the peripheral waves and the cool breeze before the sun came too high and too hot had made him human again.

And those brief words of Malachi's had smoothed the jagged edges in his brain and strengthened his determination.

He could make this work. He didn't want a benefits-only relationship with Nadia, but at least she wanted that. Or perhaps he wasn't one hundred percent sure that was what Nadia really wanted either.

She'd said she was scared. And she was certainly determined that Katie wouldn't have the childhood disappointments she'd had. He got that. But she wanted a date. She wanted to go out with him. Even a tumble in bed, which just ticked him off because he wasn't a one-night stand kind of man. But maybe he could win by stealth.

For Nadia. For him. For Katie.

By the end of Monday, the antibiotics had kicked in well enough for Lulu's Jake to improve markedly and seeing the tears of relief run down Lulu's face made Henry's own chest ache with relief as well.

Henry slipped an arm around her shoulders and hugged her. Tough being a mum.

'His condition's improved so much we could move him down to the children's ward if you're happy with that, Lulu.'

Lulu nodded. Henry knew she'd felt intimidated by the high-tech drama of the critically ill patients and their beeping, noisy machines that monitored them. And resting more easily would be better for the child than the drama that happened up here. The staff were great in either place. Yes, he could move.

CHAPTER NINETEEN

Nadia

From behind the desk near the door, Nadia watched as Jake was wheeled into the ward in a wheelchair with Lulu hovering behind. A nurse escorted the pale, drowsy boy with his intravenous fluids and the orderly pushing the chair headed for the nurses' station, looking straight ahead. Lulu kept glancing behind, and Nadia saw her face relax when she found Henry had caught up.

Nadia waved at Jake as he passed but the boy's eyes were dull and fixed on his hands, though Lulu smiled at her briefly before snapping back to her son as if she couldn't allow him out of her sight.

Nadia jumped up and hugged her, and then Tara Taylor was up and moving towards them, taking the notes from the nurse and directing the orderly to the room nearest the nurses' station. Nadia went back to her desk. They didn't need a ward clerk in their way.

Oh, poor Lulu. Her hovering fear that her son would be snatched from her still clung and clouded her worried eyes and Nadia felt her heart go out to her. Imagine if that was Katie?

The ensuing efficient organising had Jake in the bed, his IVs sorted and his mother seated in a comfortable chair beside him in minutes. A folded bed was tucked away in the corner for her in the night.

Lulu looked as if she could possibly allow herself to almost relax for the first time in a long time, and Nadia thought about that nursing degree she'd considered taking on, which she'd first considered years ago to attract her father's approval in her teens. Maybe when Katie went to school next year.

Then she thought about the shift work, and the time away from her daughter, and the missing out Katie would suffer without her mother home. Or maybe she didn't need to prove anything any more and could just read about what she wanted to know. No. This was good.

But there was no reason she couldn't study from home and learn more. She had a good brain. It had nothing to do with the fact she wanted to be able to understand Henry's work more. Not that. She knew enough now to know that Jake did look like a sick little boy. The sight made Nadia want to run to the preschool and check that her own Katie was fine.

She suspected strongly that worry about Jake had been an extra stress, along with the immunosuppressed young boy who had worried Henry so much. Being Henry, he would have worried about them both.

Which was probably why, when he appeared at her desk, his skin was pale except for the dark circles under his eyes.

Oh, Henry. She wanted to touch his face but she kept her hands firmly on the desk.

'You look as if you haven't slept since I saw you last.'

'Got a couple of hours.' He smiled at her as if she was as good as a tonic. 'How's Katie?'

'Good.' She waved him on. 'I'm glad Lulu has you looking after Jake.'

Henry smiled. He leaned down and said quietly, 'Are we

still on for our date? Friends with benefits even, if that is what you want?'

Nadia blinked with the unexpected reversal. He'd said no. Now it was okay? She didn't understand why she suddenly felt disappointed until she told herself this was a good thing.

She nodded, her cheeks pink. Not meeting his eyes.

'Wednesday. I'll pick you up at six,' he mouthed, and moved away and her gaze followed him. Stuck on his broad back. Silly to be miffed he'd decided just sex was okay. Especially when it had been her idea.

Across the room, Henry touched Lulu's shoulder and the woman turned to him with relief.

She couldn't begrudge Lulu his attention. He was there when her friend needed him the most. She thought that if something like that happened to Katie, how much she'd need to rely on someone like Henry to save her daughter.

How she already had when Katie was born. The thought gave her chills and warred with the promise to never fall for a doctor, which she'd made to herself after years of her father's neglect.

A promise that seemed a little immature and rash now, as an adult. She could feel the wall she'd built crack a little and sag. Reminded herself, *Just friends.* She had a date and she wasn't backing out. She was definitely interested in exploring those benefits...with him.

But Henry's work was important too, he was amazing at what he did, and maybe her dad was too. Imagine that.

She didn't see Henry on Tuesday because the admin clerk in the emergency department had been called home to her sick mother and Nadia had been asked if she could go across and take on that more intense job for the day.

It had been a challenge, learning new procedures, the actual drama and busyness of the emergency ward admissions position compared to her own, but she had finished the long day with a satisfaction that made her wonder just how much she was coasting in the job that she had now.

It also meant she didn't get to see Henry as no paediatric admissions came in, so by the time Wednesday afternoon came she hoped she still had a date that night.

She hadn't heard anything to the contrary, so Katie helped Nadia pack her tiny unicorn suitcase with pyjamas, slippers and dressing gown. Her toothbrush and favourite blanket, plus clothes for the morning, lay on top with Ernestine. Katie didn't sleep over at her great-gran's often, so tonight's sleepover seemed extra exciting.

Nadia felt strange banishing her daughter for a man. For Henry. For sex? Maybe they wouldn't get to third base.

And when it all boiled down Katie would only be downstairs.

When Nadia arrived at Catherine's door, her grandmother shooed her off with an elegant hand. 'Go! Relax, make yourself beautiful. We don't need you here.'

'Well…' she huffed, and escaped the excited Katie much sooner than intended and scurried back down to her unit on the ground floor and fluffed around with a smile on her face.

Good grief, a real date after so many years. Cue leg and armpit shaving, eyebrow plucking, even tooth flossing.

She couldn't quite believe she'd let herself get to this stage of excitement, but it was only a date. And thank goodness she had previous exposure to Henry over the last couple of weeks or she would have been a mess.

Only Henry. At that thought, she paused. She'd said that before and it hadn't worked then either. Her hand suspended as she mascaraed her lashes.

Just Henry? There was nothing *just* about Henry. Her belly warmed at the thought.

And for a moment, clear as if he were there in the mirror, she could see his mouth. Almost feel his beautiful, beautiful lips on hers. And what that mouth could do. The warmth in her stomach exploded into an inferno and she had to step back and breathe for a moment. Good grief. Where had she been storing those fireworks?

Her chest rose and fell as she tried to shake the all too vivid pictures and just breathe. But she tingled. Tingled?

It didn't mean they would sleep together—it just meant they wouldn't have to constantly be alert for Katie. That was all. Just a date. And she could even dress up. Wins everywhere.

CHAPTER TWENTY

Henry

HENRY KNOCKED ON Nadia's door with one hand and held the bouquet of red roses in the other. Truth be told, his heart did beat just a little faster because he'd pinned a lot of hope on tonight.

One part of him thought the flowers were all too much after they'd already been spending time together, but then his romantic side decided he wanted her to have them. He needed to give them to her.

When Nadia opened the door, her gaze met his with what looked like excitement, thank heaven for that, and relief swamped him.

Then her gaze fell to the flowers. Her eyes went round in surprise.

'Henry? Flowers?' She smiled and the delight he saw made him want to bring her flowers every time he saw her. 'How beautiful. Thank you.'

But she didn't stand aside. She stared at the flowers while he drank her in, though she still didn't move.

She was as useless as he was, and the indulgent thought calmed him. He asked a question with his hand, and the movement drew her eyes to the door.

She pulled it open. 'Sorry. Come in. You've made me flustered.'

He smiled. Good—surely it was good to be unpredictable? He offered the roses again. 'You take these, I'll shut the door.'

She gathered up the roses. They truly were an armful and the soft dark petals looked so beautiful against her brown skin. 'Thank you, they're glorious.'

She stood there holding them, as if not sure what to do next.

'You put them in water. That way, I don't get stabbed when I kiss you.'

She blinked. And for a horrible moment there he thought he saw tears in her eyes. Maybe the dead husband had brought her flowers along with pain? Had he done the wrong thing?

'I'm sure they would have been de-thorned. Is that a word?'

'Sounds plausible.' He nodded, relieved, at the roses, and she spun and carried them to the kitchen.

He shut the door and followed. Of course. Stood watching by what he was becoming to think of as his wall as she pulled out a big clear vase and filled it with water, his heart full, just drinking her in like the vase drank the water.

When she plonked them instead of taking ages to arrange them, he could not have been more pleased. He slipped up behind her when her hands were free, wrapped his arms around her waist, linking his fingers and thinking suddenly of the popcorn episode.

She spun slowly in his arms, smiling. A gentle sweep of lashes as she lifted her mouth. As he leaned down, he watched her eyes darken and her eyelids flutter closed as he swept her mouth gently back and forth with his, breathing her in, feeling her softness melt under his. He'd needed this. Needed her. Needed her to want him.

When they stepped back both breathed more quickly and, just a little flustered, he murmured, 'You know, I really like your kitchen.'

'Do you?' Her voice husky, not quite steady. Eyes still a little glazed.

He glanced around. More popcorn thoughts. 'In fact, that wall over there looks so promising.'

This time, she focused. Narrowed her eyes. And he laughed.

'Sorry, sorry. Just fantasising. You could try it?' he teased.

She looked at the wall and back at him. Her eyes lingered on his mouth and then ran down the open neck of his button-down shirt and…she had him.

Judging by the gleam in her eyes, she could imagine with the best of them. Henry felt his body heat. Harden.

Her turn to tease him. She smiled. 'We'll have to find out about that later, then. I'll just get my bag,' she said.

Henry had tried to find a restaurant with dancing. He'd even asked a few people, but the looks he'd received hadn't been worth the lack of response.

He'd asked Amelia, thinking his registrar might know. She'd grown up in the Gold Coast. Sure. She'd told him about this fabulous restaurant her mum had told her about, with a real band, and he'd been starting to feel hopeful when she'd said it had closed ten years ago.

Malachi had suggested takeaway with music on at home.

Simon had suggested one of those companies that did picnic hampers, take his own music and dance on the beach.

Who would have thought it would be so hard? In London there'd been plenty of places, but apparently not in the Gold Coast. Instead, he'd decided they'd stick with a local Greek restaurant that they could walk home from. The music would be the sound of the waves. And it was almost a full moon. And on a Wednesday night the yahoos wouldn't be out driving up and down the street in their loud cars.

He watched as she leant to retrieve her purse and he followed the line of her glorious legs to her shoes. High heels. Thinking of footpaths.

'Would you like to walk home? Will your shoes be comfortable for that?'

She turned and smiled at him, nodding. 'Thank you for asking. They should be fine, but I can fit a pair of folding flats in my bag in case.'

He guessed she'd like to walk home too. The idea pleased him.

The restaurant had been painted Mediterranean blue and Santorini white and Malachi had said it was his grandmother's favourite place.

They sat at the bar first and sipped a cocktail called Sex on the Beach. They'd both smiled at that.

When they finished their drink he asked for their secluded table with champagne, and suddenly it was easy.

He told her about London. She told him about the friendships she'd made on the Gold Coast and how she'd found her job. How she'd sometimes thought of a nursing degree, but that would leave Katie being minded too much so maybe she'd wait for a few more years and decide.

He'd always studied and gone where he wanted. A little lost without a family, but not tied down. 'I've never thought about the responsibility of children and their impact on a parent's choice.'

'Especially a single parent.' She sipped the wine, smiling at the taste. 'This is lovely.'

He was still thinking about decisions and choices. 'Is nursing something you've wanted to do for a long time?'

'To be honest, I think I wanted my dad to approve my choice. He always said Isabella should have been a doctor, but she never wanted to be.'

'He never said you should be a doctor?'

'He barely noticed Isabella, and she was the shining light. I was a shadow behind her. He just assumed I'd get married, and I did.'

He took her hand. 'You could never be a shadow.' He shook his head, looking at her in disbelief. 'You blaze every time I see a glimpse of you.' She was so beautiful, vibrant. A force he was drawn to like a lemming to the cliff. Unfortunate simile.

'Thank you.' She smiled at him. 'You are good for my ego, Henry, that's for sure.'

'I'm good for more than that.' He might have said that before.

He watched her expression change in an instant. Eyes and mouth serious. It happened fast. She squeezed his hand back.

'Yes. Of course you are. You're an absolute champion and what you did for Lulu and how you cared for Jake is wonderful. Everyone loves you in the kids' ward and Bella and my grandmother sing your praises.'

That was a little too much. He tried to squirm away from that line of conversation. Tried to joke. 'And Katie wants to know my favourite pizza.'

'Katie thinks you're wonderful.'

So, he had to ask. 'And you, Nadia. Do you sing my praises?'

'Not enough.' She held his gaze, hers troubled, and he wanted to soothe her fears. 'I'm a bit afraid you want to cosset and keep me safe. Turn me into the little woman. Look after me while you leave me at home.'

Yes. Yes, he did. He saw that now. 'And why does that make you afraid?'

'Our dad was a shadow. But he kept us safe. You couldn't even fight with him because he wasn't there. I like you, a lot, but I don't want a carer. I want a partner. Someone who's there. Or I'll look after myself and Katie.'

'I could do that.' He reached out, caught her fingers in his across the table. Her hand was soft and cool in his.

'Maybe. Maybe not.' Her voice cautiously considering. 'My grandmother thinks Bella and I were scarred by our dad's neglect. I hesitate to say scarred. I'd say wary. He gave us no priority.' She looked up. 'None.'

'You've mentioned that and I hear you.'

'Good.' She nodded. Hearing him hearing her. 'Bella has made it work with Simon, but I think I'm less willing to risk going back to being…accommodating is probably the word… to a profession. Maybe my sister understands more because she's used to shift work as well.'

'You work in a hospital. It's not new for you.' He remembered Malachi's reassurance. If she loved him.

Her eyes explored his as if she wanted to read his thoughts. He wanted to just lose himself there. But she was searching. 'Maybe I'm more selfish? For Katie. I know what I want for her.'

He didn't dispute her right. 'Well, it's hard not to be selfish when you've been responsible for everything for years. It's been up to you to be there for Katie and look after yourself and support yourself.' He shrugged and went on mildly, 'It has been about you surviving. I just happen to think you'd be thriving, not just surviving with me.'

She went to speak but he held up his free fingers. He'd hadn't let her hand get away.

'But I want to nudge in here too. I want to be a part of this.' He waved that free hand to include them both. 'Sit with you on your sofa. Make popcorn. I want to be there to carry Katie to bed at night.'

'Most times she doesn't need carrying.' Nadia frowned.

He brushed that away. 'Have you any idea how amazing it

was, feeling her weight in my arms, her little soft cheek against my neck? Her trust.'

She nodded. 'Yes, I see you genuinely like being with Katie.'

He hoped she knew he'd protect Katie with all his being.

Maybe it was time to share a few truths. She had shared hers. But he hated saying it. 'My father was an alcoholic. He left when I was seven. When I have a family, they will never want for anything. It's a factor in my wanting to succeed. My wife will not work herself to death like my mother did.'

She sat back, pulling her hand free. 'That's why you put your work first,' she said quietly. It was not a question. 'Why you're so dedicated.' She looked more sad than enlightened, and he wished he hadn't said anything now. He had the feeling that somehow that hadn't helped his cause. 'You're a good man.'

'And I agree to going slow. Except for the "benefits", if they're still on the table. I'm not that good a man.'

She whispered, 'I was hoping for something softer than a table.' He felt her gaze slide to his mouth. Even more softly, she said, 'You do kiss like a dream.'

'Tonight?' He tried to recover some of the ground he suspected he'd lost.

'I'll think about that. As for the future, you'd have to be there, and I can see how a lot of the time you might not be.'

Yes, he might need to work on that.

CHAPTER TWENTY-ONE

Nadia

OVER THE SOFT sounds of the restaurant around them Nadia's phone vibrated in her purse. Sadly, it wasn't a soft buzz like Henry's, it was a noisy one.

He sat back and she pulled it out. 'Excuse me.' Frowned at it. 'It's Bella. She knows we're out. I have to phone her back.'

'Of course.' Henry picked up his menu. 'I'll decide what to eat.'

She heard him but she wasn't listening. She was walking away from the table, waiting for the phone to answer. 'Bella, are you okay? Is it Gran or Katie?'

There was silence for too long and Nadia's heartrate picked up. Then her sister said very softly, 'Gran and Katie are fine. I need you to come to me.' The sentence was short and breathless. 'Take me to the hospital.'

'Yes, of course. Where's Simon?'

Several deep breaths later she said, 'They're doing an exchange transfusion. On a baby. And I know he can't leave.'

'Labour? You're in labour?' Had to be.

A puff of breath into the phone. Could have been an unamused laugh. 'Yes.'

'We're on our way.' She glanced at Henry and remembered

that they didn't have a car. Uber, then. Bella had a car and if they got to her, they could use hers.

'Less than five minutes. We'll be there.'

'Hurry.'

'Bella?' This sounded very unlike her calm sister. 'Maybe you should get that ambulance as well.'

'Kai's just gone to sleep. If I wake him, he'll scream and I can't do that right now.'

'We're coming. Phone the ambulance anyway.' She clicked off and spun back to Henry, who had stood. Of course he'd read her distress and was ready to go. 'Something's wrong with Bella. She said labour, but maybe more.'

She reached for her bag, which Henry had picked up as she came back to the table. 'Can you call an Uber and get us there? She's got a car we can use. I've told her to call an ambulance, but for some reason she doesn't want to.'

He nodded. Handed the concerned waiter fifty dollars and waved him away. Scanned his apps and typed for the ride, saying as an aside, 'Where's Simon?'

'Something about an exchange transfusion. At the hospital.'

The Uber pulled up as they descended the escalator from the restaurant to the street. She saw Henry glance at his phone and then the numberplate on the car before opening her door to usher her in.

When they arrived at Bella's front door six minutes later, it was open but Bella wasn't there. Heeding her sister's request that Kai should not be woken, she called out quietly, 'Bella?'

'In the lounge,' she heard.

When they entered the room Bella wasn't resting quietly in a chair or on the lounge, where Nadia expected her to be.

Her sister was on the floor and for a moment she thought she'd fallen, lying half on her side and half on her back and packed with cushions from the settee. There was even a cushion under her bottom. Bella's feet were up on the coffee table.

Henry took one look at her and knelt down beside her. 'I'm guessing cord prolapse.'

'What?' said Nadia, trying to grasp what he'd understood so quickly.

Bella smiled an unconvincing smile. 'Very good, Henry.' Then her face contorted. 'And now I want to push.'

Henry frowned. 'Any chance of waiting for an ambulance?'

'No,' she panted and pushed. When the contraction was past, she licked dry lips and whispered, 'It would be all lights and sirens and awkward positioning and people who don't really have a lot of experience like you and I about this. This way, I have some control. Different if I felt there was time for a Caesarean before the birth.'

'I don't know what I'm doing,' said Nadia softly, but she was talking to Henry.

'I do,' said Bella. 'And Henry does.'

Some of the horror and the pressure of helplessness left. She was right, Henry was here. Since everyone else was ridiculously calm, then she'd better follow suit.

'Since you're busy, Henry had better tell me what he wants me to do.'

'You could find some towels. Turn on the heaters, Nadia. Warm the room up even more for the baby. Maybe pass your sister a drink of water.'

He touched Bella's shoulder, and she opened her eyes from where she'd been breathing quietly in some calming place in her mind. 'Do you have an ultrasound Doppler to listen to the baby's heartrate? I know what you midwives are like. You've always got one tucked away in a cupboard.'

Bella laughed very, very softly, part groan. 'I do. It's on the dressing table in my room.'

Nadia felt his glance and she stood. Something else she could do, she thought as she hurried from the room. She heard him saying, 'Have you told Simon anything?'

'I tried, but I couldn't speak to the ward nurse.' She sniffed. 'I was afraid I'd just cry all over the phone and then he'd rush and not think. So I rang Nadia.'

Henry nodded. 'Good plan, we've got you covered. I'm just going to make a quick call...' His voice faded as Nadia ran into Bella and Simon's room and grabbed the little baby listener off the dressing table.

By the time she was back, Henry had called through to Simon. She heard him say, 'Bella's in labour. She says it's imminent. Cord prolapse. Couldn't talk to tell you.' He held the phone away from his ear. 'I'll see you soon, then.' And smiled down at Simon's wife. He whispered, 'I think you're in trouble.'

'No time,' she gasped. 'I'm pushing.'

Nadia handed Henry the foetal ultrasound machine. She'd found a bottle of gel too, remembering the midwives had always put it on the end before they'd listened when she'd been pregnant with Katie.

Henry pressed to the spot Bella suggested.

Instantly, they heard the galloping heartbeats, so reminiscent of the hoofbeats of a horse, and Bella must have decided it was good because she sagged with relief.

'Clever baby,' she whispered, and a tear trickled from the corner of her eye.

Henry sent Nadia a reassuring smile. 'Strong normal rate.'

So they were reassured by the strong beat. Nadia almost believed them, but her gaze was drawn to the loop of thick purple umbilical cord that was hanging between Bella's legs. She knew at least it was wrong to have the cord before the baby.

'Don't we need scissors and cord clamps? For the placenta

after?' Nadia felt useless and ill-educated. She should have studied more, but Katie was almost five and she'd forgotten all the things she'd read.

'Lotus birth until it's all over,' Bella said.

Nadia looked at Henry. 'What?'

'If it comes then just leave the placenta attached—wrap it up in a towel still joined to baby and out of the way.'

They were so calm. So in tune. And she was swirling in a whirlpool of fear which she suddenly realised wasn't helping anyone. *Stop it*, she told herself. *Have faith*. She could be calm.

Henry was saying to Bella, 'How was your birth with Kai?'

'Fast.'

'You should do that again,' Henry urged gently.

They heard a car screech to a halt outside and Bella winced. 'There'll be tyre marks on the new driveway.'

Henry bit back a smile. 'I'm guessing now you can push?'

They all glanced towards the pounding footsteps.

And then Simon was in the room, skidding onto his knees towards his wife. 'Good timing,' she breathed and pushed.

As far as Nadia could tell, even then there seemed very little progress, and as if her sister thought so too, Bella muttered, 'It's because I'm lying like this. I can't push uphill.'

'What about the pressure on the cord?' Simon spoke quietly, but with no dispute in his voice.

Bella huffed. 'Did you see the cord? It's like an anchor rope. All that fat jelly should protect for the time it will take.'

'Then move where you want to, my love, and let's see our child.' He helped her up.

As soon as Bella was kneeling on towels in front of the coffee table with her elbows resting on the table and holding Simon's hand, things started to happen.

Simon waved with his hand. 'Make a little bed for Bella,

Nadia, next to her here, so she can slide down with the baby on her skin afterwards.'

Nadia gathered a few towels and a cushion and brought the blanket over ready.

Henry was down the business end and Nadia slipped a few more folded towels beside him and marvelled at everyone else's composure.

Simon and Bella were concentrating together, as if Simon could will strength and power into his wife.

Henry knelt like a statue, a calm statue, holding an open towel and waiting. He said softly, 'We need the exact time, Nadia, Your job. Then tell me when it's thirty seconds after birth.'

Nadia nodded and moved behind him, tears running down her cheeks, a hand on his shoulder. That was all she could do to help her sister, and watch the medical people in the room save a life. 'I can do that.'

And then Henry was saying, 'Coming now, Bella, nice and smooth...' And then, 'Head's out...' And her sister heaved a sigh.

'We won't stop for this one, Bella—keep going,' Henry murmured, and Bella pushed on.

'Perfect, one shoulder and now the other.' There was a flurry of movement and shiny, tiny limbs, a splash of fluids and more cord and suddenly the baby was there.

Nadia's heart leapt at the pale child who hadn't been there a second ago and now lay unmoving in Henry's hands.

Mindful of her one job, Nadia glanced at the clock. It was a big clock, with hands and a second hand, and she said, 'Three minutes and fifteen seconds past eight.'

Then Henry was rubbing, murmuring, 'A girl. Stunned. She's not breathing, but still has tone, heartrate around eighty. So, looking good.'

She didn't look good to Nadia, but Henry was smiling as he dried the baby and put his hand again on the chest. 'Heart-rate one hundred. Grimacing like crazy. Come on, baby—a big breath. You know you can do it.'

'Ivy. Her name is Ivy. Come on, Ivy...' Now Bella wept, and Simon was rubbing her neck and shoulders, soothing, telling her she was wonderful, that baby would be fine and Henry had this.

Just as Nadia called, 'Thirty seconds,' with her chest tight—oh, heavens, when would this baby cry?—Ivy sucked in a shuddering breath, coughed, squeaked and then roared with disapproval at her rapid arrival.

Nadia burst into tears, Bella pulled off her nightie to bare her skin and, trailing the ridiculously long cord, she shifted from where she knelt to the bed Nadia had made, making give-to-me motions with her hands as she lay down.

Henry handed the baby to Simon, who placed her against her mother's skin as Bella's hands wrapped around her newborn. Simon covered them both with a towel and a blanket, tucking them in and leaving just a tiny face turned sideways against her mother's bare skin. Wailing complaints kept coming from under the blanket. The little face had already turned pink.

Finally, Ivy settled and snuffled. Henry whispered to Nadia, 'Skin to skin against the mother. Fastest way to settle heart-rate and breathing and keep a baby warm.'

'Oh.' She hadn't known that. But Henry had. And Bella and Simon. Yes, she'd start reading about midwifery and paediatrics.

Simon was stroking Bella's hair, his face aglow with the release of tension, replaced with joy. 'You always wanted a home birth,' he teased his wife as he kissed her cheek, such relief in his voice.

Bella's shoulders dropped and she breathed out a huge sigh. 'There's something to be said for all the medical equipment, my love, in emergencies. We'll go into Maternity next time.'

Nadia blinked. 'Next time?'

Henry laughed and once the afterbirth had arrived, he wrapped it and placed it beside Bella at the end of the impossibly long cord until they could sever the connection. Simon wanted samples of the oxygen and carbon dioxide levels in the umbilical cord. Even if delayed, he thought they could get them, so the men were sorting the logistics of that.

Fifteen minutes later, Nadia helped Bella shower while the men examined Ivy and pronounced her well. A midwife had arrived to sort the cord gases and Bella would be transferred soon.

Simon wanted Bella to stay one night in the hospital to rest, so the staff could watch Ivy, but still Nadia had been surprised when her sister had agreed.

'Just to keep an eye on Ivy overnight,' Bella said, 'then I'm home.'

And soon they were gone, leaving Nadia and Henry at the door.

'I was terrified,' Nadia said as they watched Simon's car pull away from the house.

'Me too,' Henry agreed.

'Oh, you were not.' Nadia pushed his arm and he smiled. 'You were as cool as a cucumber. So was Bella.'

He tucked her back into his side as they closed the door. 'You held it together well too, you know. Because we all knew that panic was more dangerous than anything else.'

Good grief. Had they really been terrified like her? Now, that was scary.

Henry went on, 'And there are protocol steps to follow for just such occasions.'

'Even when you're not an obstetrician? Paediatricians don't have cord prolapses.'

He laughed. 'Proved that wrong tonight. But we have the training in it. Still, I've seen my share, and the treatment is rapid Caesarean section. And keeping pressure off the cord until you can get to a hospital.'

'But Ivy is okay?'

'Still very lucky. But Bella had pressure, knew it was imminent. Even though the baby's hard skull crushes the cord against the bony pelvis and occludes the blood supply during birth.'

'So no oxygen gets through?'

'Some does, but less than needed, more often. The fatter the cord with the jelly, the more chance the baby has of the blood vessels inside the cord not becoming too compressed, letting good oxygen flow through.'

'Sounds risky.'

'In an imminent birth like Bella's, sometimes it's faster to push the baby out, despite cord compression. That's less desirable if it was a first baby, which could be slow. Which is why I asked Bella how her first labour went.'

Nadia remembered. 'She said fast.'

He nodded, blowing out a breath. 'Never so glad to hear something.'

Nadia nodded. 'And you said, "You should do that again".'

'Yes. Push baby out now, was what I was saying.' He smiled. 'Having such a thick cord was a big bonus. And probably why the heartrate we listened to, before the birth, was so perfect. Baby wasn't affected, despite the way the cord had been exposed to air, which makes it contract.'

She couldn't hear enough about the mechanics of this,

though Henry was looking at her as if to say, *Surely that's all you want to hear?*

'Last question. So you're saying, the thicker the cord, the more Wharton's jelly protecting the blood vessels means blood supply and oxygen from the placenta. And that's why Bella had her feet up on the table when we arrived.'

'Yes. Gravity to keep the baby's head from pressing on the cord until help arrived.'

'And Bella knew that?'

'Yes, she's a midwife. It's protocol. But the situation was dangerous for baby.'

Nadia shook her head. Her sister. 'She looked so calm. Even when the baby didn't breathe.' Nadia's remembered dread hit her. Delayed reaction. Tears flooded her eyes again. She would never forget her pale and limp little niece.

Henry put his arm around her shoulders. 'Ivy had lots of tone. And reflexes. Heartrate was there, if not fast. As long as there's a heartbeat, most babies will pull back and revive well.'

Maybe she didn't want to be a doctor or a nurse, with all this responsibility. She liked being a photographer.

He squeezed her shoulders. 'Ivy's had a feed, which is what she needed after the stress of the birth. Like Katie, Ivy's a fighter.'

Nadia slipped her arm around his waist, the man was rock-solid, and he squeezed back. She did feel better just hearing that.

In fact, she really did have so much history with this man, even though Henry had only been back in Australia a few weeks. Between them there was Katie's history. Now Ivy's. All of it with Henry being there for her.

She looked up at him. 'All I know is I'm very glad you were

here, Henry. And glad Bella was the mother who knew what she was doing.'

Henry laughed quietly. 'That she did. And with Simon arriving we had plenty of neonatal backup.'

CHAPTER TWENTY-TWO

Henry

HENRY SAVOURED THE feel of Nadia's arm around his waist. This was what he wanted. A family home like this. And Nadia to relax with after a tense medical situation.

She'd done well as a non-medical person. She hadn't panicked. She'd been quick and helpful, almost like a scout nurse in Theatre.

He smiled at the thought. He guessed she'd seen drama in the children's ward at times and that might have prepared her. Or the fact she came from medical people.

Sadly, their date had come to an end, but he wouldn't have it any other way with such a great outcome for Bella and Simon.

'How about we order takeaway while we wait for Simon to come home?'

'Sounds good. Bella didn't seem to think that Kai would wake so we can make ourselves comfortable.'

He eyed Simon's big comfy sofa. Nice idea that. 'What would you like to eat? I'm happy to ring the restaurant. I'm pretty sure they'll allow Uber Eats to pick up a Greek meal. Especially if we promise to make another booking next week.'

Nadia leaned her head against him as if thinking. 'Why don't we go back next week and try again? And order some pasta tonight. I know that Simon likes his red wine. There's bound to be half a dozen bottles of nice Shiraz in the wine rack.'

Henry grinned. 'You don't think he'll be upset if we drink his best wine?'

She giggled. He loved that sound. It was rare and lovely and he breathed her in, savouring their closeness. And there was closeness after what they'd shared tonight.

'We won't take the Shiraz he's saving for a special occasion.' She laughed. 'We'll order some pasta for Simon as well. That will cheer him up when he comes home.'

Nadia went in and checked on Kai for the second time and Henry wondered if she was missing Katie or just nervous after all the excitement.

She'd told him her grandmother had texted and said that she and Katie had had a lovely evening and now Katie and Ernestine were asleep. Nadia had texted back and told her the news and the good outcome.

As Henry searched for the number, he smiled at the inclusion the doll had in the adults' conversations. He wasn't ordering food for Ernestine, but he did like that sweet indulgence of a little girl's fantasies.

And he had Nadia to himself tonight as soon as Simon arrived. Hopefully, not too far away. The back door opened, no noisy tyre-screech this time, and Simon walked in.

He came straight to Henry and clapped him on the back. 'Thanks, Henry. For looking after Bella and Ivy. I owe you.'

'You looked after Katie and Nadia.' He grinned. 'We're square. And congratulations on your new dramatic daughter.'

Simon laughed, his voice still tinged with relief. 'Hopefully not an indication of things to come with Ivy.' He glanced up at the sky. 'Please heaven.'

He acknowledged Nadia as she came from Kai's room. 'Hey, Nadia. He's asleep?'

'Yes. Out for the count.'

'Thank you. We certainly intruded on your date night.'

She smiled, waved it away, and Henry said, 'That's okay.' He gestured to Nadia. 'Your sister-in-law suggested we borrow one of your many red wines and take it away with us when the pasta arrives.'

Simon looked hopeful. 'Pasta? There's pasta?'

'Coming. Your dinner. And ours,' Nadia said with a smile, and turned for the door when the doorbell rang.

They stayed another twenty minutes, eating with Simon, after phone calls to Gran and Nadia's father—who, strangely, hadn't asked to speak to Nadia, which Henry felt offended by—they could both see Simon needed the company for a little longer.

Eventually, his friend looked more relaxed and waved them away. Clutching their wine, they left in the Uber that arrived to transport them back to the apartments.

Henry opened the door and stood back. Nadia hadn't been to his apartment since he'd moved in and he hoped she liked it.

He watched her face as he pushed open the door and, judging by the way her eyes opened wide and she looked back at him with delight, it did meet with her approval.

Doubt was banished as she breathed, 'Oh, Henry, it's lovely. Did you put this together yourself?'

His pleasure brought a smile. 'I was going for the Hampton look. White and blue, because that's what's outside, with some sandy accents like the beach below.'

'It certainly works. I feel relaxed just looking at the furnishings and yet it's very different to Bella's decorating.'

He remembered the first time he'd seen Nadia in here and the crowd who had wonderfully forced them onto the veranda to talk. He wasn't looking to have big social events, just wanted

Nadia and Katie to feel as if they could come here any time they wanted.

Because he wanted them here all the time and he wanted it nice for them. He hadn't realised that before.

'Yes. But I took your advice and Elsa Green from downstairs, your grandmother's friend, has a cleaner who comes up and waters my plants. She housekeeps and puts the slow cooker on twice a week, so I have proper meals.'

'Lucky you,' she said, but she looked pleased he'd listened.

He'd done it for her and Katie. Wanted it perfect, and things could get messy when he was called out often.

'I know. I can't predict which delicious smells will hit me when I walk in the door on Mondays and Wednesdays.'

She sat down, leaving a space for him on the end of the couch. 'That's good. I was worried about you eating enough. I think you've lost weight since you arrived.'

She worried about him? A good start to tonight. 'It's probably loss of muscle because I haven't had time to go to the gym as often as I did in London.'

She pretended to assess him. 'Nope. None missing. Though you do spend a lot of time lazing around, eating popcorn and drinking wine,' she teased.

But, underneath the banter, something shimmered between them, and he carried the bottle she'd cadged off her brother-in-law and put it on the low table in front of her.

'Don't blame me for that. You're the one encouraging me with bad habits.'

Then he crossed back to the kitchen for the glasses on the counter, along with the candles and matches.

He'd hoped they'd come back here, hence the preparation, and lit the candles so he could turn the lights down.

On the way to the sofa, he slid open the veranda door to

allow in the breeze, and the sounds of the ocean that followed it, and set down the glasses. 'Do you still fancy wine?'

'Sure.' She patted her flat stomach. 'I don't need anything more to eat, though.'

He smiled. The pasta had been filling. 'We can have tea or coffee if you'd prefer.'

She laughed. 'No, I'd love another glass of that lovely Margaret River red. Simon really does have great taste.'

He stood for a moment, just to soak her in, sitting on his couch, before he lowered himself beside her.

She was watching him, not the wine, and he leaned in and kissed her gently. 'I've been waiting to do that all night.'

'Mm-hmm, she said and kissed him back. Not gently.

They never did have more wine.

CHAPTER TWENTY-THREE

Nadia

NADIA WOKE AT one a.m. as Henry slipped from the bed. He pressed the blankets around her and kissed her forehead. She suffered only a little embarrassed heat when she considered how he'd drawn such an enthusiastic, and loud, response from her. Several times. More than several.

'Snuggle in. I'll be back.'

He dressed quickly. Leaving? But the bed was warm, her limbs felt like simmering syrup, so she closed her eyes though her smile had dimmed. After what they'd shared, Henry was leaving. Hospital. Couldn't they have their first night without his work interrupting?

But she couldn't stay awake after the unexpected delights Henry had gifted her with and drifted back to sleep.

The next time she woke he was sliding in beside her, his skin cool and his muscular body hard, and deliciously masculine. He was back. Still half asleep, she rolled into him, pulling him closer, slipping her arms around his neck and lifting her face for his kiss.

Henry didn't need a second invitation and by the time they dropped off to sleep that time it was almost dawn.

She woke with Henry's arms around her, his gentle hands

cupping her breasts and his body spooning her back, his warm breath on her neck.

Inside, a part of her revelled in the wantonness and the delight of being here, naked with this amazing man whose company she'd come to enjoy so much, and another part panicked at how much she wanted him, loved being with him, and that he'd left her already once. She'd rushed into a step she should have slowed for.

Why couldn't she banish those ridiculous fears that this wouldn't work? So many reasons why it should. Yet a tiny panic built in her belly, though she tried to push it down.

'This is a dream come true, you know.' Henry's deep purring rumble made gooseflesh prickle her skin.

She hadn't realised he was awake and rolled onto her back so she could see his face. His hands slid away and instantly she wanted them back. 'What dream was that?'

'The one where I get called to work then come back and you put your arms around me and warm me so much we burn the sheets.'

He dreamed of being called to work?

'You leaving the bed seems a bit of a nightmare to me.'

He pulled her close against him and kissed her. 'Best kind of nightmare, climbing back in, though.'

She tensed. Cleared her throat. 'Not my dream.'

She could tell he was still in sexy land when he asked, 'What's your dream?'

'You missed the point.' Her frown deepened. 'I'm pretty sure it would be better if you didn't have a job that dragged you out of bed in the middle of the night.' And the middle of the weekend. And the middle of a lunch. But she didn't add that. With some difficulty.

'All part of the game.' Henry was moving on. 'But, dearest Nadia, it was a wonderful date night.' His voice deepened. 'And morning.'

She wasn't sure she'd moved on. But her skin heated just with that look and he dragged her along.

'Action-packed.' She tried for nonchalance despite her erratic thoughts, half annoyed, half drunk with his obvious appreciation.

'Complete with champagne, emergency birth and our bed.'

Our bed? The thought shocked her. Stupidly, she blurted, 'Your bed. Not mine. Not ours.'

'Ours. It will be here waiting for you.' He kissed her again as if he couldn't resist and slipped from *their* bed.

Yet, despite all the ups and downs of her seesaw thoughts, he was magnificent. Magnetic. But shadows lay beneath his eyes, a man who had been out in the night, many nights, and suddenly she thought of Lulu despite her own stupid angst.

'Henry?'

He turned back.

'Is Jake okay? It wasn't him that called you out, was it?'

He smiled. 'No, Jake's fine. Thank you for asking. He'll probably go home on Friday.'

'Oh.' Now she felt out of line. But her father wouldn't have answered her. 'Okay. I'm glad. Thank you.'

'Thank you,' he said, and she wasn't sure what he was thanking her for.

Once the bathroom door shut, she put her head back on the pillows and stared at the ceiling. What had she done? What had she promised by coming here? Staying. Giving herself like she'd never done before. She remembered Henry's 'our bed'.

They'd resolved nothing. Just made everything more complicated. But she'd done nothing wrong. They were both single. Nothing irretrievable. Surely.

Of course it felt awkward, but not too awkward for a first

morning after a night before. And she had discovered Henry Oliver had hidden talents because, no doubt at all, she'd never felt so satisfied and sated, ever. Or was that because she'd felt as if they'd connected on a deeper level than she'd planned for. No. It wasn't that. Please.

Because she still did have doubts that she could be happy with Henry as the man in her life. A part-time man.

She rolled from the sheets, picked up her clothes, dressed and made the bed. Finally, she smoothed the pillows and straightened the quilt—wanting, for some bizarre reason, to erase her visit? No, not erase, but make his room look as immaculate as it had last night when they'd come in.

Her mind flicked back to that moment. Not that she'd had much time to notice in the rush they'd both been in to lose their clothes. He made her feel so hot.

For goodness' sake. She was all over the place.

She wanted her own apartment, and she wanted to be there when Gran called to say Katie was ready to come home, but she couldn't just slip away. Could she?

She went through to the kitchen and put the jug on for Henry to have coffee. On the corner bench she found the latest espresso maker, not what she wanted to figure out now, but she switched it on as well, just in case he wanted to use it.

Henry arrived with little delay, hair still damp and a bead of moisture in the diamond of his throat, and her doubts morphed into a need so unexpected, so overwhelming she gripped the counter with her hands.

His shirt hung unbuttoned, broad, damp chest beneath, with his tie ready to be knotted as it draped around his collar. This morning there were dancing giraffes on the pattern, but it was the brown expanse of skin that held her gaze. Ripples of wide muscled chest.

The need to lick that tiny droplet on his neck slammed into

her, and the wanting to slide against him all over again made her treacherous fingers tighten on the bench behind her.

'If you keep looking at me like that, I'm going to be late for work.' The deep timbre of his voice raised the hairs on her arms. Who was she? What had he done to her last night?

She licked dry lips and conjured up her lost voice, which seemed to have lodged somewhere in her throat. 'I'm ready to go. Get organised downstairs.' She waved a distracted hand at the kitchen. 'I didn't know whether you wanted me to make you some breakfast.'

He crossed the room to her, and she couldn't have stopped her hands sliding under the flaps of that open shirt. His skin felt warm and deliciously damp. And so well-packed. Her face leaned of its own volition into his neck and her tongue licked the water bead that had caught her eye.

He sucked in a breath and the flesh under her hands went rigid. Lost again in a power she hadn't known she possessed, she smiled as she ran her palms around his muscle-covered ribs, couldn't have stopped herself if she'd been threatened with death. His skin felt just as hot and smooth and delicious as she'd known it would.

He groaned. 'We need to talk.'

They did and she knew she wasn't being fair.

'Talk? You mean about the fact we couldn't have one night without you being called away?'

'Not that. Not now.' He leaned down and nipped her lip. 'We're gonna do this again, aren't we? You're not going to disappear again behind the shield?'

Her watch chimed and she thought of Katie, who was probably awake now. She blinked. What was she doing? Who was this woman? She stepped back. 'I'm going for a shower.' She turned for the door, but he caught her arm.

'One more kiss,' he murmured as his arms came around

her, his turn to slide fingers on skin, and very, very gently and slowly he made her forget the world.

Before she left, he said, 'And we won't always ask your grandmother to mind Katie. She can always come over too.'

So then she and Katie could both wait until he came back to them from wherever he was called away to?

CHAPTER TWENTY-FOUR

Nadia

HENRY PHONED AT LUNCHTIME. 'Have you chosen a place for lunch?'

'I only just said goodbye to you this morning.' *And my head is still whirling*, she thought, but didn't say because her heart-rate had jumped at the sound of his voice.

'It's Thursday,' he said, as if that explained everything.

She didn't answer so he added, 'I like interrupting your work to make sure you eat.'

She smiled at that. Couldn't help it. She'd been smiling and scowling all morning, along with the swings of Will-I-won't-I?

'Well, I've lots of food here. Why don't you just come to my place? I'll whip something up.'

'Perfect. Never too early for bondage,' his voice low and liquid.

She spluttered into the phone. 'I hope you didn't say that from the children's ward.'

'I'll see you at twelve-thirty.' She could hear the smile in his voice, and she suspected he could be taking a little revenge for her comments in the kitchen this morning.

She made a quiche Lorraine and salad. Heated a couple of tiny dinner rolls and set it all out on her patio, humming. Her apartment overlooked the complex garden, behind a low wall. She could see through the foliage but people couldn't see in. Maintaining it was not her responsibility, thankfully, but definitely her pleasure, especially when the walled and paved courtyard gave an extra space for her, with a tiny table and chairs. She'd even put the umbrella up.

By twelve-forty-five she wondered if this was going to work.

The text came in at one p.m.

So sorry, Nadia. Frantic here. But I promise I'll pick up you and Katie to go see the baby at five. I'll be there.

Okay. It was an impromptu lunch. Not a planned one. And he had texted and made a real, promised plan. She picked up one of the still warm bread rolls and nibbled it. And then collected the food to put it all back in the fridge.

They could take the quiche with them to Bella's to see the baby. She'd slipped up to the maternity ward to see Bella earlier. She and Simon would be home by now, and Bella had suggested Nadia could drop in after preschool pick-up.

Henry had been busy at lunchtime. She understood. She did. He was in charge of paediatric emergency admissions and of course there would be children needing him.

She looked at the roll in her hand and suddenly tossed it into the bin. Poured herself a glass of water, drank, and went back to work.

At three o'clock Katie bounced into the car, full of talk of her friends. For the first time all day, Nadia felt like herself as she listened.

Until Katie said, 'Is Dr Henry coming for dinner?'

Was he?

'Maybe. He's coming to take us to Auntie Bella's at five o'clock.'

'In his car? Has he got a little screen for the back of my seat?'

'Yes, in his car. And no to the screen. But Auntie Bella has a big surprise to show you. We're going to visit her.'

'A surprise with Dr Henry?' Almost a happy shout. 'Is Kai there? And Mr Teeny. Is it a present?'

Nadia glanced in the rear-view mirror. Her daughter's eyes were wide with anticipation. 'Yes, Kai will be there. Yes, Mr Tierney too. And no, not a present for you. But we've got one for Auntie Bella.'

After visiting Bella at the hospital, Nadia had slipped into her favourite craft store and found a tiny handmade lemon and green sundress for Ivy. The best was a green headband stitched with tiny leaves.

She considered possible germs from childcare and vulnerable new babies. 'You can have a bath and get changed out of your play clothes and put on one of your pretty dresses.' She hoped they wouldn't have to fight about an early bath.

Katie looked thoughtful. 'I'll put on my princess dress for Dr Henry. He will like that one.'

They'd have to sort that name. Dr Henry wasn't the perfect way for a four-year-old to address her mother's boyfriend. Lover? Maybe partner? She so wasn't sure this was going to work.

By five o'clock they'd both showered and dressed, Katie complete with silver crown, and Nadia had reapplied her make-up.

At ten past five Katie was talking to Ernestine in a cross little voice with much foot stamping.

Five minutes later, the phone rang. 'I'm sorry, Nadia…' Henry's voice. She listened as he ran down his excellent reasons.

'I understand,' she said and then she hung up.

Katie cried, big rolling tears. Suddenly, Nadia had a flashback to a horrible day when her big sister Bella had cried at her tenth birthday. Their father had not made it home for cake and forgotten her birthday dinner.

Something wild and angry and determined, maybe from then, maybe from now, but fury, blossomed in Nadia's chest. *Enough is enough.* She'd known this wouldn't work. He'd hurt Katie. And she shouldn't have believed him enough to tell Katie, so it was her fault too.

'It's okay, sweetheart. We'll ask Gran if she'll come with us.' She should have done that instead anyway. So many things she'd got wrong since she'd left that man's bed this morning.

Was it only this morning?

'You know Gran loves your princess dress very much and Auntie Bella does too. You can show Mr Tierney. I bet he will love it too.' She was gabbling and made herself stop.

Half an hour later they met Gran in the car park. Katie murmured quietly, 'Is it Auntie Bella's birthday?' The exuberance gone.

'It's somebody's birthday.'

'Whose birthday?'

'If I tell you, it won't be a surprise.'

Catherine opened the front passenger door. 'Say hello to Gran.'

'Hello, Gran.'

Her grandmother cast an indulgent glance to the back of the car before she slid in. 'Hello, Katie. Hello, Nadia. Isn't this exciting?'

Katie piped up, a little brighter. 'Mummy said Auntie Bella has a surprise.'

'She certainly has.' Gran laughed. 'Goodness me.' She studied Nadia. 'You've had a big twenty-four hours.'

'Yes.'

'You seem to have lost that glow you had this morning.'

'Really? No, I'm fine.'

'Oh, dear.' Gran shook her head. 'That word. Fine. You sound like your sister.'

She had no idea what Gran was talking about. Or she pretended she didn't.

A quietly excited Mrs Tierney took them through to the sitting room, where Bella looked amazing considering she'd had a precipitous birth the day before and left hospital at lunchtime today.

Baby Ivy lay quietly content and no worse for her rapid and exciting catapult into the world as she nursed at her mother's breast.

Katie's eyes went as wide as frisbees as she stared at the little baby and the almost trim Bella. 'Your baby's out of your tummy, Auntie Bella!' she cried.

The adults laughed. 'Yes, she is, darling. This is Ivy. She's Kai's little sister.'

The aforementioned Kai, head buried under his mother's other arm, was watching the baby with suspicious eyes, but as soon as Simon came back into the room he recovered. Simon had taken leave for the next week to be the bonded parent for his son—and he tickled him until the little boy giggled and recovered his good humour as his daddy swung him on to his shoulder.

'Kai's still getting used to sharing his mummy,' Bella

said calmly. 'This is when dads come in handy for diversional therapy.'

'Is that all I'm good for?' Simon pretended to be offended.

'You stack the dishwasher well,' his wife offered, but the loving look which passed between them made Nadia even more aware of what she would not have with Henry. Done deal.

She knew how it felt to have that world ripped away.

Simon took Kai and Katie outside to play on the new capsule trampoline that Mr Tierney and Simon had set up earlier in the week and Mrs Tierney arrived with a pot of tea and three cups.

'Isn't she just beautiful?' Mrs Tierney seemed to glow with her excitement for the new arrival, as Bella sat Ivy up to burp.

Nadia nodded and smiled, and watched her grandmother carry her cup away as the two older ladies drifted from the room to see something in the kitchen.

Gran asked Mrs Tierney about her grandchildren, proving how much a part of this world the Tierneys had become already. It seemed that Bella could let people into her world without expectations. Nadia wondered why she couldn't do that herself.

She looked at her sister. Serene, glowingly happy and so in control. All her life, it had seemed that Bella had a handle on everything. Except for that one birthday. Funny how that had stuck with her today.

Nadia had thought she had control too. Until Henry. She had for a while. Sorting her life after the horror of sudden widowhood and single prem-baby parenting, to a settled and secure world after Alex's death.

But since Henry had pushed himself into her life her world had destabilised, and now she didn't feel in control at all. But then, what was control? And how much had she really had anyway? None, apparently.

Bella patted the seat beside her. 'Come sit with me, Nadia.'

Nadia hesitated. She knew Bella had recognised her unhappiness, and was going to grill her. Years of older sister counselling made her aware that she was an open book to Bella. But her sister had enough on her plate without Nadia dumping her stupid concerns and conundrums on her.

Bella patted the seat again. 'Sit. I need to thank you for all your help with Ivy's dramatic arrival yesterday.'

She blinked. Sat. And shook her head. 'I didn't do anything. Henry did it all.'

Bella raised her brows. 'Don't be silly. You did what I had complete faith you'd do. You came. Instantly. As I knew you would. Even when I interfered with your lovely date night with Henry. And you helped so much.'

Nadia waved that away. 'Coming was nothing. Of course I came. It was an emergency.'

'Yes. But you were both wonderful.' Bella touched her hand. 'I knew I could rely on you when I needed you most.'

'You were so calm.' Nadia shook her head. She'd been terrified for her sister. 'It's always been like that. You calm. Me lost.'

Bella smiled, but the smile was unexpectedly shaky. 'Not always. I wasn't calm inside. I could have lost my baby, Nadia. I made the decision not to call the ambulance and hand myself over to people I didn't know. I believed I didn't have time to leave home. I could have got that wrong.'

'But you didn't get it wrong.'

'No. I risked that Ivy was safer fast birthing here than dangerously en route in a cramped ambulance in traffic, but I'm still working through the panic about that. And I don't think Simon is much better.'

Nadia stared. She'd had no idea that her sister ever had doubts about her decisions. 'Bella, I didn't see any of that. Just you, knowing exactly what you needed to do. I think you're amazing.' She added, almost to herself, 'And I was useless.'

Bella smiled at her. 'You were perfect. I remember your determination to do everything Henry asked. You calmed me by doing all the things I couldn't do and wanted to. So—' here her sister took her hand '—thank you.'

Good grief, she'd followed orders. But her grandmother's training kicked in, despite not being convinced she deserved it. *Always acknowledge a compliment.* 'Well, thank you. You're welcome.'

But Bella wasn't finished. 'And thank you for feeding Simon dinner and staying to let him debrief. He was shocked as well, you know. Poor darling. Very scary for him.'

Nadia couldn't imagine big, calm Simon shocked at anything, but she nodded.

'Anyway—' Bella shook her head on something she decided not to say '—we certainly impacted on your date night.'

The dinner, anyway. The rest had progressed, and boy had it progressed. She still didn't know what to feel about regretting that. Now wasn't the time to go there.

'That's fine.'

Bella tilted her head. 'Something's not fine.' Her brow creased. 'Simon said you and Henry went home with a bottle of wine and two smiles. Did you go back to his apartment?'

She didn't want to do this. Not today. But Bella would drag it out of her. Nadia knew her sister's gentle but implacable persuasion.

'Yes, dear. We went back to his place.'

Bella sat forward, interested and thankfully side-tracked. 'Oh. How does it look? I'm curious to know.'

Nadia almost smiled, relieved for the respite. Bella had lived there four years. Of course she wanted to know what her old apartment looked like now.

Furnishings, she could describe. 'Totally different, very blue and white. Masculine but welcoming. He certainly has the knack for creating a relaxing space.'

'I think Henry has a knack for a lot of things,' Bella said softly then waved that away. 'Good on Henry.' She sat back. Fixed her gaze on Nadia's face. 'So, how was it? And what's happened to destroy it?'

Bella had not asked that. 'How was what?' Nadia squirmed just a little.

'Ah.' Bella shifted Ivy's weight on her lap and sat back. 'So...you stayed the night?'

And how could she tell that just by looking at her? Nadia was pretty sure she hadn't been blushing before her sister said that, but she certainly was now. Darn it.

Really no use in holding back. 'It was wonderful, amazing. Beautiful.' Then it came out in a rush. 'But it's all ruined now.'

Bella's face took on that softer, big sis, loving concern. 'What's ruined, darling?'

And that, there, was the problem in a nutshell. And how did she explain?

'Everything. Stopping just when I thought it might work. I'm too close to falling in love with a man just like our father.'

She'd said it. Oh, my, she'd said it. For a few seconds there it had felt as if she'd let it out, but then all the terror rushed back as if in a vacuum she couldn't escape.

'Yes?'

She thought of her daughter's face under the silver crown, her tears. 'He promised to come with us this afternoon, didn't arrive, and then called and cancelled from work. Katie cried when he let us down again.' She forced her breathing to slow. 'Katie cried. Like we did with Dad.'

Bella looked towards the back yard, where the happy squeals of children playing could be heard. 'Katie seems fine now.'

'Well, she wasn't.' Nadia crossed her arms.

Bella patted her baby's bottom. 'Did you cry?'

'No.' Nadia shook her head. As if. 'I was too darned angry.'

'Because he couldn't leave work?' Her sister's voice came softly.

Nadia threw up her hands. 'Because he promised.' How had she ended up on the back foot when it was all Henry's fault?

Bella laughed. 'Well, isn't he a silly man. Promising what he couldn't give. Did you pressure him for that?'

Nadia's racing mind stopped. Thought. Mulled over that. No. He shouldn't have promised. Couldn't promise. Had she forced him to that? No. Had she made him? Because what if he'd come to her and a child had died?

'Oh, heavens above.' She put her face in her hands. 'And I think I love him. Which terrifies me.' And maybe she'd blown all this out of proportion because of that. *Hell's bells.*

Bella sat quietly for a few minutes and let her think. She did that well. Always had. Then she said, 'What terrifies you the most? That he won't be there for you?'

She hated the thought of that, but it didn't terrify her. She'd been on her own for years. Which was an eye-opener. So why was she so hot under the collar?

And then… Finally, Nadia saw it. Felt it. The fear grew from the bottom of her soul and exploded into comprehension. 'What if something happened to Henry? What if he died too?'

Before Bella could say anything, Nadia whispered, 'I had no idea that was it.' She pressed her chest where the angst had gathered like a huge, hot brick. 'Henry's such a wonderful man. What if I lost him?' She closed her eyes. That was what she was terrified of. *Oh, my heaven.*

She whispered, as it all came clear, 'I suspect I would fall deeper and deeper in love because Henry's not a boy to leave me for his toys.'

'No. He's not a boy. Not at all.' Her sister smiled softly. 'Though all men are boys inside somewhere.'

Nadia blinked back sudden tears. She'd seen the boy inside Henry once. Had wanted to nurture that child. Had even imagined briefly what Henry's son might look like.

She murmured, 'When Alex died, I lost my dream of the life I imagined with him.' She couldn't think of another word for dream. That was what it had been. Just the thought gave her chills. 'If that happened with Henry...' And she had had secret dreams. She saw that now. The three of them at a theme park, like Henry had said. Walks on the beach. Maybe even a baby together. She hadn't realised she'd been dreaming as well as fighting against it.

And she could lose it all if he died. Terror shimmied inside her.

'I don't think I could pick myself up again, Bella. I'm not even game to think about that. I couldn't watch Katie go through the pain that I know will never leave her if something happened to him—because pain doesn't leave when you lose someone.'

Bella nodded with understanding. 'We saw that with Dad.'

Nadia blinked. 'What?'

'He was never the same after our mother died. And that fear is understandable,' Bella said quietly. 'There was a cost when Alex died. I get you don't want to go there again...can't imagine being back in that void. Anyone could understand that.'

Ivy squirmed and Bella lifted the infant until she was over her shoulder and gently patted her back. 'You and Simon are very similar in your fears.'

'You mean because Simon lost his wife?' Because he'd been a widower, like she was a widow? She'd forgotten that. But when Bella and Simon had fallen in love there'd been so much going on.

She'd been struggling. Leaning on Bella. Alex had been gone suddenly. Debts, she'd nearly died, her baby had been premature, and dear Gran had been unconscious.

It was as if Bella heard all the thoughts as they skipped through her mind. 'Yes. It wasn't a good time. Do you remember me telling you anything about how Simon lost his first wife?'

Nadia frowned. 'Maybe. Yes.'

'His wife and his baby both died,' Bella said softly. 'Amniotic fluid embolism while he was on call.'

'He was called back to the hospital when it happened?' She thought of the last twenty-four hours for Simon and Bella. 'Like yesterday, when he wasn't here?' Nadia thought that through and felt a chill rise the hairs on her arms. 'He was called out yesterday as well?'

Bella's eyes were shiny with emotion. 'Yes. And my waters broke and the cord came first.'

'Oh... And you could have...' Nadia's voice trailed off. Her sister and Simon could have lost their baby. While Simon wasn't here.

Bella nodded. 'Which is what knocked Simon so much, because again he was at work and I needed him.'

'Oh, my heaven...' Nadia breathed. It seemed even the best relationships had challenges. And terrifying moments.

Bella wasn't finished. 'Like you, when Simon first met me, he was afraid of risking his heart again. So he fought against his attraction. Denied the obvious pull we had to each other. He pushed me away. Firmly. Like you're doing to Henry.'

Her sister leaned forward. 'Nadia, I think Henry loves you. And you say you might love him. You have to decide if you'll risk never knowing that joy—because the chance of finding your life partner is worth all the risks—and the joy is why.'

Nadia heard the words. Felt them sink into her heart like a

new colour ink into chalk. A concept that made sense of a new beginning. Of taking risks. Of managing disappointments. For the joy that she did find in Henry's company.

Yes, Henry was colour. Light. Joy. Henry was new beginnings. Henry loved her, loved Katie, and last night, wrapped in his arms, she knew she loved him. The reality was that if she kept pushing him away she would lose him just as surely as if she denied what they had. A different type of fear sank in.

CHAPTER TWENTY-FIVE

Henry

HENRY WISHED HE'D never mentioned theme parks to Nadia because he thought he might just have jinxed himself. This relationship, rollercoaster, ride of his life with Nadia and Katie was tearing him apart.

The day had started with such a high after the night with Nadia in his arms, Henry buzzed, as if someone had pressed him into one of those recharging ports for electric cars. But he suspected he was running on borrowed time with the little sleep he'd had in the last few days.

Work had been huge this week and last night with Nadia had been overwhelmingly amazing but not restful.

This morning, Nadia hadn't done anything to alleviate his unease. One minute she was wild and wanton and the next she wanted to get away and the panic had come and gone in her blue eyes like a flashing light. He'd seen it. Tried to ignore it because he'd had to leave.

He understood they'd probably progressed faster than they should have, and if his own impatience cost him his chance he would never forgive himself.

Plus, he couldn't shake a sense of foreboding after that last phone call, when she'd said she understood but there had been finality in her tone...

He'd been stupid to promise he'd go with them. His brain had said he'd just let her down at lunch and the ward had seemed sorted. Until Emergency had phoned. He'd wanted to see Katie's eyes when she saw Bella's baby. But he'd let them down again.

Now that he could finally leave, he hadn't eaten and he needed to sleep in case he was called out tonight.

He could make some fast eggs for the protein but wondered if Nadia was home. Maybe they would be back from Bella's, and he wanted to apologise in person.

When he knocked on her door he half expected Katie to answer the tap of his knuckles, but no one came. He tried again, listening to hear the sounds of movement and voices, but nothing. At least he didn't think they were pretending not to be there.

His disappointment seemed out of proportion to the fact that Nadia had probably gone to see her sister and the new baby instead of waiting around for him. Of course.

And of course she wouldn't mention where she'd gone to him, because why would she? He was nobody.

He'd let her down again. He'd been going to organise more backup. Maybe he should look at trying to stick with just overseeing the children's ward and let someone else take over the paediatric cover in the emergency department.

If he wanted a life outside the hospital.

He wondered if Marco would be interested.

Ah, hell. Exhaustion swamped him. He looked at the stairs that led from Nadia's floor to his apartment so many floors above—he should climb them instead of taking the lift.

For a moment, he rested his head on the handrail post and sank to sit on the cold concrete and closed his eyes.

* * *

'Did you go to sleep outside our door?' the little voice said loudly.

Henry's lids flew open. Katie's bright green eyes were right in front of his face. He blinked. Straightened his cricked neck. Licked his dry lips and focused. 'Just for a minute.' But the cold ache in his backside and pain in his neck said otherwise.

He rubbed his neck. 'I might have dozed off.'

'You didn't come with us to see the baby.' Accusing. 'I put my princess dress on for you.'

'No, I had to work.' He winced at the accusing green eyes level with his own. She was wearing a silver crown. 'I like your princess dress very much.'

He climbed to his feet. He could hear Nadia coming down the hall from the garage and he pushed the hair out of his eyes and tried to look like he hadn't slept outside her door like a stray dog.

Hopefully, she wouldn't notice his dishevelled appearance.

'Dr Henry was asleep on our stairs,' said Katie loudly and with much glee.

Henry winced and groaned.

Nadia came around the corner and looked him up and down. 'I see that. I think Dr Henry was awake a long time last night and needs to sleep.'

The beautiful woman he'd been dreaming about, maybe not realistically, smiled at him. Which was a good thing. Always.

There was something different about her smile. Something warm and caring, a promise he could almost hope for, and his heart gave an extra thump like the dog's tail he might have grown while he was asleep.

She opened the door and pushed it wide. 'Come in, Dr Henry. Look at you. Have you had anything to eat today?'

He shook his head, and she shook hers admonishingly back. 'I can feed you. Only fair. You're always trying to feed me.'

And suddenly it wasn't so bad he'd been caught napping.

Henry had no idea he loved hot toasted cheese and tomato sandwiches on grain bread so much. He ate four of them. That was eight slices of melted food on bread. As soon as he finished one, Nadia slipped another steaming one onto his plate with a spatula. 'Stop,' he said. 'Stop. I'll get carbohydrate overload.'

She laughed. 'I'm sure you'll burn it off. But I'll stop.' She set down a big mug of incredibly aromatic tomato and herb soup and said, 'Drink the soup as well.'

So he did and felt almost human by the time he'd finished the mug.

He could hear Katie talking to Ernestine in the bath. Ernestine watched, she didn't bath, Nadia had said, but she certainly joined in the conversation, according to Katie's responses. Henry smiled at the thought. He could love a doll.

He hadn't realised he'd been so cold sitting on the step in the dim and chilly hall, but it was the warmth of Nadia's smile as she fussed over him that made him heat on the inside.

She tilted her head at him. 'It's lucky you're a handsome man, Henry. Even sleep creased and ruffled you're irresistible.'

He was? 'I am?'

'Oh, yes,' she said calmly as she walked back into the kitchen with his empty mug.

He stood, watched her rinse the cup, took several steps towards her and when she acknowledged he was there he slid his arms around her waist.

The scent of her filled his head. He nuzzled her neck. Whispered into her ear, 'I love you. Very much. Will you marry me?'

She leaned into him. Kissed his throat. 'I'm thinking about it.'

He thought about that. He could wait. 'I'll ask you again tomorrow. Wanna make popcorn?'

CHAPTER TWENTY-SIX

The wedding

NADIA HADN'T WANTED a big wedding. She'd had one of those and Alex had said, *'No children allowed.'* But this time she wanted a small family wedding, with little formality and Henry.

Henry just wanted them married and what Nadia wanted stood well by him.

All Katie wanted was to be flower girl.

So they set their wedding stage across the road from Bella and Simon's house on the sandy beach at Bilinga and aimed for fun.

Henry had secured council permission to erect a three-sided wedding marquee on the sandy grass and the finished landscape ended up looking more like a cross between a circus and a children's playground than a wedding reception venue.

Simon and Mr Tierney had moved the trampoline across the road and fenced off an area with play equipment and a shaded, shallow wading pool for later in the warm afternoon. Parents would be able to watch the children playing in front of them while enjoying the smokehouse at the side of the marquee when that came around with the caterers.

The whole front of the marquee lay open to the sparkling

afternoon seascape while the sun passed overhead. White tables, blue cutlery from Lulu's restaurant and flowers climbing the poles to the roof made the shady space look pretty and festive. The air was filled with the scent of flowers.

The mix of guests was adults, lots of children, two babies and a few key people from the hospital. Plus Lulu and her boys.

Henry's registrar Amelia and his two residents, plus Nadia's friends from the children's ward were there. As well as Henry's best man, Marco, a ridiculously handsome Italian with the sexiest accent, who had arrived from London and became enamoured of the Gold Coast and the weather. He completed the assembly.

Marco had taken Nadia up on her offer of renting him the ground floor unit and would be working with Simon and Henry in the paediatric practice for the next year while he sought permanent residency. He'd taken over paediatric emergency admissions. He didn't know it yet, but he was Henry's backup plan for date nights.

Nadia dressed across the road at the Purdy house, with Catherine and Bella as her assistants. They tweaked her strapless pearl-coloured sheath dress until it smoothed over her skin from bodice to her 'something new' silver sandals.

Her hair had been swept up into a tiny silver half-crown with falling golden curls and a tiny veil to float around her shoulders. A gifted and magnificent pearl-drop earring set, more than a hundred years old, was the 'old' and they matched her grandmother's pearl necklace to be the 'borrowed'. On her wrist, she wore an intricate and jewelled 'blue' bracelet, gifted from Henry, who swore the glorious aquamarines were the exact colour of her eyes.

Malachi and Lisandra's two boys, Bastian and Bennett, were the matching pageboys in black suits, looking very similar as twins often did.

And Katie was the prettiest flower girl in the world with her basket and her rose petals to scatter on the sand. And she wore her crown.

'It's time to go,' said her father and Nadia sucked in a breath.

Professor Piers Hargraves looked very distinguished in his grey suit and blue silk tie the same colour as Katie's dress.

Very softly, so nobody else could hear, he said to Nadia, 'You look very like your mother.' His voice held emotion she'd never heard from her austere dad and her eyes misted at the gentleness in his tone. 'You've always looked like your mother,' he said. 'Painfully so. I loved her very much.'

'We lost you when she died, didn't we?' she asked quietly and loving Henry now, as she did, she could see her father in a new light.

Piers closed his eyes. 'I think so. And I'm sorry. But you've grown into a beauty, Nadia, and I'm very proud of you. I wish you a wonderful marriage with this man. I think you've chosen well.'

Nadia's chest tightened and she leaned up and kissed her father's cheek. 'I think so too. Thank you.'

Across the road, Henry waited at the edge of the water with his back to the horizon, listening to the sounds of the waves as they came behind him in the surf. In front of him were the two dozen guests in white chairs they'd spread on each side of the Aegean blue carpet ready for his bride.

She'd be here soon.

Beside him stood Marco. For once, his friend looked serious. 'You're a lucky man, Henry,' he murmured.

Henry smiled. He was. 'I know it.'

He glanced at his friend and caught him studying Amelia with a discerning eye. *Oh, no, you don't.* He cleared his throat until Marco looked back his way. 'And I appreciate you being here for the occasion.'

Marco's eyes gleamed. 'I'll be here for more than that,' he said, and his gaze drifted left again towards Amelia.

'No, you don't,' Henry pretended to growl. 'I need my registrar.'

Marco laughed but Henry saw a movement across the road and his attention zeroed in.

Ah. She was coming. All other thoughts fled.

On the other side of the pedestrian crossing two figures dressed as school traffic wardens held up stop signs. Henry had to grin. The Tierneys were traffic wardens before they were guests.

The Saturday afternoon cars slowed and stopped.

When it was safe, Isabella Purdy and Catherine Hargraves each held the hand of Henry's new little daughter, Katie, all dressed in blue. She skipped with her basket between them.

After them came Lisandra and Malachi's two boys.

And finally, his love. His future wife. His gorgeous Nadia on the arm of her father, looking like the angel she was.

Henry's heart swelled and he sucked in a breath. Beside him, Marco murmured reverently, *'Bellissima.'*

'She is, indeed,' said Henry. 'My darling love.'

* * * * *

A Kiss Under The Northern Lights

Lights
Susan Carlisle

MILLS & BOON

Susan Carlisle's love affair with books began when she made a bad grade in mathematics. Not allowed to watch TV until the grade had improved, she filled her time with books. Turning her love of reading into a love for writing romance, she now pens hot Medicals. She loves castles, travelling, afternoon tea, reading voraciously and hearing from her readers. Join her newsletter at SusanCarlisle.com.

Also by Susan Carlisle

Atlanta Children's Hospital miniseries

Mending the ER Doc's Heart
Reunited with the Children's Doc
Wedding Date with Her Best Friend
Second Chance for the Heart Doctor

Discover more at millsandboon.com.au.

To Finnley.

One of the greatest pleasures in my life.

CHAPTER ONE

A KNOT HUNG in Beatrice Shell's throat. She searched the land below for the town that should be at the end of the northern Iceland fjord. The stretch of blue water grew closer as the pilot of the single-engine plane prepared to land. Ahead she could just make out a single runway of black asphalt with piles of gray stone alongside it, extending into the water. She'd never seen anything like it. Yet that wasn't a huge surprise. Coming to Iceland had been her first real trip anywhere.

The large airliner she had taken to Reykjavík had been scary, but exciting at the same time. Getting into the small plane had created a different sensation all together. Terror. The six-seater plane was nothing like the jet, the only similarity being it soared through the air. This flight had kept her hair standing on end and her heart palpitating in her chest. She would see if there was a boat out when she left. No more swooping and dipping for her. Small plane transportation wasn't her idea of a good time.

Her fingers gripped the well-worn seat as the wings tipped one way, then the other. The pilot lined up with the runway. If he missed it, he would put them in the water. She glanced at the beautiful snowcapped mountains and shivered. Into the cold water.

She brushed her finger across the small scar on the top of

her hand, then forced herself to open her eyelids. Isn't this what she'd been wanting to do since she'd learned of her rare skin disorder as a teen? To have a connection. Belong.

She'd experienced a blistering skin rash. Her foster mother had taken her to the doctor. After much discussion and other doctors being called in for their opinions, she had learned she had a skin disease called hepatoerythro-poietic porphyria disease or HEP. What intrigued her the most about the disease was it was genetic, particular to people with Nordic ancestry. Until then she'd had no hint of her background.

She recovered completely with little scarring from the flare-up of the disease. She would always carry the gene, but the illness would become nothing more unless she spent too much time in the sun or was prescribed the wrong drugs. The positive thing that came out of the experience was the knowledge of her Nordic lineage. When she had saved enough money, she'd had a DNA test done, which had led her to Iceland.

With a squeak of tires, the plane touched the asphalt, bounced, then settled to coast to a stop. She let out the breath she'd been holding. At least they weren't in the water.

When the opportunity arose to work in a clinic in Iceland for a year, she'd applied for the chance. She was tickled when she won the position. Now she could care for people with the same genetic background as herself. They might not be direct family, but they were closer than anyone else she had known.

She dared a look out the window. Another plane sat parked in front of a white block building, and they coasted beside it. The sign on the wall read Welcome to Seydisf-jordur.

Gathering her purse and her small duffel bag, Trice

climbed out of the side door the pilot had opened. He offered his hand, and she accepted it. The last thing she needed was to arrive at her new job with a busted nose from falling on her face. That wouldn't encourage the town's faith in her medical abilities.

She glanced around at the buildings lining a single road following the curve of the fjord. The town was located in the end of a narrow green valley. A gentle-looking river lead into the mouth of the fjord. The backs of the town structures hovered against a wall of rock creating the fjord. In the sunshine, the stores and houses glowed white, pink, yellow and light blue with a few having red roofs. If anything, the place was picture-perfect.

Her heart beat faster. She'd dream of coming this far north for years but never thought it would happen. Now she was here. This place she could call home. Excitement built. This could be her chance to find a link to family. No matter how distant.

"Miss, your suitcase is right here. The clinic is over there." The man pointed around the water toward the only piece of land wide enough to have a center street with buildings on both sides. "It's the white building with the red cross sign."

"Thank you." She pulled the handle up on her case, assuming she was expected to walk the half a mile. She was thankful for her warm socks and her down vest. Her new hiking boots maybe not so much. They had been a going away gift from her best friend, Andrea. "I appreciate the ride in."

The man with a beard lifted and lowered his chin and went back to the plane.

Taking the suitcase handle, she rolled it toward the small terminal building that sat securely on land. At least this part of the airport wasn't surrounded by water. Unable to see a red cross from that distance, she followed the road toward the village.

The sun shone bright, and the air was brisk. Thankfully the place wasn't covered in snow. People often mixed Greenland up with Iceland. Greenland was icy and Iceland was green.

Trice had been offered the job at the last minute because another doctor had backed out. She'd jumped at the opportunity despite the short notice. In less than forty-eight hours, she'd wrapped up her personal business, stored her few belongings and stepped on a plane bound for the far-off north. Andrea had thought she was crazy and wished her well.

She had not even had a chance to break in her new boots between yesterday and today. After a hurried last two days, a long plane ride, and the altitude, she didn't care much about the time zone changes.

Trice surveyed the area past the airport away from town. In that direction, there was some type of business located in a large red metal building next to the water. Just how much could happen in this tiny place? Compared to living in metropolitan Atlanta, where she'd spent her entire life, this town was no larger than a neighborhood. No doubt she would have culture shock. She wasn't sure if that would be a good thing or a bad thing. She was too busy trying to keep her mind off the ache of her toes to worry about how she would make this work.

Around the curve of the bay, she saw the white clapboard house. Outside it hung a small sign with the red cross on it. She headed that way.

Trudging on, she promised herself with every step she would remove her boots as soon as she had a chance. The impeccable view of the vibrantly painted wooden buildings, the vivid blue water, the green of the valley, and the white of the snowcapped mountain filled her. Here she had a chance to find her lineage and through that herself. She could feel that in her bones, just not her toes.

Drake Stevansson noticed the woman for two reasons. First, he didn't know her. Having been born and raised in Seydis-fjordur, he knew everyone. Second, even from a distance, something about the woman intrigued him. Maybe it was her vivid-colored yellow coat or the hot pink suitcase she pulled. Whatever it was, she was eye-catching.

She followed the long curve of the road into town. He handed the envelope to his aunt, the postmistress, and started in the stranger's direction and toward the medical clinic. What could possibly land this fascinating creature here? He had seen plenty of people come from a cruise ship, but there wasn't one in port. She must have been on the plane.

The woman continued on but slower now. She had a rather haggard look. Every once in a while, she stopped and shook a foot. What was that about? The road wasn't muddy. Did she walk like that all the time?

She would square her shoulders, raise her chin and start again. Something about this woman screamed, "I won't be defeated." That spoke to him. That was an Icelandic man-tra. His gut said she had the determination, the grit needed to live through so many hours of darkness in the winter, not to mention the cold. Why that should matter to him he had no idea. He would be leaving soon with the possibility of not returning except to visit.

As a boy, he had watched his grandfather die because there wasn't anyone close who could do a simple appendec-tomy. He'd promised himself then that he would become a surgeon. He would fix people's bodies. He had gotten far enough in his training that he could do the procedures, but he still need the practice hours. He had been working on those when he was called away.

Drake had returned to Seydisfjordur for the funeral of his mentor and friend, Dr. Johannsson, to learn there was no one to oversee the practice. Drake had made arrangements for a break from his surgery work so he could provide the town medical care. Locating someone to take his place had turned into a frustrating ordeal. Finally, someone had agreed to come for a year. The mayor had taken almost two years to find someone. The man was expected any day. The mayor would continue to look for someone else beyond that. In two more weeks, after settling the new person in, Drake would leave.

The only issue tugging at him not to go was Luce. She was getting older, frailer. Because of circumstances, he had become responsible for her. Yet she encouraged him leaving. "Don't worry about me. Go follow your dream." The new doctor had better be good enough to care for Luce.

Drake reached the medical clinic. He stood outside and watched the woman approach. She made the same actions once again with her feet before she reached him.

Her look focused on him as she crossed the short distance. He found her even more interesting up close. Her blond hair was as fair as any person he knew. She controlled it by twisting it on the back of her head with a sparkling hair clip. She wore a bright red shirt, baggy black pants, and had a yellow, red, orange and black scarf around her neck. An orange bag was slung over her shoulder. Everything about her screamed confidence.

"Hello. Can I help you?"

She came to a stop in front of him, again lifted a foot and

shook it from side to side "Oh, good, you speak English. I'm afraid my Icelandic is nonexistent."

"You are in luck. I happen to be one of the ninety-eight percent of the people who speak English in Iceland. I'm going to use it now." Drake leaned down so they were at eye level. He wished he could see her eyes, but they were covered by sunglasses. "Are you okay? Lost? How can I help you?"

"My feet hurt. New boots." She moaned.

With a compassionate smile, he said, "I've been there. I can help with that."

"That's okay. I just need to get them off. Mind if I sit on your step?" She was already moving to do so.

"Not at all."

She pushed the pull handle of the case down. "I just need to get my tennis shoes out." She moved to picked up the bag.

"Let me have that." Drake lifted the case. "Come inside. You'll be more comfortable here."

"Thanks. I appreciate that." She followed him inside the small wooden building. She flopped into one of the plastic chairs in the waiting room with a sigh, resting her feet on her heels.

"Here, let me help." Drake went down on his haunches.

"You don't need to do that." She pulled her feet back.

He looked into her blue eyes that reminded him of the fjord with the sun shining across it. When the few other single men in town found out about her, they would be scrambling to her door. He wouldn't be around long enough to do that. Something about this woman made him suspect he would be missing out. He reached for her foot and began unlacing the boot. "I'm a doctor. It's my job to help those who hurt."

"So you are the doctor here." Her look met his as she studied him.

"I am for at least another two weeks."

She winced as he removed her footwear.

He dropped the boot to the floor. "Easy. You must have really done some damage to your feet."

She wiggled her foot. "That at least feels better, but I have no desire to put another shoe on."

"Let's remove the sock and see what's going on." He slowly rolled the sock off. Her foot was red and swollen with blisters on both sides. "You did a job."

"I should've known better. But they were a gift, and I wanted to wear them when my friend was the one taking me to the airport." She lifted her foot with the intent of rubbing it.

"Don't do that. Then it will really hurt. Wait right here. I have just what you need." He stood.

"I'd rather take care of them myself," she called after him.

"As the medical professional here, I'd rather you let me make sure you're okay." He headed down the hall without giving her time to respond.

Soon he returned with a square plastic container and Epsom salts. He poured a generous amount of salt into the pan.

She pushed a straight length of hair that had escaped her clip away from her face. "I can do this at the place where I am staying."

He gave her a direct look. "You can't even walk there. Let me at least get you comfortable enough to do that. I'll get the warm water."

"If you insist." She grinned.

He glanced back at her. "I do. Around here we take any

injury seriously. If it gets out of hand, we have a long way to go to get treatment."

When he came back this time, she had the other boot and sock off and was leaning back in her chair with a look of acceptance.

He poured the water into the pan. "Ease your feet in. You don't want them burned on top of being blistered."

She dipped an unpolished big toe of a slim, delicate foot into the water with a sigh. Slowly her feet went into the liquid. "This feels wonderful. Thank you."

"You keep those in there for a few minutes. I'll be back with a towel." He returned with a bottle of oil. He poured a generous amount into the water.

"What's that? It smells good." She inhaled.

Drake watched her neck lengthen. He was tempted to run a finger down the length of the smooth, creamy skin. "It is something I mix myself. It's fish oil with some local herbs. I use it when hikers come by for help. We get a number of those this time of year."

"So this isn't your first time to help out like this." She fluttered her feet in the water.

"No, I see abused feet more than I'd like to."

She curled her toes. "This will be the last time you will see mine."

He took the chair beside her. "Famous last words."

She leaned back beside him. "This is amazing."

He liked this flamboyant woman's attitude. "Do you have some nice warm socks and some substantial shoes that are not brand-new?"

She nodded. "I've got my tennis shoes in my suitcase, but the thought of putting them on makes my feet hurt even more."

"I have something you can wear that will make your

feet happier." Drake went to his office and located the soft boots his grandmother had given him for Christmas. He had brought them to the clinic thinking he might like to wear them when he was doing paperwork. Finally, he would be putting them to good use. He added a pair of clean socks.

This time he found the woman with her head back and eyes closed. Was she asleep?

Seconds later her eyelids opened.

He handed her the socks. "These are made of natural fibers and will help your feet avoid getting infected." He placed the boots beside the pan.

She sat straighter. With a hand, she pushed another stray strand of hair away from her face. Raising her chin, she looked at him. "You know, I don't even know your name."

He offered his hand. "I'm Dr. Stevansson. Drake."

She jerked to an upright position. "You are? Well, now I'm completely embarrassed."

"Why?"

"Because I'm here to take your place. I'm Dr. Beatrice Shell."

That he hadn't expected. She would be his replacement. He should've thought of it first thing, but nothing about her looked—he glanced at her petite build and soft face, then her flashy clothes—like someone he would expect to live in Iceland. Or that would survive a Seydisfjordur winter. And he'd been told by the mayor that a man had been hired for the doctor position.

Drake had stayed out of the search process for his replacement, both by his own choice and the mayor's. Drake had feared that if he was involved, he would never think anyone was qualified enough to have the position. The mayor's reasoning was that since Drake didn't care enough to stay, he shouldn't have a say in who took his place.

"But I guess I'm at the right place," Beatrice said, "and you are just the person I was looking for."

Drake liked that idea too much. Still, she was coming, and he was going. Nothing would be happening between them. Just his luck. The first woman near his age and not related to him who had shown up in town in years and he'd be leaving soon.

She offered him her hand. "I'm Trice to my friends. I was expecting somebody much older."

He chuckled. "I get that quite a lot." In fact, he heard it enough for it to grate on his nerves. Dr. Johannsson had been the town doctor for years. He'd delivered Drake and most of the adults in town. Compared to him, Drake was young.

Drake had worked for Dr. Johannsson as a teen and through high school, then gone off to medical school. The old doctor had encouraged Drake to consider taking over the practice, but Drake's dream was surgery. He felt like he could help more people using those skills. But it meant leaving Luce, which he didn't like doing. She had no intention of moving from her home. Unfortunately, there was no surgery clinic near Seydisfjordur. That was an entirely different issue.

He gave Trice a good long look. No, he hadn't expected this woman with her sassy attitude, flashy clothing, and full-of-confidence outlook. She appealed to him, too much so. The last woman he'd liked couldn't leave Seydisfjordur fast enough. Trice acted thrilled she was there. "I was expecting…a man."

Her shoulders went back at that statement. "Women now make up more than fifty percent of doctors." Her brows drew together. "No one told you? The doctor who was coming backed out at the last minute. I only found out I had the job a couple of days ago."

He hadn't been told on purpose would be his guess. Drake put his hands up in defense. "That wasn't a sexist statement. It's just that we don't get many women who want to live in such a distant and hostile environment. I'm just surprised, that's all."

"I'm tougher than I look." Determination showed clear in her eyes.

His mouth quirked. "You'll need to be."

Yes, he liked this woman who seemed excited about being in his hometown. Would she still feel that way this winter? What was she looking for? Or running from? Too bad he wouldn't be around long enough to find out.

Trice gingerly put her feet on the towel Drake had placed on the floor. "Now that I have thoroughly embarrassed myself, could you point me in the direction of where I'll be staying?"

"I'll do better than that. I'll show you. I'm sure you are tired."

She chuckled. "Yeah, that would be an understatement. After two plane changes and then a prop plane to get here, I could use a rest."

"Where did you start out from?"

"Atlanta."

He whistled. "Bright lights, big city. Seydisfjordur will be a big change for you."

"So far it looks wonderful." Her eyes were glowing with anticipation. "I can hardly wait to get to know everyone."

"It won't take you long. Many will line up to see you."

That she wasn't used to. Most of her life she had gone unnoticed. It would be nice to have people actually want to meet her. She pulled on the soft, thick socks. With some trepidation, she pushed her foot into the first shoe. It felt wonderful around her abused toes. With less concern, she did the same with the other foot. "Thank you. I dreaded putting on even my tennis shoes. I promise to return them all clean."

"It's not a problem." He stood.

"I'm sure the last few minutes make me look unqualified to take over here, but I promise to have my act together tomorrow."

"Everybody makes mistakes about footwear at times. I certainly have." He smiled.

Trice doubted he had made any mistakes. He looked and sounded like the perfect guy. Kind, understanding, gentle, caring, and best of all, male. Too bad he would be leaving. Something about Drake made her believe he was different from the last guy she had dated. She stood and hobbled toward her suitcase. For some reason, she sensed this man was careful with women's hearts.

"I'll get that. You can hardly make it to the door. You can't handle the case too."

She managed to get down the steps only by holding the rail with two hands.

Drake quickly came up behind her. He placed her case on the ground, then bent in front of her. "Get on."

"You have to be kidding. You can't mean to carry me through the street on your back!" She couldn't think of a less dignified way of making a first impression than parading through town on this man's back.

"Would you rather be cradled in my arms?"

Her pride refused to let him do that.

He looked over his shoulder. "If I don't carry you, how do you plan to get there?"

She glanced around.

Drake's look held hers. "You could stay here at the clinic if you wanted."

She considered sleeping on the examination table after having been on an airplane the better part of the day. The idea didn't appeal. "Okay."

"Wrap your arms around my neck. It's just a couple houses down."

She did as he said. His arms looped under her knees. Her front pressed against his back. Heat washed through her. This was far too familiar for someone she didn't even know, but what choice did she have? Walking wasn't a good suggestion.

He pulled the handle up on her suitcase and took off at a steady stride.

She voiced next to his ear, "I can get my suitcase later."

"I believe I can handle both of you at one time. Neither of you is very heavy." He threw the words over his shoulder without any exertion indicated in his voice.

Trice couldn't help but appreciate the movement of his muscles as he walked. His broad shoulders made her confident he wouldn't drop her. This was a man who knew how to care for people and took pleasure in doing so.

They made their way down the road lined with houses and businesses no taller than two floors. Curious faces met them along the way. A few people stepped out of the buildings to watch them.

"Is everyone going to know?" She started to hide her face but thought better of it.

"Pretty much. There are only around one thousand people who live in this area, and most of them are related to me. I would bet that in an hour, everyone will have heard of your arrival."

"Good to know." She smiled at one of the ladies, who waved.

He chuckled.

People continued to stare. A few spoke to Drake as they went. He responded with a grin in return.

One older man joined in beside Drake and asked, "Who you got there?"

"The new doctor. You can meet her later. We're kind of busy right now."

The man glanced at her. "Why is she on your back?"

Trice buried her face in his shoulder. She felt more than heard Drake's laugher. His body shook.

"Isn't she a little old to need to ride that way?" The man sounded perplexed.

"Gustaf, we'll talk about it later."

Trice groaned as Drake moved on. "I'm going to have to work extra hard to earn people's respect after this show."

"You'll find people here are warm and forgiving." He stopped in front of a pink house trimmed in white.

He set the case to the side then let her legs go. She slid down his back. Heat she'd not felt in a long time washed through her. Mercy, the man had a nice body. She'd had one serious relationship, but his body wasn't as defined as Drake's.

Nor had been his strength of will. Her ex had been from a society family, and his mother made it clear Trice's background was not suitable. A foster child with no family would never do. Her boyfriend couldn't stand up to his mother, so he and Trice parted ways. A marriage between them probably wouldn't have worked anyway. Her sense of adventure and sense of humor hadn't always been appreciated. Her boyfriend had been far too serious. Worse, he had been under his family's thumb. Trice wanted a man who stood on his own two feet.

Even with her and Drake's short association, she didn't

think those were issues for him. But she shouldn't be making these observations. She had no interest in becoming involved in a relationship. She wouldn't take the chance on being second choice again. There had been enough of that in her life.

Something about Drake appealed to her. Maybe it was the fact he had been willing to carry her as he had. He seemed to enjoy the absurdity in life.

Drake's strong grip held her arm, letting her get her feet under her. He knocked on the door but didn't wait for an answer before he opened it. "Luce?"

The scrape of chair legs and shuffling of feet came from the back of the house. He carried the luggage inside. She followed, closing the door behind her. A petite stoop-shouldered woman with a weathered face entered.

"Drake, what do you mean coming into my home bellowing?" The woman's voice was gruff but held a tender note.

"I'm sorry, Luce. I brought your new boarder. This is Dr. Shell."

The woman, who must have been close to a century old, gave Trice a long look. "From America, I hear."

"Yes ma'am, I am." Was that a good or bad thing?

"Nice manners too."

Somehow Trice believed that was high praise. "Thank you. It's nice to meet you. I appreciate you giving me a place to stay."

"You have come to take my Drake's place."

There was a tone of sadness to that question. "I have come to take care of the people here for a year and do some research."

The older woman studied Trice a moment, her eyes landing on her feet. "She is wearing your Christmas present." Her accusing look shifted to Drake.

"She is. By the way, Luce is my grandmother." Drake hung his head as if in shame.

Trice liked the idea a man as large as Drake could be intimidated by this tiny woman. She had certainly called him on the carpet.

"She's just borrowing them. I had them over at the office to wear if my feet were cold while I was doing paperwork. Dr. Shell's feet hurt."

"They are very nice," Trice assured the woman. "Thank you…" She looked at Drake.

"You may call me Luce. Everyone does." The woman gave a sharp nod and said to Trice, "I'll show you where you will stay."

Trice, with Drake carrying her case, followed the older woman through the small, dim home and out the back door. In the backyard stood an even smaller cottage.

Luce opened the door. "You have everything you need in here except a full kitchen. There is a microwave and a toaster oven, but if you want to do more, you're welcome to use my kitchen anytime you please. All you have to do is to come in the back door."

Luce pushed the cottage door open. "Come in and I'll show you around."

Trice joined her. Drake entered behind her, setting the case out of the way. With him there, the place went from small to tiny. After that ride on his back, she was too aware of him. He seemed to surround her.

Luce explained everything in detail. Which wasn't much. A solid wooden bed sat in one corner. In another was a bookshelf filled with books, a chair and small table with a floor lamp beside it. Nearby rested a TV on a substantial-looking dresser with drawers. Across from that side of the room was a kitchen area that consisted of a cabinet, a table and two chairs. A small bath took up the back corner. A hoop rug created out of pastel colors lay on the floor.

As far as Trice was concerned, she'd found heaven. After growing up with little she could call her own, this would be a treat. "This really looks wonderful. I know I'll enjoy staying here."

"If you need anything, you just ask me or tell Drake. He helps take care of things around here when he's not busy seeing patients." The old woman flashed him a look. "At least, until he leaves."

"Luce, you said you wanted me to go. To be happy." He put an arm around the woman's shoulders, looking at her with a teasing grin.

"I do want you to follow your dream. I will miss you. Enough of that. You aren't gone yet. Let's let the girl settle in." She nudged him toward the door.

Drake went while looking over his shoulder at Trice. "See how I'm treated around here? No wonder I want to return to my work in London."

That far away? Why did that idea bother her? She had just met the man. Those thoughts she must squelch. They led to disappointment and pain.

"When you get ready for a tour of the clinic, you come on over. I'll be there until five o'clock. Better yet, why don't we just let that wait until in the morning?"

"Thanks for your help and for letting me borrow your shoes. And of course for the ride."

He grinned. "My pleasure."

It had been hers as well.

CHAPTER TWO

DRAKE LOOKED UP from his paperwork when the door of the clinic opened early the next morning. He saw Trice's blond hair before the rest of her. His heart did a little dip and jerk before it settled. Something about the woman charmed him. Why here and why now? He needed to keep his interest under control. There wasn't time for them to get involved. It wouldn't be fair to either of them if they did.

"Good morning," he offered as she closed the door. He pushed away from his desk that sat in the small area doubling as a waiting room.

"Hey." She looked around the area as if taking in all the details.

"How'd you sleep last night?"

"Good," she said as if in afterthought, her attention still on the space.

"I'm not surprised after the day you had." He stood. Once again she was dressed in a vivid colors. Her shirt was sunshine yellow, paired with jeans. Her hair was pulled on top of her head and bound by a piece of cloth the same shade as her shirt.

She fingered the sign-in clipboard. "I appreciate the coffee and pastry. That was very sweet of you."

"I just figured after the day you had yesterday, you wouldn't bother with buying food."

"It was nice to wake to a hot cup of coffee waiting. Along with the wake-up knock."

His chest expanded with pleasure. He felt overly pleased she had been glad to receive his gift.

She looked down the hall. "I'm ready for the tour. I need to appear professional when someone comes in after yesterday. I should try to redeem myself some."

"You have nothing to be embarrassed about." He had to have fielded at least thirty questions about that show. On the phone and in person.

"I think that piggyback ride through the middle of town might qualify under embarrassment. Too close to a Lady Godiva ride."

He chuckled. "Except you were fully clothed."

She grinned. "Thank goodness."

Drake liked she didn't take herself too seriously. He enjoyed this woman a little too much for comfort, especially since he would be leaving. His life had been on hold for so long that it felt good to trade quips with Trice. "How're your feet this morning? Do I need to give them a look?"

"They are fine. Thanks. I'm even returning your shoes." She held them up by two fingers.

"I would tell you that you are welcome to keep them, but I would suffer the wrath of Luce."

She smiled. "We can't have that."

He took the shoes from her. "Come on. I'll give the half-cent tour while I put these away. You'll know where they are if you need them."

"You're not taking them with you when you go?"

He started down the hall. "Nope. I won't need them. It's much warmer in London."

"So, what is it you're going to London for?" She slowly followed him, stopping to glance into the rooms they passed.

"I'm returning to surgery training." Drake could hardly wait. He had missed it.

"What happened, you didn't finish?" She sounded genuinely interested.

"Dr. Johannsson died. I returned for his funeral and didn't go back." He just couldn't leave.

"Why not?"

He stopped and looked at her. "After Dr. Johannsson died, the town needed a doctor. I couldn't leave them without medical care. It has taken the mayor two years to find someone to replace me. By the way, why did you decide to come here, of all places?"

"Because I've wanted to come to Iceland for years. I'm also interested in researching HEP."

His brows narrowed. "That answer I hadn't expected. Hepatoerythropoietic porphyria is an interesting condition for an American to study. Why that of all things?"

"Because I carry the gene."

His brows rose. "Really? So your family is from here?"

"My DNA test says Iceland, and other Scandinavian countries by smaller degrees."

"What have your parents told you?"

"Nothing. I went into foster care when I was three. I remember little about my mother and never knew my father. I was too young to remember anything my mother might have said. Which I doubt she did. I understand she died of a drug overdose when I was five."

His eyes filled with sympathy. "I'm so sorry."

Trice shrugged. "It is what it is. Before you ask, no, I wasn't adopted. People want babies, and I was almost six by then. It didn't happen for me. I was passed from foster home to foster home." She paused as if making a decision, then continued, "After I learned I had the HEP gene and it was explained to me how only certain people had it, I then started reading everything I could find on the subject. I made excellent grades, and that led me to medical school. I have a general medical degree, but I'm interested in research as well. I wanted to come here because it offered me a chance to do both."

Drake knew everyone in town and was related to most of them. The idea of not knowing his family was a foreign concept for him. The chance to be alone was part of the appeal of returning to London. Too often they had been involved in his business. "I didn't mean to pry."

She shrugged. "I had often wondered what my background was, and finding out I had HEP gave me a link."

He watched Trice. Her eyes had brightened. Then he understood. "You're looking for some bridge to your family."

"Yes. No. I don't know. I don't think I'll find my grandparents or anything like that, but I am interested in the people who share the disease with me."

The woman became more interesting by the minute. "That sounds reasonable. But patient care can keep you pretty busy around here."

"I can handle both. Patient care will always come first."

He liked hearing that. After all, these were his family and friends.

Trice looked at him. "You're having a hard time giving up being responsible, aren't you?"

Was he that transparent? He hung his head. "A little bit."

"That's understandable. I'm sure I will feel the same way when it's time for me to leave. It's natural."

Somehow this conversation wasn't making him feel any better. "Let me finish showing you around."

The tension in her body eased. "Thanks, I would like that."

"We aren't that busy on a daily basis. There are clinic

days for regular checkups and days for shots. Otherwise there will be those who come in to see you with the usual illnesses. Then there are the emergencies. Which reminds me, I need to call the air ambulance about an issue."

"How are emergencies handled?" She looked around the examination room as if taking stock of where everything was stored.

"I stabilize the patient the best I can. If I can't handle it here, then I call the air ambulance. If the weather is fine, then a fixed-wing plane is dispatched. If the weather is bad, which is usually in the winter, then a helicopter will be used. In the worst-case scenario, a coast guard helicopter will be sent."

Drake couldn't help but be proud of the little clinic. He had made a number of improvements during his time. "Come along this way."

She started up the hall toward the front. "I did notice you have a couple of beds here where people can stay overnight."

"I do, but that happens rarely. Most wish to go home, and I stop in to see them." Many times he shared an evening meal with the patient's family.

"So you make house calls?"

"On occasion. I also do a monthly well-child clinic and another one for the geriatric patients. On those days, a nurse flies in to help."

"That sounds straightforward." She wandered into one of the two examination rooms.

He had to give her credit. She was self-assured if nothing else. Or was she just putting on an act. Where did she get all that confidence?

"Until it isn't." He stopped in front of the open door.

She followed him down a short hallway. Doors led off to the right side.

"Back here is a small kitchen, lab and supply room. You're welcome to bring in anything you like and set it up."

"A coffee machine is all I need." She looked into the cabinets.

"Got that, but if you need special beans or flavored syrups, you'll need to bring it. Plain Jane coffee is what I have here."

She looked at the setup. "I never developed a taste for the fancy drinks. There wasn't money for that. It looks like you stay well supplied for medical work. How often do you order?"

"Once a month. Supplies come in by ship. I'll show you where all that information is."

He started back up the hall, speaking over his shoulder. "We have telecommunication with the hospital. If we can't resolve problems here, then the ambulance is called. But as you can imagine, that's only as good as the weather allows."

Trice covertly studied the handsome, tall blond man with a shadow of a beard as he showed her around. His pride for the place was evident on his face. He looked like the Nordic Vikings whose blood ran through his veins. It didn't take much for her to imagine him standing on the front of his long boat, a foot on the gunwale, his hair flying in the wind as he led his men on a raid across the water to England. His chest would be thrust out beneath a breastplate, strong legs holding him steady. Everything about Drake said he was in control of his world.

She didn't need anybody in control of her world. After years of being told where to live and what to do, her life was finally her own to oversee. Now was the time for her to find herself and what she wanted. Where she belonged.

The door opened, taking her attention away from Drake.

A boy of about eight entered, followed by a woman whose forehead was wrinkled with worry. The boy's hand was wrapped in a dish towel.

Drake stood. "What's the problem, Stavn?"

The woman spoke. "Stavn cut his hand trying to open a package with a knife." She glared at the boy. "He knew better. I'm afraid it's large enough to need stitches."

"I was trying to open the package without using my teeth." The boy sounded near tears.

Trice went down on her knees to eye level with the child. "Sometimes those things happen. I'm Dr. Shell. I'm going to be taking Dr. Stevansson's place. It's nice to meet you, Stavn. Do you mind if I have a look? I promise not to make it hurt."

Stavn hesitated, then slowly offered his hand.

Trice unwrapped the rag gently while holding pressure to his artery at his wrist, stopping the flow of blood. "Yep. That's a pretty deep and long cut. You must have been pushing really hard on the knife."

Stavn nodded, tears glistening in his eyes.

"Then I guess we better get you into an examination room and stitch that up." Drake directed Stavn and his mother down the hall. "Take the first room."

Trice accepted the hand Drake offered her. He pulled her to standing with seemly little effort.

"One of us better go make some pretty stitches." Trice grinned.

He left her to follow their patient. "I'll get the supplies while you settle Stavn."

Trice entered the examination room. "Stavn." Trice pulled a couple of plastic gloves from a box on the counter and tugged them on. She then rolled a small stool over beside the boy, who sat on the gurney. "May I see your hand again?"

The boy was quicker to let her see it than the last time.

She turned his hand over, palm side up. "Dr. Stevansson and I are going to clean it, then stitch it closed. Do you know what I mean by stitching?"

He nodded. "Yeah. Like my mother sews up my pants when I tear a hole in them."

"That's exactly right. We'll make it so it'll doesn't hurt. If it does, all you have to do is tell us, and we'll give you more medicine. There is one more thing you should know. We will have to give your hand a shot, so that might hurt for a sec. Then it'll be gone. You can hold your mother's hand, and it'll go by real fast."

Drake entered the room with a handful of supplies, making the space even smaller. He had a way of doing that. He looked at her. "You stitch and I'll bandage."

Was he testing her? "Sure." Her attention went to Stavn. "Is that okay with you?"

The boy agreed.

She took Stavn's hand once again. "I need a pan and saline."

Drake handed her the bottle. He held the pan under Stavn's hand.

She opened the bottle top. "We're going to pour this liquid over your hand. We have to wash it out really good."

Stavn sat still and rod straight as they worked. Done, Trice picked up a towel and patted the area around the wound dry while Drake set the pan aside.

"All right, let's see what we've got here." Drake pulled back the cover of the suture kit. "Stavn, if you start to feel sick in your stomach, please tell us."

His mother said, "He has a pretty strong stomach."

"Famous last words," Trice mumbled. "All right, Stavn, I need you to lie on the table. Your mom can keep holding

your hand, but she should move to the head of the bed."
Thank goodness the mother followed her advice.

Trice helped Stavn lie on the table. "I want you to look at
your mother. I have to give you that shot we talked about.
It will only hurt for a second. It's important you be really
still. After that, you can watch if you wish. If not, then look
at your mom."

Drake handed her the syringe with the local anesthetic.

"Okay, here we go. Stavn, tell me what you like to do."
She inserted the needle. "Do you like to ride a bicycle?"

The boy grunted a positive sound.

"I do too. I like to ride a mountain bike. I was sad when
I couldn't bring one with me on the plane."

"I have a mountain bike too." The boy perked up.

Trice finished deadening the area. She touched around
the spot. "Can you feel this?"

"No." The boy sounded unsure.

"Good. You are being so good. Dr. Stevansson, what kind
of thread would you go with for a boy as strong as Stavn?"

Drake acted as if he were giving the question a great deal
of thought. "I would select the heavier thread. He needs to
have it really strong."

Thankfully Drake caught on to what she was doing. Putting the child at ease. "I agree."

Stavn glanced at his hand, then back at his mother.

Trice went to work stitching first the inside of the wound
and then the outside. "Almost done." Two stitches later, she
rolled back from the table. "You can look now."

The boy lifted his hand for a second, then put it down
again.

Drake stepped forward. "Why don't you sit up while I
bandage that for you?"

Stavn moved to the edge of the table.

Drake removed gauze from a package and made quick work of wrapping it around the boy's hand. He then secured it with plastic-covered tape. "This should keep it dry. I don't want you getting this hand wet. Ask for help when you need it. I would like to see you back tomorrow for a check." Drake looked at her. "Don't you think a day out of school is deserved?"

"I do." Trice smiled at Stavn.

The mother said, "Thank you. Both of you."

"You are welcome, Mary. I'm sorry. In all the excitement, I failed to introduce you to the new doctor. This is Beatrice Shell. Mary Leesdottir."

"Nice to meet you. Please call me Trice. Sorry we had to meet under these circumstances." Trice placed her hand on the boy's shoulder. "You have a brave son. Maybe show him where the scissors are so he can use them to open a package next time."

The mother smiled and nodded as she ushered Stavn out the door.

Drake turned to Trice. "I'm feeling good about leaving the clinic in your hands. You were excellent just now. You put Stavn at ease, and I've not seen better stitching." His grin grew. "Except maybe mine."

"Thank you for the seal of approval." She had to admit she liked having it.

Two evenings later, Drake rested in his recliner, half watching TV and half reading a book. Yet his thoughts were of Trice. She had been amazing with patients young and old over the last few days.

Stavn's injury hadn't been that extensive, but after Trice's help, Drake had complete confidence she would know how to handle whatever came her way. He shouldn't be spending time worrying about the clinic since he was the one who had chosen to leave. Trice had clearly made that point. To his great irritation.

The people in Seydisfjordur were no longer his responsibility. Despite his desire not to feel any responsibility, he did. That's what caused him to agree to step in when Dr. Johannsson passed away. Drake had had no intention of being here this long. He had been on his way to becoming a great surgeon. All his colleagues had said so. He'd done his part to help his home village, but now it was time to go.

With his parents having moved across the island, and his brother and sister there as well, there was no need to remain here. Drake only anticipated returning for short visits to see Luce, but he hoped one day soon she would agree to live with his parents. He could possibly return after completing his training, but that wasn't guaranteed despite the need for a surgeon in Seydisfjordur.

He had learned that quickly. While at university, he had enjoyed much of what a larger city offered. Returning to Seydisfjordur had been more difficult than he anticipated. Finding a wife, having a family were more problematic in the remote area. And even if he did find a wife in the city and wanted to move back, she might not agree.

He'd learned that the hard way when he brought a woman he was serious about home. At the time he had been considering returning. Dr. Johannsson had been encouraging him to take over the practice. His girlfriend hadn't enjoyed the flight, didn't like that there were no serious shopping places, and hated the outdoors. That was all before she saw the area in the dead of winter. Their relationship soon ended with her red-faced, snarled remark: "Nothing would entice me to ever live here!"

The subtext was, she didn't love him enough to consider

it. That mistake he had no intention of repeating. He would take no chances. In London he could be a part of a practice, find a wife and settle down and be able to do surgery. He wanted to fulfill his dream, honor his grandfather, yet Seydisfjordur still pulled at him.

When the town needed the medical care he could provide, he had put his life on hold for them. Now that Trice was there, it was time for him to return to his training. Something that would give him a chance to help a larger number of people. Still, guilt ate at him when he thought of leaving.

He couldn't have it both ways. The discussion had been made. He would leave in little more than a week.

The next morning at the clinic, he called, "Trice, come up front when you're finished. I'll show you how to access charts on the computer. I also need to take you out back and show you how to handle the generator. It can be temperamental."

"Be right there." A few minutes later she approached the desk.

He stood and started toward the door. "We need to go outside to the back of the building."

She joined him.

They exited into the bright mid-day sunlight. The sight of the fjord and the mountain surrounding him always grabbed his attention. To Trice he said, "Tell me how you are planning to go about this research you have in mind."

"Is there a problem with me doing so?" Her tone had an edge to it as she stepped over the uneven ground.

"No, I was just curious."

"I'm particularly interested in the long-term effects HEP has on people. Studies have been done, but I believe there is more to learn. While I am here, it's the perfect opportunity to do research and write a paper. I would like to start by looking at files and then interviewing people."

He stepped up beside her and took the lead. "Files shouldn't be a problem. People might be more of one. I could help with that. Pave the way a little. Maybe I can get them to open up to you some. I know a few people who have had HEP and a couple of children. I'll need to speak to them before I share their names with you."

Her eyes brightened. "I understand. I appreciate any help you can give me before you go."

He stopped in front of the generator. "Come to think of it, there's a community event tonight. It would be a good way to meet people, to get to know them before you start asking them questions. If they interact with you some socially, then they'll be more likely to share."

Her look met his. "Is that how you are too?"

"I can be. Is there something you want to know?" He had the feeling she saw more of him than he wished.

She eyes narrowed when she angled her head to the side in thought. "I'm good for right now, but maybe I'll have something later."

"Okay. I'll honor that." Enough about him. They needed to get back to what they were doing here. "About the generator."

Fifteen minutes later after he'd explained the work of the machinery they head inside. "About tonight. Do you want to go?"

Trice smiled as if pleased with the idea She pushed the door open. "Of course. This will be my home for at least a year."

"If not more." She could get stuck here just as he had. Another doctor might not agree to take her place.

"Like you did?"

"Yes. If you are called to medicine, it is hard to pull away when you are needed." *Especially when you know the people. When it is home.*

Trice met his look. "You're doing it."

He followed her inside. There was a note of accusation in her voice. He didn't like it. "I am, but I put my surgery career on hold for two years."

She looked over her shoulder. "Why is doing surgery day in and day out so important? You already have the skills. A practice. I bet you have gotten to use your skills here."

His jaw ticked like it had earlier. Who did she think she was, questioning his decisions? "I have, but mostly I've done general medicine stuff. Earaches, gout, and stitches, as you know. If I finish my fellowship, I can return to Reykjavík if there is a position in the hospital. Most of my family is on that side of the island now. Except for Luce. At least it is less than an hour away. I need to go if I'm going to, because they aren't going to hold my spot in London forever."

"Then I guess you have to go."

"You make that sound like a bad thing."

She shook her head. "It isn't bad. I just think you don't know your value here. But I shouldn't be convincing you to stay." She huffed. "If you did, I would lose my job."

He closed the door with a thud.

"So, are we on for the community center tonight?" Drake hoped she said yes. For some reason, he wanted to escort her.

She turned to face him. "I understand communities here are big on the folk arts."

"We aren't so much this time of the year. Tonight is a special occasion, but in the winter months, when it stays dark for so long and snow is falling and the cruise ships don't come, it's our opportunity for some culture and just getting together."

"Sounds like fun." Trice smiled.

"I'll pick you and Luce up at seven then."

"We could just meet you there."

He shook his head. "Not on your life. Luce would have my hide if I didn't escort you both."

"I wouldn't want to be the cause of that. I wasn't planning on working tonight, so I'd best let you walk us over." Trice had a grin on her lips as she headed down the hall.

Drake chuckled.

Trice turned the corner of Luce's house just as Drake did.

"Oof."

Strong hands cupped her upper arms, holding her in place. "Sorry to almost bowl you over. I was afraid I was running late."

Her heart jumped just being close to Drake. Why did he appeal to her so? It couldn't possibly be the fact he was good-looking, strong, intelligent and likable.

"Good evening," he said in a low, sexy drawl. "Are you ready for this?"

She backed away, smiling. "I'm not only ready. I'm looking forward to it."

"You're a brave woman. That Nordic blood in you is coming out."

Trice searched his face. "Are you talking about the town scaring me off?"

His face turned serious. "Maybe it should."

What did he mean by that?

He stepped back. "You look nice."

She couldn't help but blush. Her effort to impress him hadn't failed. The dress she had picked out was a lime color and went almost to her ankles. A tie of the same color encircled her waist. Dress boots in tan covered her feet.

"Different boots, I see."

She put out her foot and turned it one way, then another. "These are broken in."

"Good to hear." He pursed his lips and nodded.

"I'll have you know I'm wearing my other ones every night to break them in too." She threw her shoulders back proudly. "With heavy socks."

"I'm surprised you even put them back on your feet."

She met his gaze. "I'm not easily defeated."

"I'm learning that." Drake looked rather pleased with her statement.

"I want to get them wearable so I can explore some more. I haven't really had a chance to do much of that. A good hiking trip would be fun."

"You should take some time while I am still here. You have been staying close to the clinic. We have been pretty busy, but I think most of the people who have come by the last couple of days weren't as sick as they were interested in meeting you."

Trice met Drake's look. He had such beautiful eyes. "It was nice to meet them. I hope to meet more tonight."

"Are you two going to the meeting or standing there all evening?" Luce's gravelly voice said from behind Drake.

Trice and Drake stepped back from each other.

Drake spoke first. "We were just on our way to get you."

The older woman harrumphed. She stood there with her purse on her arm, a little hat on her head and a shawl across her shoulders.

"You look lovely, Luce." Drake kissed her cheek.

"Don't you start trying to flatter me, boy," the older woman said, but she grinned.

He put his hands over his heart. "I wasn't trying to flatter you, Luce. I was telling you the truth."

"Let's go before all the good chairs are taken," the woman grumbled.

"Come on." Drake offered his arm to his grandmother. "Let's get you to the community center."

A number of people entered the low block building ahead of them. They trailed behind them. Luce left them to join a friend. She and Drake found seats on a row about halfway up. Trice couldn't help but be excited about the coming program. This was a new adventure as far as she was concerned. She had a sense of being part of the community.

After all, she would be living here. This would be her world for the next year. She was already starting to fall in love with the place. It would be different in the winter months, but something deep down in her felt like it didn't matter what the weather was. She had found her place. This might be home. Was she jumping on the idea too soon?

She glanced at Drake. Or could it be someone who made her feel that way?

Trice enjoyed working with him. He was methodical and thorough, doing his job with a smile on his face, which indicated he loved his profession. She could see Drake's skills as he took care of his patients. He had capable hands. Drake would make an excellent surgeon.

But she would miss him. She suspected the entire town would. Those weren't emotions she should be having or encouraging.

CHAPTER THREE

TRICE SAT STRAIGHTER at the sound of the guitar tuning. A group of people had settled on the stage. They looked as if they might be a family. The children were around the ages of ten and twelve. Everyone clapped, then quieted.

Trice shifted in her seat and clasped her hands in her lap. She must calm her nerves. Her hands trembled slightly. Oddly she felt a part of these people, included. Something that had rarely happened while she was growing up. She'd been lucky if she had spent over a year with a family until she was fifteen. Even with her last family, she had always been an outsider.

Drake leaned toward her. "Everything all right?"

She nodded. "Everything is wonderful."

He studied her a moment, then smiled.

She needed to appear confident in front of him. His support would be needed to get the village behind her.

"Hey." Drake placed a hand over hers for a moment.

"Yeah?"

"You'll be fine tonight."

For the next hour, they listened to the group play. The notes they could coax from their instruments were amazing. Their fingers would fly over the strings at times. Trice sat enthralled. More than once, she found herself tapping a toe.

When the concert was over, the crowd stayed for a pot-luck dinner.

Drake stood. "Let's have something to eat before they push back the chairs and tables to dance."

Dance. She hadn't expected that. Trice didn't consider herself a dancer.

They filled their plates with food stationed on two long tables.

"I didn't bring anything." Trice didn't want to look to the town as if she wasn't the type to do her share.

"Don't worry about it this time," a woman behind them said. "We will expect you to bring food next time. By the way, I'm Birta Atlasson. I heard how good you were with Stavn. I'm his aunt."

Trice said with true pleasure, "It's nice to meet you."

The line moved, and the woman's attention was caught by someone else.

Trice and Drake returned to where they had been sitting to eat. He went to get them drinks.

Returning, Drake handed her a cup. "Did you enjoy the music?"

"I did. I've never really done anything like this before. I'm enjoying it." She was too aware of him sitting close to her. The amount of attention Drake gave her both thrilled and disturbed her. Did the others notice? Maybe he was just being nice because she was new to town?

With everyone finished with their meal, the tables were pushed to the walls. Chairs circled the room. The family who played earlier returned to the stage. The rest of the crowd was invited to dance.

Trice touched Drake's arm. "I see Stavn and his mother over there." She indicated across the room. "I'm going to check on how his hand is doing."

Drake nodded and turned to speak to a man who had walked up.

Trice crossed the room, smiling at people as she went. Many returned her smile, but no one stepped out to introduce themselves. "Hey, Stavn. How's your hand today?"

He grinned when he saw her. "Look, I can move it now."

She went down on one knee, making sure her dress was tucked in at the right places. "Yes, you can. Don't get too sure of yourself until those stitches come out."

Trice stood and faced Stavn's mother. "Hi."

"Hi, Dr. Shell."

"Remember, it's Trice."

"Yes, that's right. Trice, I would like you to meet my friends." She introduced the three ladies standing nearby.

Trice had no hope of remembering their names, but she nodded and smiled. She would learn them all one day. She had been nervous earlier, but that had settled down. After a short conversation with the women, she looked over her shoulder to see Drake dancing with a young, slim, dark-haired woman almost his height. They were laughing as they moved.

"It didn't take Marie long to get Drake to dance with her," one of the women said.

"Nope. She will miss him when he's gone," said another.

"I hope he makes it out of town without her following him," the other commented.

Trice chest tightened. Her look stayed with the couple. Why did the women's words bother her? There wasn't anything going on between her and Drake. Trice had no right to feel concern. Yet she still wanted to know if Drake was involved with the pretty woman.

At the end of the song, Drake stepped away from the

woman and headed toward their group. "Ladies, do you mind if I have a dance with Trice?"

"You might want to ask her," Stavn's mom snapped.

Drake's brows rose. "You are correct. Trice, would you care to dance?"

Trice took a step back. "I'm sorry. I don't really dance."

Stavn's mom's hand on her back stopped her movement and gave her a nudge. "Go on. You'll be fine. Drake will show you what to do."

Drake offered his hand. A new tune started, and the floor began to fill up. "Join me."

Still she hesitated. Stavn's mother nudged her again before Trice placed her hand in his. "You better take care of me."

Drake looked her in the eyes. His hand squeezed hers. "I will."

Something about the statement went straight to her heart. She could fall hard for his man who was going a different direction from her. She shouldn't let that happen. No scenario made that look like a good idea. But wouldn't it be okay to act on her daydreams, just for a little while?

Drake placed his arms around her but held her at a distance. "This is an Icelandic folk song. Follow my steps."

She put a foot out when he did. He turned her and she followed. There were awkward steps, but they continued around the floor.

"You are a natural." Drake grinned at her.

"Thanks. I don't feel like one." She worked to follow his movements.

"You'll catch on after you do it a few more times." He turned her and brought her to him.

"I hope so." She missed a step and caught up.

"There will be plenty of men to show you while you are here." His words were flat as he made a move.

Trice wasn't sure she liked that idea any more than the look on his face implied he did.

When the song ended, they went right into a slow song. Drake pulled her closer. She could feel his heat. Her hand lay lightly on his shoulder and was held securely in one of his hands. His other hand lay at her waist. It almost spanned the expanse of it. They swayed to the music.

"You looked pretty popular over there talking to Stavn's mother. Here I was thinking you were nervous about being in Iceland. You have been busy winning friends and influencing people."

"Stavn's mom was kind enough to introduce me around. That was nice of her."

"Did you ask about them knowing anyone with HEP?" He led her to the right.

"No, I figured I'd wait until they got to know me better."

He gave her waist a gentle squeeze. "Smart move. I think you'll do just fine here."

"I already know I like it here." She leaned closer. "That woman you were dancing with is glaring at us."

He started to turn his head.

"No, don't look," she hissed. "I don't want her to know we're talking about her."

"It's just Marie. She's one of the nurses who comes in to help." His tone was dismissive.

She didn't look like she liked Trice much. "I'm going to have to work with her. By the look on her face, I don't think that will be much fun."

Drake shook his head. "You're being silly."

"You aren't the one she's glaring at."

Drake spun her. "You're right. She doesn't look happy."

"I think I'd better go. I don't need any drama in my days or nights. I don't need to step where I shouldn't since I'm new to town."

His grip tightened. "We've gone out a few times, but I have no claim on her or her on me."

"That's an interesting, old-fashioned way of putting things." Trice was trying to make a good impression, not become part of a soap opera.

"But it's true." Drake sounded anxious to have her believe him.

"Still, there's nothing between you and me, and I don't want her thinking there is. I better leave."

He let her hand go, and they walked off the floor.

Marie glided up to them. "Drake, aren't you going to introduce me to the new doctor?"

"Sure. Trice, I would like you to meet Marie Laxness. She will be helping you on clinic days."

Trice offered her hand. The woman took it after a moment of hesitation. "It's nice to meet you," Trice said.

Marie offered Trice a smile that didn't reach her eyes. "You too. I look forward to working with you."

Luce walked up with shawl in place, hat on her head and purse in hand. "Time to go."

"I'll get our coats." Drake left.

"Marie, how are you?" the older woman asked.

"Fine." Marie appeared unsure about Luce singling her out.

Luce's eyes narrowed. "Aren't you here a little early for a clinic next week?"

The other woman looked uncomfortable. "I came early to spend a long weekend with a friend"

"Mmm." There was no doubt from Luce's response she didn't believe that.

Drake returned, handing Trice her jacket. He pulled his on while she donned hers.Soon, she, Luce and Drake were outside in the cool air. They made their way home in silence.

At Luce's door, Trice said, "Good night."

"Give me a sec with Luce, and then I'll walk you to your door."

"That's not necessary." Trice continued on. As she turned the corner, she heard Luce say, "Don't you hurt that girl, boy. You're leaving here."

It had only been daylight two hours when Drake knocked on Trice's door. No sound. She must sleep like the dead. This time he banged on the door loud enough that he was afraid he might wake Luce. If Trice didn't answer soon, he would have to leave her. Relief washed through him at the rattle of the door handle.

Trice opened the door a crack. "Drake, what's wrong?"

"We've got an emergency. Get dressed and bring those boots you've been breaking in. You will need them. Also, the heaviest jacket you have. You got five minutes while I get supplies from at the clinic."

"I'll be ready in four." She slammed the door.

He shook his head in amazement. Trice was tough as nails. He rarely drove his truck, but he didn't have time to walk the distance to the airport. Trice hurried up as he came out of the clinic. She had a black bag with a red cross on the side in her hands.

"Let me have that." He reached for her bag. "Hop in." She did as he requested, and he placed their bags in the back of the truck.

"What happened?"

"There was an accident at Fjaroara Falls. A hiker slipped and fell. Rescue was called. As the rescuer and the hiker were being pulled up, there was a rockfall. They are both injured now. One hanging and unconscious. The other stuck on a small ledge. We are the medical care who could get there the fastest." He pulled into the airport.

"What're we doing here?" Trice tried to keep her voice even.

"We're flying there. That's why we can get there so fast." He hopped out of the truck, going around to retrieve their bags.

Trice climbed out slower.

Drake was halfway to the plane before he realized she wasn't with him. He turned to find her still beside the truck, staring at the plane. "Is something wrong?"

"I don't really do planes, and not small ones." Her voice was so low he had to strain to hear her.

He didn't have time for this. "If you are going, then you'll have to this time."

She looked around. "Where is the pilot?"

"Right here." He touched his chest.

Her voice rose an octave. "You have a pilot license?"

"I do." He started for the plane once more.

She hustled after him. "You really know what you're doing?"

He opened a storage door on the side of the aircraft and placed their bags inside, then closed the compartment. "Yes, I know what I'm doing. You better get in. I'll take care of you."

When she didn't move right away, he said, "Well?"

"I'll go," she announced, sounding braver than she felt.

Drake opened the passenger door and helped her up on the wing so she could climb in. The woman was feather-light but had a will of iron. "Get in and buckle up. I'll close the door for you."

He did so. On his way to the other side, he checked the plane and soon settled in his seat. Minutes after going through the checklist, he had them rolling down the runway.

Trice hadn't said a word or moved the entire time. He'd not had a chance to reassure her, and he felt the tension rising off her in the cockpit. They were in the air and flying steady when he glanced at her. "You know if you open your eyes, you can see this beautiful morning. You don't want to miss this view."

"If I do open my eyes, I'll also see us crash."

He chuckled. "You don't have much faith in me, do you?"

"I didn't mean for it to sound like that." She still had her eyes closed tight, and her hands clutched the edge of her seat.

"I know."

"But I'm scared."

He grinned. "That's obvious. How about trying to open one eye?"

"Oh, my." Her soft sigh a few seconds later had him thinking he would like to do something to her that would elicit that reaction.

"It gets me every time too. Keep your focus eye-level. Don't look down. But look at this land. It's beautiful."

"It is lovely. I don't see how you can leave it." As she became caught up in their conversation, she had eased her fingers off the console and relaxed in the seat.

"You would if you had planned and worked toward being a surgeon most of your life. If you wanted to live where people like Luce didn't have an opinion about what you do. If you would like to buy something and not wait a month for it to come."

"I would love to have people who cared like that about me."

He glanced at her. The vulnerability on her face pulled

at his heart. What he had, she wanted. She had a way of making him see what he would be missing when he left. "I can understand that, but it can get to be a bit much sometimes. Often."

"It's hard for me to even imagine that. Growing up as a foster kid, I never had anyone who really cared enough to offer much advice." A few minutes of silence passed before she asked, "How long have you been flying?"

"Most of my life. My father is a pilot. I learned from him but also took flying lessons. Somebody in town needs to know how to fly. I wanted to learn."

She looked around the cockpit. "Does the plane belong to you?"

"It does." He was proud of the airplane.

Trice relaxed some in her seat. "What will you do with it when you leave?"

"I'll fly to Reykjavík. John, the pilot who brought you in, will bring it back when he can."

"But doesn't it need somebody to fly it once in a while?" Her attention stayed on the view ahead.

"John will use it when he needs it. When you need him to fly somewhere, he'll take you."

"Not in my game plan to do this too often. If you weren't staying and I didn't come here, what would happen with the medical service up here?"

"A traveling doctor would come once a week. There's always somebody in a community who rises to be the go-to person for medical care. Or a nurse might even be persuaded to take the job. Just stay here full-time."

"Like Marie?"

He didn't miss the tight note in Trice's voice at Marie's name. Was she jealous despite him saying there was nothing between him and Marie? He liked the idea. It meant Trice might care. "Yes, like Marie. But she will not stay. She has already been asked." He dropped altitude.

Trice grabbed the seat. "Why're we going down?"

"Because we're almost there." He went to work landing them.

"That didn't take long."

"It never does if you fly, but it would've been a long walk and a longer drive. The roads between here and Seydisfjordur are not that well cared for. There's a short airstrip here. It's the only reason I was called. They knew I could get here."

"I won't be much help in cases like this if I'm not able to fly."

"This trip is an anomaly. You won't be called on for something this far away." He pushed and pulled a few knobs. Then adjusted the flaps.

Soon they were scooting along the runway to a stop. Drake looked at Trice. "I'm proud of you. At least you kept your eyes open."

She glared at him. "You should've been watching what you were doing instead of me."

"You were much more entertaining, and I could land the plane with my eyes closed."

"I'm glad you didn't." She unbuckled. "This was a good lesson. I'm learning to focus on things like the morning sunrise or what I want to do bad enough to try something that scares me."

"You have a point there."

Before he had turned the engines off, a truck had pulled up nearby. Drake climbed out of the plane and went around to help Trice down. She'd managed to open and close the door. Their bags were sitting on the wing. Apparently, she was determined she would be of help and not a hindrance. He liked that.

He offered his hand, and she jumped down to stand beside him.

"Stevansson?" asked the truck driver.

"Yep. And this is Dr. Shell."

"They're waiting on you up at the falls." The man pointed up the valley.

"We're ready when you are." Drake threw the bags in the back seat of the heavy-duty truck. Trice took a seat beside them, and he climbed in the front.

"Tell us what's going on. All the information I got was I was needed for backup. That a rescuer was injured along with a hiker."

"The hiker stepped over the rail before daylight, as they do when they want to get the just-right sunrise picture, and hit a slick spot and went down. Thankful he hit a ledge. Rescue was called. They went after him. On his way down, his large body caused a rockfall. Now there are two injured men. One with a head injury and the other with a broken leg. We need to get them both up. Let you do what you can before we get them out of here. A storm is coming in, and we're not sure a helicopter will make it in time. Your accessibility to a plane was why we called you. There was no time to wait. We've got to get these men out."

Relief washed through Trice as her feet settled back on the ground. When Drake had driven up to the plane, she'd thought her body would refuse to get in it. She had barely made it flying into Seydisfjordur. But she had to go. She and Drake had people needing their help waiting on them. If this was the best way to get there, then she'd have to make it work. It would have been nice if she could have kept her fear from Drake, but he'd seen it right away. He'd left her no choice but to admit to it.

He had managed to coax her to open her eyes and control her breathing.

After she had gotten over her initial fear of flying and being in such a small plane, she'd started to enjoy it. It had been reassuring being in Drake's hands. It calmed her nerves enough to at least enjoy part of the view. The beauty of the countryside in the early morning took her breath away.

This was a lifestyle she would have to get used to during the year ahead. She had wanted to come to Iceland, to find herself and her heritage. She couldn't close her eyes to that or her job responsibilities. She had to step up and do what must be done.

Now they were barreling down a narrow paved road. Ten minutes later, the man driving came to a neck-jerking stop and hopped out. She and Drake followed after grabbing their bags. He took hers from her as they started toward the group standing near the edge of the falls. Water rushed nearby with a deafening roar, creating a mist that filled the air and blew toward them.

Trice shivered. This wouldn't be much fun. But staying warm and dry would be a problem for later. Right now, the injured men were the worry.

The driver joined the group of other official-looking people. The circle opened when she and Drake approached.

Now it was time for a serious discussion. The hiker and the EMT had already been in the ravine for hours. Not only the injuries but the elements were working against them. Daylight helped, but the dark clouds gathering would not. They must be brought to safety right away.

"I'm Dr. Stevansson, and this is Dr. Shell. What can we do to help?" Drake asked.

"Glad to have you here." The man looked at her. "Both of you. We have one with a head injury hanging nine meters down, dangling from a line, and another with a possible broken leg. The rescuer, the best we can tell, is unconscious, and the one with the broken leg is another eight meters below him on a ledge. He has little mobility. We have to get some medical help down there, but the space is small. We need no more rockfalls. The conditions are wet and slippery. We're trying to work out the logistics now."

Trice said without thinking, "I'll go."

CHAPTER FOUR

DRAKE COULDN'T BELIEVE what he'd just heard. He along with the group turned and looked at her.

"Trice, I can't let you do that."

"It's not for you to say. I have some rock-climbing experience. I have the medical knowledge, and I am the smallest person here. I have to go."

Drake could do nothing but glare at her with his heart in his throat.

"Are you sure about this?" one of the men asked.

Trice squared her shoulders. "No, but I don't think there's a choice. I can do some quick triage easement and treatment if necessary, and then you can bring them up."

One of the rescue men, after crossing his arms on his chest, said, "I do appreciate your offer, but I don't think you are qualified, and we certainly don't need a third party down there making matters worse."

Drake watched in bemusement as Trice crossed her arms over her chest, too, and glared at the man. "And if you had a better plan, I think you would be executing it by now."

The man closed his mouth with surprise as if dumbfounded. He blinked.

Drake decided to intervene. "She has a point. We need to get these men up and to help before this storm rolls in."

The man shook his head. "Okay. I don't know that I have a choice. I'll get the harness."

Drake turned his back to the others and pulled her around to face him. "Are you absolutely sure? You've only been in Iceland for a week."

"I'm sure. If I don't do it, who will?" She met his look.

Drake didn't have an answer.

"I know rock climbing. I'm not afraid of heights, and I certainly know medicine. More importantly, I'm the smallest and lightest person here. That makes me the most qualified."

She had a point, but he didn't like it. "But you don't like flying."

"That's different. But we can argue about that later. Don't we want to get these people out of there safely and with as little additional injury as possible?"

Drake shook his head. "I still don't like the plan."

The mountain rescuer returned with harness and rope in hand.

"You don't have to like it to go along with it." She turned to the man.

As the rescuer rigged her up, Trice said to Drake, "Talk this through with me."

That statement told him Trice didn't feel as much bravado as she tried to show.

She didn't wait on him to begin. Her look implored him. A flash of fear went through her eyes. "Explain exactly what I need to do. I can perform the medical assessment with no problem, but what else should I look for? If those guys have been down there for hours, they'll need blankets, even heat packets to put inside their jackets to warm their cores."

"Are you finished?" Drake asked the rescuer doing her harness.

He nodded.

"Give us a minute, please?"

The man walked away.

Drake's hands went to her shoulders, and his look met hers. "You've got this. You'll be lowered slowly. Keep your feet and hands against the rock. I'll make sure you have some gloves. You will assess the injured rescuer, then see that he gets up to the top safely. Then you'll have to go back after the man with the broken leg."

"I'll need my bag."

"I will see that it is sent down to you. Along with splints and supplies." He placed a small earpiece in her ear. "Through this, you can talk to me the entire time Tell me what you need. You'll be able to hear me too. Now, how are you doing?"

"You will be there with me?"

"I'll never leave you." That wasn't exactly true. He would be leaving her in a few days. But for now, he was here for her.

Trice walked toward the edge of the cliff with Drake beside her.

She put out a hand, stopping him. "Don't go any closer. I don't want you to slip. You need to be tied off." She had been secured to a truck winch. The rope stretched across the ground.

"I don't like this plan at all." Drake's mouth went into a tight line.

"I'll have this over and done before you come up with another way, and you know it." She reassured him as well as herself.

His look bore into hers. "You be careful. I'll be right here waiting."

Trice stood in front of Drake as he switched on the light attached to her helmet. "You are going to need this."

"Step back a little bit," one of the rescuers called. "You're getting mighty close. We don't need to have another person down there."

Trice nudged him back. "He's right. It's slippery here. If people—" she gave him a pointed look with a forced grin "—would read the posted rules, then there would be no need for us to do this."

He returned her smile. "Point taken." He walked to a safe distance from the edge.

She looked at him. "Any other ideas or suggestions?"

"Other than I wish it was me going?"

Was he really that worried about her? "I'll be as quick as I can. I promise."

All her worries and fears went out of her head when he approached again, cupped her cheek and gave her a long look. For a moment, it crossed her mind he might kiss her. Then he said, "Be careful."

She blinked. "I will be."

Two of the rescue team who were tied off joined them. She gave Drake a last look and walked to the edge with the men.

Trice leaned back, holding the rope between her legs with one hand behind her back and the upper part of the same rope with her other hand, bracing with her feet against the stone wall to rappel down the cliff. She glanced below at the boulders and water rushing over them. This was nothing like rock climbing in a gym. She swallowed hard.

Drake's voice came in her ear. "You got this. Slow and easy."

It was good to hear his voice. He had a nice one. She let out the breath she had been holding. "Okay."

"How far away are you from the first man?"

"You can hear me?"

"Yes. The radio has an automatic mic."

"Oh, okay. He is about twelve feet from me…uh… I mean four meters from me now. He's just hanging there. I see no movement."

"Trice, where did you learn to rock climb?"

She moved slowly down. "In the gym of the university. I did it for exercise. Who would have thought it would have paid off like this?"

"You keep surprising me."

A few minutes later, she said, "I've reached him. He's unconscious." She hung there, balancing herself to stay upright. Then she looked down. The man with a broken leg was on the other side of the crevice. "Hey, can you hear me?"

"I hear you, Trice."

"Sorry. I'm calling to the man with the bad leg."

A man below her groaned. Then she heard a weak, "Yes."

"I'm here to help. Stay put. I have to get this man out of the way before I can come after you. But I promise I am coming."

"Hurry," came the man's low response.

"I'll be there as soon as I can." She couldn't afford to hurry. Haste could create mistakes. She fought to turn the man so she could see his face. "Drake, I'm doing the assessment on the first man now."

She pulled the digital thermometer from where it hung on her vest. Running it over the man's forehead, she read the numbers. "He has a low-grade fever. Pulse eighty over sixty. Breathing slow but pathway clear."

Wrapping her legs around the man's knees and locking her heels, she held him close enough that she could lift one eyelid. She shined her light in his face. "Pupils are fixed and dilated."

"Roger that," Drake's voice came back.

"He has a crack in his helmet, but it's still secure to his head. He took a good hit. He's too heavy for me to do much with. Tell the guys to start pulling him up. I'm coming too to guide him between the rocks. I need to stay between him and the sides so he doesn't have further injury."

"But Trice—"

"Drake, there isn't time to argue. Just don't let our ropes get tangled, and pull them at the same speed." Trice turned so her back was to the rock face. She held the man with her legs and arms. "Go slow."

With a tiny jerk, she started moving up. The man moved as well. When she could, she used a hand to push off the wall in an effort to protect her back. She misjudged an out-cropping and took a long drag over a sharp rock.

"Ouch."

"Trice?" Drake's panic-stricken voice came over the radio.

"I'm fine. Let's get this man up." She couldn't worry about her back now.

"Take care of yourself first. You're no help to that guy or the other one if you get hurt. I see you. You're almost here. Slow and easy."

"You shouldn't be so close to the edge." She didn't need Drake falling.

"I'm tied off and lying on the ground. Okay, let go of the man. We can take him from here."

She released the man, and he was slowly lifted past her until he disappeared over the top.

Drake said, "I'm going to leave you to see about this

man. I'll be back soon. One of the rescue people is going to be here with you."

Trice couldn't deny she hated to lose Drake's reassuring voice. She could get used to it. And she shouldn't.

"Hello, Dr. Shell. This is Sunna. I'll be with you until Dr. Stevansson can return. Are you going down again?"

"Please call me Trice. Send me down before I back out."

"Trice, your rope has been released to you. You are free to rappel," the woman's voice assured her.

Once again placing her hands in the correct position, Trice started down the wall again. "Please talk to me, Sunna. Are you from around here?"

"Born and raised. I understand you are from America. Heck of an introduction to Iceland being part of this show."

Trice had made it to where the first man had been. "Mister, I'm coming," she called to the injured man. Her back screamed with pain, but she kept moving. "Sunna, I'm going to have to swing over to the edge in a moment."

"I'm glad you let me know. Dr. Stevansson threatened my life if I let anything happen to you."

Warmth washed through Trice. "Nothing is going to happen to me. Okay, here I go. My rope may go slack. I'll try to sit on the edge." Trice pushed off the wall and almost made the edge.

The man half lay and half sat, his legs stretched in front of him.

Trice spoke to Sunna. "I'm too high. I'm going down a few feet and trying again." This time she was successful. She managed to reach the ledge and sit on it near the man's feet. "Made it."

Trice went to work immediately, telling the man, "We're going to get you out of here as soon as possible. What's your name?"

"Mark Richards."

"I'm Trice. I'm a doctor. Tell me where you hurt." Trice did a visual assessment using her headlamp.

"My left leg. Just below the knee."

"I need to touch it. It may hurt." Trice gently probed the man's leg from above the knee down, until the man winced. "I feel the break. It'll need to be splinted before you can be moved. I want you to lie back and take deep breaths. Sunna, are you still there?"

"Right here."

"Please send down my med bag, a blanket and the splints. Dr. Stevansson should have gotten everything ready. Also send some drinking water. You will need to swing the rope if you can in order for me to reach it."

Sunna responded immediately. "I'll have it down in a moment."

Trice turned back to the man. "I need to get your vitals. Just lie still. This shouldn't take but a few minutes." She quickly went about getting his heart rate, respiration rate and temperature. "Other than a broken leg and being stuck down here, I would say you are a lucky man."

The man grunted, clearly not impressed with her appraisal.

Sunna's voice filled the air. "Trice, the supplies you requested are coming down."

Trice looked up. The light landed on the stuff hanging from the end of a rope. "I see it. Swing it."

She missed the first pass. On the second she managed to snatch the edge of the bag and bring it in. "Got it. Don't move."

The rope slackened. Trice quickly removed the rope and set the bag and splints between the man and the wall, making sure they wouldn't be lost to the rocks and water below.

"Mark, I'm going to splint your leg. Before I do that, I'm going to give you a pain pill, because you'll need it on the way up." She located the pill bottle in her bag and was pleased to find two bottles of water tucked in the bag as well.

She handed both to the man.

"Trice?" Sunna's voice.

"Yes?"

"Everything okay? Dr. Stevansson wants to know."

"All is well. I'm getting ready to put the splints on now." She wasn't used to this much concern from one person. It would be easy to get used to. Especially when it was from Drake.

After placing the splints on either side of Mark's leg, she began to secure them with a flexible bandage. Wrapping the leg until it would not move, she soon had Mark ready to transport.

"Sunna, what is the plan for bringing him up?"

"We're sending down a harness. You'll need to strap him in."

Trice packed the leftover supplies into her bag. "Send it down. I'll need instructions. I'm getting a little punchy, and my fingers are cold. I don't want to make a mistake."

"Harness is on the way down. I'll talk you through it."

A minute later, the harness was in Trice's hands. "I'm ready when you are."

"Here we go," Sunna said. "Hold the harness by the D-ring. Shake it out so all the straps fall. Unbuckle any buckles."

"Done."

"Put the shoulder straps on first," Sunna continued.

"Hold on a sec, Sunna." Trice spoke to Mark. "You'll need to sit up as much as you can." She helped Mark with the straps while making sure she didn't go off the edge. "Legs straps next. Right, Sunna?"

"Yes."

"Mark, this is where we're going to have to be careful. You'll need to lift yourself with your arms so I can reach under you for the straps. Tell me when you're ready."

The man lifted his back and hips. Trice ran her hands beneath him until she found the straps, pulling them out between his legs. He quickly lowered his hips with a loud sigh. Trice secured the lock on one leg and then the other.

"Trice?"

The sound of Drake's voice vibrated through her. "Hey. How's the other patient doing?"

"He should be fine with time. He's off in a helicopter." His voice dropped lower as if they were alone. "Are you all right?"

"I'm fine. Will you help me lift this man up? I'm ready to get out of here."

"I'll be glad to see you." There was a pause as if he might be collecting his emotions. "So, where are you with the harness?"

"I'm locking the breast strap now." Her cold fingers worked with the metal.

"Be sure to pull out any excess in the shoulder straps. They need to be snug." Drake's voice had turned anxious-sounding.

"Done."

"Good. The rope is coming down with the caliper. Clip it on the D-ring. Make sure it closes."

"You have to swing the rope for me to reach it." She caught it on the first arc. "Got it. Clipping it on now."

With the caliper firmly closed, she said, "We're ready down here. Tell them to go slow and easy."

"Will do."

"Mark, I'll be going up with you. Making sure you don't hit the wall. Help me by keeping yourself off the wall using your hands. I'll be between you and the rock."

Mark nodded.

Trice studied him a moment. He wouldn't be the help she hoped for. He'd been through as much as his body and mind could stand. "Mark, give me five more minutes before you pass out if you can."

He muttered something unintelligible.

She was losing him quickly. Scooting along the edge as far as she could, Trice used her hand to steady his leg as he was lifted into the air. "Hold him there. Now bring me up." She swung out to take the man by the arms, making sure she was between him and the rock face. "Okay, we're ready."

They move slowly up. She said nothing for a few minutes.

"Trice? Talk to me."

"We are fine. We'll be there in a minute." She winced as her back brushed the wall.

"You okay down there? That sounded like pain."

"All's good. Just ready to be on firm ground again." She checked her patient. He had passed out. All the while, she could hear Drake giving instructions on what would be needed for the incoming patient.

"I see you."

Trice looked up. She focused on Drake's handsome face. "Hold me here and bring Mark on up. He has passed out, so he won't be any help."

Mark moved above her and was pulled over the side.

She held the man's good leg so he wouldn't swing more than necessary. "Careful of that leg. I did the best I could in the cramped space."

"Looks good to me." Drake sounded impressed.

Seconds later she was lifted over the side and drawn to a safe place away from the cliff.

A woman stood in front of her. "Nice to meet you, Trice. I'm Sunna. Dr. Stevansson is with the patient. He told me in no uncertain terms to help you and see that you were taken care of."

"I don't think that's necessary. I'm fine." Trice's fingers fumbled with the lock on her harness.

"Let me help you with that." Sunna came to stand in front of her.

Trice flexed her fingers back and forth. "My fingers seem incapable of moving all of a sudden."

Sunna reached for the breast lock. "I'm sure they are cold. We'll get you over to the truck and warm you up."

Trice was amazed at how she had managed to go from doing research to rescue work. "I should check on the patient."

Sunna held the harness in one hand and took Trice's arm in the other. "Dr. Stevansson said you would say that, but he wants you checked out, and I am to take you to the truck. Please don't get me in trouble."

Drake's heart had thumped against his chest as Trice came over the side. He only had time to glance at her to make sure she was really there before his attention returned to their patient. He hated that he couldn't go to her, but the man needed to be readied for travel.

He didn't know why he was so concerned about Trice. She wasn't anyone to him, yet the anxiety that ran through his veins screamed something different. His heart had only started to truly beat again when she had safely been pulled out of the falls.

He had instructed Sunna to care for Trice, but he was still anxious to check on her himself.

Moments later he heard her voice beside him. "What can I do to help?"

His head jerked up. "What are you doing here? I've got this." He looked beyond Trice to Sunna, who threw her hands in the air as if she had tried to stop Trice. "You did a good job down there. Go take care of yourself."

"But—"

"He's almost ready to go. I'll give you a full report in a few minutes. I don't need another patient today. Please do as I ask. If not for your sake, then mine."

Trice didn't look happy, but she joined Sunna, and they walked toward the truck he and Trice had arrived in.

Goodness, what had happened to make Trice so resilient? To think he had been worried about her being able to handle the conditions during the winter. She was more than up to it and anything else Iceland dished out. She certainly had more backbone than the other women he'd been interested in. Interested in? Yes, he was attracted to her.

He finished giving his report to the ambulance EMT. The injured man had a long, uncomfortable ride ahead of him. A big, fat raindrop landed square on top of Drake's head. It was time for them to get out of there. "He's all yours, fellows. Good luck on the drive down to the hospital. Be careful."

Drake waited until the man was loaded safely in the ambulance, then jogged to the truck just as it began to rain in earnest. A roll of thunder and a flash of lightning went across the sky as he reached for the back seat door handle.

As he climbed in beside Trice, Sunna climbed out the driver's seat. She had the truck running, and it was warm inside. "I need to go help wrap up and make a report."

"Thanks, Sunna. I owe you one." Drake climbed in beside Trice.

"Me too," Trice said.

Sunna smiled. "You are both welcome. See you around."

Trice sat with her arms across her chest, shaking.

"You need to get those wet clothes off." He shifted to look at her.

Trice glared. "Don't you get in and start giving orders. Especially when you're telling me to take off my clothes."

Drake couldn't help but grin. "There's my Trice."

Her fingers went to the zipper of her jacket but failed to bend enough to hold it. "I'm not your Trice."

Drake studied her a second. He wasn't sure that was true. "Let me help with that." He reached for the zipper pull and opened her coat, then helped her remove the wet material, dropping it on the floor.

Trice picked up a blanket from the seat.

Drake adjusted it around her shoulders. He was as damp from the mist, the rain and lying on the ground as she was, but he didn't acknowledge it. His concern remained on her.

The driver who had brought them to the site climbed in the driver's seat. "I'll see you get to some warmth and food. We really appreciate your help today." He drove along the road they had come on. "The rescue leader has already made arrangements for a room at a resort not far from here where you can warm up and rest."

Trice gave Drake a questioning look.

"There is no flying out of here today." Drake observed the pouring down rain.

Ten minutes later, the driver pulled into a gravel parking lot in front of a small cabin and handed Drake a key.

Drake climbed out and offered his hand to Trice to help her down. "I'll carry you in."

"No, you won't. I've got this."

"You don't even have shoes on." She had taken them off before he'd climbed in the truck. "It'll be much faster my way."

"No."

Drake gave up arguing. "Then I'll get your clothes and boots. Run for the porch."

She hurried away.

Drake grabbed their belongings, thanked the driver, and stalked up the steps to join Trice. "Get the door." He nudged her with a hand to her back. "We need to get in out of this."

Trice yelped.

His look searched her. "What's wrong? Are you hurt?"

"Just a scrape."

"Go inside. I need to have a look." Drake followed her, dropping her wet coat and boots in the floor along with their bags.

"Turn around and let me see your back." He reached for her.

She took a step out of reach. "I'm sure it will be fine. I'll shower and clean it well."

"Like you can take care of something on your back. I'm a professional. Let me judge." He came toward her.

"And I'm not?"

"Trice, I'm too tired and my nerves have been stretched too far for you to be so difficult. Let me see. I can take care of it easier than you can. If you could reach it."

She was impossibly independent. "Let me get out of these wet clothes first. But I don't have anything else to put on."

He pulled a blanket off the back of the sofa and handed

it to her. "Go to the bedroom and take them off, wrap up in this, lie on the bed and call me."

"Do you always make such demands on women?"

He looked at her and quirked his mouth. "You choose now to try to be funny." He took her by the shoulders and turned her in the direction of an open door. "I don't have to make demands to get a woman into bed. Now go do as I say. I'll get a fire started."

Trice disappeared into the bedroom. He went about finding a match to light the fire, which had already been laid. With that done, he removed his boots and stripped off as many clothes as possible while leaving enough to remain decent.

"Trice? Are you ready yet?"

"Yes."

Drake picked up his medical bag and headed for the bedroom. Trice lay on the bed on her stomach just as he had directed her to.

She shivered. "I don't know if I'll ever be warm again."

"You will," he assured her. "Promise. I'll try to be as fast as I can with this. Then you can get in a warm shower. Then come sit by the fire." He sat on the edge of the bed. "I'm going to bring the blanket down just low enough for me to see your injury."

She said nothing as he pulled the blanket away from her body and lowered it. He winced when he saw the angry bruised line down her back, thankful there were no abrasions or open wounds. At least her clothes had protected her some.

"When did this happen?"

"When I was bringing the first man up." Her voice was muffled against the bed.

"Oh, Trice. You should have said something. We could have figured out another way."

"There wasn't one. They were depending on me."

He knew that feeling well. Hadn't he been living that for the last two years? He pulled the blanket up, covering her to the neck, not allowing himself to step out of doctor mode no matter how much he might want to. "You don't have any broken skin. Which is good. I'll let you get a shower. Then I'll put some cream on it that Luce swears by. It has always helped my aches and pains."

Trice said nothing. The soft sound of even breathing was all he heard. She was asleep. Trice was exhausted after her heroic work. He couldn't blame her.

Drake pulled the corner of the bedcover over her, making sure her feet were tucked under. Unable to resist, he brushed her hair away from her face. "That Viking blood served you well."

CHAPTER FIVE

TRICE ENTERED THE toasty warm living room. A fire blazed in the fireplace. She pulled the blanket tighter around her. Her clothes were hung on chairs circling the fire. Drake had been busy and thoughtful.

He wasn't there, but he lingered everywhere, especially in her thoughts. He had shown such tenderness before she'd gone down over the cliff. His voice had held concern when he had spoken to her, reassuring her he was there with her. Rarely had she had that in her life.

The bravado she had shown him had been forced. She had been terrified. Relief had swept through her, and adrenaline had washed her energy away after she reached the truck. She'd done what must be done and hoped it didn't happen again. She had lived much of her life that way. The exception was that this morning, it had affected others' lives. They had needed her assistance, or they might have died.

She fingered her clothes, but they were still damp. Her boots lay on their sides with the mouths open as wide as possible. Drake had thought of everything. Taking a seat on the sofa, she brought her feet up under her. If she was this cold this time of year, how was she going to handle the winter?

A sound at the door drew her attention. Drake entered with a bag in his hand and kicked the door closed with his foot. "Well, hey. I hope you're hungry. I have some soup and sandwiches here."

"I am. Where did you get those?"

"I've been over to the main office and then to the restaurant. I have coffee going here, but would you rather have something else?"

"Hot tea would be nice."

He set the bag down on the table. "It just so happens there's some tea bags here as well, and one electric burner. I'll heat some water. How are you feeling?"

"Better now with sleep and a shower. Have you had either?" She turned to see him better.

"I took a shower. My morning wasn't as physically demanding as yours. You earned the rest." His eyes focused just below her face.

Trice glanced down. The blanket had slipped, showing a generous portion of her shoulder and the rise of one breast. She met his glaze and pulled the material back into place. The look of disappointment in his eyes satisfied in a way she hadn't expected.

He blinked, then turned to the electric eye. "I'll have this ready in a minute."

Drake acted as if he were a little uncomfortable. "Is there something I can do to help?"

"No, I've got it."

She stood and adjusted the blanket, tucking it in so it stayed in place, then pulled a throw off the sofa over her shoulders. She wasn't a fashion statement, but she was covered and warm.

"Take a seat at the table." Drake set out the food from the bag. His attention remained on his actions.

She joined him, taking one of the two wooden chairs at the small table. "Have you heard how our patients are doing?"

"The helicopter landed just before the storm broke. The man with the head injury is conscious but has a banging headache. He should completely recover. The one with the leg injury is still on his way. It takes four hours to get him to the nearest hospital, but at least he could go by ambulance."

"Sorry I fell asleep on you."

"Understandable. Your back thankfully isn't too bad. You will be sore more than anything. I need to put that cream on it before you go to bed tonight to help with the ache in the morning. How are you feeling now?"

"Like I've done all the climbing I want to for some time." She grinned.

He glanced up. "I would imagine. All of that was pretty intense."

"It was. Does the practice take part in stuff like that often?" She took the top off the bowl of soup.

"Today was more the exception than the rule."

"That's good to know. I'm not sure I could take it on if I thought it happened regularly."

Especially if he wasn't there to work with her.

"You certainly impressed the rescue squad. They couldn't praise you enough. I know of two men who were glad you were there."

"And you as well. I can't take much credit for my size, how my mom and dad created me." She hadn't thought of her mom and dad in a long time. Who they were. Where her father was. If he was alive or dead. Even what he looked like.

"Do you know anything about them?" he asked quietly.

"No. You know about my mother. I don't even have an idea who my father was or is." She didn't want to stay on this subject. "I'm hungry. Let's eat before the soup gets cold."

He took the chair across from her. Both started eating with gusto.

"This soup is really good. I was starving. I missed two meals today. One from when some crazy man woke me up before the birds to force me to fly around in an airplane, then stood around looking down as I went into a hole."

He grinned. "I might know that person."

"I thought you might." She enjoyed recovering in this cozy cabin with Drake, a flickering fire, and hot soup that filled her stomach and mellowed her mood. She liked being with him. Too much.

"We're socked in for a while. I found a few board games in the back if you want to play."

She looked at the window. Rain still came down. It only made matters worse, forcing them closer together.

"Will Seydisfjordur be okay without us?"

"I'm sure they are. You do know you won't have to be glued to the place. You can have a life too. Even be gone overnight."

She propped her elbows on the table and studied him. "What do you do with your free time?"

"I go hiking in the mountains. Even in a quiet place, you need to get away sometimes."

"Is that why you want to leave so badly?"

His eyes held a defiant look. "No, it's because I want to use my surgery skills. There isn't enough going on in Seydisfjordur for that to happen. If you haven't noticed, there is no operating theater attached to the clinic."

"Seems to me that based on today's activities, there is plenty to keep you busy. Maybe not with surgery, but certainly being needed."

"Being needed is important to you, isn't it?"

She shrugged. "It is better than no one knowing you are alive."

* * *

Drake averted his eyes. Had she really lived like that? He couldn't imagine not having someone who really cared. Seeing what it meant to her made him appreciate it more.

He had actually noticed how much he was needed. For the first time in a long time, he was rethinking his decision to leave. But he feared that had more to do with Trice than it did with the medical practice or Luce.

Still, he had made his plans, and he wouldn't let a woman he had just met derail them. Dr. Johannsson's death had done that once. Drake had no intention of letting that happen again.

"Will you tell me what it was like growing up here? Do you have brothers and sisters?" Trice watched him with expectation.

"I do. My sister lives in Reykjavík, and I have a brother who lives across the island in a small village. My parents moved a couple of years ago when my father was transferred to Reykjavík. That's when Luce became my responsibility. We've always been close. I do hate the idea of leaving her."

"It's nice to know you have a family. Everyone should have someone." She couldn't keep the sadness out of her voice.

Drake looked at her with sympathy. "You have no sense of what that is like, do you?"

"No, not really. Friendships and working relationships but no true connection."

"As much as I might complain, I'm glad to have my family, here. So many of us from Iceland are connected." He was quiet for a moment. "You know, it just occurs to me there is someone I've heard of living up here that you might like to interview for your research project. Let me make a few contacts, and we can possibly visit her before we leave." His gaze met hers. "If you'd like to? It looks as if we're going to be stuck here for the night. Maybe this evening, we could go do an interview."

"That would be wonderful." She sat straighter. The blanket slipped.

Drake took the chance to enjoy the view. He couldn't help but be disappointed when she adjusted it and curtained his show. The eagerness in Trice's eyes made his heart expand with pleasure. He had put that look on her face. "Let me make some calls, and I'll let you know if we can make the trip. I will also see if one of the women on the rescue squad has any spare pants. I have a shirt you can wear, but the pants, I'm afraid, will swallow you whole. You hang out here, and I'll be back with clothes and information." He grabbed his coat and started for the door.

Trice still sat on the sofa warming herself when Drake reentered with the damp wind and rain behind him. He quickly closed the door. "I wish I could say the weather is better, but it doesn't feel like it. We are a go, and I had good luck with clothes." He held up a bag.

"Thanks for thinking of everything."

"Before you dress, we need to get some cream on your back. I saw you wince a moment ago."

She looked at him. "Are you sure I can't handle it on my own?"

"Please just let me see to it." Drake went to his pack and removed a small jar. He sat beside her. "Let the blanket down." He tugged the material out of the way. This time he did take a moment to admire her lovely back. The urge to kiss the ridge of her shoulder almost overcame him. He closed his eyes, refocused his thoughts. This wasn't the time or the place.

"Hey, what's taking so long?"

"Just opening the jar." He lifted the cream with his index finger and slowly ran it over her spine. Trice's muscles rippled. Her skin was like touching velvet, warm, plush and elegant.

"That feels good." Trice's voice held a deep, sexy timbre that didn't encourage his control.

This was a worse idea than he had feared it might be. He took another moment to gather himself. He would and could get through this.

"All done." With a sigh, he covered her back with the blanket. He quickly stood, moving away. "Go get dressed. We must leave soon to be there on time."

That was all it took to get Trice moving. "Give me five minutes."

She returned wearing a T-shirt with his shirt buttoned over it and tied at her waist. The jeans he had borrowed from the female EMT were snug and hugged Trice's curves in a provocative way.

Drake swallowed hard. He could do this. Luce was right. Trice deserved better than being pursued by someone who had no intention of being around next week. Based on what she'd said, she had experienced more than her fair share of that in life already.

"Let me get my boots on and I'll be ready to go," she said.

"By the way, I was very impressed with your professionalism and your abilities today. Not everyone would've done what you did."

"Sometimes we have to do what scares us because it has to be done."

"Like flying?" He grinned.

"Yeah. And other things."

Was she trying to make a point? "You understand that better than most."

"I guess I do."

"That doesn't make you any less amazing." He stepped toward the door.

"Thank you. Enough about that. Who is this person we are going to see?" She followed him out, grabbing her coat on the way.

"An elder woman. She knows Luce. I visited her when I was a child. She is related to almost everyone around here. She might give you some names of people who have had HEP. Her seal of approval will take you a long way in gaining information."

"She does sound like an excellent person to get to know." Trice pulled on her coat.

He shrugged into his jacket. "Hallveig said she'd be glad to see us in about an hour. I made arrangements for us to borrow one of the rescue trucks."

"You think of everything, don't you?"

"Not everything, but I try to be thorough." That was one of the skills he had been told made him a good surgeon.

"That's what makes you such a good doctor." Trice had recognized it, and she hadn't even seen him with a scalpel.

"Thank you. You are starting to embarrass me. We've had an emotional day, so I guess we're going to brag to each other for the rest of it."

Trice laughed as she ran for the truck. She called over the hood as she climbed in, grinning, "If we don't, who's going to?"

He like the sound of her laugh. It made him want to join her in the humor. "On that note, let's get going. We have a drive ahead of us."

"Is it a long way?"

He settled behind the steering wheel. "Not so much distance. More like windy, steep roads. It just takes time to maneuver."

Half an hour later, Drake drove around another switchback. "I have only been this way once, and it was a long time ago."

"I am not complaining. I'm just glad for this opportunity. Is there anything I should know about Hallveig?"

"She's not exactly the spiritual leader of the area, but she's right up there. She's around ninety years old but doesn't know for sure how old she is. She knows most people around here, and she keeps the old Icelandic ways that have been handed down."

Another half an hour later with it still raining and the wind whipping around them, Drake pulled onto a narrow path and parked on the side of the road. "We have to walk from here."

"How did you even know where to pull over?" She looked around with eyes wide and mouth open.

He enjoyed looking at Trice when she had that bright-eyed, anything-is-possible look on her face. It made him want to see things the same way. "I got very specific instructions. Large tree with rocks in the curve."

"Interesting road signs." Trice climbed out of the truck and closed the door.

He met her at the front of the truck. "They aren't that unusual around here."

"Those I'll have to get used to. So, Hallveig lives all the way out here by herself."

"She does, which makes her that much more interesting. Despite where she lives, she knows everything going on for miles." He caught her elbow when she slipped.

"She must be fascinating."

They made their way down a single-file path with only a few trees.

"Why aren't there more trees?" Trice asked.

"Because they were all cut down and used for building houses and keeping warm through the years of settlement. Now we have a program to plant trees. It's working, but it's a slow process. It will take time to correct what we did in the past. Now we're looking for other ways to have what we need without cutting down trees."

"That makes sense."

They navigated the narrow path between two large boulders. A small house came into view. One that was little more than a shack. No light shone from within.

"I thought you said she is expecting us." She looked at him with a wrinkled brow of concern.

"She is." Drake stood before the door, giving it a light knock. He didn't want to disappoint Trice. The idea of being her hero appealed.

Time passed to the point he feared either Hallveig wasn't home or something was wrong. As he had made the decision to enter to check on her, the door was opened. A twisted, stoop-shouldered woman he hardly recognized stood there.

"I was expecting you." She didn't wait for them to respond. Instead, she turned and started back into the dim room.

The house held only a few pieces of furniture. Just the necessities. The glow from the fire gave off light along with one oil lamp sitting in the middle of a table in the center of the room. The bed was located on one side of the house and the kitchen on the other.

"Close the door and sit." The command came as little more than a growl.

"I'm Dr. Drake Stevansson. Years ago I came to see you with my grandmother, Luce."

"I remember you." She studied Trice as if she were something interesting under a microscope. "And you are?"

Trice stepped forward. "I'm Dr. Beatrice Shell."

"The new doctor."

Trice held eye contact. "Yes."

"Sit." Hallveig waved a gnarled hand up and down. She sat in a well-worn chair near the fire.

"Thank you for seeing us," Trice said. She pulled a wooden chair from the table, faced the woman and lowered herself into it.

Drake chose to stand on the other side of the fireplace from Hallveig.

Trice didn't appear taken aback by the woman's abrupt manner. "The reason I am here is that I am doing a medical study on people carrying the HEP gene. Are you familiar with the genetic disorder?"

Hallveig nodded.

"I understand you know everything that happens around here and everyone." Trice watched Hallveig intently.

She nodded but offered no encouragement to talk.

Trice moved to the edge of her seat. "Do you know anyone who has HEP or has been diagnosed with it?"

The question hung in the air for a minute. "I had it as a child. I recovered with a few scars. My brother had many."

"May I ask you some more questions and draw a small amount of blood?" Trice pulled a notebook out of the pocket of her coat.

Apparently, she had taken a few minutes while he was gone earlier to prepare for the meeting. Trice continued to impress him.

"Questions, yes. Blood, I'm not sure." Hallveig leaned back in her chair and picked up her knitting.

Trice leaned forward, looking earnest. "I could make it just a finger stick, if you would allow?"

Hallveig took so long to nod, Drake worried she might not.

"I would also like to talk to members of your family if I may. I would ask them the same questions I am going to ask you." Trice almost vibrated with her excitement.

Hallveig looked at Drake.

He nodded. "You can trust her, Hallveig."

The woman nodded too. "I heard what she did at the falls."

Drake smiled. How it had reached the old woman all the way up here so fast, he might never understand. "Yes, she was impressive."

Hallveig's attention returned to Trice. "I will agree. But I must ask my family if they agree."

"Will you tell them to contact me at the clinic?"

"I will."

Over the next few minutes, Drake stood quietly by while Trice conducted her interview. Once again, he was impressed by her consideration and scholarly manner. More than that, she was patient and kind with the older woman. Where had Trice been all his life?

"That's it for the questions," Trice announced. "Thank you so much, Hallveig. I only need one more thing. Just a little bit of blood." She pulled a blood sample kit out of her pocket.

Drake grinned. Trice used that pocket like a magician used a hat to do a trick. What else did she have in there?

"Hallveig, may I see your finger?"

The older woman offered her hand.

"There will be a little prick and squeeze." Trice suctioned the drop of blood into a small plastic tube and closed the top. It went into the pocket. She then carefully placed a Band-Aid over the spot. "That's it."

With the efficiency he had come to expect from Trice, she finished with Hallveig. "Thank you so much for doing this."

The woman nodded.

Now it was his turn. "Hallveig, when was the last time you had a checkup?"

"I don't know." She continued with her knitting.

"That long. Would you mind if I had a look at you since I am here?"

"I don't need one." The woman's hands didn't slow down. She wasn't going to agree without some coaxing.

"Would you please do it for me? It won't take but a minute. It will not hurt at all. I'll just have a quick listen to you."

She considered him long and hard, then nodded.

Drake smiled. He looked at Trice. "May I borrow your stethoscope?"

She reached in her pocket, found the instrument and handed it to him.

Minutes later he pronounced, "Hallveig, you are in remarkable health. May we all be doing as well as you."

Hallveig gave him a toothless grin. "I knew as much."

Drake returned her smile, then winked at Trice before handing back her stethoscope. "I bet you did. We must go now."

Trice stood.

"Dr. Stevansson leaves soon," Hallveig stated more than questioned.

"I do." Drake placed his hand on the woman's shoulder briefly. He was no longer saying that with the confidence he once had.

"Hallveig, do you ever come to Seydisfjordur?" Trice asked quietly.

"Once a year. It is a long way for me."

"I understand. I hope you come while I am still there. It would be lovely to see you again. You will talk to your family?"

"I will." Hallveig narrowed her eyes as she looked at Trice once more. "You have the Viking ancestry."

Trice smiled. "I do. Somewhere. Sometime."

"Come closer," Hallveig demanded. The woman took her chin, gripped it, then moved it back and forth. "You are a Bjonsson."

"What?"

Drake said, "That's a last name. We put *daughter* or *son* on the end of the father's name. The Bjonssons are well known in this area. There's even one in Seydisfjordur."

"I am a Bjonsson." The pleasure in Trice's voice said it all. Her world had been made complete. In an odd way, he wished he had been the one to put that pleased look on her face.

"Are you sure?" Trice asked with tears forming in her eyes.

The woman nodded.

"I would never doubt Hallveig," Drake assured Trice with a squeeze on her shoulder.

Hallveig looked perplexed. "She did not know?"

He smiled at the old woman. "No, she did not know. You have made her very happy."

Trice gave the fragile woman a gentle hug. "Thank you."

Hallveig put her hands on Trice's shoulders and looked into her face. "You are good. We will be glad you are one of us."

Drake let Trice exit before him. "Thank you, Hallveig."

"Young man." She stopped him.

Fear washed through him at her tone.

"You do not know your heart or your place. You think on that before you make a mistake."

CHAPTER SIX

TRICE STOOD IN dumbfounded silence outside Hallveig's house. She couldn't believe it. She was a Bjonsson. She had family. No matter how distant. Roots. A history.

Hallveig pronounced it with such confidence. Could it be true?

Drake stood close beside her. "Are you okay?"

She looked into his concerned eyes and gave him a huge smile. "I'm better than okay." She wrapped her arms around his neck. "I have family. Real, breathing family."

His hands came to her waist. "Yes, you do."

"I'm so excited. I can't believe it." She hugged him tighter, then pulled away.

"Isn't that part of why you wanted to come to Iceland, to find family?"

She liked being held by Drake. In fact, she wanted him to hold her more. "It is, but I never really thought I would find anyone that might belong to me."

He chuckled. "We better get out of this weather and back to the truck or you may be too sick to find them."

"Never." She started down the path. "This has been the best day. Do you know the Bjonsson who lives in Seydis-fjordur?"

"I have met him." His tone was flat and dry.

She stopped walking and studied Drake. "That didn't sound very encouraging."

Drake twisted his mouth. "He isn't the most approachable person."

All the air went out of her lungs. "Oh. You don't think he will speak to me?"

"I'm just afraid you might not get a very warm welcome." Drake took her elbow and directed her on down the path.

"I'll take my chances." She would get the man to at least see her. Make him understand how important to her it was to meet him.

They reached the truck. Trice climbed in, shivering.

Drake slid behind the steering wheel, then turned a knob. "It'll be warm in here in a few minutes."

Trice huddled close to the warm air coming out of the vent. "By the by, I'm sorry I didn't even think about giving Hallveig a checkup. All I was concerned about was what I wanted."

"That's what we went for. I just thought since we were there, she needed to be seen. We've had more than a big day. Let's go back to the cabin and get some rest. We'll leave at daylight if the weather will let us. I'll see about us visiting old man Bjonsson when we get home."

That's what he thought of Seydisfjordur. As home. Soon he would have a new home. A new life. A new career. He would prove to himself and anyone else watching that was where he belonged. He would keep his promise to himself and his grandfather to help people. But wasn't he helping people here? Hallveig's words came to mind. *You do not know your heart or your place.*

Trice rubbed her hands together. "You know you don't have to take what little time you have left in town seeing about me. Give me some directions and I will go see him."

Drake looked at her. "I like spending time with you."

"OK, thank you."

"After we get back and see things settled around the clinic, we'll drive up the valley to visit him. I just don't want you to get your hopes up. He's not what you would call a family man. In fact, he has run all of them off that I know of."

"Oh, then he may not welcome me." The idea made her sad.

He glanced at her, then returned his attention to the road.

Less than an hour later and not soon enough for her aching back, Drake pulled into the road by the cabin. "I sure would like to know how our two patients are doing."

"So would I. Would you like to go to the restaurant for dinner and see what we can find out?"

"That sounds good."

Drake drove along a road she didn't recognize, then parked in front of a long building. "Since there's only light rain, we'll leave the truck here and take the path back to the cabin."

"If anybody's learned their lesson about the importance of staying on a path, that's me." She climbed out of the truck, taking a moment to stretch her back.

"I can't say it enough. You did impressive work this morning. Far above what you were expected to do." He held the door for her to enter the building.

"I think it was more about me being scared than anything." She stepped by him to stop in what was obviously the lobby of the resort.

"Many people don't do things because they're scared." A low fire burned in a rock fireplace. He started down a hall.

She joined him. "Are you scared of something?"

"Yeah. I'm afraid of never having the chance to do what I love."

Trice regarded him. "Surgery?"

"Yeah. I am so close to finishing my training." He stopped at the door of a room filled with tables and chairs.

"Why did you go into medicine?"

"Because my grandfather died when there wasn't someone close who could perform surgery. He was too sick to fly, and the road would have taken too long. I watched him suffer. I made up my mind then that I'd become a surgeon so others wouldn't have to watch their loved ones die."

A woman came to show them to a table.

"But if you leave, won't the people around here be in the same situation?" She weaved between tables of people to their spot.

When they had settled in their chairs, Drake leaned over the table toward her. "Leave it to you to ask the difficult questions. No, because I have no place to do surgery, no theater. The clinic would need to be enlarged. There's no money for that."

"I can understand that, but I can also understand the significance of what you do here."

Drake had obviously made up his mind about leaving. It wasn't her place to try to change it. Even if she could. He deserved his chance at his dream just as she was getting hers. Yet it still made her sad to think of him leaving. She would miss him. Too much.

The woman taking their order brought her attention back to the here and now. Their discussion went to subjects more general over dinner. They strolled back to the cabin.

Trice pulled her coat off and hung it up before turning her back to the smoldering fire. "I'm glad our patients are doing so well."

"I am as well. I just wish you hadn't gotten hurt in the process."

She twisted her back. It had eased since they got out of the truck. "It's not that bad, but I know I'll be sleeping on my stomach."

Drake made a noise that sounded like a groan.

She considered him, eyes narrowed. "Are you okay?"

"Yeah. Fine." He didn't look at her. "I should put some more cream on your back. Otherwise, you'll have a difficult time sleeping the night through. I'll build the fire while you get ready for me to do that."

"Are you planning to stay here tonight?"

"I was. Unless you have a problem with it. We are lucky to get this cabin. All of them are taken with the rescue crew and tourists. I can see if I can bunk with someone else if you aren't comfortable with me being here. I promise to be a perfect gentleman."

"What if I don't want you to be a gentleman?" That popped out. Was her subconscious speaking for her now? What would be wrong with them enjoying each other while they could? Would that be so awful? He would be gone soon. She gave him a sideways look to see what his reaction was to that. Had she shocked him?

Drake stopped midmovement to look at her. "Trice, you need to think carefully about what you are saying."

She faced him. "I know what I'm saying. I'm attracted to you. I thought maybe you were to me too."

He looked at her for a moment. Saying nothing.

That was a gamble that didn't pay off. She started toward the bedroom. "I'm sorry. Am I being too blunt? Just forget I said anything."

"Trice."

"Yes." She glanced back.

His voice dropped low. "You didn't misread anything."

She continued into the bedroom with a smile on her lips. A few minutes later she called, "Ready." Trice had slid under the covers to her waist, her back bare. She hurt and looked forward to having Drake's fingers moving across her in a gentle glide. A creak in the floor told her Drake had entered.

"Scoot to the middle some."

She did as he requested, being careful not to show more of herself than necessary.

The bed dipped. Drake sat on the edge of the mattress. "This still looks painful."

"Yes, Mother Hen," she grumbled.

"There's nothing wrong with being careful." He smoothed cream over her skin.

She shivered from the coolness of the cream, or Drake's touch, she wasn't sure which. "Never said there was."

"Yet you're making fun of me."

She considered him over her shoulder. "I do appreciate your concern."

His gaze met hers. It was soft, caressing and enquiring. His fingers journeyed down her back. She quaked. He blinked, and the look disappeared. He quickly stood. "You need to get some good rest. I'll see you in the morning."

She held the blanket to her as she rolled so she could see him. "Where are you planning to sleep?"

"I'll take the sofa. You are in pain."

"But there's plenty of room in this bed."

"You do know what will happen if I do that, and you are in no shape for that amount of activity."

She couldn't let him sleep on an uncomfortable sofa. "Don't make me feel guilty about sleeping in this comfortable bed. You've had a hard day, and you need your rest too." Why was she pushing this? "Look, there's plenty of room for both of us. We're adults. I believe we can control our actions." She hoped she spoke for them both, especially herself. "Don't we have to be up early?"

Drake looked at her long enough that she had become convinced he wasn't going to take her up on the invitation.

"All right. I will, but if I disrupt your sleep or hurt your back for some reason, then I'm off to the sofa."

He headed for the bathroom.

By the time Drake returned, she'd pulled on a T-shirt and settled on her stomach. She was aware of the dip in the mattress as he climbed in beside her.

Drake faced away from Trice, trying not to move until his muscles had locked into place. He would be sore in the morning from trying not to touch her. Sleeping on the floor might have been more comfortable than having a warm woman next to him and being unable to touch her. His life kept taking turns he hadn't expected. And currently didn't enjoy.

You do not know your heart or your place. Those words echoed again. "Trice, about what we were talking about earlier."

"Mmm."

"What do you think we should do about it?" He sure knew what he wanted to do. But he wanted to hear her say it.

"I thought a hot no-strings fling as long as you are here would be superb."

Drake's stomach muscles tightened at the idea. His manhood twitched in anticipation.

"We aren't going the same direction in life," she said. "I don't see either one of us settling down anytime soon. We have plans we want to accomplish. Let's make it clean and simple so that when you leave, we part as friends."

He winced. Had she been so hurt in the past that she didn't want any strings? Her background had made her that way. She had no ties to anything, and his entire life was filled with strings. He had to give her credit. Her fortitude impressed him.

If she could put what she wanted ahead of everything, then he could too. "I like that plan. But not tonight. I want you feeling better and in no pain."

She rolled, and her fingertips brushed along his bicep.

His hand stopped hers. "You rest, and we will talk about it more tomorrow."

"Promise?"

"You can count on it."

Minutes later, he heard her even breathing. She was asleep.

A groan awakened him. There was movement from Trice's side of the bed. She rolled to her back, yelped, then returned to where she had been, releasing another groan.

His hand hadn't touched her skin before he felt the heat. Trice had a fever. He rested the back of his hand on her forehead. It was a high one.

She relaxed for a moment.

Drake turned on the bedside lamp, then went to the main room and retrieved his medical backpack. After finding his thermometer, he ran it over her head from ear to ear. The reading flashing in the tiny screen was one hundred two degrees. He searched for the fever-reducing medicine and shook out a couple of tablets before he filled a glass with water.

Placing the glass on the table beside the bed, he took a seat beside Trice. "Trice, you have a fever. Can you sit up and take some medicine?"

She rolled her head back and forth.

He slipped an arm under her shoulders, being careful not to touch her injury, and lifted her forward.

She moaned and opened her red, glassy eyes. "I was having a wonderful dream. You were kissing me."

He wished he had been. Trying to ignore her statement and his urge to do just that, he said, "You need to sit up and take these. Open your mouth."

She did.

He quickly brought the water to her lips. She eagerly drank. Some of it dribbled down her chin and dropped on her chest. "Finish the water, sweetheart."

Trice did as he instructed.

He dabbed the stray water from her chin with the sheet. "Now, lie back. I'm going to get a cool compress for your head. You'll be fine in the morning."

"Don't go." Her eyelids slowly closed.

"I'll be right back." He hurried to the bathroom, found a washcloth, wet it and returned to Trice.

She lay back on the pillow, her eyes still closed.

Drake placed the cloth across her forehead.

Trice sighed. "Feels good. Back hurts."

"I know, sweetheart. I know. I need to have a look at it. Can you roll over?"

"I don't want to." Her eyes fluttered open.

"Your back won't hurt as bad if you get off it." She muttered something he couldn't understand. "I'll help you." He pulled at the blankets. All she wore was the T-shirt and light pink panties, but he wouldn't allow himself to dwell on that fact. He raised one shoulder and pushed her hip, encouraging her to shift. She moved to her stomach without a noise.

Drake lifted her shirt and winced. The bruises had turned darker. Trice said nothing and didn't move.

"I'll need to check things in the morning. Try to get some sleep." He carefully lowered her shirt. Taking the rag to the bath once more, he ran it under cool water and placed it on her forehead. Trice felt cooler now. Turning off the bedside lamp, he lay down.

Trice took his hand. Her hot breath flowed over his arm. "You're a nice man."

Drake couldn't see her clearly in the dim light. He smiled. Had there been no one who took care of her when she was sick?

"Sorry I woke you." She wiggled next to him.

"Not a problem. Hush now. You need to sleep."

She pushed into his side. "You do too. I'm cold."

Her fever was breaking. He put his arm beneath her neck. She rested her head on his chest. He was careful not to touch her back.

Her lips touched his chest. "Thank you for taking care of me. I wish I felt better."

He groaned. "Trice, don't do that. You are not up to it, and I can't resist you if you don't help me."

She wiggled against his side again and sighed.

Trice had fallen asleep, but that wouldn't be happening for him for a long time to come. He had been trying to keep some space between them, but that wasn't working. Trice had a way of pulling him closer. His fingertips brushed the top of the curve of her hip. He hadn't anticipated being shaken by the instantaneous combustion between them in such a short period of time.

He wanted her. It was time for him to accept that, but he didn't have any business letting himself fall for her. Her back hurt, and he planned to leave in five days. His thoughts had gone crazy since Trice had arrived. No matter what he did, they circled around to her.

That would end when he left. His emotions would settle down again. He'd get involved in his work and adjust to life in London. Would she even want him to stay? If she did, would he be just another person on the long list of people who had let her down?

Drake reminded himself of that idea throughout the night while he held Trice. Somehow, he didn't think it would be that easy anymore. He didn't want to leave Trice alone. And oddly, leaving Seydisfjordur didn't have the same appeal. Luce was right. It didn't seem fair to Trice. Yet he had to. There were commitments to honor. His dream to pursue. Returning to Seydisfjordur had only been a detour.

Trice woke to the warm reality of a hard body next to hers. She lay on her side, and a heavy arm rested across her waist.

A soft snore came from above her head.

She opened her eyelids just enough to look over the plane of Drake's chest covered by material.

Another snore made her grin. She looked up, seeing the dark shadow along his jaw. She really liked his jaw. Her fingers twitched to trace that dark line, but she stopped them. She shouldn't start anything that she wasn't physically capable of carrying through with.

She needed her life to move forward. There was a chance she might find a family member, a distant one, but family none the less. She couldn't become wrapped up in a man who would leave and never look back. That wasn't the type of relationship she wanted or needed. She wanted a sturdy and healthy one. There had been enough partial relationships in her life already. But to spend a few lovely hours in his arms with no strings attached would make for nice memories. "Drake."

His eyelids fluttered. His fingertips brushed the curve

of her breast as he removed his arm. Looking at her, he said, "Hey."

The temptation to kiss him right then grabbed her when his sexy morning voice flowed over her.

"Did you sleep any last night?" He studied her.

She yawned. "Best ever. How about you?"

Drake's warm, caressing look found and held hers. "Best ever. How's the back?"

"Hurts."

"Roll and let me have a look." He shifted, making the mattress dip.

"I don't think this—"

"Trice, let me see."

She did as he said. Satisfaction went through her when she heard the tight intake of his breath. She hadn't bothered to pull the covers up. Her bikini underwear was clearly in view.

Drake pushed her T-shirt up her back in a slow, revealing way. The sizzle in the air made her breath catch. She remained still.

"Trice." His voice sounded hoarse.

She said softly, "Yes?"

"You may want to breathe. I don't want you to pass out." A teasing note surrounded the words.

She rolled enough that she could see his face. "I'm breathing." She took a deep breath, letting it out slowly. Drake's eyes widened and focused on her breasts.

"Trice." His tone matched a father disciplining a child. "I'm trying very hard to remain a doctor here. You are not making it easy. Now stop playing and let me see your back."

She settled on her stomach again, pleasure filling her. Drake struggled with their attraction as much as she did.

"This looks better than it did last night." The tip of a finger ran down the length of her back to the dip of her waist. Cool, dry lips rested a second on the back of her shoulder. In a low voice Drake said, "Two can play the same game."

She rolled to her side. Her gaze locked with his. "Do you really want to play?"

Drake climbed out of bed and regarded her. "I'm leaving. You're staying."

"You didn't answer my question."

"Which one? Do I want you? Yes. You are the sexiest woman I've ever seen. The most amazing one. The bravest. The most beautiful. Hell yeah, I want you."

"You mean that?" Did he really feel that way?

He looked into her eyes. "Every word of it."

Trice slipped from the bed, not caring about the skimpy clothing she wore. Walking to Drake, she put her arms around his neck and kissed him. "Thank you for that. No one has ever said anything like that to me."

Drake gently placed his hands on her waist, but the tension in his body said he held himself under control. His mouth found hers. He pulled her secure against him. His manhood stood strong and thick between them. His tongue ran along the seam of her lips. That was all the encouragement she needed to open for him. Drake invaded with the eagerness of a person thirsty for water. Their tongues tangled. She gripped his shoulders. His hands remained on her waist, but his fingers tightened. How like him to always be mindful of her injury.

She'd been kissed before, but none had been like this one. This went to her soul, captured her.

Drake cupped her butt and lifted. She wrapped her legs around his waist. Her center rested against the stiffness of him, making her tingle with desire. She whimpered. His thumbs slid beneath the elastic of her panties.

A knock on the door stopped any further exploration. Drake's mouth left hers. His heated eyes held want, disappointment and something she couldn't define. He let her deliberately slide down his body.

"I should get that." He stepped away, jerked on his jeans, and headed for the door.

She heard Drake talking to another man but couldn't make out the words. Quickly she pulled on her clothes, taking special care with her shirt, not applying too much pressure to her back.

Drake returned. "We need to get moving. That was one of the rescue squad. They are leaving and wanted to know if we needed a ride to the plane. I told them we would appreciate one. We shouldn't make them wait."

"I'll be ready in ten minutes. Will that do?"

He didn't look at her as he spoke. "That will do. The sky looks nice and clear. The flight home should be smooth."

She shuddered.

Drake narrowed his eyes. "What was that for?"

"The thought of going up in an airplane again." She pulled on her pants.

He pulled on his shirt. "You know, you could hurt my feelings."

She wasn't clear if he was teasing or not. "I don't mean to. It's just that I'm not a big fan of flying in general."

"Or my plane in particular. Yet you jumped at the chance to hang ten meters above roaring water and rocks."

"I didn't jump at the idea. I did what had to be done." Why did she feel the need to defend herself? He'd been there. Knew the situation.

He stepped to her, his eyes predatory.

Would he kiss her again? She would like it if he did.

"And you were magnificent. I was proud of you." He

placed his hands on her shoulders and gave her a kiss on the forehead. "Now to see if you do as well getting home."

She sagged with disappointment when he moved away.

"Do you have everything?" He looked around the room.

"Yep. I didn't come with much."

"You will need your jacket." He pulled it off the back of a chair and handed it to her. "It's time to go home."

She hadn't thought about it, but she was going home. Seydisfjordur was as much her home in a little over a week as any other place she had ever been. "Yes, let's go home."

An hour later, Drake had the engine warmed up and prepared for takeoff. He pushed the throttle forward, and the plane ran down the runway.

As he made movements with his hands and feet that were now second nature to him, he was aware of Trice trying to cover her anxiety. It wasn't working. She held her breath, and her fingers bit into the seat cushion.

"I wish you'd settle back over there. It's a beautiful day for flying." He turned the plane toward the east.

"So you say," she grumbled.

"Look out at how beautiful it is." For some reason he wanted her to enjoy flying.

"I can't yet."

"For a woman who hung over the side of a cliff for hours yesterday, I can't understand why you're so scared being in an airplane with me."

"It's not your flying."

"Thank goodness. Would you like to fly over the waterfall where we were yesterday?"

It took her a moment, but she said, "Yes. I would like to see it."

He made a turn.

"Wow, I didn't mean for you to do that." Her hand gripped his arm.

His look met hers. "I'll take care of you. Now, be looking down, because here it comes."

"Oh, wow."

She let go of him. He missed her touch immediately. "This is one of the most beautiful waterfalls in Iceland."

"Look at those boulders below. I'm glad I didn't know of their size yesterday. You might have had to push me over the side."

He had known. That had been one of the reasons he'd not wanted her to go. "It is deep. This is a wonderful tourist spot, but it has to be respected. It's also dangerous."

"I'm going to read up on it when we get home."

At least she no longer looked terrified and was speaking to him normally. "You might enjoy a book I have about Iceland's history and special sights. You need to visit some of these places if and when you have a chance."

Her face turned eager, eyes bright. "I'd love to read the book. I promise to leave it with Luce to return to you, or I could even mail it."

"You don't have to do either of those. I would like to give it to you." He made a banking turn to the left, leaving the falls behind them. He loved seeing her enthusiasm about what he considered commonplace. It made him see the sights in a different light. With wonder and anticipation. Being with Trice had him experiencing what he'd always known but with renewed pleasure.

"Thank you. That's nice of you. I will cherish it."

He like the idea of her having something that had been his.

They continued toward Seydisfjordur. Drake did a few subtle dips and turns so Trice could see the mountains.

"I love the snow-tipped mountains," she said as much to herself as him.

Drake chuckled. "After six months or more, you may not see them the same way. You'll be looking for spring like everyone else around here."

"But not you. You will be in England with rain."

They had reached the fjord. He flew over the water. Trice's fingers turned white as she held the door handle. The tires touched the runway with a screech, and they rolled toward the building.

Trice released her grip and breathed a sigh of relief. "Were you trying to impress me just now with those maneuvers?"

"What if I was?" He pulled the plane to a stop.

"Why would you?"

He looked at her. "Isn't that what a guy does when he likes a girl?"

Pink spotted her cheeks. "Drake, are you flirting with me?"

He grinned. "About ninety percent of the time."

CHAPTER SEVEN

TRICE CLIMBED FROM the plane as Drake exited the other side. Relieved to have her feet back on the ground, she had still enjoyed being with Drake. She especially enjoyed him flirting with her. And most of all his kiss.

"I know you must be tired. I'll drop you by Luce's and head over to the clinic to see if there's anything I need to do."

"I work there. I should be there as well." She pulled her bag out of the storage compartment.

He grabbed his too and closed the door. "You are a tough person to be nice to. I might have made a few more dips and turns if I had known you could be so contrary."

"You would have done that?" She looked at him with a mock shocked face that included an open mouth.

He shrugged. "Sure. I have already admitted I was showing off some."

She glared at him. "If you were trying to impress me, that wasn't the way."

He stepped closer, watching her. "If I wanted to impress you, how would I go about doing that?"

"I don't know. Maybe by taking me out for a nighttime picnic to watch the stars. Something that was less likely to make my stomach roll."

"Then how about joining me tonight? I know just the

place. And just the sky to find them in. Wear warm clothes and the socks I loaned you."

"Okay. I'll take that dare, or date, whichever you're making it." They started toward his truck.

"I like the idea of a date." A look of satisfaction came across his face.

They climbed into his truck.

She smiled. "I like the idea of a date as well."

Excitement he'd not experienced in a long time ran through him. Just the idea of spending time with Trice had a way of doing that. He made the short drive to the clinic.

They were only there five minutes before they had three patients. They were simple matters of a child with an upset stomach, an older woman complaining of a bad cold, and a man who had a bunion that needed attention. They divided the cases between the two of them and soon finished.

After yesterday's adventure, every problem seemed easier.

Trice hadn't complained of her back hurting despite her discomfort in the plane. When she returned home, she would give it some attention. She had almost finished cleaning the exam room when Drake came to the door.

"Your turn."

"What?" She faced him.

"It's time for me to give your back a look. I saw the way you shifted in the plane seat. You were in pain." He entered the room.

"Not pain. Uncomfortable. I'll look at it when I get home."

"You know you can't reach it if you need to care for it. Now stop arguing and let me see." He stood beside the gurney.

She huffed. "I think you're enjoying this."

He grinned. "I think you might be right. I do like looking at your lovely back, but right now I'll focus on giving a medical evaluation."

She turned her back to him and lifted her shirt.

"You will be glad to know it's much improved. You have a rainbow of colors. You can pull your shirt down now." He stepped away from her.

She did and turned to face him. "Satisfied?"

"With your recovery, yes." He walked toward the door. "I think we have everything settled here if you want to go home. I'll be leaving in a half an hour as soon as I put in the reports."

"I can do those and close up." She didn't want him to see her as a slacker.

"Trice, wouldn't you like to get out of those clothes?"

She looked down at what she'd been wearing for the better part of two days. "Are you saying you would like me to freshen up before you see me again tonight?"

His look remained on her. "I don't think it would hurt either one of us to clean up."

"Okay. I'll go. What time should I expect you?"

He stopped on the way to the office. "Eleven o'clock too early?"

"Wow, that late?"

"It takes a long time to get dark here this time of year."

"I will be ready." The idea of seeing him again made her giddy.

"You sure you're up to it tonight? It can wait until tomorrow."

She was eager to spend as much time with him as she could. "If you're up to it, I'm up to it. I might have another social engagement if we wait."

They both laughed.

"This isn't a place where there's a nightclub on every corner or even a movie theater."

Like he would have in London. "I'd rather look at the stars anyway."

"Then I'll see you in a few hours. Don't forget to wear warm clothes."

She was curious now. "Where're we going?"

"That's my surprise."

Drake was astonished he hadn't seen Luce. He expected her there with her disapproving look. A tinge of guilt filled him. But he was an adult and so was Trice. They didn't need Luce to make their decisions for them.

Still, he suspected she was right. This probably wouldn't end well for one or both of them. He held his head high and walked to Trice's door. Knocking, he waited until she opened it.

"You still feel up to an evening out?"

"You bet. Let me get my coat." She went back into the house and returned with the coat in hand.

He led her to the truck and helped her in. Five minutes later, they were on the road leading into the valley.

"Shouldn't we be going up the mountain?" Trice looked ahead of them.

"You just sit back. I'll do the driving. We're higher than you think."

After another two miles, he turned off the paved road and drove along a gravel one. A few minutes later, she realized how high they had gone, causing her to hold on to the door handle.

Drake glanced at her. "High enough for you?"

She continued to focus on the outside view. "I'd have to say yes."

Drake chuckled, pulling to the side of the road and parking the truck.

"We're stopping here?" She looked around them as if expecting more.

He opened the door and hopped out. "This is where we're going."

"Oh."

He wanted to show her the best of Iceland. She said she loved the stars, and there was no better place to see them than here. The sky would be a regular festival of lights tonight. This was the perfect place to see the show. Once again, he had to remind himself this wasn't some relationship where he had to impress the girl. Yet he wanted Trice to remember him well. Why was it so important that she did?

She climbed down from the truck to meet him. "This view is amazing without stars."

"I think so." He reached in the back for the picnic basket, blanket and plastic ground cover. Closing the door, he said, "This way."

"Can I help you carry something?"

He handed her the blanket. "Up for a little stroll?"

"Sure."

He led the way up a path. They walked for ten minutes until they came to an open field. By this time, it was dusk. They were surrounded by nothing but sky.

"I didn't think it could get any better, but it has."

Drake knew from the sound of Trice's voice he'd impressed her. He liked that idea. What would her reaction be in a little while? It was fun showing his homeland to someone who appreciated it.

"How did you find this place?" she asked.

"It wasn't too hard. My house is just right over there." He pointed behind him toward a rise.

She gave him a suspicious look. "So what was all the driving and walking about, then, if your house is right over there?"

Drake shrugged. "Because it was the easiest way to get to this spot." He kicked a couple of rocks out of the way, then flipped the plastic sheet out, laying it on the ground. Taking the blanket from her, he positioned it over the plastic. In the middle, he placed the picnic basket. From the basket he pulled a candle in a glass. He lit it and set it to the side.

"Join me? The light show will start in a few minutes." He sat with his legs crossed.

Trice joined him on the blanket, a grin on her face. "Why, Doctor, this is impressive."

"I'm glad you like it." He opened the basket and removed food containers, placing them within reach. Last he took out plates, utensils, wine and glasses.

"You thought of everything."

"I tried." He served their plates, handing her one.

She tasted each item. "This is wonderful."

"Thank you." He bowed his head.

She took another bite. "Did you make it?"

"No, I asked Marta at the café to put something together, so I can't take credit for it." He opened a container.

"It's a relief to know you aren't perfect at everything." She ate a spoonful of pasta salad.

"I had no idea you thought I was." He rather liked the idea she believed that. "Now you know my secret." He grinned. "Eat up. We'll need to blow out the candle to really appreciate what we see."

She took a large bite. "I've lived in cities all my life. Until I came here, I'd never really seen stars without some light. I've heard people talk about them but have never seen them myself. I'm so excited."

With their meal finished, Drake took a few minutes to pack their leftovers away in the bag, leaving the wine out. He blew out the candle and lay back on the blanket with his hand beneath his head and legs stretched out and ankles crossed. "Come join me. This is the best way to see the sky."

Trice lay beside him in the same manner. "Oh, wow. I had no idea the sky could be so big."

"Yeah, this I will miss living in the city," he said softly.

"It's just beautiful." She continued to look up.

He admired Trice. "It's not the only thing."

Trice glanced at him to find him watching her. Her skin heated. She looked back at the sky. A pink wave of light emerged. Then a green one. They appeared to dance with each other. A vivid blue joined them.

"Oh, wow. The aurora borealis. I never thought I would ever see it." She couldn't take her eyes off the show in the sky. "I love it." She would remember this forever. She couldn't believe the colors. The view was everything she ever thought it might be. It went on forever.

She grabbed Drake's hand. "You knew, didn't you? Of course you did."

Drake held her hand. "The lights are a regular this time of year when it is clear."

"They look like they are dancing. Or fabric flowing across a black backdrop. Oh, I know. Like those trapeze artists who wrap themselves in silks and twist and turn."

Drake laughed. "And the list goes on."

"I can't help it. They are amazing."

He couldn't stop grinning. "I love watching you. Hearing you express your pleasure."

"Thank you so much for bringing me here. Next to finding out I might have real family here, this is the best." She wrapped her arms around his neck, kissing him. Just as quickly, she pulled away, and her attention returned to the sky.

He nudged her back to him. "Come lie beside me. Rest your head on my shoulder. Get comfortable."

Trice did what he suggested with a sigh and snuggled close. He was warm and hard and felt like security. This she could do for the rest of her life. Except they didn't have that long. And she refused to get attached.

They said nothing for a long time.

"Drake, are you asleep?" She placed a hand on his chest.

"No." The word brushed her ear. "I was just enjoying knowing you were beside me, sharing this beautiful sky."

"We didn't have to do this tonight if you were tired." Still, she was glad they came.

His hand ran up and down her arm. "There's not too many more nights left to do it."

He sounded as sad as she felt. "I don't want to think about that."

Drake didn't respond. Had she said the wrong thing? Yet it was the truth. She should've kept the thought to herself. Now that she had said it, she had no choice but to speak. "I will miss you."

In the dark, she felt more than saw him roll toward her. Her heart plummeted.

Drake placed his large hand on her stomach.

Her muscles rippled. Her nerves shot like live wires in response. "It's been fun getting to know you," she said.

"How's your back feeling?"

Even in the poor light, she could tell his face hovered over hers. "It aches a little bit."

With a minimum of movement, he pulled her on top of him. "Is this better?"

"Much."

"Trice, may I kiss you?"

"Why don't I kiss you instead?" Unable to make out his features clearly, she still knew every dip and rise, curve and angle of his face. Her lips found his without searching. As if pulled to them by a string.

His mouth was firm, warm and welcoming. He took. He gave. He suggested. He accepted.

She'd found heaven.

The tip of his tongue ran the width of her lips. She opened for him. Their tongues danced like the colors in the sky. Blending, meeting and swaying to each other and then away. The heat between them built.

His hand moved to her back. She winced.

His head jerked back. "I'm so sorry. I didn't mean to hurt you."

Trice planned to kiss his lips, but her mouth landed on his nose. "I'm fine."

"I just got caught up—" His voice sounded anxious.

"I can't think of anything more flattering. Kiss me again." She leaned down.

His hands came to her shoulders. "Not until I've checked your back. I would never forgive myself if I hurt you."

She sighed and crawled off him. "You're making too much of it."

"Maybe so, but that's the way it's going to be. I'm going to need good light. Do you mind if we go to my place? There are pillows and a big porch with rocking chairs where you can sit in comfort for as long as you like without your back hurting."

She wanted to go with him to his home, to his bed if he wanted her. She wanted to know all there was about Drake, see how he lived, feel his arms around her again. "Okay, my back would appreciate that."

He flipped on a flashlight.

"You think of everything."

"Experience."

She didn't like the idea. "Do you bring women up here often?"

"Why Trice, are you fishing for information about my love life?"

She was confident that his teasing tone was meant to ease her thoughts, but it didn't. She might have been concerned, but she would never admit it. "Dr. Stevansson, don't let your ego get ahead of you."

"To keep the peace, I can say I have never brought another woman to this spot. Now, does that calm your ruffled feathers?"

"My feathers aren't ruffled." They were though. She didn't like the idea of him sharing something as special as the last hour with anyone else.

"It didn't sound that way to me." He returned to putting the wine and glasses away.

She stood out of the way, holding the flashlight as he folded the blanket.

"I'm flattered you wanted to know." He gave her the blanket, then turned his attention to the plastic sheet. "The question you really want the answer to is, do I think you are special?"

"You are so…egotistical." He was making her mad now. Maybe that was the plan. It would put some space between them. She had to remind herself not to let emotions get involved.

He stepped to her, into her personal space. "That may be true, but it's also true that I do think you're special. Very special. I would like to show you how much if you will let me. But no pressure. I'll only go as far as you wish."

Drake pulled up his drive. Trice hadn't said a word since leaving their picnic spot. He wasn't sure if this was a good or bad thing. Worry had started to nag at him. Had he come on too strong? He only had a few more days with Trice and didn't have the time to miss out on a minute of them.

He had left one interior light on, which made the A-frame house glow on the high hill.

"Drake, what a wonderful place. I can imagine the view during the day."

"It's a nice one. You can see almost the entire fjord." One he would miss when he moved away. He drove to the house and around to the back and pulled under a carport. He turned to her. "Still want to come in?"

"Of course I do." Trice grabbed the door handle and got out. She walked round to his side of the truck. "Let me help carry stuff in."

"I've got it. Just the food bag. The blanket and the plastic sheet I'll leave for later."

Drake went ahead of her, flipping on the light switch. He set the bag on the kitchen counter.

Trice entered more slowly. "What a kitchen. I might learn to cook if I had one like this."

"You are welcome to use it anytime." He moved further into the one large room, kicking off his shoes near the sofa. "Come on out to the porch. I'll get you a pillow for your back."

She wandered in his direction as if taking it all in.

"You are thinking mighty hard over there."

"This place is amazing." Trice trailed a finger along his leather sofa.

"I'm glad you like it. Make yourself at home. I'll be right back." Drake soon returned with a pillow. He offered his hand, and Trice took it. After leading her outside to the front porch, he settled her in a rocker with the pillow behind her back. "You enjoy the lights while I get us something hot to drink."

Drake quickly put together hot chocolates from supplies his mother had left behind the last time she had visited. He hadn't had it since he was a child, but he thought Trice might enjoy it. She seemed like that type. He soon returned to her with mugs in hand.

She took hers with a smile on her face. "Hot chocolate. With a marshmallow even." Lifting the mug to her lips, she took a sip. "Perfect."

He sat in the rocker next to hers. "I'm glad you like it."

"Do the lights go on like this all night?" She looked out beyond them.

"They do. They lengthen and get thinner with the season. Then leave to return." Was that what he would do? His grandmother lived here. He would be back, but would Trice be here? She could come and go, but for him it was more complicated.

"With time everything changes." Melancholy hung in her voice.

"It does." Drake didn't want to talk about him leaving. He wanted to live in the here and now. With Trice.

They sat in silence for a while.

Drake liked that. It was rare to find someone he felt comfortable enough to just find pleasure in just being with. "Trice?"

"Mmm?" She sipped her hot chocolate.

"I know the timing is all wrong. I'm going away, and

you are staying here. There are only four days left before I leave."

"Are you trying to depress me?"

"No. What I'm trying to say, poorly obviously, is that I don't want to waste what little time we have together by pretending I don't want you in my bed."

Trice looked at him. She stood and offered her hand. "I'm getting cold, and I haven't had a tour of your house yet."

This wasn't going the way he had hoped. After baring his soul, he hadn't expected she'd ask for a tour. He wasn't sure whether to laugh or be insulted.

She walked around him and headed inside.

He picked up the mugs and followed. Trice wasn't in the living room where he thought she would be waiting. He took the dirty dishes to the kitchen sink. "Trice?"

"Up here."

He tracked her voice up the stairs to the loft master bedroom. What was going on?

"Drake? Are you coming?"

He stopped in the bedroom doorway. His heartbeat bumped up three paces. Trice wore one of his dress shirts and stood in the middle of the room. Sexiest sight he'd ever seen. He hoped he wasn't reading this view wrong.

"I thought we could start the tour here. If you don't mind?" Her sweet voice pulled him to her.

He looked at her from head to toe. His gaze captured hers, held as he deliberately walked her direction. "You better not be teasing me, Trice."

A Mona Lisa smile graced her lips. She placed a hand on his chest over his heart. "I would never tease about something so important."

Drake's anticipation went up. Being with him was important to her. One of his hands went to the hem of his shirt, his fingertips brushing the smooth skin of her outer thigh.

Trice's intake of breath told him she was as aware of the sexual tension in the room as he was. Yet she didn't move. Instead, her expression dared him. "I don't think my shirt ever looked this good on me."

She stepped back a couple of paces. "This old thing?"

He moved toward her. "That happens to be my newest shirt."

"That must be why it was hanging on the closet door." She took another step back.

"I was planning to pack it." He moved forward.

That took some of the light out of her eyes. "Let's not talk about that."

"Agreed. What would you like to talk about?"

"I'd rather you kiss me. I like your kisses."

Drake reached for her. His mouth found hers. Trice's arms circled his neck. His hands at her waist pulled her to him. She used her fingers on his shoulders to come up on her toes to reach his lips.

This time he made sure his hands stayed on her hips, not touching her back. Trice didn't make him request she open her mouth. She invited and welcomed him. He might combust right then if he wasn't careful. She never stopped surprising him.

Trice ran her fingers through the hair at the nape of his neck, urging him to deepen the kiss. He didn't disappoint her. His tongue twirled with hers. She pressed against him. His manhood throbbed with desire.

His hand slid over her hip to her thigh. He ran his palm along it, then up and down again to return. The last time he stopped at the elastic of her panties. His index finger nudged under the panty line.

Trice moaned and shifted her hips, her lips placing kisses along his jaw.

His finger moved lower toward the junction of her legs. Heat dwelled there. She shifted, opening her legs. An encouragement. One he didn't need but appreciated. He retreated. This time her moan was more of a complaint.

"Patience, my eager lovely." He went down on a knee and reached under her shirt until he found the top of her panties.

Trice's hands came to rest on his shoulders for support. He slowly removed the material as if revealing a present at Christmas. A perfect present. One he had asked for.

She shimmied and the panties fell to her feet. He had to focus on a spot beyond her for fear he might explode right then. Trice had him thinking and acting like a man starved for a woman. He was. For her. Hooking the tiny piece of clothing on her foot, she lifted it and flung it across the room.

He captured a thigh with a hand.

"Drake." His name was nothing more than a whisper.

He kissed the inside of her thigh. "Sweet."

Trice quivered. Her fingers brushed the hair at the top of his head.

"Liked that, did you?"

She tugged on his hair.

He stood. Her lips found his. Her hands went under his shirt and lifted it. He stepped back and scooped it off, letting it drop to the floor. Trice's palms rested on his pectorals. She ran her hands up and along his shoulders. He remained still, soaking in the pleasure of her touch. His hands rested on her hips. He was ever mindful of her back.

"This is nice," she murmured across his chest before she kissed him just below his neck.

His lips found hers. Tasted and absorbed the brilliance

of her. The feel of her against him. Drake wanted this to go on forever. He paused. But it couldn't.

Trice studied him a moment. "Everything okay? Did I do something wrong? You want me to go?"

She acted so secure, yet with the slightest suggestion she might not be wanted, she overcompensated. He forgot how vulnerable her background made her. "Sweetheart, if you left now, I would have to follow you."

A soft smile formed on her lips. "Would you?"

"All the way to your front door, begging you to come back."

She grinned. "I like the idea of seeing the whole town watching you."

His gaze fixed on hers. "I'm not ashamed of everyone knowing I'm crazy about you."

Trice's smile grew wider. "I'm crazy about you too. Please kiss me again. I like it when you kiss me."

He cupped her face. His lips touched hers, wanting her to know he meant everything he had said. Her arms came around him, and she hugged him as if he were her lifeline. Her hands roamed his chest, then his back. He loved being in her arms. Couldn't get enough of it. Drake wanted to trace her smooth, hot skin once more. Running his hands down her neck, over the ridge of her shoulders, he then moved them to her waist. There he gathered the shirt until his fingers found what he searched for. His hands traveled over the spheres of her butt, pulling her to him, raising her to her toes.

She brushed her center against his solid length. It strained, held in check by his jeans. He lowered her along him. She kissed his neck, then nibbled at the same spot. Holding her with a hand at the waist, he eased his other hand to her center. Wet heat waited for him. Heated his blood. Thrilled him.

Trice's breath caught. She widened her stance, giving clear access. He accepted it. Slipping his finger inside, he felt her tighten around him. She stilled, gripping his shoulders. He pulled his finger from her and entered again.

Trice leaned against him. He held her low on the waist, still aware of her injury. She lowered against his finger and rose again. He gave her what she wanted, pushed upward.

Finding her small nub, he teased her with the tip of his finger. She tensed and groaned, wiggling against his manipulations. After three quick inhales, she ground out, "Drake, please."

Picking up the speed of the movement of his finger, he held her pressed against him. With a sound of joy, she plummeted over the edge to her release.

Drake grinned when her knees buckled and she went limp against him. He swept her into his arms and carried her to the bed. Laying her carefully on it, he came down beside her.

CHAPTER EIGHT

TRICE BASKED IN the gratification of Drake's lovemaking. She lay on the bed with her eyes closed, regaining her breath and composure. Her dazed look met Drake's. A grin rode his lips. The man was pleased with himself. He should be.

She reached for him. He came to her. "It's time I return the favor."

"That sounds nice."

"Lie back." He did. She kissed him. Her hands roamed his chest and stopped to remove his belt. She released it and tugged it from the belt loops, dropping it to the floor.

"Let me help." Drake sat up beside her, then quickly removed his socks before standing to take off the rest of his clothes. They were dropped to the floor.

She watched with appreciation. His body was well taken care of. Drake stood in front of her in all his bare splendor, then came down beside her. Trice sucked in a breath. She'd seen many male bodies, but none were as magnificent as Drake's. The thought that he wanted her humbled Trice. He looked into her eyes as if he really saw her.

Trice shifted. "You are staring. You're starting to embarrass me."

Drake cupped her cheek. "I was just marking you in my memory, thinking how beautiful you look." His finger drifted away from her face to travel along her neck to the first button of the shirt. He flipped it open.

Trice's breath came faster with every movement of his fingers. She squirmed.

"Please don't move." His focus shifted lower. With each empty buttonhole, the shirt revealed more of her to his view. Drake's eyes burned bright with desire, which fueled her own.

Drake stopped the descent just below her belly button. He ran the back of his hand slowly back up, ending between her breasts. Using only a finger, he pushed the shirt away enough to reveal a breast.

Her center throbbed as Drake lowered his mouth to cover her nipple. Heat flooded her. Her breath came in jerks. Could she stand much more of this? Could she live without it?

Drake nudged her gently to her back, shifting the shirt to reveal both her breasts. His mouth moved to her other breast. Could anything feel so wonderful as having Drake's lips on her? Her fingers played in his hair as he teased and lavished attention on her nipples.

His hand rested on her middle. He found the last two buttons on the shirt and released them, leaving her completely exposed.

"You're so amazing." Drake kissed her belly button. His mouth whispered over her skin until his lips found hers. His hand dipped lower to tease her center.

Two could play that game. Trice's hand wrapped his solid length.

Drake stilled. A moment later, he removed her hand. He looked at her. "Trice, I want you and can't wait any longer to have you. Say you want me too."

"I want you."

Drake rolled away and pulled out the bedside table

drawer. He removed a square package, covered himself and turned to her. Reaching beyond her, he placed a pillow beside her. "I don't want to be responsible for hurting you further. Let's put the pillow behind your back."

"I have a better idea." She tugged on his hand. "You lie down."

He did. She straddled him. Drake's eyes widened a second before a wicked gleam entered them. She leaned down to kiss him, her hair creating a curtain. His hands found her waist and skimmed upward until he held a breast in each hand.

Trice lifted on her knees, bringing her center over the tip of his manhood. Slowly she lowered herself down on him. With a sharp lift of his hips, she captured all of him. She moved in a steady up-and-down motion.

She looked at Drake. His eyes were closed, and his face was twisted in a look of unspoiled pleasure. Suddenly he flipped her, braced on his hands he rose over her and re-entered with gentleness. Even during his fierce desire, he showed concerned for her injury. He plunged full-hilt and sent her spiraling into the clouds. She hung there, absorbing the bliss and slowly floating back to reality.

Drake's look locked with hers. He retreated and returned, as he drove toward his release. He groaned her name long and reverently before he fell to the bed beside her. With his breathing still deep and quick, he pulled her close and kissed the top of her ear.

Trice smiled and placed her hand over his resting on her stomach.

Drake woke in a panic in the middle of the night. He was in trouble. Big trouble. Like nothing he had ever known. Worse than the fifth grade when he had two girlfriends at the same time. He cared for Trice, far more than he should. This time he couldn't just break up with her and move on. Trice wouldn't be easily pushed away or dismissed.

He had plans. Plans he needed to keep. Important plans. But he couldn't have it both ways. Trice wanted what he was leaving. More than that, he needed to use his skills. He needed to finish his training. That would never happen in Seydisfjordur. There just wasn't the population to give him enough experience.

Could he ask her to come with him? Would she? Did she care for him enough to do that?

"Hey," Trice said from where she slept curled against his side. "Something wrong?"

"Nothing." And everything. "Except I'm not making love to you."

Her hand ran across his chest and back, caressing him, encouraging. "You can remedy that, Doc."

He rolled toward her. "You think I'm just the medicine you need."

She kissed him. "I know you are."

He groaned when she ran a finger along his already hardening manhood. "You keep that up and I'll be the answer to all your problems."

Her look turned sassy. "Who says you aren't already?"

Drake wished he was. He feared he had created more problems, but he couldn't have stop himself. Trice made his heart swell and his body hum. "Back okay?"

"I'll be fine. Just kiss me."

He would take the here and now and worry about later—later.

That morning, he slipped out of bed, leaving a soft, warm Trice behind. Maybe if he went into another room, he could think clearer. Figure out how to complete his surgery training and have Trice at the same time.

In the kitchen he prepared a light breakfast. He had his head straightened out by then. His determination was back in place. He would be leaving in a few days. He had his spot waiting on him in London. If he didn't take it, then it might be years before he had another chance. Trice would be a wonderful memory. With that decided, he would make the most of the time he had with her.

He jerked to a stop in the doorway. She still lay facedown on his sheets. The sun streaming across Trice's bare skin made it glow. The sight had him filing it away in his memory.

Drake recognized the moment Trice woke. She stretched like a feline, coming up on her hands and lifting her behind in the air, and then bringing her abdomen to the sheets again. His manhood shot to ready in seconds, watching her erotic movements. His flannel sleep pants did little to cover his reaction. The tray in his hand shook. He carried it with the steaming mugs of coffee, boiled eggs and toast to the bedside table. "Good morning, sleepyhead. I was starting to think you were never going to wake."

"Good morning. What have you been up to?"

"I thought you might like something to eat." He placed the tray on the bedside table before he dropped it.

"You are always so considerate." Her hand brushed his arm from elbow to wrist. "Where's my...uh...your shirt?"

"Don't feel like you need to put something on for me." Drake found the shirt and handed it to her.

She turned her back to him, slipping her arms in the sleeves, then buttoning it. "What time is it?"

Disappointment filled him, but it was probably just as well. He needed the distraction. "It's still early."

"We should be at the clinic on time since we were gone a day and a half. I still have to prove myself. I want the town to know I'll be there for them."

Unlike what he would be for his grandmother. Still, she was the one pushing him to go. Trice would be here. She would be here to see to Luce. But it was his responsibility. He had to move past this. Up until ten days ago, he'd had it all settled in his mind. Now uncertainly had creeped in. Slowly Trice had become the center of his world. That had to end.

Trice raised her arms in the air for another big stretch. She looked at the tray. "What do you have here?"

"Our breakfast." He picked up the tray and set it in the center of the bed.

"Looks good. We'll get food all over your sheets." She picked up a napkin.

"Like I care about that."

She grinned. "You might not until you wake with crumbs all over you." She took a bite of toast, making sure to keep it over the tray.

Drake enjoyed a nice view of her breasts in the gaping shirt.

She looked toward the window. "This I could get used to, waking up to this green valley with the ice blue of the fjord surrounded by the snow-tipped mountains. I can imagine watching a storm coming is magnificent."

He knew all the views well. But he must give those and other things up to reach his goal. "Almost as magnificent as the view I have now."

Trice followed the direction on his look. She sat straighter. "I don't see how you can leave this house either. Are you going to sell it?"

"No. My family will come here for holidays and visits.

My parents built this house. For the view. I bought it when they moved." He took a bite out of a boiled egg.

She added butter to her bread. "I've seen nothing in the village like it."

"No, all the materials had to be shipped in. It took a couple years before we could move in. Everyone said Dad was crazy to put all the glass in the house since it's so cold here, but my parents wanted to feel like a part of nature. They felt like the view was worth it. There is special wire in the glass to warm it. They also added special insulation and thick drapes that disappear into a wall pocket that are used for heat and light control on the long days."

Trice shook her head. "I don't see how you can leave it."

"You're not making this any easier."

"I'm sorry. That isn't my intent." She took a sip of coffee looking at him over the rim. "Do you think you will have a chance today to call Mr. Bjonsson?"

"For you I will make a point to. I'd like to be the one to introduce you."

She put her mug down on the tray. "I better get dressed so you can take me home to get changed." She moved to get off the bed.

"Before you do that, let me check your back." He went to her side of the bed.

"You're still worried about my back?"

"I hope I didn't make it worse."

She looked directly at him. "It is fine. If it weren't, it would have been worth it."

"I'll take that as a compliment." He grinned. "You'll have to take the shirt off."

She looked over her shoulder with a teasing grin. "Are you sure you're not just doing this to get me to undressed?"

"I can't deny the idea has appeal. But I actually want to

have a look at your back." He moved the tray back to the bedside table.

"You didn't hurt me, I promise." She lowered the shirt over her shoulders while looking back at him.

"Quit arguing. I would like to see for myself." He kissed her shoulder and down her back. "I think you'll recover nicely." He reached around her to cup her breasts.

She leaned against him. Her warmth met his heat. "How much time do we have?"

He turned her to face him. "Enough."

Trice watched Drake put the last stitch in the nine-year-old boy's head. The child had fallen and busted his head open. Drake had great surgery skills. He hadn't hesitated about handling the emergency. He had swiftly and confidently prepared the area while at the same time putting the boy and his mother at ease.

As much as Trice hated to see him leave, she understood he had commitments he must honor. His skills were too great for a small clinic that would see little need. Still, she dreaded the time she had to watch him go. She had made a deal with herself not to think about how many days Drake had left. Her plan was to make the most out of the time they had together.

She had to remain strong and detached if she wanted to survive.

That morning after breakfast, they had made love in the sunshine. Never had she been quite as free or bold in her lovemaking, confident in her body. She spent most of her life insecure in her personal relationships because she had had so few, but with Drake she had opened up and given her all. He had given her that security and confidence. For that she would always be grateful.

The next man in her life would have a lot to live up to after Drake. As if by a silent mutual agreement, they had decided not to discuss him leaving, as if they were going to pretend he would always be there.

She stood there and watched Drake tie off the last stitch and snip off the thread like a lovesick teen. Love? Was she in love with him? She had only known him a little over a week. She couldn't be. Love took longer than that to develop. Yet the moments they had shared had been more intense than any she had ever felt.

The bell ringing on the door of the clinic refocused her attention. She stepped out of the exam room and walked down the short hall to the front. "Can I help you?"

"We are here to see Dr. Stevansson." A middle-aged woman stood there with a preteen girl beside her.

"I'll be taking over for Dr. Stevansson." Trice didn't like the taste of those words on her tongue. She wished Drake would be here tomorrow, the next day and all those that would fellow. "I'm Dr. Shell."

"You're the woman who saved those two men's lives," the preteen stated.

"That was more of a team effort." Trice looked between the woman and the girl. "Now, what can I do for you?"

The woman lifted her foot. "I have foot pain. I thought it was getting better, but this morning I could hardly stand."

"Come back this way." Trice turned toward the examination room.

The woman hobbled across the floor, supported by the girl.

Trice pointed to the examination room. "Please have a seat in the chair. What's your name?"

"Maude Traustason. This is my daughter, Lula."

The girl stood beside the woman.

"Nice to meet you both. Well, Maude, can you tell me what's going on with your foot?" Trice pulled the stool forward and took a seat.

"Drake says I have plantar fasciitis. He told me to soak it, but I don't have time. I have to work at the cannery and take care of my kids. Is there something else I can do?"

"Please take your shoe and sock off and let me have a look." While the woman removed them, Trice continued, "Do you stand on cement all day? Or sit at a desk?"

"I walk on cement most of the time." The woman dropped a shoe to the floor.

"Have you been taking an anti-inflammatory?"

She peeled off her sock. "I did for a while."

"Did it help?" Trice looked at the woman.

"It did."

"May I see your foot?" Trice rolled the stool closer and placed the lifted heel across her legs. The red angry skin made her flinch. It had to hurt. "I'm going to touch it." She looked at Maude. "Please don't kick me."

"It really hurts." Maude's face twisted up.

"I don't doubt it." Trice examined the foot with a gentle hand, then lowered it to the floor. She picked up the woman's shoe. "Is this what you wear to work?"

"Yes."

"Then I would suggest you get a pair with more support. Especially in the heel area. Did Dr. Stevansson give you some exercises to do?"

"He did."

"Good. Be creative about when you do them. At work when you have a moment, do just one or two at a time. At night I want you to soak your feet. Others will have to help—" she looked at the girl "—or you'll just have to let something go, or this won't get better. I also want you to take an anti-inflammatory on the days you work, and come back to see me if you aren't better in two weeks. I can't stress enough that soaking your feet is important."

The woman nodded. "Okay."

"And you really should buy some better shoes."

"All right."

She glanced at Drake standing at the door. He had been listening. She felt him come up a few minutes earlier. Her body had a way of knowing he was around. He had a way of muddling her mind as well. She needed to concentrate on what she was there for and not Drake.

Trice placed Maude's foot on the floor. "May I ask you a medical history question?"

"Okay." Maude looked at her.

"Do you or any of the members of your family have HEP? I'm doing a research project on HEP and would like to interview anyone who has it."

Maude looked at her, not saying anything for a moment, as if deciding if she would offer any help. "I carry the gene. My sister does too."

Trice worked at containing her joy. "Would you be willing to answer a list of questions and allow me to view your medical records?"

Maude appeared unsure but said, "I guess so."

"I'll let you put on your sock and shoe while I go get the questions." Trice hurried toward the door.

Drake stepped out of the doorway to let her pass.

She returned with her electronic pad. Drake ended his conversation with Maude's daughter and left the room. Trice handed the pad to Maude. "Here, if you would answer these, it would be wonderful. Do you mind if I take Lula for a soda while you're working?"

"That's fine." The woman went to work on the questions.

Trice led Lula toward the back of the building. "I know where Dr. Stevansson hides his soda."

They went to the kitchen area. Trice handed the girl a can of drink. In a falsetto high voice she said, "Don't tell Dr. Stevansson. It's our secret."

"What's going on in here?" Drake popped out from behind the doorframe.

Trice and Lula jumped.

"Caught you. Are you in my snacks again?" He looked from one to the other, then grinned. "Help yourself." He looked directly at Trice. "Since you already have."

"Lula, let's go see if your mother is finished." Trice ushered the girl out of the room as if they had gotten away with a crime.

Lula laughed.

Her mother handed the electronic pad to Trice when they entered. "All done."

Trice took the pad. "Thanks so much, Maude. I really appreciate it. Would you mind letting your sister know about my research and ask her if she would participate?"

Maude's lips thinned. "She doesn't come to town often."

"Do you happen to know any other people who might have the syndrome?" Trice needed to move forward with her project.

"I can ask at my knitting circle tonight. Maybe somebody there does or knows of somebody who does." Maude stood to leave.

Lula headed out the door with soda in hand.

"I would appreciate that." Trice smiled. "Come by and let me know how your foot is doing."

Maude stopped at the door. "Do you knit?"

Trice shook her head. "No, but I've always wanted to learn."

"Why don't you come to our circle tonight? You can meet everyone and give it a try."

Trice looked at Drake, who leaned against the doorframe, talking to Lula. She had planned to spend the evening with him.

He gave her a smile that didn't reach his eyes. "You should go. You will have fun."

She wasn't sure if she was disappointed he didn't discourage her or glad he was unselfish enough not to say anything. She needed to move beyond him anyway. What they had now wouldn't last. She had her future to consider.

Trice's attention returned to Maude. "Thanks. I'd love to come."

Maude smiled. "Good. We meet at Unndis Hanson's house. See you there."

"I don't have any supplies." Where would she find needles and yarn on such short notice?

Drake volunteered, "My mom left some of hers. They're at the house. I'll get them for you."

Trice could have kissed him. "Thanks, Drake. That would be nice."

Maude moved toward the door. "I'll call my sister on my way home. Thanks for your help."

"Come back if the foot doesn't get better. I'll be here to help." Trice saw her out the door. "I look forward to seeing you this evening."

Drake wanted to disagree with the evening plans, but he had no right. Trice needed to become a part of the community, find her own way, one that didn't involve him. He had made the choice to leave town. He shouldn't, wouldn't hold her back. Asking her to forgo the knitting group to spend time with him would be selfish. Her research was important to Trice, and more than, that it was important to people who had the disease. Yet he wanted Trice with him as much as possible.

After Maude and Lula had left, Trice kissed him, her eyes bright. "I am making progress. I'm so excited."

"I never doubted you. I think you can do anything you put your mind to."

She wrapped her hands around his bicep and pressed against him. "You're just being nice because you like me."

"True." He gave her an indulgent look.

"I'm going to clean up the examination room, then log in Maude's answers and get ready for tonight."

Trice sound so happy, he couldn't bring himself to complain about the plans. "I have some paperwork to do as well if I don't want to stay late tonight. I better get busy."

She gave him a searching look. "You're not angry, are you, about me going to the knitting meeting instead of spending the time with you?"

"No, no. You need to go to the knitting meeting. I understand that."

"I hope so. My research is really important to me. And I want to fit in here."

"I know." He did. What he'd taken for granted all these years, she desperately craved. "You should go."

She kissed him again. "I'm glad you understand."

He pulled her close. "I would understand better with another kiss."

For the next hour, they worked without interruption. Then Drake knocked on the office door where Trice worked. "How about having lunch with me?"

She looked up. "Shouldn't one of us be here?"

"I'll put a note on the door about where we are."

"Okay then." Trice stood.

Before they went out the door, he pulled her into his arms and kissed her. She wrapped her arms around his waist and returned his kiss.

Drake pulled away, looking into her eyes. "Let's forget lunch and lock the door."

Trice giggled, which only made him want to really do what he'd suggested.

She pulled away from him. "That wouldn't do much to instill faith in me. I need to make a good impression on the town."

"I believe you have that covered already." She'd proved her abilities more than once. Luce would be in good hands.

"I can't take any chances on messing that up. And I fear once I get started kissing you, I won't stop."

"Mmm. I like that idea." He gave her another quick but heated kiss.

She placed her hands on his chest. "We better have some lunch and stay out of trouble."

He opened the door. "It's too late for that."

Trice grinned, her look warm. "Maybe."

They headed down the street. Drake was tempted to take her hand but resisted doing so. He didn't know if Trice would appreciate everyone knowing something was happening between them. He was confident that if anyone saw him looking at Trice, they would know right away he was crazy about her.

"Where are we going?"

He pointed down the street. "To the diner for a sandwich."

"We could go to my place. I'll fix you a sandwich." Her eyes held a mischievous light.

"Dr. Shell, are you trying to lure me into bed in the middle of the day?"

"I was just trying to offer you lunch. No agenda." She stopped and fixed him with a twinkling look. "Unlike you, who had me come look at the stars, then lured me to your house to take advantage of me."

His look locked with hers. "I lured you? If I remember correctly, it was you waiting in my bedroom."

Her face pinked sweetly. "I hope I wasn't too bold."

Heat from the memory covered his body. "I couldn't have asked for a nicer welcome."

They continued walking. At the café, he held the door open. The noisy place went quiet. Everyone stopped what they were doing and clapped.

Trice looked at him, perplexed.

He said just for her ears, "They appreciated your work the other day. Come on, let's find a table." He directed her to one in a back corner. Trice took a chair on one side, and he took a chair on the other. He would have liked to have sat next to her, but that would have made his feelings too obvious.

A waitress came from the bar to take their order.

"I'm really looking forward to learning to knit. I'm amazed at all the community activities the town has." Trice was almost buzzing with excitement.

"In the dead of winter, we have to make our own entertainment. We have something almost nightly. In the nice months, we still like to get together. We especially enjoy our folk dancing and singing."

Trice sat forward. "You sing? I know you can dance."

"It's folk dancing. And yes, I do both well enough." He would miss that comradery when he moved to the large city.

"I'd like to hear you sing."

The eagerness in her eyes made him smile. "Maybe I'll

sing for you sometime." He looked around, "But it won't be in the middle of lunch."

"And I had so hoped…"

He laughed. "Trice, I think you could get me in trouble."

"Maybe you could teach me a folk dance."

He was impressed with her efforts to acclimatize to the town. He wasn't sure someone else would make the effort. He shouldn't have been surprised. She gave all of herself, and people responded to that. She certainly had to him last night. Like no one else ever had. His greatest fear was that he might not find someone who would ever give so freely again.

How could somebody possibly not want her in their life? He wanted her badly. The problem was, he had made plans that didn't include her. If he did stay, having Trice beside him would make it easier.

The waitress brought their meals, stopping his out-of-control thoughts.

"I meant to tell you on the way over here that I called Bjonsson."

She sat forward. "You did?"

"I didn't get to talk to him, but I left him a message with a woman who answered. She told me she would see to it that he got my message. I will try again before I leave, maybe drive up there."

"Hopefully he will contact you. I won't give up. I'll keep trying even after you are gone."

"I never doubted you would for a minute." He put his sandwich down. "Tomorrow night the town is throwing me a going-away party. Would you like to come?"

The light went out of her eyes. She raised her chin. "I've already been invited. Luce said something about it a few days ago."

"I should've known. It's hard to get ahead of her. Are you planning to come?"

She shook her head. "I don't think so."

He met Trice's eyes. "I'd like for you to be there."

Trice said nothing for a long minute. "I will come if you really want me there."

He moved his legs so hers fit between them and gave them a gentle squeeze.

"You know," she said, "I'm starting to have a very busy social life. I may get busy at the last minute."

"My party is going to be the event of the year, so I don't think I need to worry." At least her good humor had returned.

"It will be another good opportunity for me to meet people."

"I agree. And I promise to help you in that area." He leaned forward so only she would hear him. "Now, how do you plan to repay me?"

She put a finger to her chin as if considering. "I haven't thought about it."

He leaned forward. "Maybe an early thank-you?"

"Like?" She acted innocent.

"I was thinking I could come by after the knitting meeting." Dared he hope she would agree?

"It'll be kind of late."

He crossed his arms and laid them on the table, putting him that much closer to her. "Are you trying to get rid of me already?" He was half teasing and half serious.

"No, I'm trying to figure out how to live without you."

Those words were like a punch in the chest. He hadn't meant to hurt her. Had tried not to. Luce had been right. He should have stayed away.

"I've been thinking maybe we shouldn't see each other

again. I'll be alone in a couple nights anyway." Her eyes remained downcast.

"I'm sorry. I just made this assumption that we would see each other every night until I left. My apologies. I shouldn't have done that. I know this isn't easy for you."

"I should be used to it. It has happened enough in my life."

"It wasn't my intention to hurt you." His hand covered hers. He no longer cared what others saw or thought. Trice was hurting because of him.

Trice pulled her hand away and put a smile on her face. "Enough of this. I knew the score when I arrived. After all, I came here to take your place." She shook her head. "Let's enjoy what time we have and not talk about the future."

They both returned to their meal.

He gave a curt nod. Despite the pleasant conversation he tried to participate in, the food in his stomach had soured.

CHAPTER NINE

AFTER THEIR LUNCH, she and Drake strolled back to the clinic. There he left her to oversee the clinic while working on her research. He drove home, returning with a cloth bag containing two knitting needles and a skein of navy yarn.

"This is wonderful. Thank you so much. Are you sure your mother won't mind?"

"Positive. Now you're all set for this evening."

She wished his support reached his eyes. "I have to say I'm looking forward to it."

"Mind if I walk you to the Hansons' later?" He looked like a puppy left behind.

Trice had to give him something. "Oh, course not."

That brightened his face. She would miss him tonight. Still, she didn't enjoy being a foregone conclusion for the next few nights. Maybe it was just as well they let things stay at a one-night event. Still, she hated seeing Drake look disappointed. "I'm actually nervous about this. I've never had a chance to socialize with a bunch of women. What if they don't like me?"

He roared with laughter. "Like that's going to happen. Everyone you meet likes you."

At the knock on her door, she opened it to Drake. She grabbed her sweater and the knitting bag and stepped outside.

He grinned. "You are excited about this evening."

"I am." She headed toward the street.

His hand on her arm stopped her. "Hold on a minute. I have something I need to do."

Drake's gaze held hers before his face came down to hers. The kiss was sweet, tender. Unlike any other kiss they had shared. With this one, he was trying to tell her something. Did she dare believe he really cared?

He pulled away and rested his forehead against hers. Her breathing had increased. She placed a hand over his heart. The rapid thump there matched hers. "Luce is going to be watching."

"I have no doubt. Luce knows exactly what we've been doing. She knows everything. She'll have something to say about it. She has already gotten on to me."

"For what?"

"She told me not to hurt you."

Trice straightened. "I'm tougher than that."

"I wish I could say the same."

She studied him a moment. "What do you mean by that?"

He met her look. "I'm going to miss you, Beatrice Shell. A lot."

"I will miss you too." She hurt at the thought.

"Maybe our paths will cross again one day."

Many families and temporary friends had said the same to her over the years. None of them had she ever seen again. People got busy. They didn't care enough. She was just forgotten. "Let's enjoy knowing each other now." She stepped out of his reach. "I need to go. I don't want to be late."

A few minutes' walk later, she hesitated at the Hansons' front door.

Drake's hand on her waist was warm and reassuring. He

gave her a nudge. "Go on. They will love you. You will have a good time. I'll see you in the morning."

She wanted to turn and walk away with him, but she didn't. Drake didn't even look back to see if she had gone inside. If he had, she would have run to him. Bracing herself, she knocked on the door.

A woman opened the door and invited her in. The living area was bright. Women stood around in groups talking. She moved further into the room without anyone making eye contact or speaking. Worry started to creep in.

Some people could be reserved about talking to anyone new. Trice understood that well. She had hoped tonight would be different. A moment later, Maude hurried toward her.

"Come sit beside me." Maude returned to a chair across the room. "I see you brought something to work with. Good."

The other women in the room moved to their chairs as well.

Trice waited, watching the other women remove their needles and yarn. As if in unison, they began moving their needles, creating a click-click sound while looping yarn. Moments later, they were in conversation about someone she didn't know.

Maude said, "Let me show you."

Trice removed her materials.

Maude said, "Take the needles and hold them in your fingers like this. Attach the yarn."

Trice followed the instructions the best she could. After a couple of false starts, she managed the basics. Soon she had created a row of stitches.

"Now you have to go back the other way."

Trice almost groaned, but she made the effort. Minutes

later, she had another row, but with a number of uneven loops. Still, she was proud of her efforts.

While knitting, she listened to the conversations about who was pregnant, who was sick and who would be marrying soon. These were all parts of life within a community. People she would be caring for over the next year, the baby she would help deliver. Her eyes watered. This was part of belonging. A life she had never known. But might have found.

"Dr. Shell, did you really climb down and save two men?" one of the younger women asked.

Trice laid her knitting in her lap. She wouldn't be able to concentrate and talk at the same time. There had been medical problems to solve that had been less frustrating than figuring out how to make identical loops. "I wouldn't exactly put it that way, but yeah. I was the one who climbed down, only because I was the smallest. I could fit in the crevice. And please call me Trice."

She had the entire room's attention. Someone said, "That must've been scary."

Another lady said, "I couldn't have done it."

Trice gave them an indulgent smile. "It was scary more after the fact than at the time. I just did what needed to be done."

"That's pretty impressive," someone else said.

The entire time, their needles never stopped.

Trice cleared her throat, hoping it wasn't too early for this conversation. "As I'm sure you know, I'm taking Dr. Stevansson's place for the next year. While I'm doing that, I will also be doing some research work." This was her chance to say something about HEP. "My research is studying HEP."

The blank faces of the women told her more explanation would be needed. Trice took a moment to explain the disorder. A number of the women nodded, now understanding what she was referring to.

Trice leaned forward. "In fact, I could use your help. I need to speak to anyone who has had HEP or is willing to be tested for it. If you have had it or know someone who has been tested for it, I would really appreciate you letting me know. I promise there will be nothing or very little that is painful involved."

The room went quiet. The circle just looked at her, saying nothing. Watching.

Trice broke the silence. "I have it. I learned about it when I became sick. That's when I became interested in the disorder. I want to learn more about the disease. I can do that by talking to people."

Suspicion filled the women's eyes. Maybe Trice should have waited on Drake to say something about it. But he had his own life to worry about. He was packing to leave and tying up business. She couldn't depend on him. He would soon be gone.

A woman shifted in her chair. "I was sick with it as a child, and my daughter as well."

Excitement filled Trice's chest. Maybe this would work. "Will you come to see me one day next week? Bring your daughter as well."

The mother nodded.

"Thank you. That would be wonderful."

Another said, "I think my neighbor had it. I'll tell her to come see you."

"I would appreciate it." Trice couldn't help the thrill going through her. She had made progress. Picking up her knitting again, she tried to get in the groove.

Nobody else said anything for a couple of minutes as they returned to their work. Finally, one of the older women said with a sly grin, "What do you think of Drake? He seems to like you."

Each woman eagerly watched her. Their hands automatically moved the needles, but their looks stayed with her. Trice's body warmed. Her hands shook, causing her to drop a loop. "I think he is a great doctor. I know you will miss him."

"He seems smitten with you," a woman with a toothless grin said.

"We are friends." Trice should have expected this. Prepared herself for it.

A giggle went around the room.

"Maybe she could get him to stay," a woman on the other side of Maude said.

Trice looked at each of the women. "I won't be doing that."

Maude took pity on Trice and asked one of the women a question, moving the attention away from her and Drake. Trice wasn't interested in sharing what was happening between them. It was too new and was going to be too short.

The meeting broke up. Trice packed her knitting carefully away. She would continue to practice. Maybe make something for Drake and send it to him. No. They had agreed their fling would end when he left. That would mean no contact.

Trice stepped out into the dim light, fully expecting to find Drake waiting for her. He wasn't. She couldn't help but be disappointed. He was doing as she'd asked. She started home. This time she wished he hadn't abided by her request.

It didn't take her long to walk past Luce's front door and round the corner toward her own home. Her home. She liked the sound of that. It was a small space, but she'd never had a spot all her own. She had always shared with someone else. All her personal belongs could fill her suitcase, but here she had more. It was a place that needed her and where she could belong.

Trice opened her door to the lone light she'd left on. Again a sense of disappointment went through her. Drake wasn't there. She had to move past this expectation. He would be in a matter of days. She had to learn to do without him.

She went about getting ready for bed, and still there was no knock on the door. Wearing her warm pajamas, she climbed under the covers, then turned off the light. She tossed and turned, thinking of how little time she had to spend with Drake. Worse, she had told him she wouldn't see him personally again. Why had she insisted on doing that? To protect herself.

She was only hurting herself. Early in her life, she had learned not to let anyone close because she would soon leave, but this time she wanted as much of Drake as she could get. They had so little time. She wanted to create more happy memories.

At the tap on her window, she jerked straight up. Another tap. She walked to the window. A face was pressed against it. Drake.

He pointed toward the door.

She hurried to it. "What are you doing here in the middle of the night? Is something wrong?"

He stepped into her personal space, far enough that she stepped back. He kept coming, closing the door behind him. "Yes, there is."

"I'll get dressed."

"I was thinking you need to get undressed."

Trice met his look. His eyes held a predatory gleam. "What are you up to?"

"I came to see you. I missed you. I couldn't sleep." He sounded pitiful.

She liked the idea of him needing her. "Why were you tapping on the window instead of knocking on the door?"

"I was trying to be quiet." He moved toward her again. This time her back came up against the wall. "Luce has ears like a twenty-year-old." His lips brushed hers. His cool hands came to rest under her pajama top at her waist.

She shuddered. "Your hands are freezing."

"How about warming them up?" He nuzzled her neck.

She gave him a light slap on the shoulder. "You're crazy. People are already talking about us."

"So? We're adults." His lips found hers before they traveled down her neck, leaving kisses along the way. "You will let me stay the night, won't you?"

She couldn't resist him. "What kind of doctor would I be if I didn't take care of a man in need of warming?"

"My thoughts exactly." His lips met hers as he brought her against him. He began walking her backwards towards the bed.

Sometime later, Trice lay beside Drake, her head resting on his shoulder and her hand tracing circles on his chest. Why couldn't she have this all the time? Life seemed to always be shoving her out of the way.

"You know, I could do this forever." Drake gave her a gentle squeeze.

"It is nice."

"I wish we had longer. We only have tomorrow night left, and part of that will be taken up with my going-away party." He sounded as if he'd like to forget about the party.

She kissed the side of his jaw. "We agreed not to talk about you leaving."

"I know, but I think we should." He rolled so he could see her face.

"And accomplish what?" She didn't want to go down this road. It was too muddy, sticky.

"I was hoping for a compromise. Will you come visit me? I could come here some." Even he didn't sound confident about how that would work.

Her hand fell away from his chest. "I would like that. But soon it would become difficult for us to get away. Then slowly we would get too busy to see each other at all. We would just be prolonging the inevitable. I've lived it all my life."

Drake's face turned to one of hurt and disappointment. "You don't even want to try?"

"I have tried—before. Everyone says they will stay in touch, but no one does. It's a lot more painful to let things drag on. To hope for a phone call. To look for a letter. To make plans that must be canceled. You need to leave here and embrace your new life. It's what you want. I need to find my place in the world. Let's make the most of the here and now." She brushed her fingertip across his chest.

"You don't have much faith in people, do you? I'm not one of those who will forget you. You don't have to be alone all your life. Have you ever thought it was a two-way street? That you could have tried to stay in contact as well?"

"I was a child—"

"But what about those you went to medical school with? How many of those people have you tried to stay in touch with? Or your last foster mother?"

"I…uh…"

"Exactly. I think we have something worth trying to build on. But both of us have to want it. To work at it. Have faith that we can do it. I know your past tells you that there are no lasting relationships, but I care about you. I won't let you go."

She shook her head.

A deep sadness filled his eyes. "You won't even try, will you?"

"You have an intense year ahead of you. You won't have time to come here. You shouldn't have distractions. I'm not going anywhere at least for a year. I can't just leave anytime I want, and neither will you be able to."

A stream of anger went through Drake. "I have agreements and obligations as well. I've been trying to get back to my surgery training for two years. If I don't go now, I might never get to go. Space may not open up at another time. What I learn could make the difference in someone's life. Even my grandmother's. She isn't getting any younger. Now is my chance to get that training."

Trice pushed up on an elbow so their looks met. "I don't blame you. Your skills are needed. That's how I felt about coming here. It was something I had to do."

"It would be too difficult to get another placement." He needed the training to bring it home to Iceland.

"Hey, I'm not asking you to stay for me. I would never do that no matter how tempted I am to do so. We need to face it. The time just isn't right for us."

He wanted to shake her. "I don't want to accept that. You're too important to me."

She lay beside him again. "You can't accept it because you've never had to live it."

"I'm not one of those who will forget you when I'm gone. You don't give me enough credit."

Trice offered him a wry smile. "I have to go with what I know."

"I can and will prove you wrong. What will you do when you leave here?"

"I don't know. I'll be trying to get my research paper published. Then find a place to practice medicine. If they will have me, I might stay here."

She wanted what he was giving up. Why had he found her now? "Why here?"

"I really like it. I feel at home."

Just as it had been to him. "You wait until you spend a winter here. You might change your mind. I was hoping you might come to London. We could come back to Iceland when the time was right."

"You know that isn't easy for an American."

"Could we at least stay in contact? Online. Write."

She sighed and rolled over on him. "Why don't we concentrate on another form of communication right now?"

He ran his hands gently up her smooth back while she gave him a wet, hot kiss. He must find a way to keep her in his arms.

Trice woke when Drake left her bed early, before daylight, with a sweet kiss that had her reaching to hold him to her. How would she survive when he left? She didn't want to consider it, but that was all she could think about. She wanted to forget about their conversation. It had hurt too much to tell him no. To discourage him. Some of what Drake had said was true. That wasn't what really bothered her. The problem was, she had been left after promises had been made to keep in contact. Too many times that had failed.

All she said was true. In time they would get too busy for each other. Distance would kill what they had. It was easier just to shut it down now. She had never intended for it to get this complicated.

In fact, it should've been only for one night and that's it. They had both known the score going in. The plan had been for their relationship to remain short and sweet. They should have kept it that way, but she couldn't. She wanted Drake too badly. Now she would put it all behind her. Her life had given her plenty of experience in how to do that.

He would be gone in little more than twenty-four hours. After that, she would figure out how to survive. If he managed to return for a visit or they had a chance to see each other, she would make the most of that as well. She had no doubt he would soon find somebody in the big city of London. It wouldn't take much for him to forget her. Of this she was confident.

Drake's surgery training should take priority. He had made it clear what his dream was. That meant he needed to leave Seydisfjordur. She wouldn't be a part of making him unhappy. That she promised herself and him as well.

Not a person to scare easily, she was terrified now. With knowledge of a few relationships, and none of those ending well, she had no doubt she and Drake would end the same way. Yet she dared to dream they could be different. That they might really have something worth fighting for.

He'd been more than a wonderful distraction. This was the first time she'd been in love. Drake's leaving would hurt. Deeply.

Entering the clinic, she found Drake in the storage room with his iPad in hand. "Hey."

His face lit up. He set his pad down and wrapped his arms around her. His lips found hers. She clung to him. He kissed her breathless. Her knees had gone weak by the time he let her go. "Will you come to my house after the party tonight? I still have that book to give you."

"How could I say no after that kiss? And I do want to read that book."

He grinned. "You are going to miss me."

Heaven help her, she was.

The rest of the day, she vacillated between walking on air and deep depression. She could hardly concentrate on her patients. To her great delight, two people came in to help with her research.

"You must have won them over last night," Drake commented after a man left.

Trice sat in the office. "I don't know about that."

"I've never known them to open up to a stranger like they have you. But you do have a way of bringing that out in people." He sounded proud of her, and she liked that idea.

"I wouldn't have thought that. It hasn't happened before." How many homes had she been in where she'd just blended into the background? They had decided she wasn't a good fit for them. In Seydisfjordur, she seemed to have blossomed.

"Will you be going back to the knitting circle?" He continued to lean against the doorframe.

"I think I will. I started a project, and I would like to try to finish it." She would return to the circle if for no other reason than being part of the group.

"And what is your project?"

She grinned "I hope it's the beginning of a hat."

"I'm impressed. I look forward to seeing it finished."

A hush filled the air. They both knew that wouldn't happen.

Trice quickly tried to cover up the heavy moment. "My knitting leaves a lot to be desired. I just have never been asked to be a part of something."

His brows rose. "Never? How could somebody not notice you are amazing?"

"Maybe a study group, but come to think of it, I asked them. It doesn't matter. It's just nice to have a place to belong."

Drake placed his arm around her shoulders, held her tight and kissed her temple. "Seydisfjordur is lucky they have you."

What had she done to deserve Drake? She was in trouble.

CHAPTER TEN

IT HAD BEEN a long time since Drake had been nervous before any event, especially one taking place in his hometown. Yet here he was, getting ready to face his family and friends, and tonight his hands were damp.

He couldn't believe he was this close to getting what he'd been dreaming of for so long. But the gloss was off because of Trice. How was he going to leave her? Her hand holding his bicep only reminded him of how much he wanted her close.

Drake opened the door to the community center. The group gathered must have been the entire town and surrounding area. The clapping started and continued to the point that he hung his head and shook it with embarrassment.

Trice moved off to the side, leaving him standing in the middle of a horseshoe of smiling people.

The longer he looked into the smiling faces of people he'd known all his life, the more overwhelmed he became.

The mayor stepped forward and commanded everyone's attention. It took a moment for the noise to die down. "We're going to have our meal and then the program."

Program? He hadn't expected that. The meal, yes, but that was all. He looked at Trice to see if she knew anything about that.

She pursed her lips and shrugged her shoulders. He wasn't getting any help there. Then Trice's mouth formed a smile. She apparently liked seeing him unsure. His grandmother proved even less help.

The mayor said to him, "Now, you and the new doctor go first. We have a place for you right up front at the main table."

He and Trice moved to the table that had so much food on it, he feared he heard it groan. He asked into Trice's ear, "Do you know what's going on?"

Over her shoulder, she said sweetly, "I have no idea. I believe most of this must've been planned a long time before I came. Here you had me believing you were a man who had his ear to the ground and knew everything going on in town."

The smile left his face. "Apparently not. Because I haven't heard a word about this."

"Just sit back and enjoy it. They're only showing you how valuable you have been to the community."

Why hadn't he put more value on that? He'd certainly known it where Dr. Johannsson had been concerned. He just had never thought of himself in the same terms.

Trice went about filling her plate. She stopped and looked at him. "Are you okay?"

"Yeah, yeah, I'm fine."

With food in hand, they were directed to the front table.

Trice hesitated. "I shouldn't be seated up here."

"You're with me. My guest sits beside me." He needed her there.

People began filling the other tables. A number of them approached him to share how much they had appreciated him. Helga Olafsdottir told him thanks for taking care of her broken arm. Einar Abelsson said thanks for stitching up his hand. Lydia Einarsson, with her daughter on her hip, voiced her appreciation for delivering her baby. Mr. Jonsson hobbled up with his gout. Drake couldn't eat for the interruptions. Almost everyone in the room was a patient he had seen at one time or another.

A grizzly-looking man came to stand in front of Trice. He watched her. Said nothing. It took Drake a moment to recognize him. Drake had last seen him when he was a teenager. Even then it hadn't been but for a moment or two when Drake helped him out of the clinic.

She glanced at Drake, then looked at the man again. "Can I help you? Is there a problem?"

"I am Olafur Bjonsson."

Trice went statue-still, then jumped up and cut around the table. Drake hurried after her. He feared she might scare the man off.

Drake came to stand beside her, putting out his hand. "Mr. Bjonsson. Thank you for coming. I would like you to meet Dr. Beatrice Shell. As I said in my message, there is a chance you are related to each other."

Trice looked as if she wanted to throw her arms around the man. Her eyes glistened. Was she going to cry?

Olafur continued to study Trice. Then he grunted. "She looks like my aunt, Lilja Andresson, who ran off to America when I was a child."

Trice stared at the man. Her mouth opened, closed and opened again. Finally, she found her voice. "Can we talk sometime? Please. I would really like to get to know you. Learn about your family. Possibly mine."

He nodded.

"Thank you so much. I promise to call you."

Olafur nodded again, then walked away.

Trice hugged Drake. "Can you believe it? I really might have family."

He smiled indulgently. "It is wonderful. I wasn't sure he even got my message. I hated to leave when you had not made contact with him. I never imagined he would show up here."

"I can hardly wait to talk to him. I'll call him tomorrow. Do you think he has any pictures?" Her words were tumbling over each other.

"May I make a suggestion?"

"Sure." She watched him, all smiles.

Drake gave her an earnest look. "I would be careful not to overwhelm him. Go slow and easy."

She took a moment before she spoke. "You're right. I'll be careful. And go slow."

Another person came to speak to him. When that person left, he and Trice returned to their seats. People continued to stop and speak to him, give their thanks.

Trice said, "It must be gratifying to know you have meant so much to so many people."

"It is."

The mayor joined them on the other side of Drake and drew his attention away from Trice. Drake would have rather spent his time with Trice. This would be their last night together. He was too aware of time slipping away. If he wasn't careful, he would become melancholy.

He had spoken to the surgery program leader in London that afternoon. They were expecting him in three days. He had just enough time to get settled in a leased flat.

Drake had eaten little of his food when the mayor stood and tapped on his glass, calling the place to order. "Quiet, please. I have a few words. Drake Stevansson was born and raised here. He went off to college and medical school and returned to help us when we were in desperate need of a doctor. Now it's his turn to go off again and succeed in his training as a surgeon." He looked at Drake. "We are thankful you put your life on hold for these past two years for Seydisfjordur. I don't know what we would have done without you.

"In appreciation, we've all contributed to this gift wishing you the very best." The mayor handed Drake a thick envelope. "Use this to help with whatever you need."

Drake's throat had a knot in it. He worked to swallow. He was overwhelmed with the generosity. He stood. "I don't know what to say. This wasn't necessary. It's too kind. I've enjoyed being your doctor. I will be leaving you in good hands with Dr. Shell."

The entrance door burst open. In a frantic voice, a man yelled, "There's been an explosion at the cannery!"

Trice was right behind Drake as they exited the door. As he passed the mayor, he thrust the envelope back into the man's hand for safe keeping. He called over his shoulder, "Trice, go to the clinic and bring anything you think would be needed in an emergency. Just fill any bags you can find. We can send others after them. Then bring my bag." With that, he picked up his pace, leaving her behind.

Ahead of them, gray smoke billowed from the cannery located on the fjord on the other side of the airport. The blue sky framed the plume of smoke.

She ran to the clinic, wishing for more stable shoes than the ones she wore. Throwing open the door, she hurried down the hall to the supply room. She picked up a large duffel bag and began dumping gauze, antiseptic and tape into it. Soon she had almost cleaned out the supply bins.

She took a moment to pull on Drake's shoes, which she

had already borrowed once. With as much weight as she could carry, she started toward the door.

A man entered. "Drake said to come help you. I have a truck."

She thrust the bags at him. "Take these. I'll get the others. We're going to need blankets."

"People are gathering them. We should have some when we get to the cannery." The man headed out the door.

She returned to the supply room and picked up more supplies. With those in the truck, she climbed in the passenger seat.

The driver sped around the harbor. He honked the horn, clearing the people so they could get past. Three minutes later, they were traveling through the iron gates of the long red building.

Before the truck driver could pull to a complete stop at the front door, Trice had opened her door. She yelled, "Drake."

Another man loped up to them. "He's around this way."

"Hey, I need those two black bags on top," Trice stated.

The man reached over the side of the truck and grabbed the bags. Seconds later she was following him into the dim light of the building.

People were running around every which way.

"He'll be up these stairs in the boiler room." The man indicated the metal steps, and putting down the bags. "I'll go back for the supplies."

Trice hurried up the stairs. The area was almost dark. "Drake?"

"Here."

Relief filled her at the reassuring sound of his voice. She hurried forward.

"Trice, be careful. There is debris on the floor."

Her toe caught on a piece of metal. With luck, she remained upright. She kept moving. Finally she just made out the shape of Drake.

She dropped their bags beside him, then joined him on her knees. "How many people injured?"

"Ten that I know of. There are still eight missing." The pain of loss rang clearly in his voice.

She gave him an anxious look, grateful he was still in town for this event. She could have handled it, but she was glad to have his help. "What do you need me to do?"

"I need you to organize triage. Send four men to me with blankets. I'll have them carry some people out and lead the others. Set up triage as far away from the building as possible in case something is unsteady. So far, I've seen mostly minor things and breathing difficulties."

Trice stood. "I'll get started now." She turned away, then back again. "Drake. Be careful."

"I will." He refocused his attention on the man he cared for.

Trice hurried back outside. She found the man who had driven her. "I need you and three more men to go to Drake. He needs you to bring patients out here. I'll be setting up the triage area." She looked around her. "Over there in the parking lot for the injured. Bring them to me."

"Will do." The man called other men's names and headed inside.

A group of women came up to her. One said, "What can we do to help?"

"I'm setting up a triage station in the parking lot. I need the supplies in the back of that white truck and all the blankets you can find." Trice went to work seeing about the men and women Drake sent to her.

Marie, the nurse from the night of the dance, came to Trice. "What do I need to do to help?"

"See this patient gets oxygen." Trice moved on to the next patient. "This one needs stitches." She called to Marie. "Those—" she pointed to the patient's right side "—will have to wait. She will need to be moved to the clinic."

"A hospital has been set up in the community center. There are a few who live here with some basic medical skills. They are working there. She will be well taken care of until you or Drake can see her again." One of the women who had been helping Trice waved a man over. He loaded the patient in the back of a truck.

Trice liked being a part of a community who came together during a disaster, no matter how large it was. The people didn't wait on one person to make all the decisions. They saw a need and jumped in to fill it. This was the type of place she would like to call home.

Trice quickly assessed the next man's broken hand. Marie joined her. "This one needs his hand wrapped until we can x-ray it and set it."

The next man lay on a blanket.

"Where does it hurt?" Trice asked.

"My foot. Part of the tank fell on it."

Trice pulled his pants leg up to see the man's calf, which had started to swell. "Your foot is most likely broken. Leave it in the boot, which will give it support. We will set it later." She waved to one of the men helping. "Over here." The man stood above her and the patient. "This man needs to be put with the group who need an X-ray. Do not remove his boot. Understood?"

The man nodded.

Trice returned to see patients. The next had a superficial injury to the ankle. She left him for Marie to bandage. Thankfully the patients coming in were slowing. Since they had eased, Trice sent Marie to the community center to organize it and listed who needed to have care first. She also made lists of those who should be sent home after she or Drake saw them and people who needed attention overnight.

One of the men who had been helping Drake hurried up to Trice. "Drake needs your help inside. Can you come now?"

Fear went to her throat. "Is he okay?"

"Yes. He has a patient he needs help with."

Trice snatched up her bag. "Show me."

Drake hated to call Trice into such a dangerous situation, but he had no choice. He needed her assistance. He couldn't do this without her. Even then he wasn't sure they would manage to save the man's life.

"Drake. I'm here. What can I do?" She moved as fast as safety would allow.

He turned the flashlight on the man crushed between a large boiler and a beam.

"Oh, Drake. Is he still alive?"

"He is. I'm treating him for shock. He needs a blood transfusion." His voice held concern.

"Do you know his blood type? I'll start typing blood and getting more donated." She would see to that as soon as she returned to the outside.

"I'm going with O. I already have some of the men rounding up people."

"Send them to the clinic. I'll see about it," Trice assured him.

"The problem remains that if moved, he may bleed out. He would never make it to Reykjavík. He needs an exploratory laparotomy immediately if he even has a chance to survive. It needs to be done here and soon."

She placed her hand on his arm. "You can do it."

"There is no theater. No one to put him to sleep. No recovery."

"We'll use one of the exam rooms. I'll assist along with Marie."

"Marie?"

"She's at the community center, overseeing it. You have the skills. Use them."

Drake didn't have a response to that statement. Wasn't surgery what he had been wanting to do? But under these conditions?

"You stay with him." She placed her hand on his shoulder. "I'll go to the clinic and get things ready. I'll let you know when to bring him."

"There isn't much time." His look met hers.

"We'll hurry."

Time flew by and crawled at the same time as Drake waited to hear from Trice. His patience was almost gone by the time the blood came. He had spent the time regularly checking vital signs and rigging a system to deliver the blood along with helping the cannery workers form a plan to move the huge boiler.

When a man arrived with two pints of blood Drake immediately went to work administering it. It would be too little too late if Trice didn't hurry.

His phone rang. He put it on speaker, needing both his hands for his patient.

Trice's voice said, "Drake, we'll be ready for you when you get here."

"We're on our way." He hung up the phone. "Okay, guys. Let's go to work." With two men on each side of him to lift his patient, he directed the man on the crane. "Lift slow and easy."

The groan of metal made him fear they might be damaging the man further, but they had to get him out. Not soon enough, the space opened so the men could pull the injured man out.

"Slowly. Lay him on the blanket." Drake managed the blood still flowing. Trice had better have plenty of blood waiting at the clinic. They would need it.

They made it out of the building without a mishap. Waiting near the door sat a truck with the motor running and padding for the patient in the back. The men placed the patient on the bedding, and Drake climbed in beside him. To the driver he said, "Keep it slow and steady."

Trice was waiting for him at the clinic door. She rushed to meet him when the truck stopped. "How is he doing?"

"Just hanging on." Drake jumped from the back of the truck.

"You go get scrubbed in, and I'll see about prepping him. Everything you need is lying out in the restroom." She went to work overseeing the unloading of the patient.

Drake glanced into the first examination room. It was filled with furniture. The next one had the door closed. He continued to the restroom. Just as Trice had said, a gown, surgical hat and gloves waited.

Minutes later, he opened the door to the examination room. It had undergone an obvious makeover. Everything that was unnecessary had been removed. He could smell a hint of disinfectant. No doubt Trice had made sure the walls and equipment had been sanitized.

A gurney sat in the middle of the room with his patient on it. A tray with instruments stood beside it. The examination light had been positioned near the bed. With two swift steps, he stood beside the man. He pulled on his headlamp. It felt good to have it on again.

"I located what gas I could find to use to put him to sleep." Trice wore surgical gear as well. "I went through your office and found your surgical headlamp."

Behind her stood Marie.

"We are ready when you are, Doctor," Trice announced, taking her position on the other side of the patient from him. Marie stepped up beside him.

"Vitals, please," he said.

Trice rattled them off. "He's being given blood now."

"We need to get him to sleep." Drake picked up the gas mask and placed it over their patient's face. "Trice, monitor vitals."

Her gaze met his. She nodded.

Confidence he wouldn't have said he possessed filled him. He could do this in this makeshift theater. He had excellent support.

"BP is ninety over sixty," Trice announced.

"That's to be expected with internal bleeding. But it's time to stop that. Let's find those bleeders. Scalpel."

Marie placed it in his palm.

Slowly and carefully, he made a midline incision in the man's abdomen.

"Suction?" What were they going to do for suction?

Marie handed him the end of the tube to the stomach pump machine. He looked at her. "It was Trice's idea."

His gaze met Trice's. The woman never ceased to amaze him. He went to work removing the blood pooled in the man's middle section. "We're going to need more blood."

"It's on the way. People all over town are giving." Trice moved to check the transfusion site.

There was knock at the door. A voice called, "Blood is here."

Trice went to the door to take it. She returned to hook it up to the man after checking the IV.

Drake searched the internal organs. "I wished we had a way of taking X-rays."

"You don't need them." Trice's voice held complete confidence. "You'll find the problem."

He suctioned the area as well as he could. "Sponge."

Maria handed him one. "Keep count. We don't want to leave one lying around somewhere. In fact, keep a written tally."

"There's a pad and pen in that drawer." Trice point to the small cabinet in the corner.

Maria found it and made a notation.

Drake couldn't believe what Trice had managed to pull off in less than an hour.

She had created a full operating theater. He couldn't think of many situations more dire than doing surgery with rudimentary equipment in an examination room turned theater in a remote area.

"We need to find the bleeders or bleeder and get him closed. The helicopter will be here in a few hours after we know he is stable enough to move to Reykjavík. Suction." He cleaned the area as well as possible once more. "Sponge. Trice, vitals."

She rattled off precise and to-the-point numbers.

"Now move the spleen aside and let me see if the bleeding is from there." He searched the area. "There is one. Clamp."

Maria handed him something close to what looked like a surgical clamp.

"What is this?"

Trice spoke up. "A hair clamp. I couldn't find any surgical clamps anywhere. I had to improvise."

"Nicely done." She was wonderful.

She had a smile in her eyes.

"Let's get this stitched up and look for more. Marie, you handle suction. Trice, you help with holding the two sections together while I stitch."

Both women went to work.

It felt good to command a theater. There was no room to argue with the man's life in the balance.

Marie opened a suture kit and handed him the needle already pre-threaded. She suctioned. With the area clear, he carefully joined the two ends of the vessel. "Hold it right there, Marie. Almost done. Suction."

"Excellent. Got it." He nodded to Marie.

Blood still pooled in the man's cavity.

"We've got another somewhere." He went looking, gently moving organs around in a mythical order. He lifted a lobe of the liver. "There it is. This is going to be tricky. Vitals."

Trice gave him the numbers.

"Okay. He's holding his own. Marie, I want you to hold the liver like this." He positioned it where he wanted it. "Trice, I need you to clamp this off the best you can." He held the vessel. "Then help keep the area clear so I can see and get it attached. We're going to have a devil of a time because of the angle."

They all took their positions, and Drake went to work. It might have been the most rudimentary of theaters and the job the most difficult he'd had to perform, but he did some of his finest work.

He stepped back. "Suction one last time. Marie, count those sponges. We can't afford an infection or left behind sponge."

Trice and Marie followed his directions while he searched for further issues.

"Well done. Let's close. Any broken bones will have to

wait until he can be x-rayed." Drake checked his watch. "The evacuation helicopter should be here in an hour. We couldn't ask for better timing."

In a silent room, he closed the man's abdomen.

While Marie covered the man in blankets and checked his vitals every fifteen minutes, Trice and Drake cleaned the room.

Trice said, "You've got some skills with stitches."

"I practiced long enough." He grinned behind the mask. "Marie, thanks for your help. You go get some rest. You've done a night's worth of work," Drake said.

"It was amazing to watch you. Both of you. Trice will make a great local doctor. I'm glad I'll be working with her. I going to check on those injured at the community center before I get some rest."

Trice pulled off her gown and hat. "Thanks for your help. You were amazing. You've earned a rest. I'll see about the community center."

"But—"

"I've got it. If you want to, you can come in later today and oversee what's going on. And Marie, thank you. I wouldn't have wanted anyone else's help."

"Thanks. I feel the same about you." Marie smiled and headed for the door.

With her gone, Drake said, "Apparently Marie has become one of your fans as well."

"An emergency helps people see others in a different light. Plus, I think she knows something is going on between us."

Drake would agree with that.

Trice finished putting away supplies. "I've got to go now. I need to check on things at the community center. I'll have work to do in the morning."

"I'll be right here until the evac arrives." He stood over the patient.

She hesitated at the door. "Don't you have to leave this morning?"

Her sad eyes were almost his undoing. "I'm postponing for at least twenty-four hours. I can't leave you with all this to do by yourself. You've got your hands full."

"We had some last night together."

It wasn't what he had planned. "Story of my life. There's always something getting in the way of my plans."

Trice gave him a quick kiss on the lips. "I'll check the other patients. After you see this patient off, why don't you go to my place and get some sleep? It's closer than yours, and you'll be nearby in case you're needed."

"You'll join me?"

His hopeful look warmed her heart. She nodded. "As soon as I can."

Trice trudged to the community center. Exhausted, she still had work to do. In the two weeks she'd been in Seydisfjordur, she'd done more, felt more than she had in her entire life. She wasn't sure she could keep up this pace, but she was exhilarated by the idea of seeing if she could.

Here in this remote place, she'd found herself. A place to belong, a place to grow, and place she could call hers. If only Drake stayed...

At the center, she entered to find patients lined up in orderly rows. One wall was a food area. "Good morning."

The women working there greeted her with tired looks.

"Would you mind fixin' a plate for Drake? I'm going to check on the patients here. Then I'll take it over to him."

"You have done enough. I'll see about that," the older

of the two women said. "Thank you for all you have done for us."

"You are welcome. And thanks for taking a meal to Drake. I'm sure he'll be happy to see it."

Over the next hour, Trice reviewed charts and ate a bite herself. She heard the whirl of the helicopter approaching. Her and Drake's patient would be leaving soon. They had done good work together. Pretty amazing stuff in fact.

And the town. They had come together and organized as if they had practiced it. They knew each other so well, they knew whose skills to call on. Those who had some medical experience led those willing to help.

Trice told the lady who came in for her shift of overseeing care that she was leaving to get some rest. "Call me or send someone after me if there's the slightest problem. When I return, we'll see about discharging patients."

In the early sunlight, she walked home. The lights were off in the homes, and a few businesses were opening.

She was turning the corner of Luce's house when her door opened. "You did good last night. You okay?"

"I'm fine."

"You need to rest. He is already doing so." The old woman carried no censure in her voice.

"He'll leave tomorrow." Trice wasn't as good at removing emotion from her voice.

The old woman looked sad but resigned. "It has to be."

"I know."

"One must learn what they really want." Luce stepped inside her house and closed the door.

Trice had found what she wanted. Caring, support, and a place where she gave and got it in return. She'd found those here with or without Drake. She had also found love despite the fact it was leaving her. Her heart squeezed at the idea of losing him. Yet he had to go, just as she had to stay. He needed a chance to find what he wanted.

She opened the door of her home to find Drake sound asleep on his stomach in her bed. He snored softly. She went to the bath and showered. Pulling on an oversize shirt, she headed for the bed as well.

Giving him a shake, she said, "Scoot over." She wiggled in next to him, pushing him to give her room using her behind.

Drake rolled to his side and pulled her to him. He murmured next to her ear, "Everything okay at the center?"

"Under control."

"Mmm."

A soft snore filled her ear. She snuggled into him. He would be gone in less than twenty-four hours. She would take what she could get for as long as she could get it.

Hours later, she woke to Drake nuzzling her neck while his hand under her shirt fondled her breast. "I'm sorry. I can't help myself." He nuzzled her ear again. "Reconsider us staying in contact."

Trice was flattered. She snuggled closer. She would miss this time and intended to absorb as much of it as possible. Trice didn't want to have this discussion now. She wanted him to make love to her. "We've already talked about that. I have responsibilities here, and you have training in London."

"I'll come here when I can. You come to me when you can. We can talk and write, call often."

She hated being the one to voice reality. "It won't work."

His lips followed her brow. "You won't even try?"

Trice kissed his chest. "It's not that."

"Then what?" He looked at her.

"I'm tired of having only half of what I want. I don't want crumbs. It's time I demand to have the whole cake. To be the center of someone's attention. To come first. You can't do that in London, and I won't ask you to stay here."

"Come on, Trice. It'll only be for a little while. If we both work at it, we can make it work. We can get through the year, and then we can be together."

Would that be what she wanted to do? She already knew what it was like to be anonymous. She liked being included in a knitting circle. The fact that people helped others without question. She had no desire to return to what she had before. No longer would she settle for part-time. Trice looked away.

"You think you belong here?" He pulled away and lay back on the pillows.

"I don't know for sure, but I believe so. But it's not all about Seydisfjordur. It's about me." She pointed to her chest. "Me standing up for what I want. Finding my place in the world."

"You don't think you can do that with me?" Drake growled.

"Not in London. Not when you are focused on surgery." She raised a hand before he could speak. "Which you should be. This was supposed to be a fling for a reason. I care too much for you to hold you back. I would never want that. You need to go. I won't hold you here. I can't."

"You sound like Luce. She pushes me to go, yet she knows I worry about her."

"I will take care of her. You need to go. If you don't, think of all the people who might not get the care they need. You owe it to yourself, and your future patients to finish your training."

All Drake's hurt showed in his eyes. Her heart broke. She hadn't wanted it to end this way.

He threw the covers back. "You finish getting some sleep.

I'll go check on the community center and see if I can send some of the patients home. I'll be busy the rest of the afternoon tying up business and packing. Bye, Trice."

Through tear-filled eyes, she watched him dress, then walk out the door and out of her life.

CHAPTER ELEVEN

TRICE DIDN'T SEE Drake for the rest of the day. She stayed busy at the clinic and then later at the community center. He had discharged a number of the patients at the center, but there were still others that needed to stay at least another day.

Day turned into night, and she returned home lonely and sad. She'd been both of those before. She would survive. She would work through them again.

By the time she went to bed, there had still been no word from Drake. More than once, she had thought of going to him. What would she say? That she had changed her mind. But she hadn't. She couldn't lead him on to believe that.

She wasn't surprised he was hurt, even understood it, but she knew what it was like to have promises made to stay in touch and then there be nothing. She didn't want that. Refused to live like that ever again. It was better to cut it off clean and remember each other well.

Trice wanted him to concentrate on his surgery. Getting his career started. To have his dream. Worrying about her wouldn't make that happen. He wouldn't intend to hurt her, but it would happen. Not once had they discussed forever. Had he even considered that?

Returning to her house, she tried to get some rest, but it never came. In a short amount of time, she had become used to sleeping next to Drake. Even that she would have to adjust to, and it might be the hardest to accomplish.

She couldn't figure out a way to make their situation different. For them to have a future, one of them would have to give up their dream. She wouldn't ask Drake to do that. His skills were needed. But she also couldn't agree to give up what she'd finally found—a community. Exhausted, she walked from the clinic to her house.

The next morning, Trice strolled to the front of Luce's house on her way to the clinic. Luce's front door opened, and the old woman stepped out. "He came by earlier to say goodbye. He left you this." She handed Trice a paperback book. "He said for you to keep it."

Trice had heard the plane taking off. She had hurried outside and watched as he circled over the town and headed south.

The older woman said quietly, "Drake needed to go so he can know his mind. His heart is here. He must learn that. Then he will come home."

"I'm sure he'll come back for a visit."

The way Luce looked at Trice told her the woman's words had another meaning. "You must work to stay busy. Time will go by."

Not fast enough to heal her heart.

"That way you will not notice him being gone." Luce patted Trice's arm.

Trice would notice Drake being gone no matter what she did. "Thanks. That's good advice." She would start today. Determined, she squared her shoulders. She walked to the clinic, went in and proceeded with business. She was here to do a job, and she would do it and do it well. She had her research to review and a call to Olafur to make.

Yet that heavy block of sadness and loneliness weighed her down.

Over the next week, he didn't call, nor did she receive a letter. She didn't like being cut off any more than she had the times it had happened before. Yet Drake was doing as she had asked.

Trice worked to fill her days, but her nights were long and sleepless. As the hours crawled into days and those into weeks, it didn't get any easier. She just pushed forward. Every time she heard the engine of a plane, her heart palpitated with the possibility it was Drake, then crashed when it wasn't.

Drake had circled Seydisfjordur the day he left.

Had Trice looked up, hoping to see him one more time? Had she been as disturbed by him leaving her behind as he was by doing it?

He had studied the little town nestled on the water below him. It had been his home forever. He had gone knowing he had left part of himself behind. Trice might not still be in town when he did return, but he knew well the others who made up Seydisfjordur would be there just as they always were.

He hadn't liked the way he and Trice had parted, but he couldn't help his anger. She didn't even want to try to work out something between them. It wouldn't have been easy, but they could have tried. Her problem was she had no faith in anyone wanting her.

If they both wanted the relationship, they could have figured out how to make it work and overcome the complications. They didn't have to become part of the negative statistics that said it was next to impossible. She wanted stability. To be the center of someone's world.

Had he made her think she could be? No, he hadn't offered her that. Not once had he offered her anything permanent, especially with him. Drake blinked. Was that what he wanted? Trice in his life forever?

He had been gone for three weeks. He wished he could say he was happy and had adjusted well to returning to the structure of hospital schedules and the requirements of surgery. But that wasn't the case. Thankfully, his skills weren't lacking.

He disliked the noise and lights of the city. They were nothing like he remembered. Now they irritated him. He missed the quiet of a starry night. The peace of the wind.

To make matters worse, he longed for Trice. He couldn't get beyond that. Or that he had all but demanded everything be his way. That she come to London. That she work there. She would have been giving up everything for him. He'd been unfair to even think she might follow him when he'd seen how happy she was in Iceland. Above all, he wanted to see her happy. Yet what he'd asked for wouldn't have done that.

He had been so confident that when he reached London, he would be so caught up in his work that the pain of losing Trice would ease. That hadn't been the case. He had planned this move for so long, had looked forward to returning to surgery so much, that he shouldn't be this miserable. He was horribly lonely for Trice. And he missed Seydisfjordur.

He recognized happiness. He had it with Trice. What he felt now wasn't it. Still, this was what he needed to do, to hone his surgical skills. Then he could return to Iceland prepared to do more for his homeland than he had been doing. He just had to give his feelings time. To hope that it worked. He had made a commitment, and he would stick with it.

He had just finished his third surgery of the day. He

had seen inside three humans' bodies, yet he couldn't say what they looked like or their names. He couldn't say what they did for a living, or how they had come to get a scar on their hand or what nickname their mother called them or what their favorite folk dance was. All of that he knew about most of the people in Seydisfjordur. His patients in the hospital were just people passing through the OR who he would never really know. He missed the personal connection of working in a small clinic.

You do not know your heart or your place. Hallveig's words marched through his head.

He did know now where his heart was, and his place as well. It was time he went home to Trice and Seydisfjordur. With that decision made, the weight he had carried on his shoulders fell to his feet. Finally, the center of his back relaxed for the first time since circling Seydisfjordur the last time.

An hour later, Drake said to the balding, stern-looking man standing beside him as they scrubbed their hands, "Dr. March, may I speak to you in your office after this procedure?"

The man observed him a moment and nodded. "That will be fine."

Drake sat in the chair across the desk from the older surgeon. "How can I help you, Stevansson?"

"Sir, I'm sorry to tell you this, but I will not be staying with the program."

The man sat forward. "And why not? We held a place for you. Why would you leave us after only three weeks?"

"Thank you, sir, for doing what you did, but the two years I've been gone have changed things. I've learned to appreciate knowing my patients. By name, not as a number. I love surgery, I do, but I need more. More interaction."

The older man leaned back in his chair. "Your work is impeccable, but I have to admit I've been unsure about your happiness with working in a hospital."

Drake wasn't sure how to respond, so he remained quiet.

"I realized how much you wanted to rejoin the program and how patiently you waited until you could, but you seem to go through the motions, which are better than par, but your heart doesn't seem to be in your work."

Drake sat straighter. "I assure you—"

The man held up his hand. "This is not a criticism but an observation. Please speak freely."

"Working in a large city just isn't for me anymore. I belong in Seydisfjordur." And with Trice.

"You're going to give up surgery to return to your small-town clinic? It will be a waste of talent."

"I'm sorry you feel that way, sir. But this isn't the right place for me. I'm sorry to have taken your time and a space, then let you down."

"There is no way to change your mind?"

"No sir, there isn't." On that Drake had no doubt. He was going back to Seydisfjordur and begging Trice to have him.

"Then I guess all I can do is wish you well." The man stood and offered his hand. Drake shook it. "I hope you aren't making a mistake."

Drake squared his shoulders. With complete confidence he said, "I am not."

As the days went by, Trice became less confident about having made the right decision regarding Drake. What she had was nothing. No phone calls, no notes, no interaction. She'd requested it be that way. He was honoring his word.

Yet everything in her mind, body and soul clambered to hear his voice, to know how he was doing.

Maybe he was right. They could compromise. She had only a year's commitment to Seydisfjordur. The town hadn't asked her to stay longer, and if they did, she didn't have to agree. Yet by then, how she and Drake felt could be completely different. Only she knew it wouldn't be for her.

Was he as lonely as she? She felt like Seydisfjordur was home, but without Drake, she wasn't as sure as she had once been. She should be with him.

The only true bright moment in her life was when she had spoken to her potential cousin, Olafur Bjonsson, at length and requested a DNA test. She was waiting for it to return. Still, she felt deep in her soul it would be positive. He was her family. He had a sister who had three daughters, but they lived on the other side of the island. Trice hoped to meet them one day. Just knowing they existed filled her heart. She had blood connections in a world where she had never had anyone. Yet something was missing. Drake was the connection her heart longed for.

Would he even respond to her if she called? He'd been angry with her when he had left. How would he react if she dared to call him? Would he be glad she did?

One afternoon, she dared to call his number. Her heart almost beat out of her chest. Would he answer? Her heart settled into its place when the call went to voicemail. She sank to the chair while she listened to his voice. At the beep, she hung up. Tears flowed like they never had before. Maybe it was best to leave well enough alone.

Three days later, the sound of a plane made her head pop up from where she worked at her desk. Would she ever move beyond that reaction to a plane engine?

Since she didn't have any patients, she walked outside

to the front steps. The sun shone brightly. She watched the plane circle, then line up for landing. The plane had markings like Drake's, but she knew that was just wishful hoping. The plane came to a stop near the terminal.

A man came around the front of the plane. His mannerisms reminded her of Drake. Hope had her imagining things. But the idea it might be him pulled at her enough to keep her standing there. The pilot looked her direction, but the distance was too far to really make out who he was. Still she stared.

The man walked toward the terminal. John, who ran the airport, met him and shook his hand. The man slapped him on the shoulder just like Drake would have. Trice slowly went down the steps and started walking toward the airport. She wanted to run, but controlled her actions, not wanting to embarrass herself if it wasn't Drake. Her heart quickened. What if it was him?

She started down the road. He moved so much like Drake, but he was in London doing surgery. Her feet kept moving of their own accord. Her pulse ran wild in anticipation. He walked toward her along the road around the harbor. The closer he came, the more he looked like Drake. She picked up her pace. His strides lengthened.

It was Drake!

She broke into a run. He loped toward her. He was close enough now for her to clearly see him.

He dropped the pack from his back and opened his arms. She ran as fast as she could the last few yards, not stopping until she slammed into his chest. Drake rocked back with the force of her reaching him. His arms tightened around her. Her arms went around his neck, and she clung to him. He squeezed her tighter. If it was up to her, she would never let him go.

They remained wrapped in each other's arms for a few

minutes. Trice fought the moisture filling her eyes. She focused on absorbing the fact that Drake's heat warmed her, and he was there with her again.

"I've missed you." Her voice was gruff with emotion.

"I've missed you too." He sounded as if he were having a difficult time controlling his emotions as well.

She pulled away enough to see his handsome face. "I'm sorry I was so stubborn about us not having anything to do with each other."

"I'm the one who should apologize to you. I wanted everything to go my way." His look held nothing but sincerity.

She cupped his cheek. "I wanted you to have your dream."

"Honey, when you're in my arms, I have my real dream. I love you."

"Drake, I love you."

He kissed her, long and sweet and perfect. Her heart swelled. All her life she'd been looking for connection, roots, love. This man in her arms gave her all of that and more.

Drake picked up his pack and pulled it over one shoulder. He put an arm around her waist and directed her toward the clinic.

Trice slipped her arm around his waist, too, laying her head against his shoulder. "Luce said you would be back."

"Somehow Luce always knows."

"She seems to. Why are you here? How long can you stay?"

"Can't a guy say hi before you start grilling him?" He grinned. "Can't I just come visit you?"

She gave him a sheepish look. "I'm so excited you are here."

"Why don't we ride up to my house, where we can talk uninterrupted?"

She stopped and studied him a moment. "Because I don't think you have talk on your mind when we're at your house."

His grin turned wolfish, predatory. "Well, you might be right about that, but I'd like for you to come with me anyway."

"Let me close the clinic and put out the sign about where to find me." Trice hurried ahead.

A few minutes later, they climbed into his truck, which had remained parked behind the clinic. He had left it for her to use when needed. Drake drove up the steep, winding road to his house. He opened the front door, letting Trice enter first. He closed the door behind him, grabbed her and kissed her so tenderly she came close to crying.

He rested his forehead against hers. "I didn't want us to be interrupted at the clinic. Sometimes the town doesn't know boundaries."

"Drake, shouldn't you be in London? Is something wrong?"

He gave her another deep kiss. "Everything was wrong. You weren't there. I came home for you."

Her eyes narrowed. "For me?"

He cupped her cheek. "Yes, for you. Sit. I'll explain."

Trice wasn't confident she would like what was to come, but she did as he requested. "I need to say something."

He sat beside her, but not close enough for her to touch him. His look turned earnest. "I gave up my surgery fellowship. I want us to be together. I'll do whatever it takes to make that happen."

Trice wanted to wrap her arms around him but remained where she was, her hands tightly clasped together. Her voice turned stern. "Drake, I won't let you give up your dream. You are a surgeon. You should be doing surgery. What you love."

"I love you more." He pulled her into his lap.

Placing her hands on his chest, she pushed back so she could see his face. "I don't want you to one day resent me because you gave up something you love for me."

"That will never happen. You are the most important thing in my life."

She searched his face. "We can make it for a year writing, seeing each other over the internet, visits."

"I want more than that. I want us to really be together. Right here." His eyes were bright with the possibility.

"How?" Her brows rose.

"I'm back here to stay." He grinned.

"But Drake, you can't to that. You were born to be a surgeon. I hope you didn't leave for me."

"I left for me. And because what we have together is more important to me."

"I can come to London after I finish here. We can find a place outside of the city where we can have the best of both worlds."

He studied her with a look of amazement on his face. "That's not what you want. I know you well enough to know that."

"I would do it for you. I could make it work."

"I don't want you to make it work. I want you happy. This is your happy place. It is mine as well. I have found it has a hold on me no matter how much I might try to say it doesn't. No matter where I am, it will always be here, calling me. With you here, it screams, *I belong here*. One of many things I have learned lately is that I can be invaluable wherever I am. It just may not take the same form."

She kissed him. "It took you long enough to figure that out."

He smirked. "Some of us are slow to get the idea."

Trice cupped his cheek. "Yes, they are." She dropped her hand. "If you come back here, I will need to find a job elsewhere. I won't be needed."

"I'm not coming back to take your job. I was already

packed and ready to head this way when a representative of the Reykjavík Hospital phoned. He wants me to start a pilot program for local surgical clinics. The first one would be right here. I would handle the simple surgeries and emergencies as needed in the surrounding area. I also discussed it with the town council through the mayor. I want to use the money they gifted me to help buy a small CT machine. They agreed. Iceland's medical commission hopes you would be willing to stay and oversee the clinic and continue to help me when your year is over. They heard how efficient you were when we did surgery."

It was almost too perfect. Trice appreciated the excitement on Drake's face and how animated he was talking about the plan.

"We can be together. Right here where you want to be and where I have realized I belong."

Trice didn't know what to say, she was so overwhelmed.

Drake took both her hands. "What do you think? Would that make you happy?"

"That would be wonderful. I can't think of anything more wonderful."

"Nothing?" He watched her with a smile on his face.

"What's going on, Drake?"

He continued to look into her eyes. "This is a personal matter, not a medical issue."

"Are you sick?" She looked at him, suddenly concerned.

"I'm fine except for one thing. My heart hurts."

She sat forward. "What's wrong with your heart?"

"It hurts for you. I've missed you. I love you, Trice." He went down on one knee. "I love you so much. I know we haven't known each other long, but I also know I love you and I want to marry you as soon as possible."

She threw her arms around his neck, squeezing him tightly. "I love you too. I always will."

"So, what do you say?"

Drake looked so unsure, she had to take pity on him. "Yes, yes, yes, yes, yes, yes, yes! A million times yes!"

He kissed her with such tenderness that expressed his love clearly. She sighed when he released her.

"I can get my family here in a couple of weeks," he said. "Do you think you could be ready to marry me by then?"

She grinned. "I bet I can call a meeting of the knitting circle and have it done in no time."

He threw back his head and laughed. "I'm sure you're right."

Her gaze locked with his. "One more thing. Having a family is important to me. I know you are good with children, but how do you feel about having some of your own?"

"If they're with you, I want them. In fact, I think we should start practicing right away." He took her hand and tugged.

In the doorway of his bedroom, she stopped him. She met his questioning look. "I came here hoping to find blood family, and I found so much more. You are the real family I've been looking for. Thank you for that."

"Honey, I'll always be here for you. Seydisfjordur has always been my home, but with you here, it's where I belong."

* * * * *

MEDICAL

Life and love in the world of modern medicine.

Available Next Month

Best Friend To Husband? Louisa Heaton
Finding A Family Next Door Louisa Heaton

....

The GP's Seaside Reunion Annie Claydon
A Kiss With The Irish Surgeon Kristine Lynn

....

Nurse's Baby Bombshell Charlotte Hawkes
The Single Dad's Secret Zoey Gomez

Keep reading for an excerpt of a new title
from the Intrigue series,
MOUNTAIN CAPTIVE by Cindi Myers

Chapter One

Rand Martin had built his reputation on noticing details—
the tiny nick in an artery that was the source of life-threat-
ening blood loss; the almost microscopic bit of shrapnel that
might lead to a deadly infection; the panic in a wounded
man's eyes that could send his vitals out of control; the
tremor in a fellow surgeon's hand that meant he wasn't fit
to operate. As a trauma surgeon—first in the military, then
in civilian life—Rand noticed the little things others overlooked. It made him a better doctor, and it equipped him
to deal with the people in his life.

But sometimes that focus on the small picture got in
the way of his big-picture job. Today, his first call as medical adviser for Eagle Mountain Search and Rescue, he
was supposed to be focusing on the sixty-something man
sprawled on the side of a high mountain trail. But Rand's
attention kept shifting to the woman who knelt beside the
man. Her blue-and-yellow vest identified her as a member
of the search and rescue team, but her turquoise hair and
full sleeve of colorful tattoos set her apart from the other
volunteers. That, and the wariness that radiated off her as
she surveyed the crowd that was fast gathering around her
and her patient on the popular hiking trail.

"Everyone move back and give us some space," Rand

ordered, and, like the men and women he had commanded in his mobile surgical unit in Kabul, the crowd obeyed and fell back.

SAR Captain Danny Irwin rose from where he had been crouched on the patient's other side and greeted Rand. "Thanks for coming out," he said.

"Are you the doctor?" Another woman, blond hair in a ponytail that streamed down her back, rushed forward.

"Dr. Rand Martin." He didn't offer his hand, already pulling on latex gloves, ready to examine his patient. The blue-haired woman had risen also, and was edging to one side of the trail. As if she was trying to blend in with the crowd—a notion Rand found curious. Nothing about this woman would allow her to blend in. Even without the wildly colored hair and the ink down her arm, she was too striking to ever be invisible.

"My dad has a heart condition," the blonde said. "I tried to tell him he shouldn't be hiking at this altitude, but he wouldn't listen, and now this has happened."

"Margo, please!" This, from the man on the ground. He had propped himself up on his elbows and was frowning at the woman, presumably his daughter. "I hurt my leg. It has nothing to do with my heart."

"You don't know that," she said. "Maybe you fell because you were lightheaded or had an irregular heartbeat. If you weren't so stubborn—"

A balding man close to the woman's age moved up and put his hands on the woman's shoulders. "Let's wait and see what the doctor has to say," he said, and led Margo a few feet away.

Rand crouched beside the man. He was pale, sweating and breathing hard. Not that unusual, considering the bone sticking out of his lower leg. He was probably in a lot of pain from that compound fracture, and despite his protestation that nothing was wrong with his heart, the pain and shock could aggravate an existing cardiac condition. "What happened?" Rand asked.

"We were coming down the trail and Buddy fell." This, from another woman, with short gray curls. She sat a few feet away, flanked by two boys—early- or preteens, Rand guessed. The boys were staring at the man on the ground, freckles standing out against their pale skin.

"I stepped on a rock, and it rolled," Buddy offered. "I heard a snap." He grimaced. "Hurts like the devil."

"We'll get you something for the pain." Rand saw that someone—Danny or the blue-haired woman—had already started an intravenous line. "Do you have a medical history?" he asked Danny.

The SAR captain—an RN in his day job—handed over a small clipboard. Buddy was apparently sixty-seven, on a couple of common cardiac drugs. No history of medication allergies, though Rand questioned him again to be absolutely sure. Then he checked the clipboard once more. "Mr. Morrison, we're going to give you some morphine for the pain. It should take effect within a few minutes. Then we're going to splint your leg, pack it in ice to keep the swelling down, and get you down the mountain and to the hospital for X-rays and treatment."

"But his heart!" Margo, who'd shoved away from the balding man—her husband, perhaps—rushed forward again.

"Are you experiencing any chest pain?" Rand asked, even as he pulled out a stethoscope. "Palpitations?"

"No." Buddy glanced toward his daughter and lowered

his voice, his tone confiding. "I had a quadruple bypass nine months ago. I completed cardiac rehab, and I'm just fine. Despite what my daughter would have you believe, I'm not an idiot. My doctor thought this vacation was a fine idea. I'm under no activity restrictions."

"Your doctor probably has no idea you would decide to hike six miles at ten thousand feet," Margo said.

Rand slid the stethoscope beneath Buddy Morrison's T-shirt and listened to the strong, if somewhat rapid, heart-beat. He studied the man's pupils, which were fine. Some of the color was returning to his cheeks. Rand moved to check the pulse in his leg below the break.

"Chris, come hold this," Danny called over to the young blue-haired woman after he had hooked the man's IV line to a bag of saline. She held it, elevated, while he injected the morphine into the line. Rand watched her while trying to appear not to. Up close, she had fine lines at the corners of her eyes, which were a chocolatey brown, fringed with heavily mascaraed lashes. She had a round face, with a slight point to her chin and a Cupid's bow mouth with a slightly fuller lower lip. It was a strikingly beautiful face, with a mouth he would have liked to kiss.

He pushed the inappropriate thought away and focused on working with Danny to straighten the man's leg. Buddy groaned as the broken tip of the bone slid back under the skin, and the gray-haired woman let out a small cry as well. Margo took a step toward them. "What are you doing?" she asked. "You're hurting him!"

"He'll feel a lot better when the bones of the leg are in line and stabilized," Rand said, and began to fit the in-flatable splint around the man's leg. Once air was added, the splint would form a tight, formfitting wrap that would make for a much more comfortable trip down the mountain on the litter.

The splint in place, Rand stood and stepped back. "You can take it from here," he told Danny, and watched as half a dozen more volunteers swarmed in to assemble a wheeled litter, transferred Buddy onto it, and secured him, complete with a crash helmet, ice packs around his leg and warm blankets over the rest of his body.

While they worked, another female volunteer explained to Buddy's family what would happen next. In addition to the family and the search and rescue volunteers, a crowd of maybe a dozen people clogged the trail, so each new hiker who descended the route was forced to join the bottleneck and wait. The onlookers talked among themselves, and more than a few snapped photographs.

Danny moved to Rand's side. "It's a little different from assessing a patient at the hospital ER," Danny said.

"Different from the battlefield too," Rand said. There was no scent of mortar rounds and burning structures here, and no overpowering disinfectant scent of a hospital setting. Only sunshine and a warm breeze with the vanilla-tinged scent of ponderosa pine.

"Thanks for coming out," Danny said again.

"You could have handled it fine without me," Rand said. He had heard enough from people around town to know Eagle Mountain SAR was considered one of the top wilderness-response teams in the state.

"The family calmed down a lot when I assured them we had a 'real doctor' on the way to take care of their father," Danny said. He glanced over to where Margo and her mother were huddled with the balding man and the two boys, their anxious faces focused on the process of loading

Buddy into the litter. "But I won't call you except in cases of emergency, if that's what you want."

"No. I want you to treat me like any other volunteer," Rand said.

"You mean, go through the training, attend the meetings, stuff like that?"

"Yes. That's exactly what I mean. I like being outdoors, and I need to get out of the office and the operating room. I'm in good physical shape, so I think I could be an asset to the team, beyond my medical knowledge."

"That's terrific," Danny said. "We'd be happy to have you. If you have time, come back to headquarters with us, and I'll introduce you around. Or come to the next regular meeting. Most of the volunteers will be there. I'll give you a training schedule and a bunch of paperwork to sign."

"Sounds good." Rand turned back to the crowd around the litter as it began to move forward. He searched among the dozen or so volunteers for the woman with the blue hair but didn't see her. Then he spotted her to one side. She stood in the shadow of a pine, staring up the trail.

He followed her gaze, trying to determine what had caught her attention. Then he spotted the man—midforties, a dirty yellow ball cap covering his hair and hiding his eyes. But he was definitely focused on the woman, his posture rigid.

Rand looked back toward the blue-haired woman, but she was gone. She wasn't by the tree. She wasn't with the volunteers or in the crowd of onlookers that was now making its way down the trail.

"Is something wrong?" Danny asked.

"The volunteer who was with Mr. Morrison when I arrived," he said. "With the blue hair."

"Chris. Chris Mercer."

"Has she been a volunteer long?"

"Off and on for four years. Her work has taken her away a couple of times—she's an artist. But she always comes back to the group." Danny looked around. "I don't see her now."

"She was just here," Rand said. "I was wondering where she went."

"There's no telling with Chris. She's a little unconventional but a good volunteer. She told me she was hiking about a mile down the trail when the call went out, so she was first on the scene," Danny said. "She's supposed to stick around for report back at the station. Maybe she's already headed back there."

"Looks like she left something behind," Rand said. He made his way to the spot where she had been standing and picked up a blue day pack, the nylon outer shell faded and scuffed. He unzipped the outer pocket and took out a business card. "'Chris Mercer, Aspen Leaf Gallery,'" he read.

"That's Chris's," Danny said. He held out his hand. "I'll put it in the lost and found bin at headquarters."

"That's okay. I'll take it to her." Rand slipped one strap of the pack over his shoulder.

"Suit yourself," Danny said. He and Rand fell into step behind the group wheeling the litter. Morrison's family was hiking ahead, though the daughter, Margo, kept looking back to check on their progress. Every twenty minutes or so, the volunteers switched positions, supporting the litter and guiding it down the trail or walking alongside it with the IV bag suspended. They continually checked on Mr. Morrison, asking him how he was doing, assessing his condition, staying alert for any change that might indicate something they had missed. Something going wrong.

Rand felt the tension in his own body, even as he reminded himself that this was a simple accident—a fall that had resulted in a fracture, free of the kinds of complications that had plagued his patients on the battlefield, and the motor vehicle collision and gunshot victims he often met in the emergency room where he now worked.

Heavy footfalls on the trail behind them made Rand turn, in time to see the man in the dirty yellow ball cap barreling toward them. The man brushed against Rand as he hurried by, head down, boots raising small puffs of dirt with each forceful step. "Hey!" Rand called out, prepared to tell the man to be more careful. But the guy broke into a run and soon disappeared down the trail.

"Guess he had somewhere he needed to be," Danny said.

"Guess so," Rand said, but the hair on the back of his neck rose as he remembered the expression on Chris's face as she had stared at the man.

She hadn't merely been curious or even afraid of the man.

She had been terrified.